ALSO BY CARLOS FUENTES

Aura
The Buried Mirror
Burnt Water
The Campaign
A Change of Skin
Christopher Unborn
Constancia and Other Stories for Virgins
The Crystal Frontier
The Death of Artemio Cruz
Diana: The Goddess Who Hunts Alone
Distant Relations
The Eagle's Throne
The Good Conscience
Happy Families
The Hydra Head
Inez
Myself with Others
A New Time for Mexico
The Old Gringo
The Orange Tree
Terra Nostra
This I Believe: An A to Z of a Life
Where the Air Is Clear
The Years with Laura Diaz

DESTINY AND DESIRE

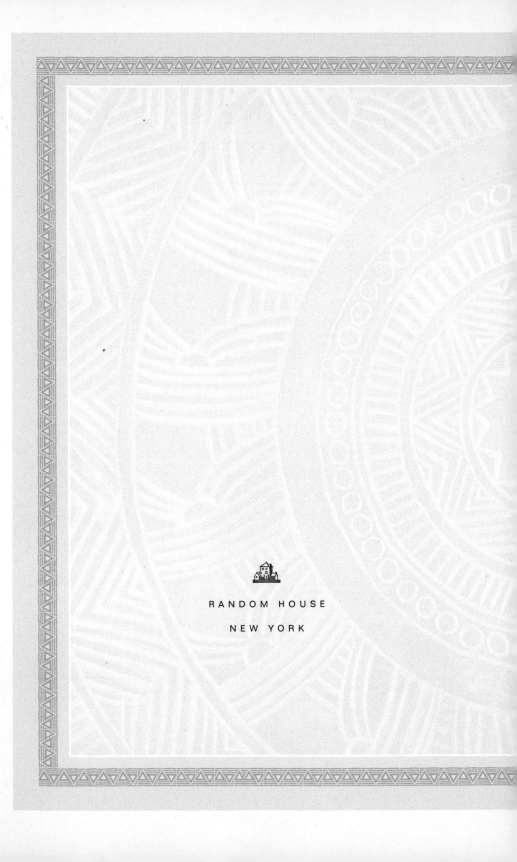

RANDOM HOUSE

NEW YORK

DESTINY AND DESIRE

A NOVEL

◇◇◇

CARLOS FUENTES

TRANSLATED BY

EDITH GROSSMAN

English translation copyright © 2011 by Edith Grossman

Published in the United States by Random House, an imprint of The Random House Publishing Group, a division of Random House, Inc., New York.

RANDOM HOUSE and colophon are registered trademarks of Random House, Inc.

Originally published in Spanish as *La voluntad y la fortuna* by Alfaguara, Mexico City, Mexico, in 2008, copyright © 2008 by Carlos Fuentes.

Library of Congress Cataloging-in-Publication Data
Fuentes, Carlos.
[Voluntad y la fortuna. English]
Destiny and desire : a novel / Carlos Fuentes ; translated by Edith Grossman.
p. cm.
Originally published in Spanish as La voluntad y la fortuna by Alfaguara, Mexico City, in 2008.
ISBN 978-1-4000-6880-7
eBook ISBN 978-0-679-60445-7
1. Grossman, Edith, 1936–   II. Title.
PQ7297.F793V6413 2011
863'.64—dc22   2010015078

Printed in the United States of America

Title-page image copyright © iStockphoto.com / © Jhason Abuan

www.atrandom.com

2 4 6 8 9 7 5 3 1

First U.S. Edition

For my children
Cecilia
Natacha
Carlos

Contents

Prelude: Severed Head 3

PART ONE   Castor and Pollux 7

PART TWO   Miguel Aparecido *115*

PART THREE   Max Monroy 237

PART FOUR   Cain and Abel 289

Epilogue: Ascent to Heaven 407

DESTINY AND DESIRE

Prelude

SEVERED HEAD

At night the sea and the sky are one and even the earth becomes confused with the dark immensity that envelops everything. There are no chinks. No breaks. No breaches. Night is the best representation of the infinitude of the universe. It makes us believe that nothing has a beginning and nothing has an end. Especially if (as is the case tonight) there are no stars.

The first lights appear and the separation begins. The ocean withdraws to its own geography, a veil of water that conceals deep-sea mountains, valleys, ravines. The ocean bottom is a chamber whose echoes never reach us, least of all me, during the small hours.

I know that day will destroy the illusion. And if dawn never breaks again, then what? Then I'll think the ocean has stolen my form.

The Pacific really is a tranquil ocean now, as white as a large basin of milk. The waves have warned it that earth is approaching. I try to measure the distance between two waves. Or is it time that separates them, not distance? Answering this question would solve my own mystery. The ocean is undrinkable, but it drinks us. Its softness is a thousand times greater than earth's. But we hear only the echo, not the voice of the sea. If the sea were to shout, we would all be deaf. And if the sea were to stop, we would all be dead. There is no unmoving sea. Its perpetual motion gives oxygen to the world. If the sea doesn't move, we all suffocate. Not death by water but by as-phyxiation.

Dawn breaks and daylight determines the sea's color. The blue of the water is merely a dispersion of light. The color blue means that the solar sphere has conquered the clarity of the water, provid-ing it with a covering that doesn't belong to it, that isn't its skin, if in fact the ocean also has skin . . . What will the new day illuminate? I'd like to give a very fast answer because I'm losing the words to tell you, the survivors, this tale.

If the newborn sun and the dying night don't speak for me, I'll have no history. The history I want to tell all of you who still live. I believe the sea lives and that each wave that washes over my head feels the earth, touches my flesh, looks for my gaze and finds it, stu-pefied. Or rather bewildered. Incredulous.

I look without looking. I'm afraid of being seen. I'm not what you would call a "pleasant" sight. I'm the thousandth severed head so far this year in Mexico. I'm one of fifty decapitated heads this week, the seventh today, and the only one in the past three and a quarter hours.

The rising sun is reflected in my open eyes. My head has stopped bleeding. A thick liquid runs from the encephalic mass into the sand. My lids will never close again, as if my thoughts will con-tinue to dampen the earth.

Here is my severed head, lost like a coconut on the shores of the Pacific Ocean along the Mexican coast of Guerrero.

My head torn away like the head of a dead fetus that has to lose it so the headless body can be born in spite of everything, quiver for a few moments, and die as well, drowned in blood, allowing the mother to be saved and to cry. After all, the efficacy of the guillotine was tested first by severing the heads of corpses, not kings.

My head was cut off by machete blows. My neck is a cloth that unravels into shreds. My eyes are two open beacons of astonish-ment until the next tide carries them out and the fish swim into my head through the sacrificial orifice and the gray matter spills in one piece onto the sand, like an overturned bowl of soup, lost in the earth, forever invisible unless a fee is paid by national and foreign tourists. We're in the tropics, damn it! Don't you know that, you people who are still alive or who believe you are living?

My brain stopped controlling the movements of a body it can no longer find. My head abandoned my body. Without a body, what good does it do to breathe, circulate, sleep? Even if these are the oldest areas inside my head, do new zones await me in the part of my brain I didn't use in life? I no longer have to control balance, posture, respiration, the rhythm of my heart. Am I entering an unknown reality, the one the unused portion of my brain will soon reveal to me?

Those who have been guillotined don't lose their head right away. They have a few seconds—perhaps minutes—to move their bulging eyes, ask themselves what happened, where am I, what's waiting for me, with a tongue that, separated from the body, does not stop moving, loquacious, idiotic, about to lose itself forever in the mystery of finding out what happened to my trunk instead of focusing urgently on the greatest duty of a severed head, which is to recreate the body in its mind and say: This is the head of Josué, the son of unknown parents, who is searching for his living body, the one he had in life, the one he felt night and day, the one that woke every morning with a life's plan negated, of course it was! by the image in the first mirror of the day. I, Josué, whose only concern at this moment is not biting my tongue. Because although my head is severed, my tongue attempts to speak, freed at last, and succeeds only in biting itself, biting itself as one bites a sausage or a hamburger. Flesh we are and to flesh we return. Is that how it goes? Is that the prayer? My eyes without sockets look for the world.

I was a body. I had a body. Will I be a soul?

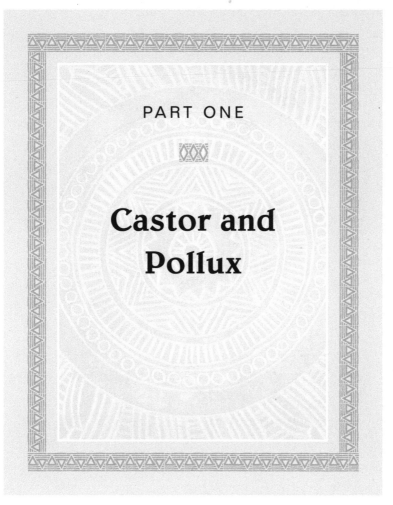

PART ONE

Castor and Pollux

Permit me to introduce myself. Or rather: introduce my body, violently separated (you know this already) from my head. I speak of my body because I've lost it and will not have another opportunity to introduce it to all of you, gentle readers, or to myself. In this way I can indicate, once and for all, that the following narration has been dictated by my head and only my head, since my detached body is nothing more than a memory: one that can be transmitted and left in the hands of the forewarned reader.

Forewarned indeed: The body is at least half of what we are. Still, we keep it hidden in a verbal closet. For the sake of modesty, we do not refer to its invaluable and indispensable functions. Forgive me: I will speak in detail about my body. Because if I don't, very soon my body will be nothing but an unburied corpse, a slaughtered fowl, an anonymous loin. And if you, being very well bred, don't want to know about my bodily intimacies, skip this chapter and begin your reading with the next one.

I am a twenty-seven-year-old man, one meter seventy-eight centimeters tall. Every morning I look at myself naked in my bathroom mirror and caress my cheeks in anticipation of the daily ceremony: Shave my beard and upper lip, provoke a strong response with Jean-Marie Farina cologne on my face, resign myself to combing black, thick, untamable hair. Close my eyes. Deny to my face and head the central role my death will be certain to give them. Concentrate instead on my body. The trunk that is going to be separated from my head. The body that occupies me from my neck to my extremities, covered in skin the color of pale cinnamon and tipped with nails that will continue to grow for hours and days after death, as if they wanted to scratch at the lid of the coffin and shout I'm here, I'm still alive, you made a mistake when you buried me.

This is a purely metaphysical consideration, as is terror in its passing and permanent forms. I ought to concentrate here and now on my skin: I ought to rescue my physical being in all its completeness before it's too late. This is the organ of touch that covers my whole body and extends inside it with acts of anal mischief both modest and permissible if I compare them to the female gender's major jokes, the incessant entering and leaving of foreign bodies (notoriously the male's penis and sacredly the body of a child, while from my masculine wrappings only semen and urine come out in front and in back, just like *chez la femme,* shit and in cases of constipation, the deep communion of the suppository). Now I hum: "The bullock shits, so does the bird, and the best-looking babe will drop her turd." Broad, generous entrances and exits in the woman. Narrow, mean ones in the man: the urethra, the anus, urine, shit. The names are clear and brutal, the nicknames obscure and laughable: Bellini's duct, Henle's loop, Bowman's capsule, Malpighi's glomerulus. Dangers: anuria and uremia. No urine. Urine in the blood. I avoided them. In the end, everything in life is avoidable except death.

I used to sweat. In life my entire body would sweat except for my eyelids and the edge of my lips. My sweat was clean, salty, with no bad odor, though sweating and urinating were human products distinguishable by the different quality of their smell. I never needed deodorants. I had noble, clean armpits. My urine did smell bad, of abandoned hovels and lightless caves. My shit varied according to circumstances, depending especially on diet. Mexican food brings us dangerously close to diarrhea, North American to stomach cramps, British to constipation. Only Mediterranean cuisine assures us of a healthy balance between what comes in at the mouth and what goes out through the asshole, as if olive oil and vinegar from Modena, the produce of the gardens of Southern Europe, peaches and figs, melons and peppers, knew beforehand that the pleasure of eating should be balanced by the pleasure of shitting, very much in accordance with Quevedo's lines: "I love you more than a strong desire to take a shit."

In any case—in my case—shit is almost always firm and brown, sometimes artfully coiled like the clay turds sold in the markets, sometimes diluted and tortured by our hot national spices: O shit of mine. And rarely (above all when I travel) reticent and ugly-looking.

I know that with these diversions, my dear survivors, I am putting off what is most important. Getting to my head. Telling you what my face was like after making it clear that the buttocks, as everyone knows, are man's second face. Or are they the first?

I've already indicated, when combing my hair, that I have a good Indian thatch of dark hair, more deeply rooted than a maguey. I have to say that my eyes are dark and set deep in the sockets of a bony facial structure that would be almost transparent if not for the dark mask of my skin. (Dark skin hides feelings better than white. That's why when they are revealed, they are more brutal though less hypocritical.) In short, I have invisible eyebrows, a pleasant, slender mouth, almost always smiling for no reason other than courtesy. Ears neither large nor small, barely adequate to my extremely thin face, skin adhering to bone, the roots of my hair springing up like nocturnal thickets that grow without light.

And I have a nose. It isn't just any nose but a large proboscis, slender, fortunately, but long and thin, like a periscope of the soul that precedes the eyes to explore the landscape and find out if it's worth disembarking or if it's better to remain withdrawn deep in the sea of existence.

The wide Sargasso of anticipated death.

The sea that ascends in small waves, obliging me to swallow it before it reaches the orifices of my large nose, jutting out between the beach and the dawn tide.

I am a body. I will be a soul.

BIG BEAK. MONSTER schnoz. Elephant honker. Anteater snout. Pinocchio. Tapir. Dumbo (despite normal ears). The uproar in the schoolyard showed no preference among the epithets hurled at me by the mob of identical snot-noses in their uniforms of white shirt and blue tie, always badly knotted, as if not using the top button at the collar were a universal sign of rebellion controlled in the long run by the double discipline of teacher and religion. Blue sweater, gray trousers. Only at the extremities did this gang of schoolboys display their indolence and brutality. Leather shoes scuffed by the habit of kicking, kicking balls in the schoolyard, kicking desks in the classroom, kicking trees on the street, using kicks to demonstrate that though it might be without words they were protesting, they were born to protest, they were not conformists. Should I have been grateful to be the only thing they attacked with words and not blows?

I don't know. The jeering ferocity of their faces was such that, in spite of my esthetic intention to single out from the ugliest not the best-looking—there were none of those—but the least "ferocious," when they attacked I saw a single beast, a single face with bared teeth and eyes with metallic lids, as if they were protecting a strong-box of unspeakable emotions behind prison bars, for I never lost sight of the fact that these same assholes who were assaulting me on account of my big nose would be praying later with heads bowed and singing the national anthem, chins trembling with pride.

At the Jalisco school, so named since revolutionary liberalism prohibited the teaching of religion and revolutionary conservatism turned a blind eye and permitted it, but only if the schools proclaimed not their faith but their historical or geographical patriotism: Columbus, Bolívar, Homeland, Mexico were transformed into pseudonyms for schools run by Jesuits, Marists, Christian Brothers, and, in the case of the academy I was sent to, Catholic Presbyters, and therefore, among ourselves, the school was known as the Presbytery and not as Jalisco. It was a way of mocking the shared hypocrisy of the government and the clergy. Jalisco on the outside. Presbytery on the inside.

Big Beak, Pinocchio, Monster Schnoz, the insults rained down on me, obliging me to retreat as they moved forward like a column of troops led by a horrible kid with a shaved head, piggy eyes, a beet-red mouth, ears stuck to his skull, and the attitude of a great high-wayman, a forward-thrusting stance, a posture of defiance not only toward me but toward the world: He was the most nonconformist of nonconformists; his tie was knotted on his chest and wrapped around his neck, accentuating his air of a bandit. It was strange. This being the apparent head of the mob of schoolboys, a feeling whose origin I could not determine told me the guerrilla leader was waging war not against me and my nose but against something else, something closer to him that made my presence disappear as soon as the bell rang and recess was over—or as soon as one of the teachers intervened who, until that moment, had not even noticed what was happening to me, as if assaulting a student, even verbally, were not very different from playing basketball, telling jokes, or eating a piece of cake.

I gave instructions to my spirit. "Hold on, Josué. Don't give in. Don't return their insults. Arm yourself with patience. Defeat them with your self-control. Don't even think about hitting anybody. Whoever gets angry loses. Stay serious and calm. They'll end up respecting you, you'll see."

Until the day my good advice was betrayed by my evil impulses and I hauled off and socked the baldest of the bald. The conflict of San Quintín broke out (students of history: In this battle, Philip II defeated France and was covered in glory) in the midst of a colossal confusion that eventually turned into defeat, and also recalled Rosario de Amozoc, when a free-for-all dissolved all doubts in a brawl worthy of saloon fights in westerns. Or a donnybrook, the British version of a brawl, fracas, mêlée, brouhaha, uproar, tumult, hullabaloo, pandemonium, charivari, turmoil, logomachy, and, in general, chaos pure and simple. That is, the bald kid fell back against his comrades, who threw him back at me, though the guerrilla fighter had slipped and hit his face on the paving tiles in the yard, which provoked an argument between two, then four, then seven comrades about who had made the champion fall, and then another boy boldly stood at my side, faced the crowd of schoolboys, and shouted that the next blow would be struck not at me but at him.

The self-assurance of my defender was transformed into authority over a herd that counted its own strength in numbers and not in courage. The professorial whistle for order finally sounded that afternoon, which otherwise was stormy because the morning sun was leaving to bathe in cataracts of punctual twilight rain.

"It's the rainy season," said my smiling defender, resting his hand on my shoulder.

I thanked him. He said he could not stand cowards who fight only in a gang. He became distracted and offered his hand to the bald kid to help him up.

"Don't be late for class, asshole," he said.

The bald kid wiped the blood from his nose, turned his back on us, and ran away.

Together my new friend and I walked the length of the large yard, a space surrounded by two floors of classrooms and auditoriums, with a frontón court at the end.

"If they were a little more educated, they'd have called you Cyrano."

"They're sons of bitches. Don't give them any ideas. They'd call me Sir Anus."

"And if you were lame, Nureyev."

My savior stopped and looked at me astutely.

"You don't have a big nose. It's only a long nose. Don't let that bunch of bums get to you. What's your name?"

"Josué."

I was going to add the standard "at your service" that dates from colonial Mexican courtesy, when my protector threw back his head and began to laugh.

That's how I always want to remember him, the way he was at that moment. My height, but the reverse side of my coin. A face tending to plumpness, with the cheeks of an infant not yet weaned. Yes, the mouth of a nursing baby, and eyes so tender and bright they almost demanded a pacifier. His body, on the other hand, was vigorous, his walk decisive, perhaps too sure of his strong step and firm forward motion, while my movements tended to slip away from me, subtle and even a little hesitant, as if they weren't sure if at my feet they would find earth or the void, solid ground or swamp, light or mud . . .

It was the first thing I noticed. My uncertain, short steps. The martial, even imperious walk of my friend.

I realized he hadn't told me his name. I introduced myself again.

"Josué," I said, still walking.

He stopped like a mock statue. I looked at him with some surprise.

"Josué. Josué," I repeated, somewhat uncomfortable. "Josué Nadal."

My friend convulsed. Laughter seized him, doubled him over, eventually it obliged him to raise his head, look at the increasingly cloudy sky, then look at my astonished face, laugh even more when he saw me, and provoke in me a certain feeling of annoyance at not being in on the joke, a pleasantry that was somewhat unpleasant for me.

"And you?" I managed to say to him, hiding my irritation.

"Je . . . Je . . ." he in turn managed to say between outbursts of laughter.

I was becoming angry: "Listen, I don't find the joke . . ."

He took me by the shoulder: "It's not laughter, compadre . . . It's surprise . . ."

"Then stop laughing."

"Jericó. My name is Jericó," he said, suddenly serious.

"Jericó what?" I insisted.

"Just Jericó. No last name," said my new friend with an abrupt, definitive air, as if in the act of opening a book the entire text had disappeared, leaving only the first name of the author but not his last.

"Jericó . . . We'll get along like clockwork."

THE RIVER OVERFLOWS its banks at harvest time. Now it is dry and the tribes can cross over. But first spies must be sent out to reconnoiter the area. Joshua crosses the Jordan disguised as a merchant and hides in a brothel in the city. The harlot lives there with her family. She is a simple woman and a generous one. With her body, her affection, her protection. She is accustomed to hiding fugitives, antagonistic husbands, drunkards who need time to recuperate. Impotent men who linger and wish to demonstrate the virility recovered with the affection and patience only a whore can offer because it is her vocation and not merely her profession. Does the harlot know that Joshua and his men are members of a wandering tribe halted on the banks of the Jordan, searching for the promised land? The whore, whose name is Hetara, does not believe there are promised lands or lost paradises. She knows about the madness of Israel and its prophets. They all want to leave the land that offers them hospitality and move on to the next nation of promise. But when they reach it, they immediately begin to dream of the next promised land and so on and so forth until they become exhausted in the desert and die of thirst and hunger. The great whore of Jericho does not want her city to be the final port of the tribes of Israel. Not because she despises them. On the contrary, she loves them because she loves the wandering vocation of Israel and does not want them to stay here only so they can go forward in fulfilling their interminable destiny.

Because she knows these things, the brothel's clients consult her and she recounts fables. Some she has dreamed. Others she has remembered. But most of them she improvises in the heat of the visitors she receives. She is a sorceress, say her intimates who, like abandoned dogs, seek shelter in her sensual charity; she amazes whoever speaks to her and tells the fortune of her clients only on the basis of who those clients are. She is a realist. She would never give a man a destiny not already found in that man's future. Because all she needs is a hint of each client's past to imagine his future with certainty. She is not a cruel woman. She is prudent. When the future appears happy, she decreases the joy because she knows that any change in a life can unexpectedly darken it. When, on the contrary, the future is unhappy, she interjects a small dose of optimism, slips in a joke, shrugs her shoulders, and passes from prognostication to prostitution: her flesh, her mouth, her legs, these are the future . . .

Joshua came to Jericho with a pure intention: to explore the city and then take it in order to continue the reconquest of the land of Israel begun by Moses, whom Joshua served as a son and to whom he promised, at the hour of his death, to continue the tenacious path from the plains of Moab to the mountains of Nero to the summit of Pisgah. To conquer all the visible land from Gilead to Dan, the lands of Efrain and Manassas and the land of Judea to the sea. But first the city in view had to be vanquished, the first city, the city of palm trees: Jericho. Which is why Joshua was there, his purpose to reconnoiter the land and conquer it the next day. He felt protected in the generous brothel, with its pungent odors of sweat and excrescence, spilled wine, fried food, burned animal hair, smoke from slow fires, red roofs. He recalled, however, the admonition of Moses, his protector and guide, against the pleasures of sex and the orgiastic cult of Balaam. But the caresses of the great whore of the desert told him that thanks to her, her disloyalty, her protection, the city of Jericho would fall and the Jewish people could continue to follow their path of strength with justice and justice with strength. Joshua asked the prostitute what was at play that night, love or war. And she said that in each coupling in the world life and death were at play, pure, gratuitous pleasure alongside the obligation to give birth to the product of the coupling, the temporary suspension of obligation in the name of pleasure and its fatal resumption when the erotic couple separates and the world's law is imposed. And beyond that? asked an eager Joshua, already captured between the legs of Hetara, which is what he decided to call her, in the fire of his pleasure and with the understanding that here, in the bed of this woman, he was preparing as much for victory as for defeat.

Would he attribute one or the other to this hour of pleasure? Would the victim forgive him his fleeting lust? Would it cost him dearly at the hour of defeat? Joshua hurried the act and Hetara felt authorized, sitting with her legs crossed on the straw pallet, to tell him, Joshua, you will win the battle but will not exhaust your fate. Your people will debate forever either remaining in one place or the promise of the next place to conquer, a place better than the previous one. And on and on forever. The exodus will be endless. And new. In their successive exiles, your descendants will enrich the land they walk on. They will be doctors and heal. They will be artists and create. They will be lawyers and defend. They will be successful and envied. They will be envied and persecuted. They will be persecuted and suffer the worst tortures. The great weeping of your people in which, for one tragic, happy moment, all the men, women, and children in the world will recognize themselves. All this I see, Joshua. I also see your people immobile, certain they have found a country and have no obligation to move on. That will be a deception. Israel is condemned to migrate, move, occupy lands in the same way you, tomorrow, will occupy mine. Our bodies have joined just as tomorrow my land and yours will be joined.

Think, Joshua: How will you return my land to me? How will you avoid making my destiny tomorrow the one that is yours forever? Will you occupy my land only in order to forget that no one gave you one of your own?

Joshua listened attentively to Hetara and told himself that this night of forbidden pleasure was the price of permitted victory. Hetara knew everything and forgave nothing. Joshua saw it in her dark eyes, he pulled the red ribbon from her dark hair and said:

"Do me one last favor. Hang the red ribbon from the roof of your house."

"Will my family be saved, and my clients?"

"Yes, you will be saved. I swear it."

In this way Joshua justified his night with the whore of Jericho, returned to the mountain, and told the Jews: Truly, Jehovah has delivered the land into our hands. And they all followed him to the banks of the Jordan and shouted with a great shout, convinced that God had promised them victory in battle, and the priests sounded the trumpets. Then the walls of Jericho fell with a great noise, as if the voices and the trumpets were the arms of God, and the Jews entered Jericho and destroyed the city, put men, women, and children to the sword, old people, oxen, sheep, and asses, respecting only Joshua's order:

"Do not touch Hetara the prostitute."

And Hetara went to live among the Jews and learned that her

city would never be seen again, because Joshua decreed that whoever rebuilt it would be cursed in the eyes of the Lord.

THIS WAS HOW Jericó and I became friends. We discovered everything we had in common. Our age. Sixteen and seventeen years old.
Books we had read, not only as children but those we shared now,
though he had a year's advantage on me, which in adolescence is a
great deal. He lent me—annotated—books he had already read. We
commented on them together. And a similar attitude in and out of
school. Being independent. We discovered that we would not permit
anyone to inculcate in us opinions that weren't ours or had not at
least been screened by our own critical sense. Further, we thought
our opinions were not opinions alone but doubts as well. This was
the firmest ground of our friendship. Almost instinctively, Jericó and
I understood that each line we read, each idea we received, each
truth we affirmed, had its opposite, as day had night. In that final
year of secondary school, we did not allow a single line, idea, or
truth to pass without submitting it to judgment. We had not yet calculated how much this attitude would help us—or hurt us—when
we were out in the world, away from the sheltered nest of school.
For now, being dissidents inside it distinguished us with a still adolescent, pedantic, excessive air from the student mob that surrounded us and then, after Jericó's defense of me and the bloodied
nose of the bald aggressor, stopped interfering with me or my nose
and looked for new odious marks to fight, as long as they could isolate the victim and present themselves as an unidentifiable and consequently unpunishable mass.

Eventually even the famous bald kid approached us with an
amusing false piece of news.

"They're saying you two are always together because you're fags.
I want to be your friend and see if they dare to say that about me
too."

He accompanied his words with terrible grimaces of ill will and
the torpid agility of a budding champion.

We asked him with false astonishment if he was safe from all aggression and he said yes. Why? we insisted. Because I'm very rich

and don't brag about it. He pointed, his hand perpetually bloodied or covered with scabs, to the street:

"Do you see a black Cadillac parked there at the exit?"

Sure. By now it was part of the landscape.

"Have you seen me get into it?"

No, we had seen him waiting for the bus at the corner.

"Well, it's my father's car. It comes for me every afternoon. The chauffeur sees me come out and he gets out and opens the door for me. I go to the bus stop and the Cadillac goes home empty."

I thought about the useless waste of gasoline but said nothing, thinking that for now the boy deserved all our curiosity. He placed his hands on his hips and looked at us with an appealing—or perhaps pathetic—need for approval. Lacking our applause, he gave in and introduced himself.

"I'm Errol."

Now Jericó and I did smile, and our friendly smile was a request: Explain that to us.

"My mother has been a fan of Errol Flynn her whole life. Now nobody even remembers Errol Flynn. He was a very famous actor when my mother's mother was young. She told her she never missed an Errol Flynn movie. She said he was very handsome and "nonchalant," that's what they called him in movie magazines. He was Robin Hood, and he swung from tree to tree dressed in green, as camouflage, ready to steal from the rich and give to the poor, an enemy of tyranny. And my mother inherited her mother's taste."

A dreamy look passed over the eyes of the aggressive bald kid who was introducing himself now as Errol Esparza and offering us both his friendship and a summary of his life, the three of us sitting on the steps of the schoolyard during the final year of our secondary education, ready to assume the duties (and the airs) of the preparatory school in this same building, with the same professors and classmates, no longer identical to themselves but to the changing mirror of early youth, when a thousand insistent signs of childhood persist in obstructing the face that struggles to break through and tell us: We've grown up. Now we're men.

That is why the final year of secondary seemed so long and the first of preparatory so uncertain and distant. Not because of essential realities in one or the other level of education, but because of the accidental facts that we were ourselves: chubby-cheeked Jericó, bald Errol, and me, skinny Josué, the three of us surprised at the changes our bodies and souls were experiencing, though all three, each in his own way, pretended to accept the transformations without amazement, with natural dispassion, even with a certain indifference, as if we knew beforehand what we would be in the coming year and remained overwhelmingly ignorant of what we still were.

Errol suggested the real pitfall. He invited us to his house. It was an invitation made with a strange air of irony mixed with indulgence concealing a poorly disguised embarrassment. Implicitly, he was expecting to be invited to our houses, believing that our friendship would last only if we knew a sixteen-year-old boy's worst secret: his family. With this trauma overcome, we could move on to the next stage. Being adults and being friends.

The good Errol's good faith—not to call it innocence—was beyond any doubt. I knew that everything unsaid by the boy with the shaved head did not live in the basement of bad faith. Errol behaved honorably. In any case, Jericó and I were the ones walking twisted paths.

"Errol Esparza."

"Josué Nadal."

"Jericó."

You who survive me can imagine that when I became Jericó's friend, I asked him what his last name was and he replied Just Jericó, no last name. I wasn't satisfied, I felt curious, I went to the admissions secretary at the school and asked outright,

"What's Jericó's last name?"

The secretary was a young, attractive man who seemed out of place in the small records office, behind a corrugated glass panel near the school entrance, where half his face and an entire hand would appear, upon request, to attend to the public. He hastily withdrew hand and face and his voice acquired a neutral but forced tone.

"That's Jericó's name: Jericó."

Although it was during office hours, the secretary closed the small window. Soon afterward I sensed both an offensive and defensive attitude in my friend Jericó. I attributed it to the secretary's indiscretion, though I had no proof. The fact is that Jericó, letting a few days pass through the sieve of an unaccustomed seriousness in our dealings with each other, which I attributed to my own indiscretion as well as the secretary's (a position normally filled by embittered women in their forties with no hope of finding a husband), asked me to go with him to the café on the corner, and once we were seated in front of two tepid, tasteless, decaffeinated concoctions, he gave me an intense look and said that during the past semester he and I had naturally cemented a friendship that he wanted to know was solid and lasting.

"Do you agree, Josué?"

With a good amount of enthusiasm, I told him I did. Nothing in my past—my very brief past, I said with a laugh—promised a friendship as close as the one Jericó and I had created in the past few months. His concern seemed to me unnecessary, though welcome. We were sealing a pact between comrades. I wished that instead of Nescafé we each had a glass of champagne. I felt the warmth of satisfaction that as adolescents we discover in the friendship of a kindred spirit who rescues us from the solitude reserved, without pity, for the incomprehensible boy who stops being a child overnight and no longer fits into the careful world his parents prepared for him under the illusion that a child so indulged would never grow up.

That wasn't my case. Then Jericó said that between the ages of seventeen, which we already had reached, and twenty-one, which was yet to come, he and I ought to establish a project for life and study that would make us close forever. Perhaps there would be separations, trips, women, for example. The important thing was to seal, right here, an alliance for the rest of our lives. Knowing that he would always come to my aid, and I would come to his. Knowing which values we shared. What things we rejected.

"It's important to make a list of obligations . . ."

"Sacred ones?"

Jericó agreed energetically. "For us, yes."

Where would we begin?

First, with a shared decision to reject frivolity. My friend took a gossip magazine out of his backpack and leafed through it with displeasure and disgust.

"Look at this succession of idiocies in full color on glossy paper. Are you interested in knowing that the rock-and-roller Tarcisia married the Russian millionaire Ulyanov, both of them barefoot, with Hawaiian leis around their necks, on the Playa del Carmen, and that the guests began the day dancing to hip-hop on the sand at seven in the morning, when they gorged on a savory tripe stew in honor of the bride's father, who is a native of Sonora? Would you have liked to be a guest? Would you have accepted an invitation? Answer me."

I said no, Jericó, not at all, I'm not interested in being—

He interrupted me. "Not even if it was your own wedding?"

No, now I smiled, I thought that taking the matter as a joke was the best thing and I admired Jericó's intense ability to take life very, very seriously.

"Do you swear never to go to a *quinceañera,* a *thé dansant,* a baptism, or grand openings of restaurants, flower shops, supermarkets, bank branches, the celebration of university alumni, beauty contests, or meetings at the Zócalo? Do you promise to despise a couple who have their picture taken in color and published in the paper when she is eight months pregnant and wearing a bikini with the proud husband caressing her belly and announcing the imminent arrival, baptism, and sanctification of *Raulito* in the midst of a storm of flashbulbs (which is why they were announcing the emotional event now)?"

I made the mistake of laughing. Jericó slammed his fist down on the table. The coffee cups rattled. The waitress came over to see what was going on. The hostility in my friend's eyes frightened her away. The café began to fill up with patrons thrown up after a day of work that perhaps differed for each one but still imposed an identical fatigue on all of them. Public or private offices, businesses large or small, the merciless traffic of Mexico City, the nonexistent hope of finding happiness when they reached home, the weight of what was not. All that began to come into the café. It was seven in the evening. We had begun talking at five-thirty, when the place was empty.

And together we had agreed on a plan for a shared life. Did we speak only of avoiding the stupidities of social and political festivities and celebrations? Not at all. Before what Jericó contemptuously called "the herd of oxen" came in.

"Oxen," Jericó repeated. "Never say 'oxes.' "

"Oxen?"

"No. Oxes. Never say oxen are oxes."

"Why?"

"So as not to give in to the vulgarity, stupidity, and camouflaging of mental poverty by means of deadly buffoonery."

We settled on a plan of readings, of selective and rigorous intellectual self-improvement, which, survivors, you will not find out about today because at that moment Errol Esparza walked into the café and reminded us, boys, today's the day you visit my house. Let's go.

"Like clockwork," Jericó said, as usual.

THE ESPARZA FAMILY lived in the Pedregal de San Angel, an ancient volçanic bed, a remnant of the eruptions of Xitle, on whose dark, bulky foundations the architect Luis Barragán attempted to create a modern residential district based on strict rules. First, that volcanic rock be used to build the houses. Second, that they would assume the monastic forms of the Barragán style. Unadorned straight lines, clean walls, with no variant other than the colors, evocative of folklore, associated with Mexico: indigo blue, sourcherry red, and sun yellow. Flat roofs. No visible water tanks as in the rest of a chaotic city where so many styles cohabitate that in the end there is no style unless it is the triumphal repetition of squat houses, one-story businesses, paint shops, auto repair shops, tire shops, garages, parking lots, and miscellaneous candy stores, taverns, and retailers of all the daily necessities of this strange society of ours, always controlled from the top by very few and always capable of organizing itself from the bottom, with the majority living independently.

I have said all of this because the pure order desired by the architect did not last as long as a snowball in hell. Barragán had closed the Pedregal with symbolic sentry boxes and gates, as if to dictate a public anathema: *Vade retro, Partagás, you will not pass.*

Impure disorder in the name of the false freedom of residents and their accommodating architects—all of them subject to another tyranny, the tyranny of bad taste and assimilation of the worst in the name of a robot's autonomy—finished off the fleeting effort to give at least one metropolitan residential district the unity and beauty of a district in Paris, London, or Rome. So that in the midst of the naked beauty of the original framework there erupted like malignant chancres fake Colonial, Breton, Provençal, Scotch, and Tudor residences, not to mention the inconceivable California ranch and the nonexistent tropical "adobe hacienda."

Still, the Esparza family had not brought to Pedregal the architecture of their previous districts. They had accepted the severity of the original monastic design. At least on the outside, Barragán triumphed. Because once Jericó and I walked into the home of our new friend, Errol Esparza, what we found was a baroque disorder inside a neobaroque chaos inside a post-baroque clutter. In other words, one horror did not suffice in Esparza's house. The bareness of the walls was a summons that could not be denied to cover them with calendar art, mostly still lifes, picture after picture, not merely contiguous but incestuous, as if leaving a centimeter of empty wall were proof of barefaced miserliness or the crude rejection of an invitation. Articles of furniture also fought for the prize of space. Massive sofas from cheap furniture stores designed to fill large empty spaces: six griffin claws, three cushions of embossed velvet for the back, tables with dragon feet and surfaces covered with ashtrays taken from various hotels and restaurants, rugs with Persian intentions and the appearance of straw sleeping mats contrasted with salons of a Versaillesque nature, Louis XV chairs with brocade backs and deer feet, glass cabinets with untouchable *souvenirs* of Esparzan visits to Versailles and Gobelin tapestries of recent manufacture. Everything indicated that the first room, with its gigantic television screen, was where the Esparzas lived and the "French" room where, in the evenings, they *received.*

"Make yourselves comfortable," the good Errol said without a hint of irony. "I'll let my mother know we're here."

We were looking at the shaggy purple rug whose obvious intention was to grow like an interior, crepuscular lawn, when Errol reappeared leading a "simple" woman who announced her simplicity with her old-fashioned hairdo—I think it was called a "permanent"—down to her low-heeled shoes with black buckles and moving—now upward—to her cotton stockings, one-piece flowered dress, short apron on which the lady listlessly rubbed her red hands, as if drying them after a domestic flood, to pale, barely made up features. Her face was the blank canvas of an artist undecided whether to conclude it or leave it, with impatient relief, unfinished.

The lady looked at us with a mixture of candor and suspicion, still drying her hands like a domestic Pontius Pilate, and said in a dull voice, Estrella Rosales de Esparza, at your service . . .

"Tell them, mother," Errol said brusquely.

"Tell them what?" Doña Estrellita asked with no pretense of surprise.

"How we got rich."

"Rich?" the lady said with authentic confusion.

"Yes, mother," the bald kid continued. "My friends must be amazed at so much luxury. Where did it all come from, this . . . junk?"

"Oh, son." The lady lowered her head. "Your father has always been very hardworking."

"What do you think about papa's fortune?"

"I think it's fine."

"No, its origins."

"Oh, son, how can you be—"

"Be what?"

"Ungrateful. We owe everything to your father's efforts."

"Efforts? Is that what we call crime now?"

His mother looked at him defiantly.

"What crime? What are you talking about?"

"Being a thief."

Instead of becoming angry, Doña Estrellita maintained an admirable composure. She looked at Jericó and me with patience.

"I haven't welcomed you. My son is a very impetuous boy."

We thanked her. She smiled and looked at her son.

"He insults me because I'm not Marlene Dietrich. As if that were my fault! He isn't Errol Flynn either."

She turned her back, bending her head, and went back to the mysterious place she had come from.

Errol burst into laughter.

He told us his father had been a carpenter, first in one of the poorest districts in the city. Then he began to make furniture. Soon he was selling beds, chairs, and tables to several hotels. Then he established a furniture store downtown, near the Avenida 20 de Noviembre. With so much furniture on his hands, the only thing he could do was put up a hotel, and then another, and yet another, and since the guests wanted entertainment close by—television was still in diapers, that is, black-and-white—he took an old movie house in San Juan de Letrán and turned it into a live-performance theater, decorated in the style of a Chinese pagoda just like the one in Los Angeles, and since man does not live by art alone, he opened a furniture store and then another and another and yet another until he had a chain of hotels and that's what we live on.

Errol sighed while Jericó and I—and certainly all of you who can hear me—put on a polite face and listened without blinking to this lightning account of a career that culminated in this shambles of a house in the Pedregal de San Angel with a boy who refused to get into the Cadillac driven by a uniformed chauffeur and delighted in humiliating a defenseless mother and attacking an absent father.

"He hired gangs of bums to put mice inside rival movie houses, break his enemies, and take over their theaters."

"How nice," I dared to say, but Errol, enveloped in the cloud of his own rhetoric, didn't hear me.

"He sent salesmen to distract employees in the businesses of his rivals."

"Very smart," Jericó said with a smile.

"He sent evangelists to convert them to Protestantism."

"The religion of capitalism, Errol," I said for the sake of saying something.

"Have you read *Protestantism and the Modern World* by Ernst Troeltsch?" Jericó commented, increasing the aberrations of the conversation. "Without Protestantism there is no capitalism. In the opinion of Saint Thomas, capitalists went to hell. Consequently, all capitalists are Protestants."

I swear it hurt me to see Errol's bewilderment when right after that Jericó and I looked at each other, thanked him, and left the walled house through a garden with no trees where workers were raising something like a statue onto a pedestal.

"Let the chauffeur drive you home."

We agreed and left. Relieved, but without saying a word and exchanging a complicit glance that said: He's our friend. We won't stop talking to him.

Were we talking to ourselves, Jericó? Didn't we leave the Esparza house secretly thinking that all this horror, this inanity, this dissatisfaction, this grief, takes place *en famille,* it occurs because *a family* exists—like a tray of rotten fruit, a cup of poison, a sewer capable of receiving it all, digesting it, purifying it, bringing it back to life from a near-death final injury?

You and I avoided looking at each other, Jericó, when we left the residence in Pedregal. Neither of us had a family. We were what we are because we were, are, will be orphans. What is orphanhood? No doubt not the mere absence of father or mother or family but inclemency, the ruination of the sheltering roof for reasons that sometimes are clearly attributable to abandonment, to death, to simple indifference. Except that you and I did not know any of these reasons. Perhaps you do, but you've kept them to yourself. And my situation was equivocal, as I'll recount later.

He's our friend. We won't stop talking to him.

Although perhaps, privately, we envied Errol his family situation no matter how violent or pathetic it was.

"He didn't need to say what he said," was the secret message Jericó sent me when I got out at Calle de Berlín.

"That's true. He didn't," I remarked, more to confirm our friendship than for any other reason.

ON THE OTHER hand, months later, when we graduated from secondary to preparatory, we found not a pretext but an opportunity to speak for hours on end with a new instructor who had just joined the faculty. Until then we had not felt admiration or scorn for the group of teachers who, with far too much discretion for our demanding spirits, taught not very imaginative classes based on acts of serial (like a crime) memorization of history, geography, and natural sciences. The biology instructor was amusing because of the subterfuges he summoned and the rough terrain he walked in order to sublimate the facts of nature by means of an explicit final reference, the crown of his reiterated discourse, to the act of divine creation, the origin and destiny of our physical realities and transcendent mortality.

There were, no doubt, other excesses that broke the gray neutrality of our classes. The headmaster, an irascible Frenchman with unpronounceable Breton family names, whom we called "Don Vercingetorix," regularly opened the school year by standing on a dais with a gladiolus in his hand. After perusing the assembled student body with a severe look worthy of Torquemada, he would proclaim, "This is a young Christian before he goes to a dance and kisses a girl." Immediately afterward he would throw the flower on the floor and stamp on it in a kind of holy can-can until he had pulverized the innocent flower, which he would then pick up from the floor and show us the vegetable tatters in his hands, concluding: "And this is a Catholic boy after he goes to a dance and kisses a girl." Of the moribund gladiolus, all that survived, with a symbolism surely not desired by the enraged Vercingetorix, was the erect stem. A pregnant silence and a final warning: "Think. Confess your sins.

Break ranks." All that was missing was for him to warn, "And don't break into laughter," though the formal severity of the school lent itself not to jokes but to a kind of Christian resignation when we got ready in the locker room to play basketball, knowing that at the opportune moment Professor Soler would come in, saying "Let's see, let's see, everybody ready?" as a pretext to look at us before we pulled on our shorts and approach, "let's see, let's see," to adjust the jockstraps needed to protect our sex from blows on the court, to heft with touching reverence, on his knees or bending over, the testicles of each student to check that we were well protected as we went out to athletic encounters and, if we were lucky, sexual combat.

We students forgave this innocent pleasure of Father Soler, whose red face was the product not of any shame but of an inheritance that can give to the product of the mixing of Indians and blonds a sanguine appearance very apt for disguising the blushes of embarrassing emotion. In other words: Collectively the students forgave the life both of the ostentatious Vercingetorix and the silent Soler, considering that they did not have many opportunities to express themselves in public, subject as they were to long hours of prayers and rosaries, early suppers, fleeting breakfasts . . . They would have put out the sun with the smoke of incense.

Everything changed when the new philosophy instructor came on the scene.

Father Filopáter (that's how he was announced and how he introduced himself) was a small, agile man. He moved with a combination of juvenile athleticism and spiritual animation, as if in order to demonstrate one you had to celebrate the other. He walked with varying rhythms. Very quickly when he went from one task to another. Very slowly when he strolled around the yard accompanied by one or two students to whom he listened with intense concentration, offering the paradoxical idea of a short man who grew as he thought, as if his ideas—for he seemed *to think* more than *to talk*—were flying over him, creating an unusual halo, not round but long, though always shining.

It goes without saying, you who are still alive and can contradict me with no risk or confirm everything I say out of curiosity, that Jericó and I immediately fixed on the new arrival and imagined how we could approach him and determine who he was—in addition to being a philosophy instructor—by what he thought and said. He was ahead of us.

Always together, he said, approaching with his quickest step, like Castor and Pollux.

The mythological allusion did not escape us, and both Jericó and I instantly looked at each other, knowing he spoke of the twins born of the same egg, for their father was a god disguised as a swan. Always together, the twins took part in great expeditions, like the exploits of the Argonauts under the command of Jason, searching for the as yet undiscovered soul they called the Golden Fleece.

Filopáter read in our glances that we already knew the legend, though neither he nor we had the courage, on that sunlit October afternoon, to conclude the story of the young twins. A legend can end badly, but the conclusion should not be anticipated at the beginning of life (Jericó and Josué) or what soon would become a friendship (with Father Filopáter). And yet how could it not illuminate for me, no matter how tacitly, the suspicion of an ending that was, if not desired, ultimately fatal? Perhaps the affinity born immediately between the instructor and ourselves was due to a kind of shared respect thanks to which we knew the outcomes but held them off with friendship, ideas, in short, life, since for friendship the outcome always was ideas, life, and the death of the *real* dialogists. If Socrates survives thanks to Plato, Saint Augustine, and Rousseau because they confessed, and Dr. Johnson because he had Boswell as his secretary and clerk, what opportunity for survival did we three—Father Filopáter, Jericó, and I—have beyond a luminous October afternoon in the Valley of Mexico? Would we be capable, like poets and novelists, of surviving thanks to works that, though they are ours, escape us and become the property of everyone, especially the reader not yet born? This was the challenge that began to filter, like a pure breeze separating us from the overwhelming pollution of the traffic, the smog, the movement in the street of desolate bodies, the mere proximity, here in the schoolyard, of noisy students at recess. No, the breeze was not pure. It was an illusion of our affinity.

Jericó and I were not (I must inform you) beings separate from the school community. On the contrary, knowing ourselves (as we knew ourselves) superior to the gregarious collectivity of the institution, fortuitous companions in earlier readings perhaps well thought out and digested, our meeting owed a great deal to chance, which is accidental, but also to destiny, which is disguised will. In cafés and classes, on long walks through the Bosque de Chapultepec or the Viveros de Coyoacán, we two had compared ideas, evoked readings, each one filling in the lapses of the other, recalling a book, condemning an author, but in the end assuming an inheritance that eventually we shared with the unrepeatable joy of intellectual awakening that is a fact in every society, but especially in ours, in which true creativity is rewarded less and less while economic success, celebrity, television appearances, sex scandals, and political clownishness are valued more and more.

The difference between us, I admit right now, was one of exigency and rigor. I also admit, for the eternal record, that in our relationship I was more indolent or passive, while Jericó was more alert and demanding.

"Demand more of yourself, Josué. Until now we've moved forward together. Don't lag behind me."

"Don't you lag either," I replied, smiling.

"It's hard," he responded.

After gym, which was required, we all showered in the long, cold, solitary bathrooms in the school. Unlike the nuns' schools, where girls have to wash dressed in gowns that turn them into cardboard statues, in schools for boys, showering naked was normal and attracted no one's attention. An unwritten law dictated that in the shower we men would keep our eyes at face level and no one, under penalty of suspicion of unhealthy curiosity or simple vulgarity, would look at a classmate's sex. Naturally, this rule was overseen by the one who observed it least: timid, impertinent Father Soler, who would walk up and down the bathroom with the mixed gaze of an eagle and a serpent—very appropriate to our nation—and in his hand a threatening, symbolic rod that he never, as far as we knew, used on the boys' wet backs and lustrous buttocks.

Those who are still alive and reading me will agree that I am telling them something as unusual for them as it was for us. Jericó decided that the temptation of our looking at each other naked existed, but the way to overcome it was not by physical effort but by expressing ourselves intellectually. For that, he said, let's choose two thoughts that are opposite and therefore complementary and invoke them in the shower—which was icy, those who still enjoy their senses should know, for that was demanded by our mentors' code of physical rigor and aspirations to sanctity.

It still causes astonishment, as well as sensual delight, to remember that by common agreement, when it was time to shower, standing side by side, not looking at each other, soaking wet and naked, with the incessant drip of delicious water falling on our heads, one would repeat aloud the constituent, formal ideas of Catholic philosophy as if they were at once dogmas and anathemas, while the other recited the theory of their absolute negation. Jericó maintained that the Christian philosophy of Saint Augustine and Saint Thomas Aquinas was the basis of the authoritarian, oppressive system of the Iberian nations. The ancient dispute between Saint Augustine and the British heretic Pelagius in the fourth or fifth century set the pattern. The heretic proclaimed the freedom to approach God by means of our own sensibility and intelligence. Saint Augustine stated that there is no personal freedom without the filter of the ecclesiastical institution. The Church is the indispensable intermediary between individual faith and divine grace. By contrast, the heretic claimed that grace is within reach of everyone. Grace, the saint responded, requires the power of the institution to be granted. From this ancient dispute in ruined oracles between a child of Roman Africa and an obscure northern monk grew, said Jericó in the rain of the shower, first the division between Catholics and Protestants and then the difference between Latin Americans and North Americans: We had the Middle Ages, Augustinian and Thomistic, and they didn't; they had Pelagianism brought up to date by

Luther and the imperatives of capitalism, and we didn't. For North Americans, history begins with them and the past was invented by Cecil B. DeMille with the help of Charlton Heston. For us, the past is so old that it has to be lived again.

If enunciating medieval Catholic contentions in the shower was a singular but unifying act between two naked eighteen-year-old boys, it was no less demanding to make the nihilistic argument in its Nietzschean dress (or in this case, nakedness), for it was up to me to allege that there is no freedom if we don't emancipate ourselves from faith and from every foundation or acquired rationale, lifting the veil of appearances and adopting the impulse toward the truth, whose first step . . .

"Is the recognition that nothing is true."

I said these words "in the rain," and I confess I felt desolate and in those moments wanted to possess the certainties enunciated by Jericó, for not only did the stream of water on my head blind me, but so did the grief of the loss of all certainty. Still, my role in this fraternal dialogue, which distanced us from false modesty or unhealthy curiosity, was that of a transformer of values by means of false values, saving my dear, my beloved friend Jericó from Christian culture, which is the culture of renunciation.

"And when have you ever seen a Catholic renounce pleasure if in the end it's enough to confess to a priest to free yourself of all guilt?"

"Or money, something that once was the occupation of Jews or Protestants?"

"Or fame, as if modern sanctity was granted by the magazine *Hola*?"

We left the bathroom laughing, happy to have surmounted sexual temptation, proud of our intellectual discipline, prepared to exchange roles the next time, when I'd be Catholic, he'd be nihilist, and in this way we'd sharpen our weapons for the inevitable encounter—it would be the greatest dispute of our early youth—with a man—the only man—capable of challenging us: the recently arrived Father Filopáter.

———

WE RETURNED TO Errol's house. Because of Jericó's permanent curiosity and, in my case, not only for that reason but because of something I haven't mentioned yet and that profoundly affected my life.

The fact is that the Esparzas were entertaining that night. Don Nazario had acquired a chain of hotels in Yucatán and was celebrating with a party. Our classmate the bald kid (though I should say the ex-bald kid, since Errol had let a mane of hair grow that, he told us, was the sign of rebellious youth in the sixties) invited us, as he remarked, to inspect the flora and fauna. Conforming to manners they deemed "distinguished," Errol's parents welcomed their guests at the entrance to the Versailles salon. Don Nazario, whom we had never seen, was a florid man, tall, red-faced, with eyes that were someplace else. He seemed full of bonhomie, distributing embraces and smiles, but looking off into the distance, almost fearful that something forgotten, menacing, or ridiculous would appear. He wore green gabardine and a large Hawaiian tie lavish with palm trees, waves, and girls dancing the hula. He looked like a man in costume. He dressed in accordance with his origins (carpentry, furniture, hotels, movie houses) and not with his destiny (a mansion in Pedregal and a bank account safe from bruising). Was it an act of sincerity and pride in his humble past to display himself as he had been, or the cleverest disguise of all, almost a challenge: Look at me, all of you, I reached the top but I'm still the humble, easygoing man I always was?

He greeted us as if we were his oldest friends, with great embraces and mistaken references, since, with his heart in his hand, he thanked us for the "service," that is, the favor or favors we had done him, which, of course, were nonexistent, leading us to one of two conclusions: Either Don Nazario was out-and-out wrong, or he was treating us in a manner that would not offend but did save him from the possible mistake of owing us something and having forgotten it.

In any event, the confusion passed as rapidly as the speed with which Señor Esparza, radiating cordiality, pushed us forward and repeated the ceremony of the joyous, grateful embrace with the guests behind us, freeing us from the welcome of his wife, Doña Estrellita, who was there, no doubt about that, we saw her, we greeted her, though at the same time she was absent, hidden by the powerful presence of her husband as well as by a desire for invisibility that duplicated, in a certain sense, the desire to disappear altogether.

Was the attire of the mistress of the house the result of her own taste or an imposition by her husband? If the second, we were approaching uxoricide. The lady seemed dressed, if not to go to heaven or hell, then to inhabit a gray limbo, as gray as her mouse-colored tailored suit, her eternal cotton stockings replaced by old-style nylons, her low-heeled shoes by ones of patent leather with ankle straps. Her discomfort at standing on line and receiving in public was so evident that it immediately classified her husband as a sadist who, when he saw her from time to time, would say with a ferocious look, utterly foreign to his affability as host:

"Laugh, you idiot! Don't make me look bad!"

Patently clear because Señora Estrella gave forced smiles and looked for approval in the eyes of a husband who did not need to look at her: He dominated her, we realized, through pure anticipatory habit. Doña Estrellita knew that if she didn't do one thing or another, she would have to pay dearly when the guests had left.

I confess that my understandable fascination with the couple separated me from the rest of the crowd, which was dissolving behind a veil of noises, inaudible conversations, the clink of glasses, and the passing of canapés offered by a short, dark-skinned waiter costumed in a striped shirtfront. I could not help admiring the discipline of Errol's mother in playing the part of the present absent woman. In her fixed, dead eyes there appeared from time to time a lightning flash that commanded her:

"Obey."

I don't believe it was difficult for her to do so. She knew she was easy to ignore, and I suppose that from the time she was young her comments, timid in and of themselves, were extinguished to the beat of her husband's brutal orders, shut up, don't play the fool, you're always out of place. Why worry about it?

"Leave the zoo, guys. Let's go to the den," said Errol. "My refuge."

The "den" was the disordered room we had already seen. Errol took off his jacket and invited us to do the same.

"After what you've seen, do you feel capable of betting everything on art and philosophy?"

I think we laughed. Errol didn't give us the chance to respond. Sprawled on the most comfortable armchair in his shirtsleeves, legs spread, he freed himself of tasseled loafers and seized a guitar as if it were the willing waist of an obedient woman.

"You'd be better off getting into politics. Let's hope you can find a path between what you want to be and what society permits you."

I was going to answer. Errol did not allow himself to be interrupted.

"Or are you suddenly going to wager on destiny?"

He held up a hand to silence us.

"Just imagine, I've already bet on a destiny."

He observed us; we were polite and interested.

He told us, without our asking, that even though we didn't believe him, once—a long time ago—Nazario and Estrellita might have loved each other. At what moment did they stop? What would you call the night he no longer desired her, or didn't see her as young anymore, and she knew he was watching her grow old? In the beginning everything was very different, Errol elaborated, because my mother Estrella was a convent girl and my father wanted a wife without blemish—that's what it's called—because in his life he had known only sluts, and whores know how to deceive. With Estrella there was no doubt. She traveled from the convent to the bed of her lord and master, who used her up in one night, demonstrating to her that he didn't care a fig about convents—that was his outmoded expression—and it would be better if his wife, being chaste, behaved like a whore to please a macho like Nazario Esparza.

Her family handed over Estrellita, received a check and some properties, and never concerned themselves about her again. Who were they? Who knows. They charged a good price to give her, chaste and pure, to a voracious, ambitious husband. The passion ended, though sometimes he looked at her with an intense absence.

It wasn't enough to avoid the repetition of the same battle every night, when Estrella still retained a shred of courage and dignity that served only to infuriate Nazario. The same battle every night until they found the reason for the next dispute, which was to postpone the obligation of sex that she needed not only as something new but because of the chaste obligation of the matrimonial sacrament and that he, perhaps, wanted to put off because of a strange feeling that in this way he was honoring the virginity of his wife, though it was clear to him that Estrella had come to the marriage bed intact and if she was impure, he had been the reason. None of this endured or had too much importance. He was plunging into a gross vulgarity, which Jericó and I had observed that night and Errol now expanded on for us.

"I loved her ten thousand enchiladas ago" was the husband's response.

She took refuge in the renunciation of sex in the name of religion and set up a pious little shrine in the matrimonial bedroom that Nazario wasted no time in getting rid of with a swipe of his hand, leaving Estrellita resigned to finally seeing herself one night as her husband saw her. She no longer looked young to herself and was certain she looked like an old woman to him.

"Ten thousand enchiladas ago, while she prayed on her knees: 'Neither for vice nor fornication. It is to make a child in Thy holy service.' "

She replaced the saints with pictures of Errol Flynn, whose erotic proclivities were unknown to both Estrellita and Nazario.

"Do you know what?" Errol continued. "I bet I can have a destiny that lets me overthrow my father. Do you like that word? Don't we hear it every day in history class? Tom took up arms and overthrew Dick hoping that Harry would overthrow somebody else and so forth and so on. Is that history, dudes? A series of overthrows? Maybe so."

He seemed to take a breath and say: "Maybe so. Maybe not . . ."

Without letting go of the guitar, he raised his glass: "I bet I can have a destiny that overthrows my father's. Overthrowing a destiny, as if it were a throne. Maybe so! Suddenly! Or maybe not . . ."

He stretched out his arm and played the guitar, beginning to sing, very appropriately, the ballad of the disobedient son:

"Out of the way, father, I'm wilder than a big cat, don't make me fire a bullet that'll go straight through your heart . . ."

Voices rose, angry and gruff, in the hall between the Versailles salon and the refuge where we were sitting.

"Are you crazy? Give me that camera."

"Nazario, I only wanted—"

"It doesn't matter what you wanted, you've made me look ridiculous taking pictures of my guests! That's all I needed!"

"*Our* guests, it's also my party—"

"It's also your nothing, you old idiot."

"You're to blame. I don't like receiving. I don't like standing on that line. You do it just to—"

"If you did it well, you wouldn't humiliate me. You're the one who makes me look ridiculous. Taking pictures of my guests!"

"What does—?"

"You can blackmail somebody with a photograph. Don't you realize?"

"But they all appear on the society pages."

"Yes, you moron, but not in my house, not associated with *me*."

"I don't understand . . ."

"Well, you should, you fool!"

Errol stood up and hurried to the hallway. He put himself between Nazario and Estrella.

"Mama, your husband is a savage."

"Shut up, you bum, don't butt into what doesn't—"

"Drop it, son, you know how—"

"I know, and I can smell the vomit in the mouth of this old bastard. He stinks like a cave—"

"Shut up, go back to your asshole friends and keep drinking my champagne free of charge. Damn freeloaders! Dummies!"

"Leave us alone. This is between your father and me."

Nazario Esparza's eyes were as glassy as the bottom of a bottle. He put his hand in his pocket and took out (why?) a ring with dozens of keys.

"Get out, you're a curse," he said to Errol.

"I'd like to imagine you dead, Papa. But not yet a skeleton. Slowly being devoured by worms."

These words not only silenced Don Nazario. They seemed to frighten him, as if his son's curse resonated with an ancient, prophetic, and in the end a placating voice. Doña Estrella put her arms around her husband as if to protect him against their son's threat.

Errol returned to the room and his parents dimmed like an empty theater. Jericó and I followed with wooden faces.

"You see," said Errol. "I grew up like a plant. I've lived outdoors, like a nopal."

It was obvious: Tonight was his and he wasn't going to let us slip in a word.

He was as insistent as a rainstorm.

"Do you know the secret? My father wants to get rid of himself. That's why I behaved the way I did. I have him all figured out and he can't stand it. He'd like to be the product of his own past, denying what happened earlier but taking advantage of the results. Understand?"

I said no. Jericó shrugged.

"Who were those people?"

"Ah!" Errol exclaimed. "That's the sixty-four-thousand-dollar question. Do you know why my father forbids photographs at the parties he gives at home?"

"I have no idea," said Jericó.

"You can't imagine. Why do you think he gets all these people together, offers them champagne, but bans photographs? I can tell you because I secretly go through his papers and tie up loose ends. It just so happens that Don Nazario deducts—that's what I said—he deducts these so-called 'parties' from his taxes. He classifies them as entertainment expenses and 'office expenses,' business meetings disguised as 'cocktail parties.' "

"Who comes to a cocktail party to be 'deducted'?" I insisted, interested in not having my sentimental education cut short.

"Everybody," Errol said with a laugh. "But only my father is so clever that he bans publicity and closes the deal."

His laughter sounded hollow and sad.

"I've got the old man by the balls! The old fucker!"

I managed to squeeze in a question: "Do you think you're going to negate your father's offenses?"

"No." He shrugged. "I only want to push my differences with him to the limit. Understand? I'm rich, you're poor, but I have more misery to overcome."

He emptied his glass in one swallow.

"You should know you're born with privilege. You don't make it."

And he looked at us with an intensity we had never seen in him before.

"Everything else is robbery."

I TOLD YOU, my dear survivors, I went to the Esparza house that night to avoid my own home, if it can be called that. Dysfunctional and all the rest of it, Errol's family was in the *have* column, if Cervantes was right—and he is—when he quoted his grandmother: There are only two families in the world, the one you have and the one you don't have. Now, how do you quantify familial possession or dispossession? People's opinion of the fair is based on whether they had a good time. I ought to explain—I owe it to those who are still alive and gather in cities, neighborhoods, families—that I grew up in a gloomy house on Calle de Berlín in Mexico City. Toward the end of the nineteenth century, when the country seemed to settle down after decades of upheaval (though it traded anarchy for dictatorship, perhaps without realizing it), the capital city began to spread beyond the original perimeter of Zócalo-Plateros-Alameda. The "colonias," as the new neighborhoods were called, chose to display mansions in various European styles, especially the Parisian and another, more northern one whose origins lay somewhere between London and Berlin and its destiny in a district patriotically called Juárez, though devoted to baptizing streets with the names of European cities.

My first memory is of Calle de Berlín and a three-story house with parapets and towers proclaiming its lineage, a meager stone courtyard, no plants, and only two residents: the woman who took care of me from my infancy, and myself. My name is Josué Nadal, something that readers have known since my decapitated head began to ramble, resting like a coconut and lapped at by the waves on a beach in Guerrero. The name of the woman who cared for me from infancy was María Egipciaca del Río, a name with Coptic resonances that should not be surprising in a country where baptisms are a fertile part of the popular imagination: In Mexico there is an abundance of Hermengildos, Eulalios, Pancracios, Pánfilos, Natividades, and Pastoras, Hilarias, and Orfelinas.

Her name being María Egipciaca and mine Josué should not attract any particular attention if we recall the biblical names that North Americans had from the very beginning: Nathaniel, Ezra, Hepzibah, Jedediah, Zabadiel, not to mention Lancelot, Marmaduke, and Increase.

Attribute this nomenclature, if you like, to the naming vocation of the New World, baptized once at the dawn of time with indigenous names and rebaptized with Christian and African ones throughout its history.

I'm saying all this to situate María Egipciaca in a sovereign territory of proper names that go beyond the designations "mother," "stepmother," "grandma," "aunt," "guardian," or "godmother," which I didn't dare use for the woman at whose side I grew up, but whose identity she always hid from me, tacitly forbidding me to call her "mother," "godmother," or "stepmother" because the mixture of attention and distance in María Egipciaca was like an alternating current: When I displayed mistrust indulgence overflowed from her, and when I showed affection it provoked a hostile response. I'm explaining this game since there is something ludic in every close, solitary relationship that constantly has to choose between amity and enmity; it became clearly established only as I grew and situated in my surroundings this small, severe woman, always dressed in black with a belt and a wide, starched white collar, though her hair was styled coquettishly with short reddish curls in what used to be called a "permanent" (and was repeated like a temporal oracle on the head of Errol's mother). The severe dress did not go well with the high-heeled shoes María Egipciaca wore to disguise her short stature, though this was more than compensated for by the energy she displayed in the huge house on Calle de Berlín, which was like an elephant's cage occupied by two mice, for it had three floors but she and I lived only in a space bounded by the vestibule at the entrance, the living room, the kitchen, then two bedrooms on the second floor and a kind of mysterious ban on the third floor, where neither one of us went, as if the madwoman in the attic lived there and not the odds and ends left by previous residents in the course of a century.

Furthermore, the house on Berlín had suffered a great deal in the 1985 earthquake and no one had bothered to repair the cracked walls or restore the airy garret that served as the mirador and crown of the residence. So that when I came to live there, while I was still an infant, forgotten, forgetful, and forgettable (I suppose), its condition was not so much abandoned or forgotten as adrift, as if a house were a stream lost in the great tide of a city that had always been ravaged by military destruction, poverty, inequality, hunger, and revolt, and in spite of, or because of, so much catastrophe, determined to come back more chaotic, energetic, and brazen than ever: Mexico City would give a gigantic finger to the rest of the country, which was attracted to it like the proverbial fly to the spider's web where it will be trapped forever.

Were there two María Egipciacas? I don't remember the moment my life began in the light green mansion on Calle de Berlín, because no one remembers the moment of my birth, and lacking other references, we situate ourselves in the environment where we grew up. Unless in a fit of sincerity or imaginary health, the person who shelters us says:

"You know something? I'm not your mother, I adopted you right after you were born . . ."

María Egipciaca never did me a favor like that. And yet I recall her with the passing affection that gratitude imposes. It's one thing to be grateful for something and another to be grateful forever. The first is virtue, the second stupidity; favors can be renewed but gratitude is lost if it doesn't turn into something else: love that is a high-flying bird or friendship that is not (Byron) a bird "without his wings" but a fowl less fleeting than love, with its high passionate flight and its low carnal passion. María Egipciaca was part of my childhood landscape. She fed me and had the peculiarity of offering me the spoon accompanied by incomplete proverbs, as if she were waiting for the Holy Spirit of Homilies to descend and illuminate my childish brain:

"No matter how early you wake up . . ."

"If you eat and sing . . ."

"Let it rain, let it rain . . ."

"A closed mouth . . ."

"An old woman died . . ."

I believe that whatever the real identity of María Egipciaca, for her, mine was that of perpetual infancy. As a little boy I didn't dare ask her Who are you? since I had adjusted, in the gloomy solitude of this greenish house, to *where* I was though I didn't know *who* I was. The fact is she never called me "son," and if she said it by accident, it was in the way someone says "listen," "boy," or "kid." I was an asterisk in the daily vocabulary of the woman who took care of me without ever explaining or clarifying her relationship to me. I didn't feel worried, I was used to it, I nullified any question about María Egipciaca's status and was sent to the public school on Calzada de la Piedad, where I made some friends—not many—whom I never invited to my house, and I was never invited to theirs. I suppose I had a forbidding aura, I was "strange," what others intuitively know about—a family, a home—did not stand behind me. I was, in fact, the orphan who, like the mailman, comes and goes punctually, without provoking a response to what would later, in secondary school, be my watchword: my large nose, or as Jericó, the friend who came to fill all the loneliness of my childhood, would say, "You don't have a big nose. Your nose is long and thin, not big. Don't let that bunch of bastards get to you."

Since the nose is the advance guard of the face and goes before the body, announcing the other features, I began to smell that something was changing in my relationship to María Egipciaca when, fatally, she discovered my shorts stiff with semen in the hamper. My alarming first ejaculation was involuntary, as I was glancing casually at an American magazine at the stand on the corner, which I acquired with embarrassment and leafed through with excitement. I thought I was sick (until on subsequent occasions alarm was transformed into pleasure) and didn't know what to do with my dirty underwear except toss it in the hamper as naturally as I tossed in shirts and socks, and with the certainty that the laundress who came to the house once a week was not very concerned about finding signs of one kind of filth or another in underwear: that's why it was "under."

What I didn't know is that before handing it over to the laundress, María Egipciaca carefully went over each item. She didn't have to say anything to me. Her attitude changed and I couldn't attribute the change to anything but my stained shorts. I imagined that a mother, without any need to refer to the fact, would have come to me affectionately and said something like "My little boy is a man now" or some similar foolishness, would never have referred to the concrete fact, much less with a desire to punish. That's how I knew María Egipciaca was not my mother.

"Pig. Dirty pig," she said with her most sour face. "You make me ashamed."

From that moment on, my jailer, for I could no longer view her any other way, did not stop attacking me, isolating me, cornering me, and eventually arming me with total indifference in the face of the expert fire of her censure.

"What are you going to do with your life?"

"What are you preparing for?"

"What goals do you have in mind?"

"If only you were more practical."

"Do you think I'm going to take care of you forever?"

"What do you want all those books for?"

This culminated in a nervous ailment that in fact signified the collapse of my corporeal defenses before a reality that held me under siege without offering a way out, a great wall of enigmas about my person, my goals, my sexuality, my family origins, who my father and mother were, what good it did to read all the books shown me by the secondhand book dealers with whom I was friendly for a while, and knew later, thanks to Professor Filopáter.

The doctor diagnosed a crisis of nerves associated with puberty and said I had to rest for two weeks under the care of a nurse.

"I know how to take care of him," María Egipciaca interjected with so much bitterness that the doctor cut her off abruptly and said that starting tomorrow a nurse would come to care for me.

"All right," María Egipciaca said with resignation. "If the señor pays . . ."

"You know the señor pays for everything, he pays well and he pays on time," the doctor said with severity.

That was how Elvira Ríos came into my life, the young, brown-skinned, short, affectionate nurse who immediately became the object of the concentrated hatred of Doña María Egipciaca del Río, for reasons not far removed from the similarity of their fluvial last names and in spite of the fact that my caretaker was singular and my nurse a true delta.

"Look at her, so dark and dressed all in white. She looks like a fly in a glass of milk."

"Ay, there's no lack of idiots!" the little nurse responded with inconsequential speed.

But now, to be more grateful than ungrateful, I should return to Father Filopáter and his teachings.

FILOPÁTER DIXIT:

The philosopher Baruch (Benoît, Benito, Benedetto) Spinoza (Amsterdam 1632–The Hague 1677) attentively observes the spiderweb spread like an invasive veil over a corner of the wall. A single spider dominates the space of the web that, if Spinoza remembers correctly, did not exist a few months ago, has existed for only a very short time, going unnoticed, and now demanding attention as a principal element in a monastic room, bare and perhaps barren for someone, like Spinoza, who does not have a vocation for superior detachment.

There is nothing but a cot, a writing table with papers, pens, and ink, a washbasin, and a chair. There is no mirror, not for lack of means or an absence of vanity. Or perhaps for both reasons. Books thrown on the floor. A window opens on a stone courtyard. And the spiderweb ruled by the patient, slow, persevering insect that creates its universe without help from anyone, in an almost astral solitude that the philosopher decides to break.

He brings in from the street a spider (they abound in Holland) identical to the one in the bedroom. Identical, but an enemy. It is enough for Spinoza to place the street spider delicately on the web of the domestic spider for it to declare war on the intruder, for the stranger to let it be known that its presence is not peaceable either, and for a battle between the spiders to begin that the philosopher observes, engrossed, not really knowing which one will triumph in the war for living space and prolonged survival: The life of an arachnid is as fragile as the silk its spittle produces when it makes contact with the air, and as long as its probable patience. But the introduction of an identical insect into its territory is enough to transform the intruder into the Nemesis of the original spider and unleash the war that will end in a victory that interests no one after a war that concerns no one.

But in fact, not lacking in imagination (whoever says he is?), the philosopher adds strife to strife by tossing a fly onto the spiderweb. Immediately the spiders stop fighting each other and walk with a patient, dangerous step to the place where the immobilized fly lies captive in unfamiliar territory that imprisons its wings and lights up its greenish eyes (green like the walls of the house on Berlín), as if it wanted to send an SOS to all the flies in the world so they would save it from an inexorable end: to be devoured by the spiders that, once they satisfy their hunger to kill the intruder by their poisonous endeavors, will devour each other. That is death: an unfortunate encounter. That is a spider: an insectivore useful to man the gardener.

Spinoza laughs and returns to the work that feeds him. Polishing lenses. Cutting glass for spectacles and for the magic of the microscope invented a short time earlier by the Dutchman Zacharias Jaussen, master of the brilliant idea of joining two convergent lenses, one for seeing the real image of the object, the other for the augmented image. In this way we consider the immediate image of things and at the same time the deformed image, augmented or simply imagined, of itself. The philosopher thinks that just as there is a world immediately accessible to the senses, there is another, imaginary world that possesses all the rights of fantasy only if it does not confuse the real with the imaginary. And what is God?

Spinoza is very conscious of the period in which he lives. He knows that Uriel de Aste was condemned by the ecclesiastical authorities in 1647. His crime: denying the immortality of the soul and the revelation of the world, because everything is nature and what nature does not give, neither the Pope nor Luther will lend. He knows that in 1656 Juan de Prado was excommunicated for affirming that souls die in their bodies, that God exists only philosophically, and that faith is a great obstacle to a full life on earth.

Baruch himself, a Jew descended from the Portuguese expelled in the name of the political madness of Iberian unity, an Israelite by birth and religion, wasn't he thrown out of the synagogue because he did not repent of his philosophical heresies that—the rabbis were correct—led to the negation of the dogma of the doctors and opened the way to what was most dangerous for orthodoxy: free thought, without doctrinal bonds?

No: Spinoza was expelled because he wanted to be expelled. The rabbis pleaded with him to repent. The philosopher refused. The rabbis tried to keep him. They offered him a pension of a thousand florins, and Spinoza replied that he was not corrupt and not a hypocrite but a man searching for the truth. The fact is that Spinoza felt dangerously seduced by Israel and, threatened by that seduction, turned his back on the synagogue. This was how the chief rabbi declared Spinoza *nidui, cherem,* and *chamata,* separated, expelled, extirpated from among us.

Which is what the philosopher wanted in order to postulate an independence that would not let itself be seduced, in retaliation, by the rational liberalism of the new Protestant bourgeoisie of Europe. A rebel before Israel, Spinoza would also be a rebel before Calvin, Luther, the House of Orange, and the Protestant principalities. In any case, he told his friends: Keep my ideas secret. Which did not prevent a fanatic one night from attempting to assassinate him with the ragged stab of a knife. The philosopher placed the cape ripped by the knife in a corner of his room.

"Not everyone loves me."

He did not accept positions, sinecures, or chairs. He lived in furnished rooms, without *things,* without *ties.* He did not accept a single compromise. His ideas depended on a dispossessed life, his survival on modest manual work, badly paid and solitary. Thought must be free. If it is not, all oppression becomes possible, all action blameworthy.

And in that isolated solitude, polishing lenses and performing the historical drama of the spider that kills the spider and the spiders that join together to devour the fly and the big fish that eats the small one and the crocodile that eats them both and the hunter who kills the crocodile and the hunters who kill one another for the skin that will crown the helmets of soldiers in battle and the death of thousands of men in wars and the extension of the crime to women and children and old people and the selection of the crime applied to Jews, Muslims, Christians, rebels, libertines, those who, heretics all, choose: *eso theiros,* I choose: heresy, freedom . . .

What is everything, in the end, but an optical effect? Baruch (Benoît, Benito, Benedetto) asks himself as he bends over his lenses, convinced a man is a philosopher only if, like him, he gives himself up to asceticism, humility, poverty, and chastity.

But isn't this the greatest sin of all? Isn't the rebellion of Lucifer in its high degree of humility the most awful of crimes: being better than God?

Baruch Spinoza shrugs. The spider devours the fly. Death is no more than an unfortunate encounter.

Thus spake Filopáter.

A SHORT WHILE after that terrible family scene in the mansion in Pedregal, Errol left home. We found out because he left school in the first year of preparatory at the same time, and we decided to call at his house, as curious as we were concerned about a boy whose destiny seemed so different from ours that, in the end, it represented what Jericó and I could have been.

That afternoon the house in Pedregal seemed dismal, as if its extreme bareness of austere lines had become overloaded with the internal accumulation of things I've already described. As if the simple contrast of sun and shadow—a taurine architecture, after all, an essential reduction of the ritual—had ceded light to a somber sunset so that the interior of the house infected the exterior despite its resistance.

We didn't have time for the front door to be opened for us. It opened and on the doorstep a young, robust woman appeared accompanied by the weak-looking, dark-skinned waiter we had met at the reception. Each carried a suitcase, though the woman also had, pressed to her bosom, a small porcelain statue of the Virgin of Guadalupe. They were not alone. Behind her appeared Errol's mother, Señora Estrellita, drying her hands on her apron, looking at the servants with a passionate intensity we did not recognize and enduring the downpour of insults from her husband Don Nazario, dressed for the beach in shorts and leather sneakers.

It was like a cataract of hatreds and recriminations on feedback; turbid waters, contaminated with urgencies and excrescences that had their muddy source in the words of the father, were calmed in those of the mother and eventually found a strange backwater of silence in those who should have been angriest, the two servants dismissed by Señora Estrella to shouts of good-for-nothings, scoundrels, you've abused my confidence, get out, I don't need you, I can run the house and prepare the meals better than you, lazy Indian beggars, go back to the mountains, and unaware of our presence, she hurled a misguided domestic fury at the pair of servants but it turned back on Jericó and me, the invisible spectators, and her husband, Don Nazario, a kind of distant but omnipotent Jupiter dressed to go jogging who, in fact, was running around his wife as he stepped on the toes of his employees, whose obstinate silence, stony glances, and immobile postures bore witness to their passive resistance and announced an accumulated rage that, without the mitigation of daily release, would spill over in one of those collective explosions that the Esparzas perhaps could not imagine or perhaps believed they had warded off for long periods of time with the rules of obedience and submission to the master, or it may be they desired it as one desires an emotional purge that sweeps away indecisiveness, secret guilt, the omissions and faults of those who hold power over the weak.

Doña Estrella shoved the dismissed employees. Don Nazario insulted Doña Estrella. The servants, instead of picking up their suitcases and walking away—she praising the Virgin—remained stoic, as if they deserved the storm of insults raining down on them or enjoyed without smiling those the master directed at the mistress in a kind of chain of recriminations that most resembled eternity as a prison sentence.

"Where was the Chinese vase?"

"Stupidities are celebrated in a girl and even forgiven . . ."

"Admit that you two broke it!"

". . . not in an old woman."

"And the canary?"

"You were a fool when you were young . . ."

"Why did it die?"

". . . but you were cute . . ."

"Why did you leave it dead in its cage?"

"You were pretty, you moron!"

"Why was the cage door open?"

"What happened to you?"

"Are you trying to drive me crazy?"

"What frightens you more?"

"Don't stand there like lumps."

"Living alone or staying on with me?"

"Move away, I'm telling you."

"Don't be stupid, tell them to come back. In a minute you'll—"

Doña Estrella whirled to face, with mouth open and eyes closed, her husband. She stepped to one side. Don Nazario turned his back. The servants walked back into the house, as if they knew this play all too well. They returned armed with the dagger of the insults the

master had directed at the mistress. They would hang them, like tro-
phies, in the damp, dark back room, always reserved for the staff,
with a wall, it did have that, so they could tack up the print of the
Virgin and, as a kind of curse, the photo of the Esparzas.

How long, how long! Errol would exclaim the next day when we
went to see him in his tiny apartment: barely two rooms on Calle del
General Terán, in the shadow of the Monumento de la Revolución.
The dark-skinned servant gave us our friend's new address, swearing
us to silence because young Errol's parents didn't know where he
was living.

"When did he leave?"

"Ten days ago."

"How did he leave?"

"Like a soul chased by the Devil."

"Why did he leave?"

"Please, ask him."

It didn't surprise us that he had gone. We were interested in his
reasons. The small apartment in the shadow of the great revolutionary gas station was bare of furniture, just a mattress on the floor, a
table, two chairs, a bathroom with the door half open, our friend
Errol, whom we sometimes envied and sometimes felt sorry for. The
guitar we already knew. A new drum set, a neglected saxophone.

Did rage drive him away? he asked us rhetorically, sitting on the
floor, his arms crossed, with his long hair and shortsighted eyes. No,
fear drove him away, no matter how justified his anger with his parents. Fear of becoming, in the company of his family, what his father
and mother already were: two backward, spectral, avaricious beings.
Two enemy ghosts who left a dead smell behind them. Estrellita
with that eternal face of someone going to a wedding who does not
renounce the happy ending regardless of all evidence to the contrary. Her inconsequential bliss. Her weeping out of sheer habit.
The imaginary coffin waiting for her in the hallway to the bedroom.
Yes, what's my mother good for? Distrusting the servants? Is that her
only affirmation? Weeping when she imagines the death of others, a
vague *others,* in order to put off mine?

"But I'm here, Mama."

He strummed the guitar.

"When my father scolds her, she goes into the bathroom and sings."

Her only devotions are to death, the only certain thing in life, and the Virgin. She doesn't consider the fact that faith brings her closer to the despised maid. How is it possible to be a Christian and despise believers who have the same faith but are socially inferior to us? How do you reconcile these extremes, shared faith and separate social position? Who is more Christian? Who will enter heaven through the eye of the camel? Who through the lock of the strait gate?

Jericó and I looked at each other. We understood that Errol needed us in order to give external words to his internal torment, which transcended his relationship with his parents and settled, eventually, in the relationship of Errol to Errol, of the boy to the man, the sheltered to the homeless, the artist he wanted to be to the rebel that, perhaps, was all he could be: a rebel, never an artist, because personal insurrection is not a sign of esthetic imagination. And he immediately referred to his father.

"What can you think of a man who travels abroad with a money belt filled with silver pesos around his waist to make certain no one steals them? A man who travels with a special case filled with chiles to season insipid French cooking?"

He was silent for a moment. He didn't invite us to comment. It was clear his diatribe had not yet ended.

"Do you remember when I told you how my father made his way? The man of action, the faithful husband, the strong head of the family? First a carpenter, in a poor district of the city. A furniture maker. Selling chairs, beds, and tables to various hotels. Furniture stores, hotels, movie houses. Remember? The modern Saint Joseph, except that his Virgin Mary didn't give birth to a savior but to an informer. I didn't tell you everything that time. I skipped over the link that joins the chain of my revered father, like the key ring in his pocket that he rattles with so much authority. Between the furniture store and the hotels are the brothels. The first chain of my fortune is made of whorehouses. That's where the mattresses went, that's where the beds were used, that's where the Catholic, bourgeois, and respectable fortune of a couple who insult their servants and ignore their son was founded. In a brothel."

What could we say? He didn't expect anything. His confession didn't affect us. It was his business. For him, obviously, it had been transformed into an open wound, and that was when we knew that because of our disinterest in this matter, the value Jericó and I shared with regard to the geographies of families or the supposed "crimes" of individuals, it did not concern us. Right then Jericó and I confirmed something we already knew, the necessary product of our readings assimilated to the philosophical and moral leap that the instructive friendship of Father Filopáter signified. A lesson for us, for him the recognition of losses and gains in the ancestral game between parents and children, forebears and descendants. About whom could I speak except women who weren't related to me, María Egipciaca, my nemesis, and Elvira Ríos, my nurse? And Jericó, who remained silent about family antecedents about which he may have been completely ignorant? And about whom except ourselves could we speak, he and I, Jericó and Josué, regarding the familial relationship that in our lives was ultimately identical to the relationship between friends? This apparent solitude was the condition of our absolute solidarity. The small saga of Errol and his family confirmed in Jericó and me the fraternity that was a sure sign of the orientation of our lives. Brothers not in blood but in intelligence, and knowing this, we realized (at least I did), joined us early on but perhaps put us to the test for the rest of our lives. Would we always be the intimate friends we were now? What would the twelve strokes of noon leave us? And what the prayer murmured at the end of the day?

Perhaps it was unfair to call us what Filopáter named us— Castor and Pollux—simply in contrast to the real orphanhood of our friend Errol Esparza, voluntarily estranged from his parents though perhaps more devoted than we were to the eternal struggle between talent and solitude.

Then he came out of the bathroom, naked, his head wet, the young man who greeted us and sat in front of the drum set while

Errol picked up the guitar and the two of them began their rock version of "Las Golondrinas."

A few mariachis to the wise.

I ALWAYS KNEW she would spy on us. The presence of Elvira Ríos was offensive to María Egipciaca, even before the nurse set foot in the house adrift on Calle de Berlín. In the mind of my caretaker, this enormous residence had room for only two people, her and me, in the chastely promiscuous relationship I have already told you about. It was as if two enemy animals occupied, with no other companion, an entire forest, and one fine day a third animal appeared to throw into confusion a couple that in fact did not love each other. Was there hatred between my guardian and me? I suppose there was, if the perpetual dissimilarity of affections and sympathies determines an antagonism that moves people in conflict to do what they have to do only so the other, as soon as he is aware of what is going on, will occupy the adversarial position. If I complained or woke up in a bad mood, María Egipciaca lost no time in asking what is it? what's wrong? what can I do for you? If, on the other hand, I woke brighter than the sun, she hurried to wield a poisoned rapier, it's clear you don't know what the day holds in store, have you thought about your assignments for today, why didn't you finish them yesterday? now you'll have more obligations and since you lack not only time but also talent, you won't get anywhere: you'll always be a *raté* . . . Where María Egipciaca had gotten this French word led me to wonder what kind of education my caretaker had received, since I never saw her reading a book, not even a newspaper. She didn't go to the movies or the theater, though she did have the radio on day and night, until the day itself became a kind of annex to the programming of XEW, "The Voice of Latin America from Mexico." That the poor woman learned something is evident because on the day, at the crack of dawn, that the nurse Elvira Ríos appeared, María Egipciaca remarked:

"How silly. That's the name of a bolero singer."

"Isn't it just that you're Del Río and she's Ríos? Does that irritate you?"

"From current to current, let's see who drowns first."

The days preceding the arrival of the nurse were perhaps the worst of a confinement that previously, at least, had doors open to the street and school. Now, confined by doctor's orders and waiting for the imminent arrival of the nurse, my "stepmother's" manias were exacerbated to the point of cruelty. She found a thousand ways to make me feel useless. She prepared meals making so much noise it could be heard all through the house, she came up to my bedroom with the tray resounding like a marimba orchestra, she sighed like a tropical hurricane, deposited the meal outside my door with a groan of cardiac exertion, picked it up, came in without knocking as if she wanted to catch me at the solitary vice that, since the incident of my undershorts, had fixed her opinion of my impure person. If she didn't drop the tray on my lap it was because her vocation of service would have obliged her to pick up and clean without asking me to do the same, since that would have denied María Egipciaca's sacrificial function in this house where, however, all the dirt accumulated for seven days until the competent maid came in once a week, drew the curtains, opened the windows, aired out and let in the sun, washed and ironed, filled the dispensers for the necessities of the next few days, and left as she arrived, without saying a word, as if her work did not depend in any way on the apparent mistress of the house, María Egipciaca. On only one occasion did the cleaning woman speak to my caretaker to say:

"I know a nurse is coming to take care of the boy. If you like, I'll bring some flowers."

"There's no need," María Egipciaca replied severely. "Nobody died."

"It's to cheer up this tomb a little," the servant said in a bad humor and left.

I must admit to those who survive that my taking to a sickbed made me very happy. I saw it as an opportunity first of all to devote myself to "the unpunished vice," reading, and second, to oblige María Egipciaca to serve me with no pleasure, irritated, making an unnecessary racket but obliged, beyond any other consideration, to tend to me for reasons that had nothing to do with the affection or duty a mother owes her child, but merely to remain in the good graces of "the señor," that mysterious patron to whom the doctor had referred with unqualified severity and categorical words.

I should confess that the allusion to "the señor," which I heard for the first time on that occasion, produced a conflicted feeling in me. I realized that María Egipciaca was not the source of my material existence or physical comfort but simply followed the orders of a person who had never been mentioned before in this house. Was the physician's indiscretion really an indiscretion? Or had the good doctor intentionally put María Egipciaca in her place, revealing that far from being the lady of the house, she too, like the weekly maid, was an employee? I wanted to gauge the effects of this revelation on my guardian's attitude. She was careful not to vary in the slightest the behavior I already knew. If I was sick and sentenced to rest, she would heighten, without modifying in its essentials, her irreproachable conduct as a señora charged with lodging me, feeding me, dressing me, and sending me to school.

But since at the same time the doctor had announced that the nurse would come to take care of me on the instructions of the señor who "pays for everything, pays well, and pays on time," María Egipciaca had on the horizon of her suspicions a new and weaker propitiatory victim. The nurse and I. I and the nurse. The order of factors etcetera. The outcome foreseen by María Egipciaca was a relationship that excluded her from her good governance of the house and care of my person. How to reaffirm one and prolong the other? Sometimes the questions that pierce our spirits escape through our eyes, just as my encephalic mass spills out of my skull today, when I woke up dead on a Pacific beach.

Fourteen years ago Elvira, if she did not prevent my death, did renew my life. My routine as an early adolescent in secondary school promised, in my young but limited imagination, to repeat itself into infinity. It is curious that at a time of such great physical changes, the mind insists on prolonging childhood, since the belief that adolescence itself will be eternal is only the mirror of the tacit conviction (and convention) of childhood: I'll always be a little girl, a little boy, even though I know I won't. But I'll be an adolescent with the mentality of a little boy, that is, of a survivor. In the end, what age belongs to us more than childhood, when we truly depend on others? Everything is longer when we are children. Vacations seem deliciously eternal. And class schedules too. Though subject to school and especially the family, at that time of life we have more freedom with regard to what binds us than at any other period. It seems to me this is because in childhood freedom is identical to imagination, and since here everything is possible, the freedom to be something more than the family and something more than school flies higher and allows us to live more separately than at the age when we must conform in order to survive, adjust to the rhythms of professional life, submit to rules inherited and accepted by a kind of general conformity. We were, as children, singular magicians. As adults, we will be herd animals.

Can't we rebel against the gray sadness of this fatality? I evoke this feeling because I believe it is what joined Jericó and me as brothers. And I'm also of this opinion because it was the nurse Elvira Ríos who came before anyone else to break the habitual formations enclosing me in the house on Calle de Berlín under the tutelage of María Egipciaca. It isn't that the nurse had proposed to "free me" or anything like that. It was simply a question of a presence different from everything I had known until then. María Egipciaca constantly praised the Caucasian race, the "whiteys," almost assigning to them the destiny of the world or, at least, the monopoly on intelligence, beauty, and strength. She suffered from an unfortunate mental confusion that led her to say things like "If whites governed us, we'd be a great country"; "Indians are our burden"; "See, the Americans killed the Indians and that's why they could be a great nation"; "Those blacks are only good for dancing." When she leafed through my history books, she would sigh over the blond Emperor Maximiliano de Habsburgo and deplore the triumph of "that Indian" Juárez. She didn't know much about the war of 1846–48 with the United States, though her prejudices were enough for her to wish that North Americans had taken over the entire Mexican territory once and for all. When I dared to remark that then we would be a Protestant country, she was confounded for the moment and not until the next day did she come up with an answer: "The Virgin of Guadalupe would have converted them to religion," because for her, Protestantism was, at most, "a heresy."

The arrival of the nurse Elvira Ríos, very dark-skinned and dressed in white with a black valise in her hand and an active professional disposition that would not tolerate insolence or interruptions or jokes, became a challenge to Doña María Egipciaca. I felt it from the moment the nurse prohibited my jailer from entering my room.

"And the tray with his food?" María Egipciaca said haughtily.

"Leave it outside."

"Better yet, you carry it up."

"With pleasure."

"And if you like, cook it too."

"That's no trouble, Señora."

Each of Elvira's responses seemed to corner María Egipciaca a little more, and in the end she prepared the meals and brought them to the door of my bedroom, attempting to cross the threshold, not counting on the nurse's will.

"The patient needs rest."

"Listen, Señorita, I'm not going to—"

"That's an order."

"We've lived together his whole life!"

"That's why he has a nervous ailment."

"You're arrogant!"

"Just professional. My job is to protect the young man from any nervous disturbance and restore his tranquillity."

"It's my house!"

"No, Señora. You're only an employee here, like me. Please close the door."

"Arrogant! Presumptuous Indian!"

From this delicious exchange (which avenged all the years of tension in the house on Berlín) was born my admiration for the small, agile, slender nurse. I attempted to converse with her in a less professional manner. She wouldn't allow it. She was here to take care of me and restore me to health, not to chat. I looked at her with a look I did not recognize but the mirror confirmed as "the eyes of a lovesick calf."

My gaze obtained only one response: Elvira placed a thermometer in my mouth with a gallant gesture.

The truth is that this agile, self-assured presence in a young, small body excited me more than if Elvira had shown herself naked. I learned right then, during the first few days of my nerve cure, first to guess at and then immediately to desire the flesh hidden behind the nurse's snow-white uniform. What would she be like naked? What kind of underclothes would a señorita like her wear? Was she still a señorita? Did she have a boyfriend? Was she married? And as young as she was, did she have children? All these questions resolved, eventually, into a single image. Elvira naked. My eyes stripped her of clothing, and she did not resemble the paper dolls in the magazines that had first excited me. I understood one thing: Seeing her dressed, all in white, moved me more than seeing her without clothes, because the uniform stimulated my imagination more than nudity.

The earlier routine disappeared. It was replaced by a new routine joined to the presence of the nurse, my imagination whirling between her slender hips and the succession of thermometers, pills, checks of blood pressure, and conversations that revealed my juvenile lack of experience and vague desire to prolong childhood without showing my dread of adulthood.

She seemed to observe it all with an intelligent gaze that María Egipciaca, intruding from time to time, called (from behind the door, like a ghost that no longer frightened me) "black squirrel eyes," or "her with the little mouse eyes," words that did not disturb the young professional, no doubt accustomed to things worse than a muttering, rabid old woman displaced by the facts of life from her customary dominant position. I was grateful to Elvira that her presence had translated into my liberation. The house would not be the same again. The tyranny of my childhood lost its powers with every passing hour.

"Wakes earlier."

"Gets up crazy."

"No flies come in."

"Shuffling."

Elvira completed the interrupted proverbs of María Egipciaca, who listened to them hiding behind the door, betrayed by a moth-eaten sigh. She was defeated.

A week went by. Ten days went by. The period of my convalescence was growing short, and one night, when the famous peace of the graveyard reigned, Elvira said to me:

"Young man, you need only one thing to settle your nerves."

And immediately she undressed in front of me and I could bear witness to my own imagination. What one thinks can be superior or inferior to reality. I feared, when Elvira unfastened her shirt, that her breasts would not be as I had imagined them. That her belly, her pubis, her buttocks, would contradict my fantasy. This was not the case. Reality surpassed fiction. Elvira's silence during our fifteen minutes of love was barely broken by an earthly little sigh from her and a prolonged *ay!* from me, which she stifled, with delight, by covering my mouth with her hand.

Better than my pleasure was the feeling that I had given it to her. No matter how Elvira picked up again not only her clothes but her nurse's attitudes, I knew from then on that I could give pleasure to a woman and believed at that moment it was the greatest wisdom in life and everything I learned from then on would not be better or wiser than this, although this, I also found out, would never be repeated exactly the same way. There would be in my life loves that were longer, shorter, more or less important, but none would replace my sexual dawning in the arms of Nurse Elvira, healer of my youth and quadrant of my maturity.

And so it happened that on the same day I got up from bed and Elvira very seriously said goodbye, I went into the bedroom of my almost forgotten jailer Doña María Egipciaca and found an unmade bed and an abandoned mattress.

FATHER FILOPÁTER HONORED us with his friendship. Of all the assholes running loose in the schoolyard, he selected Jericó and me to talk, discuss, and think with him. We knew it was a privilege. We didn't, however, want to be seen as something exceptional, enviable, or, by the same token, laughable or open to ridicule by the mass of students more interested in dozing or kicking a ball than in demonstrating that man is a being who thinks when he walks. Because our conversations with Filopáter were all peripatetic. With absolutely no desire to evoke Aristotle, Filopáter made it clear that in the act of walking, one establishes an active friendship without the hierarchies implied when we sit at a table or receive the lesson from the altar—civil or religious—of the teacher-priest (or as Filopáter would say, not without a touch of pedantry, the *magister-sacerdos*).

I suppose that speaking while walking was the intuitive way in which the teacher put himself on our level and invited us to speak without his looking down at us from on high. Sometimes we stayed after class in the yard. Other times we walked the streets of Colonia Roma. Rarely did we reach the Bosque de Chapultepec. The truth is that in the act of holding a dialogue, the city tended to disappear, changing into a kind of agora or academy shared through the word. And the word, what was it? Reason or intuition? Conviction or faith? Provable faith? Rational intuition?

The first thing Father Filopáter set forth for us was what he considered a danger. He knew about our readings and intellectual enthusiasms. From the very first, he warned us:

"Be careful of extremes."

The invitation to debate was formulated from the moment the priest proposed that we talk to him. We respected him enough—and I suppose we respected ourselves enough—not to question his right to think, ours to refute him, and his to respond. Moreover, I confess that Jericó and I wanted and needed this, I at the age of eighteen and he at nineteen, and both of us fertile ground for receiving another's seed in the mental fields we had been cultivating at least since sixteen and seventeen with impassioned readings, debates between ourselves, and a feeling of enormous emptiness: Why did we think, for whom did we think, who would dispute our proud youthful knowledge, who would put it to the test?

Because nothing inspires pride comparable to that of a young person's intellectual awakening. The darkness dissipates. Day dawns. Night is left behind. Not because the earth moves around the sun, but because *we* are the sun, the earth is *ours*. We knew it.

"Drinking from the same fountain, you and I can be left dry, Josué, we can turn into intolerant individuals without someone to put us up against the wall and make us doubt ourselves . . ."

I am transcribing and fixing these words of Jericó's because I will have occasion to invoke them very often in the future.

Now, as if he had read our thoughts and deciphered our disquiet, Filopáter approached us in the schoolyard, tacitly asked us to join him in his slow walk among the arches of the building, without attracting attention, with pensive references to the weather, the changing light in the city, the quality of the day, the ability to hear and take pleasure in urban music, and thought.

"I'm not mistaken if I say you're very involved in two authors."

He saw our books, hidden sometimes in our book bags, sometimes displayed defiantly on our desks or read with youthful ostentation at recess, when the presence of my friend Jericó defended me against the old assaults on my innocent nose and we were both consigned to a kind of student limbo. We were "strange" and didn't know how to get a ball into a hoop.

The two authors were Saint Augustine and Friedrich Nietzsche. In an intuitive and reasoned way, Jericó and I, like iron unattached to a magnet, had headed for opposing thinkers. We wanted, more accurately, to learn to think on the basis of extremes. Our purpose was transparent to someone like Father Filopáter and his rapid attraction to an unoccupied center: for us and, in contrast to what we could imagine, for himself.

"It matters a great deal to you to think as you choose, doesn't it?"

"And also to express freely what we think, Father."

"Authority has no right to intervene?"

"Of course not."

"Of course not when it's a question of a religious institution? Or never?"

"We want it never to interfere if it's a question of a secular state."

"Why?"

"Because the state is secular in order to dispense justice, and justice is not a question of faith."

"And charity?"

"It begins at home," I allowed myself to joke, and Filopáter laughed along with me.

He began by situating our extremes. He clarified that Jericó and I chose two authors who would teach us to think, not two filiations who would oblige us to believe and defend what we believed. In this we agreed with him. It was the basis of our dialogues. We weren't wedded to our philosophers except insofar as we read and discussed them. Was Filopáter tied to the dogmas of his Church? Thinking this was our initial advantage. We were mistaken. In any event, our thinking was opposed to faith and wagered on the clash of ideas. Our decision was that these ideas were diametrically opposed, and Filopáter situated them in a pellucid manner.

We read Saint Augustine: God creates all things and He alone sustains them. Evil is only the absence of a good we could have. When it fell, humanity lost its original values. Recovering them requires divine grace. Grace is inaccessible to human beings, fallen and in disgrace, on their own. The Church is the intermediary of grace. Without the Church, we remain joined to the dis-grace of the human mass, which is *massa peccati.*

Saint Augustine defended these ideas and fought without respite the heretic Pelagius, for whom salvation was possible without the Church: You can be saved by yourself.

At the other extreme of these youthful ideas, Nietzsche proposed freeing us from all metaphysical belief, abandoning any acquired truth, and accepting with bitterness a nihilism that rejects a Christian culture impoverished by the need for renunciation and yet masked by false values that consecrate appearances and hinder the impulse toward truth.

"What truth?"

"The recognition of the absence of any truth."

Father Filopáter was not lacking in astuteness and I don't believe he suspected, beyond a couple of *peripeteias,* that his religious investiture would lead him to instruct us in the virtues of faith and the error of our deviations. Today merely thinking that makes me ashamed, and I let that kind of suspicion fall useless to the sand where my decapitated head lies. Filopáter did not condemn Nietzsche or praise Saint Augustine. And he did not pull another Catholic theologian from his sleeve. We should not have been surprised, in short, that the lesson he set aside for us would bear the name and imprint of a thinker condemned as a heretic by both his original Hebrew community and eventual Christian one.

Therefore, before expounding the philosophy of Baruch (Benedetto, Benito, Benoît) Spinoza, Filopáter, as he placed on his head not a biretta or a cap but a black zucchetto, reminded us of the origin of the word "heretic," which was the Greek *eso theiros,* which means "I choose." The heretic is the one who chooses. Heresy is the act of choosing.

"Then heresy is freedom," Jericó hastened to say.

"Which obliges us to think, what is freedom?" the priest shot back.

"Fine. What is it?" I came to my friend's assistance.

To obtain an approximate answer, Filopáter asked us to retrace the path of the heretic Spinoza.

"You have just told me you believe in freedom of thought."

"That's true, Father."

"Is the thought of believing in God free?"

We said it was.

"Then, can faith be free?"

"If it isn't consumed in obedience," said Jericó.

"If it affirms justice," I added.

Filopáter adjusted the black calotte.

"If it doesn't, if it doesn't . . . Don't be so negative. Do you believe in the will? Do you believe in intelligence?"

Again, we said we did.

"Do you believe in God?"

"Demonstrate it to us, Father," Jericó said, arrogantly, brazenly.

"No, seriously, boys. If God exists, He is a God who does not demand obedience and offer justice, but a God positively intelligent and possessing will."

"Our differences aside, I would say I agree," I affirmed.

The priest playfully pulled my ear and placed the zucchetto on my head.

"Well, you're mistaken. God is not intelligent. God has no will."

I laughed. "You're more of a heretic than we are!"

He removed the zucchetto.

"I am the most serious of orthodox believers."

"Explain yourself," said the very haughty Jericó.

"Believing that God has intelligence and will is to believe that God is human. And God is not human. I do not say with vulgarity 'He is divine.' Only that He is other. And we gain nothing by turning Him into a mirror of our virtues or a negation of our vices. God is God because He is not us."

"Why?"

"Because God is infinitely creative."

"Isn't that what we humans are, individually, collectively, or traditionally?"

"No, because our creativity is free. God's is necessary."

"What do you mean?"

"That God is the cause of Himself and of the finite beings—you, me, everything that exists—derived from Him. God is active not because He is free but because all things necessarily originate in Him."

"Then he isn't the bearded man in the sky?"

"No, just as light isn't the light of a candle or a lightbulb."

"And Jesus, His son?"

"He is a human form among the infinite forms of God. A form. Just one. He could have chosen others."

"Why?"

"To let us see Him."

"And then return to nothing?"

"Or to everything, Jericó."

"What do you mean?"

"That God is vast, not intelligent. God is infinite, not divisible."

"But He can be human, material . . ." I apostrophized.

"Yes, because the body is one thing and matter another. We are only body, the stone is only matter. But God, who can be body—Jesus—can also be matter—creation, seas, mountains, animals, plants, etcetera, and also everything we don't even know or perceive. What we do manage to see and know, touch and smell, imagine or desire, are for God only modalities of His own infinite extension."

I believe he saw us looking somewhat perplexed because he smiled and asked:

"Do you subscribe to a theory of the creation of the universe? In reality, there are only three. The one of the divine *fiat*. The one of the original explosion, which derives from the theory of evolution. Or the one of the infinite universe, without beginning or end, without an act of creation or apocalypse. Pascal's vast sidereal night. The infinite silence of the spheres. Earth as a passing accident whose origin and extinction are equally lacking in importance."

I don't know if Filopáter was proposing to us a kind of menu of the origin of the universe, and if he expected us to subscribe to one or the other of his three theories he was mistaken and knew it. He wanted only to force us to think on our own, and in the course of our talks we realized our initial error. Filopáter did not want to convert us to any orthodoxy, not even his own. And I confess I ended up wondering what, then, if not religious faith, the philosophical reasoning of our teacher could be.

What was he saying to us?

"If you don't believe in God, believe in the universe. Except that the universe is identical to God. It has no beginning and no end. That is why God alone can see a thousand-year-old tree grow."

In the admonitory reference to Spinoza, however, we encountered a personal resonance that Filopáter could not, or would not, let us hear. Spinoza was not expelled from Judaism because of persecution. He expelled himself because of love of solitude, and he loved solitude—Filopáter explained—in order to think. He wanted to be expelled from the Hebrew community to demonstrate that religious believers care more about authority than about truth.

"What do you think?"

After consulting with each other, Jericó and I told the priest he would have to answer the question himself. We were disrespectful.

"If what you want, Father, is to set a trap for us so we commit today to what we won't commit to tomorrow, we believe the one who has been trapped is you."

"Why?" the cleric said with great, with real humility.

How to tell him that whatever happened, whatever he thought, Filopáter would never renounce his religious fidelity? He would be faithful to it no matter how *heretically* he might think—no matter how much he might *choose*.

Perhaps he guessed the answer we didn't give to his "why" loaded with responsibilities for two young students who were alert but immature.

"Why?"

He looked at us with the gratitude, confidence, and affection we would always have for him.

"Listen, don't be satisfied with telling me what I might want to hear. And don't challenge me out of mere negativity. Be serious. Don't exaggerate."

It was another way of telling us he had chosen a path but it was up to us to choose our own. He said it in the indirect way I'm saying it now. He left us with a permanent feeling for the unavoidable difficulties in living life seriously. Spinoza engaged in rebellion and scandal intentionally, in order to be expelled and be independent. Filopáter had not done the same. In the light of his experience, was the venerated Baruch (Benoît, Benito, Benedetto) a coward who, instead of breaking with his Church, looked for the way in which his Church would break with him? And was Filopáter another coward who knew a good many intellectual options outside the Church and settled for the protective cupola of the ecclesiastical dome?

"I avoid rebellion and scandal," he told us the last time we saw him, Jericó and I both knowing that when we left school we would not visit Filopáter again, or the students, Professor Soler and his restless hands, Director Vercingetorix and his trampled gladioluses. Why? Because it was simply a rule of life that the attachments of adolescence are lost in order to become adults, without weighing the loss of value this can signify. Filopáter would become the object of our self-satisfied contempt because his instruction consisted of teaching the thought of others, with no contribution of his own.

But wasn't the inquiry itself, the ability to ask and to ask *ourselves,* an indispensable part of the education that would allow us to be "Jericó" and "Josué"? Only later, much later, did we learn that Filopáter resembled Baruch more than we had imagined at school.

"He did not accept his family's inheritance. He died in poverty because that is what he wanted. He left with nothing."

"Nature is happy with very little. So am I."

The candles drip wax on a barrel filled with blood.

MARÍA EGIPCIACA'S EMPTY bed became the symbol of my being abandoned inside the mansion on Calle de Berlín. Nurse Elvira had disappeared, I suppose forever. The imperious doctor had no need to return. Now the lawyer named Don Antonio Sanginés put in an appearance. I wanted to solve the mysteries that surrounded me. Where was my warden, María Egipciaca? What did the empty bed and rolled-up mattress mean? Where were her clothes, her cosmetics (if she had any), her basic possessions: dentifrice and toothbrush, hairpins, brush, comb? The bathroom was as empty as her bedroom. There were no towels. And no toilet paper. It was as if a ghost had lived in the room of a woman whose physical reality was obvious to me.

The mystery of her absence was no greater than my sense of it, except that the enigma of the woman never became anything else, while in my own case, absence signified solitude. It was strange. The customary presence of Señora María Egipciaca somehow filled the empty spaces of this mansion untouched by reversals or novelty. It wasn't a beautiful house, or historic, or evocative. It was huge, and I had to admit that the occasionally amiable though almost always hateful presence of my jailer filled all the spaces that now were not only empty but solitary, for hollowness as sidereal as the universe evoked by Father Filopáter is not the same as a disappearance of the concrete and customary, no matter how odious it may have seemed to us. I imagine the worst injustices, the concentration-camp universe created by the Nazi regime, and try to imagine something that might have been a consolation. Suffering with others. The prisoner in Auschwitz, Terezin, or Buchenwald could see his death in the eyes of other prisoners. Perhaps that is the mercy no one could tear away from that group of victims.

How could I, wretch that I was, compare my insignificant abandonment in the mansion on Berlín to the fate of a victim of Nazi racism? Was my vanity so great it placed my minuscule abandonment above the gigantic abandonment of the millions of men and women whom no one could or wished to help?

Well, yes. You can attribute it, now that I, a victim myself, am nothing more than a severed head lapped by the waves of the Southern Sea, to the failings of self-pity, the rupture of the customary, even a certain nostalgia for the presence, odious or amiable but at least habitual and constant, of my old guardian, to calibrate the solitude that invaded me at the time with a sense of being abandoned that brought me dangerously close to the sin of believing that the world was my perception of the world, that my particular image of things was as momentous as the injustice committed against an entire people, religion, or race.

I'm being sincere with you and make no apology for my absurd anguish but do criticize my narrow perception and arrogant presumption in believing that because I was solitary I was persecuted. But who, in a situation comparable to mine, does not project his personal misery onto a greater screen, a collective experience that saves us from the sadness of the trivial and insignificant? Perhaps, looking back, I realize that what I perceived was inside me, and what lay outside was so small that to endure it I had to sketch it on our time's large collective screen of grief, abandonment, and despair.

Forgive me for saying what I have just said, you who still live and give definitive value to your existence. I do it to punish myself and situate the small crises of my youth within their real limits, which are limits only because we first extended them to the entire universe, turned our small problems into matters of universal transcendence, and compared ourselves, grotesquely, to Anne Frank or, more modestly, David Copperfield. All this is to say that the disappearance of María Egipciaca, preceded by my illness, the incident with Nurse Elvira, and the suspicion I was not who I believed myself to be, confused my existence and left me, like a shipwrecked sailor, wanderering in the solitude of the mansion on Berlín. Waiting for a solution to this new stage of my life, fearful it wasn't a stage but an insurmountable condition. What would become of me? Following my guardian, would I disappear too? Would I be expelled? How long would a wait continue that was a torment and brought me to the ludicrous extreme of comparing myself to a victimized Jewish girl or an abandoned English boy?

The attorney, Licenciado Don Antonio Sanginés, appeared one Saturday morning to explain the situation to me. Which was what it had always been. Except that Señora María Egipciaca would no longer look after me.

"Why?" I dared to ask in the unyielding presence of the lawyer, a tall, imperturbable man who looked at me without seeing me, so heavy were his eyelids and so meager the light that came in or went out through those curtains.

"That's the way it is," was his only response.

"Did she die? Move away? Was she dismissed? Did she grow tired of the work?"

"That's the way it is," Licenciado Sanginés repeated and proceeded to lecture me about my new situation, as if nothing had happened.

I would continue to live in the house on Calle de Berlín until I finished my preparatory studies. Then I could select my course of study and stay in the house until I completed it. At that time, new instructions would be given to me. I would receive a stipend sufficient to my needs. Matters would be arranged in accordance with those needs.

The lawyer read the document containing these instructions,

folded it, placed it in the jacket pocket of his blue pinstripe suit, and rose to his feet.

"Who will look after me?" I said, alarmed at not having anyone to fix my food, make my bed, prepare my bath, and ashamed at having to admit to this catalogue of requirements.

"That's the way it is," Sanginés repeated and left without saying goodbye.

I asked myself if I could live with so many unanswered questions. I saw myself lost in the big old house, left to my own devices and the question Sanginés had posed: What were my needs?

As soon as the lawyer had left, the usual maid came in and, without saying a word, began her work. I believe it was this resumption of custom in the midst of an unaccustomed situation that disconcerted me more than anything else. The attempt to mollify me by assuring me everything would be the same did not resolve the mysteries I found troubling. Who was María Egipciaca? Where was she? Had she died? Had she been dismissed? Would I see Nurse Elvira again? Who was I? Who was supporting me? Who was the owner of the house I lived in? How did those proverbs end?

". . . does dawn come earlier."

". . . wakes up crazed."

". . . the old woman's in the cave."

". . . lets in no flies."

". . . shuffling the deck."

Jericó completed the proverbs María Egipciaca had left dangling and gave me an order:

"Come live in my apartment."

"But the lawyer—"

"Pay no attention to him. I'll arrange it."

"And if you can't?"

"That can't happen. You have to learn to rebel."

"And be left without—"

"You won't lack for anything. You'll see."

"You're pretty rash, Jericó."

"Sometimes you have to take a risk and ask yourself: Who needs whom? Do they need me or do I need them?"

"Us?"

He looked with contemptuous eyes at the empty rooms in the house on Berlín.

"You'll go crazy here. It'll be like clockwork."

JERICÓ LIVED ON the top floor of a crumbling building on Calle de Praga. The green tide of the Paseo de la Reforma could be heard in perpetual conflict with the gray traffic of Avenida Chapultepec. In any event, living on the seventh floor of an apartment building with no elevator had something about it that isolated us from the city, and since on the other floors there were only offices, after seven in the evening the building was ours, as if to compensate for the cramped arrangement of a living room integrated with the kitchen—stove, refrigerator, pantry—separated only by the high counter we used as a table, integrated in turn by two high stools that resembled the racks where they placed heretics, to the derision of the people, and the punished, to the mockery of their masters.

What else? Two bedrooms—one smaller than the other—and a bathroom. Jericó offered me the larger room. I refused to displace him. He suggested changing beds every seven days. I accepted, not understanding the reasoning behind the offer.

We also shared the closet, though I brought from Berlín to Praga (from Döblin to Kafka, one might say) more clothing than the very few items my friend had.

And we shared women. I should say, a single woman in a single house on Calle de Durango, the brothel of La Hetara, a name of ancient lineage, according to my friend, for at the dawn of Mexican time two women fought for control of whoredom in the city: La Bandida, a famous madam celebrated in boleros and corridos and, much more discreet, La Hetara, to whose house Jericó took me one night.

"You're like a lamb going to slaughter, and I know why. You fell in love with the nurse Elvira Ríos. You didn't realize that the nurse, the doctor, the entire house on Berlín, and of course your jailer Doña María Egipciaca were all passing illusions, phantoms of your childhood and early youth, destined to disappear as soon as you reached the 'age of reason.' "

"How do you know that?" I asked without too much surprise, since to me the speed of my friend's associations and conundrums was already proverbial.

"Aaaah. The fact is your case is mine . . . I believe . . ."

With growing perplexity I asked him to explain. I had grown up in a mansion in the care of a strict tyrant and he, apparently, had been freer than the wind, giving the impression—underscored by his apartment, his vital ease in speaking, living, going to see whores, walking between the Zona Rosa and Colonia Roma as if there were no (were there any?) urban frontiers—that he had appeared in the world totally prepared, with no need for family, antecedents . . . or a last name.

All the entrance bells at the building on Praga had the names of individuals, companies, legal offices. The top floor said only PH—Penthouse. Ever since school, and above all after the incident with the young administrator whom I asked about Jericó's last name, I did not have the courage to investigate any further. It cost the administrator his job. After my question we didn't see him again, not even hidden behind his officious little window. I deduced that just as the school secretary had vanished, I could disappear too if I inquired about the last name and therefore the origins of my straightforward though mysterious friend Jericó.

And yet, here we were together in the garret (penthouse) on Calle de Praga between Reforma and Chapultepec, sharing roof, bathroom, meals, readings, and, finally, women. Or rather, woman. Just one.

Jericó pushed aside the beaded curtain and moved easily among the twenty or so girls gathered in the parlor of La Hetara. He told me—noticing my glances—to close my eyes. Why? Because we were going directly to the room where our friend was waiting for us. Friend? Our? Our whore, Josué. Our? Mine is yours. I forbid you to choose. I already chose for you, he went on, opening the door of a bedroom that had a thick, mixed aroma (perfume, sweat, starch) slathered on the walls, which no one and nothing, except the collapse of the house, could eliminate.

It was a room overloaded with heavy curtains on the walls, an effort at the kind of Oriental luxury I would later appreciate in the paintings of Delacroix crowded with silks, draperies, carpets, incense burners, fans, odalisques, and eunuchs . . . except in this room everything was sensually olfactory and barely visible, so great was the pileup of pillows, carpets, poufs, mirrors with no reflection, and the smell of cat piss and fast food, as if, when the act was over, the prostitute's solitude was compensated for only by an appetite contrary to the insatiable hunger that is the rule for the modern woman, molded by models who look like broomsticks and lead the daughters of Eve to bounce back and forth between bulimia and anorexia.

What awaited us? Was she fat or thin? Because in the darkness of the room, which was not even half-lit, it was difficult to find the dependable object of Jericó's desire transformed, with fraternal tyranny, into my own.

I allowed myself to be led. I recognized my position as student with barely one flower in my buttonhole, the deflowered and lamented Elvira, while Jericó strolled through this brothel like a sheikh in his harem with an unpleasant self-assurance that owed a good deal to his nineteen years. He was the sultan, the *qaid*, the chief, the top dog. Would his age humble him or exalt him even more on this, my first night as an eighteen-year-old adolescent in a whorehouse?

With a dramatic gesture, Jericó took a heavy silk bedspread and pulled it aside, revealing the woman protecting herself beneath and behind this large scenic device.

How much was revealed to me? Very little. The woman was still covered from the waist down, only her bare back gleamed, in the dusky light, like a forgotten moon, and her face was covered by a veil that concealed her from nose to shoulder. The only things visible were the eyes of a winged beast, black, large, cruel, mindless, and indifferent, as mysterious as the hidden half of her face, almost as if from the nose down this woman had an appearance that denied the great unknown of her gaze with a vulgarity, simplicity, or stupidity unworthy of her enigmatic eyes.

I didn't see much more, as I say, because as soon as we were undressed, the woman disappeared amid Jericó's kisses and my timid caresses, the two of us naked without any previous order or decision, naturally stripped of everything except our skin, avid to kiss the woman, touch her, in the end possess her.

And never speak to her. The veil that covered her mouth also sealed it. She did not allow a sigh, a moan, a reply to escape. She was the object-woman, something volunteered, made for the pleasure—that first night—only of Jericó and Josué, Castor and Pollux, here and now again the children of Leda, whore to the swan, born in this instant of the same egg, the Dioscuri in the act of being born, crushing the flowers and grass, shattering the eggs of the swan so that from her would be born love and conflict, power and intelligence, the tremor in the thighs, the fire on the roofs, the blood in the air.

We followed each other in love.

Only later did I try to reconstruct in memory what existed outside my body, as if in the act itself any impression other than pleasure would extinguish it. The woman behind the veil was inanimate though endowed with a labored indolence. She adopted mechanical poses that left the initiative to the two of us. Even so, my love was abrupt, spasmodic, obliging me to imagine Elvira's lack of haste.

"Can you say something to her that will make her tremble?" Jericó whispered in my ear, he and I facing each other with the woman between us, the two friends head to head, panting, trying in vain to smile, naked in our carnal blindness, our hands resting on the woman's waist, fingers touching, I looking out of the corner of my eye at the bee tattooed on one of the whore's buttocks, our mouths joined by respiration that was shared, yearning, suspicious, shy, ardent.

"Can you imagine all the men who've had her? Doesn't it excite you to know the road of her body has been traveled by thousands of cocks? Does it bother you, interest you, repel you? Only you and I become emotional? Are we going to find our pleasure separately or at the same time?"

I would like to believe, at a distance, that those nights at La Hetara on Calle Durango sealed forever the fraternal complicity (that had already existed since school, since our readings, since our conversations with Filopáter) between Jericó and me.

Still, there was something else. Not only the postcoital sadness I didn't feel with Elvira and did now, but an ugliness, a vulgarity that Jericó himself took care to point out to me.

"Do you want to believe?" He coughed with a caricatured, pompous cough while the woman lay facedown in the bed. "Do you want to believe that sex is like a great baroque poem whose exterior is the insidious ornamentation on limpid profundity?"

He made a disagreeable face so I would laugh.

"Then take a look at Hetara at dawn, without the night's makeup. What will you see? What will it taste of? A roll dipped in perfume. And what will you find if you tear off the veil? A revolting face."

He indicated the woman's backside. She had a queen bee tattooed on her left buttock. He didn't know I had seen it, which is why he pointed it out to me.

"Everything's varnish, my dear Josué. Lose your illusions and say an affectionate goodbye to the veiled woman."

Only later did I remember that when I made love to her I closed my eyes, knowing that he, Jericó my friend, made love with his eyes open and came without making noise. Even though he came. She did not.

"Like clockwork."

WHEN WE GRADUATED from prep school, we would matriculate in the Faculty of Law. We took that for granted.

Our earlier philosophical meanderings—the reading of Saint Augustine and Nietzsche, the discussions with Father Filopáter, the magnet of Spinoza—convinced us that the framework of ideas was like the skeleton in a body that now required the flesh of experience. And without having read Spinoza, experience could be had by a bus driver or a cook. We—Jericó and I—ran the risk of believing that ideas were enough in themselves: splendid, eloquent, astral, and sterile. To give reality to our thoughts, we decided to study law as the option closest to our shared intellectual vocation.

Because we could share a woman or an apartment. This was almost child's play compared to the brotherhood of thoughts—Castor
and Pollux, children of the swan, the Dioscuri born of the same
ovary, causing flowers and grasses to burst forth in the world, at-
tending the birth of love and conflict, power and intelligence. Because they were so united, they decided our next step: to be lawyers
in order to give reality to our ideas.

I was certain about our shared purpose. Still, I noticed in my
friend, during the months of vacation between our leaving prep and
matriculating at the university, a growing disquiet manifested in isolated phrases when we ate, showered, walked through the neighborhood, went into one of the increasingly rare bookstores in the city,
and invaded (or allowed ourselves to invade) spaces devoted to popular music, videos, and gadgetry. There was no lack of street life on
the way to our old prep school. Vast, swarming, moving like an
undisciplined army of ants, the street gave an accounting of increasingly greater differences of class. There was an abyss between the
motorized world and the world on foot or even between those in cars
and those on a bus. The Mexican contrast, far from ebbing, increased, as if the country's "progress" were an optical illusion, calculated on the number of inhabitants but not the sum total of their
welfare.

The working-class city increased its numbers. The privileged
city isolated itself like a pearl in the urban oyster (cloister). Jericó
and I went to a cineclub and saw Fritz Lang's *Metropolis*, with its
two rigidly separated universes. Above, a great penthouse of games
and gardens. Below, an enormous underground cave of mechanized
workers. Superficially gray, at bottom black. Or rather, without light.

In our city, the young who were neither poor nor rich rubbed elbows with the wealthy in discotheques and wandered solitary and
joyless through the commercial centers, the large groupings of
stores, movie houses, and cafés under the common roof of provi-
sional protection. Outside, an option was waiting for the young in
stylish clothes: Move up, move down, or stay where you are forever.

For all these reasons, Jericó and the one who is narrating this
story to you, gentle survivors, felt privileged. I had lived in protected

comfort in the house on Berlín. Now, I shared the apartment on Praga with my friend. I hadn't known the source of Jericó's income. Now I had a suspicion that I didn't have the courage to share with him. On the fifteenth of every month an envelope appeared in the mailbox with a check made out to me. I confess I cashed it in secret and didn't tell Jericó. But I imagined that periodically he received similar assistance and even went so far as to think, with no proof at all, that the source of our controlled income might be the same. The truth is that the amount I had at my disposal was enough for my immediate needs and nothing more.

Since my friend and I led twin lives, I supposed his income was not very different from mine. What we did share was the mystery.

I was saying that during the months of vacation, Jericó began to let slip phrases without precedent or consequence. They seemed directed at me, though at times I considered them mere expressions in viva voce of my friend's thoughts and concerns.

In the shower: "What do we fear, Josué?"

At breakfast: "Never leave yourself open to an ambush."

Having lunch at three o'clock: "Don't let anyone impose opinions on you. Be independent."

Walking together through the neighborhood: "Don't feel superior or inferior to anybody. Feel equal."

Back in the apartment: "We have to make ourselves equal to everything around us."

"No," I replied. "We have to make ourselves better. What makes us better also challenges us."

Then we fell into a frequent debate, our elbows leaning on the table, my hands supporting my head, his open in front of me, at times he and I in the same posture, both joined by a fraternity that, for me, was our strength . . . as we drank beer.

"What undermines a man? Fame, money, sex, power?"

"Or, on the contrary, failure, anonymity, poverty, impotence?" I hurried to say between sips of brew.

He said we ought to avoid extremes, though in case of necessity—and he smiled cynically—the first was preferable to the second.

"Even at the cost of corruption, dishonesty, lies? I give up!"

"That's the challenge, dude."

I took his hand affectionately.

"Why did we become friends? What did you see in me? What did I see in you?" I asked, returning with a certain dreamy melancholy to our first meeting, when we were both almost children, in the school officially named Jalisco and in reality Presbytery.

Jericó didn't answer. He remained silent for several days, almost as if speaking to me were a form of treason.

"How to avoid it?" he murmured at times. "I give up!"

I smiled as I said, so the conversation would not be sidetracked in the usual way: Either you learn a trade or you end up a highway robber.

He didn't smile. He said with punctual indifference (that's how he was) that at least the criminal had an exceptional destiny. The terrible thing, perhaps, was to give in to the fatality of the evasive, the conformity of the common and ordinary.

He said the vast *masa pauperatis* of Mexico City had no choices but poverty or crime. Which did he prefer? Criminality, no doubt about it. He stared at me, as he had when we made love to the tattooed woman. Poverty could be a consolation. The worst commonplace of sentimentality, he added, removing his hands from mine, was to think the poor are good. It wasn't true: Poverty is a horror, the poor are damned, damned by their submission to fatality and redeemable only if they rebel against their misery and become criminals. Crime is the virtue of poverty, Jericó said on that occasion I have not forgotten, looking down and taking my hands again before shaking his head, looking at me now with a restrained happiness:

"I believe that youth consists of daring, don't you agree? Maturity, on the other hand, consists of dissimulating."

"Would you dare, for example, to kill? To kill, Jericó?"

I pretended terror and smiled. He went on with a somber air. He said he feared necessity, because hunting for the necessary meant gradually sacrificing the extraordinary. I said that all of life, for the mere fact of being, was already extraordinary and deserving of respect. He looked at me, for the first time, with a wounding contempt, lowering me to the condition of the commonplace and lack of imagination.

"Do you know what I admire, Josué? Above all things I admire the man who murders what he loves, the thief who steals what he likes. This is not necessity. This is art. It is will that is free, supposedly free. It is the opposite of the herd of complaining, stupid, bovine, directionless people, the ones you pass every day in the street. The filthy herd of oxen, the blind herd of moles, the thick cloud of green flies, capeesh?"

"Are you telling me it's better to have the extraordinary destiny of a criminal than the common destiny of an ordinary citizen?" I said without too much emphasis.

"No," he replied, "what I'm praising is the capacity for deceit, disguise, dissimulation of the citizen who murders in secret and turns his victims into strawberry marmalade!"

He laughed and said we wouldn't matriculate together at the Faculty of Law in the Ciudad Universitaria. Next week Jericó was going to France on a scholarship.

That's how he told me, without preambles, amiable but cutting, with no warning and no justification. That's how Jericó was, and at that very moment I should have put myself on guard against his surprising nature. But since our friendship was, by this time, old and deep, I thought the reappearance of my friend's Nietzschean "brutalities," contrasting the world with the perception of the world, was merely a momentary return of the options that mark youth, similar to a circular plaza from which six different avenues emerge: We have to take only one, knowing we sacrifice the other five. Will we know one day what the second, third, fourth, or fifth roads held in store? Do we accept this, thinking it didn't matter which one we chose because we carry the true path inside us and the different avenues are mere accidents, landscapes, circumstances, but not the essence of ourselves?

Did my friend Jericó understand this when he abandoned me so suddenly in search of a destiny he could separate from me, but even more, from himself?

Or was he taking an indispensable step so Jericó could find Jericó, and to do that it didn't matter to him—or in the end, to me—if his trip to Europe distanced him forever or brought him closer than ever to me? I didn't know the answer then. Only now, cut down, on a remote Pacific beach, do I return to that moment of our shared youth, trying to resume life itself, beyond our personalities, as a premonition of postponed horror: a youth of external violence and internal desolation. An age that disappeared, fragile but perhaps beautiful.

My absurd preoccupation was different then, different.

What name would Jericó travel with?

What last name would be displayed, of necessity, on his passport?

PROFESSOR ANTONIO SANGINÉS stood out, in every sense, in the Faculty of Law. Tall, distinguished, endowed with an aquiline profile, melancholy brows, and eyes at once serious, cynical, mocking, and tolerant under heavy lids, he appeared in class immaculately dressed, always in three-piece suits (I never saw him combine an unmatched sports jacket and trousers), double-breasted, buttoned to emphasize the high, stiff collar, the monochrome tie, and his only concessions to fantasy, light brown shoes and cuff links won at raffles or bought with love, for it was not impossible to imagine Licenciado Sanginés buying cuff links decorated with the figure of Mickey Mouse.

I do not need to add that a figure like his made a devilish contrast with the increasingly popular style of our time. The young dress the way beggars or railroad workers once did: torn jeans, old shoes, threadbare jackets, shirts with announcements and slogans (KISS ME, INSANE, I NEED A GIRLFRIEND, TEXAS LOST, I LIKE TO FUCK, I'M ABANDONED, MY PORK RINDS CRACKLE, MÉRIDA METROPOLIS), sleeveless T-shirts, and baseball caps worn backward and all the time, even in class. Even sadder was the sight of mature, not to say old, men and women who assumed a borrowed youth with the same sports caps, Bermuda shorts, and Nike sneakers.

With it all, Professor Sanginés's elegance was seen as an anachronistic eccentricity, and he repaid the compliment by viewing the style of the young as decadence unaware of itself. He liked to quote the Italian poet Giacomo Leopardi and his famous dialogue between Death and Fashion:

FASHION: Madame Death, Madame Death.
DEATH: Wait until the right time, and you will see me without
    having to call.
FASHION: Madame Death!
DEATH: Go to the Devil. I will be ready when you are not.
FASHION: Don't you know me? I am Fashion, your sister.

This was what, with a certain macabre, decadent air, attracted me to this teacher who taught the class in International Public Law with a degree of meticulousness far above the abilities of the students, for he, far from filling us with facts, expounded on two or three ideas and supported them with reference to a couple of fundamental texts, inviting us to read them seriously though convinced—a glance at the flock was enough—no one would follow his advice. That is: He did not order, he suggested. It did not take him long to realize I not only listened to him but for the next month responded to his questions in class—until then simply a cry in the desert—with respectful alacrity. Sanginés suggested *The Prince*. I read Machiavelli. Sanginés indicated *The Social Contract*. I immersed myself in Rousseau.

First he invited me to walk with him through the Ciudad Universitaria, then later to go to his house in Coyoacán, an old residence from the colonial period, only one floor but very extensive, where in room after room, books supported, in a manner of speaking, the wisdom, if not of the ages, then of the end of the world. He noticed my delight and also my nostalgia. The encounter with Professor Sanginés reminded me of our conversations with Father Filopáter. It also brought to mind the absence of my friend Jericó and the lonely need we sometimes feel to share what we see and do with a brotherly friend. I don't know if Jericó felt in Europe what I felt in Mexico. The pleasure would have doubled with his presence. We would have been able to comment on Antonio Sanginés's lessons, compare them with those of Father Filopáter, and proceed, as we had done then, with our intellectual formation on the solid foundation of our friendship.

Professor Sanginés's residence breathed the air shared by the man and his books. Both were joined in an internationalist ethic very much opposed to the new global laissez-faire. Globalization was a fact and its momentum swept away old frontiers, laws, and discourses, antiquated habits and defenses of sovereignty. The teaching of Antonio Sanginés did not deny this reality. It merely pointed out, with elegant emphasis, the dangers (for everyone) of a world in which international decisions were made without competent authority, just cause, juridical intention, or proportionality, and with war as the first, not the final, recourse. The catastrophic intervention of the United States in Iraq was the probative example of Sanginés's theories. The authority had been nonexistent, fragile, and usurped. The cause, a true potpourri of lies: There were no weapons of mass destruction in Iraq, overthrowing the dictator was not the reason behind the resolution, the dictator fell and terror made its entrance, the region passed from maximum order (tyranny) to maximum chaos (anarchy), and the catastrophe did not ensure the flow of oil or confirm the lowering of prices. The little match on the Potomac became the conflagration in Mesopotamia.

"The only ones who win," Sanginés concluded, "are the mercenaries who profit from the beginning and ending of wars."

If this was Antonio Sanginés's practical lesson in class, in private I discovered that his condemnation of international crime merely reflected his interest in crime *tout court*. I was discovering that half his library dealt not with the noble thoughts of Vitoria and Suárez, Grotius and Pufendorf, but with the obscure though profound examinations by Beccaria and Dostoyevsky of crime and criminals and, even more somber, the books of Butterworth on the police and of Livingstone and Owen on prisons.

When he explained the prison system, Sanginés offered details about subjects like security, living conditions, recognized privileges, health, access to the outside world, correspondence, legal contacts, family and conjugal visits, repatriation, internal discipline, punishments, segregation, cells, life sentences, and discretionary sentencing.

"Prison is like a mummy bandaged from head to toe in laws and institutions. The prison authorities, for the most part, behave, for good and for evil, in accordance with 'regulations.' Except there are so many 'regulations' that they allow great discretion in applying them and even in ignoring or violating them, creating a set of unwritten laws that, especially in the case of Mexico, eventually replace written law."

I don't know if he sighed: "Throughout Latin America homage is paid to the law only to violate it more thoroughly. Prisons in Mexico are no worse than the ones in Brazil. In Colombia the guerrillas impose their own prison law, mocking national statutes. In Central America, the disasters of war have created so many de facto situations that the legal code is a dead letter."

The professor's three little boys came in and, dressed as pirates and shouting about boarding and blood, they climbed on his head, his shoulders, his chest, making him laugh, and as soon as he had affectionately freed himself, he made a final comment as he adjusted his jacket and tie.

"Everything I tell you, Josué, about theory and laws does not matter if you do not observe life in our prisons up close."

He looked at me in a sly manner I hadn't seen until then, for our relationship had always been as direct as the association of a student with his teacher can be. I believe Sanginés attempted to dim the gleam in his eyes without waking my suspicions by lowering his lids—which he naturally did when he thought—and remarking that among the classes in the jurisprudence curriculum, one was required as a course but elective as to subject: forensic practice. It was up to me to decide the field in which I wanted to do this practice. Commercial or civil suits. Divorces, evictions, estates, seizures, bankruptcies, mergers, land boundaries, jurisdictions, appraisals, all of this the professor enumerated without referring to the internationalist subject of his class and, eventually, anchoring in prison law.

Did he sigh? Did he command?

The fact is that, motivated by Don Antonio Sanginés, I requested and secured permission to do my class in forensic practice in prison.

And not in any prison but in the most feared, most famous, but most unknown, visible in its strange name but invisible in its even gloomier (I supposed) interior. The grave of the living. The house of the dead, yes. The Mexican Siberia, a wasteland within a wasteland, a cave within another cave, a labyrinth with many entrances and no exit, an altar of consecrated blasphemies and profanations. The black hole. The metaphor of our life imprisoned in the womb at first, in a shroud at the last, in the deepest secrets of the domestic prison between tango and tomb. The prison built with the stones of the law. Hope, the prison of Zechariah. Liberation, the hope of Isaiah.

And so, with these thoughts, I commenced the conclusion of my law studies at the Palacio Negro de San Juan de Aragón, built underground in the bed of the old Río del Consulado, beneath the footsteps of the urban crowd which, I never suspected, could be heard as one more torture in the depths of this prison of prisons.

LA CHUCHITA APPROACHED and, with tears in her eyes, gave me her hand. In the other she carried a small mirror into which she looked from time to time with a mixture of serenity and alarm. Dress me, she said. I replied that she was already dressed. The girl cried out and began to pull off her clothing, I mean the long nightshirt of coarse homespun worn by all the girls imprisoned in the depths of San Juan de Aragón. I hate it, she screamed, tearing at her tangled hair flattened by grime, I hate seeing myself naked. You're dressed, I said innocently. She leaped at me, trying to scratch me. They have to dress me, she screamed, they have to dress me. Then she bowed her head and withdrew while a blue boy, at her side, bent over the cement floor picking up something invisible, and a little farther on, another adolescent scratched incessantly at his back and complained of the pimples that itched, that burned, that never healed no matter how his bloodied nails scratched at dark skin.

The girl Isaura had a fixed idea: the volcano Popocatépetl. I sat beside her for a while. She spoke of nothing else. She repeated the name of the mountain over and over again, smiling, savoring the syllables. Po-po-ca-té-pel. I corrected her. Po-po-ca-té-petl. The word was Nahua—I corrected myself, wanting her to understand me: Aztec. She repeated: Po-po-ca-té-pel. I insisted: té-petl. She looked at me with sustained, inexplicable fury, as if I had violated a secret chamber, a sacred corner of her existence. I would have preferred the girl to attack me physically. She merely observed me with a distance that wanted to wound me and the entire world, the world that had sent her here, the empty swimming pool of children imprisoned in San Juan de Aragón. What would I say to her? There was no open pathway between my presence and her release. When she walked away repeating Po-po-ca-té-pel, she no longer was looking at me.

I wasn't told the name of the next creature I approached. Its sex was indecipherable. It couldn't have been more than six or seven years old, but something had been engraved on its face. Indeterminacy, or rather, a gentle, undefined astonishment. Who was it? Alberto. A boy. No. Albertina. A girl. It looked at me with tears in its eyes.

Another boy of about fifteen showed off a scar at his waist. I say "showed off" because he displayed it with a self-satisfied mixture of misfortune and valor, pointing at it with his index finger, look at me, touch me, just try . . .

I was distracted by a boy with a very sad face. I didn't dare ask him his name. He couldn't have been more than eleven, but in his gaze an ancient guilt was revealed in small lines between his eyebrows, a grimacing mouth, the defiance suggested by very white teeth in a filthy mouth from which the remains of a tortilla and scrambled eggs were dangling. Like a flash of lightning, sadness transformed into aggression when he realized I was observing him.

"Félix," he shouted. "Felicity."

He threw himself at me. Only the intervention of a guard stopped the charge.

Others were more eloquent. Ceferino told me he wasn't guilty of anything. The crime lay in being abandoned. He was abandoned in a wretched neighborhood where not even the dogs could find anything to eat in the garbage dump. He wanted to eat a dog to see what it tasted like. It would have been better if he had eaten the parents who abandoned him in the neighborhood of the garbage dump. He looked for them. No way. Where did they go? The city is enormous. What did they leave behind? The tag on his overalls. The name of the store where they bought him overalls. There they told him where his papa and mama had gone. He walked an entire day from neighborhood to neighborhood, searching until he found them at a little stand on the Xalostoc road, there on the highway to Pachuca, that is, right on the fucking road. Papa, mama, I was going to say to them. It's me, your son, Pérez. He realized as soon as he looked at them that they had abandoned him because the child was a burden, another mouth to feed, a hindrance, and now, in their small business, his papa and mama had forgotten him completely. They believed—he believed—that if they had prospered just a little it was because they didn't have to feed a boy named Pérez. He looked at them, if not smiling then satisfied, self-satisfied. Not free of guilt. Just forgetful of everything that happened before they emigrated from the neighborhood and found a suitable way to survive. They were unaware of his existence. They didn't know he was there, at the age of eleven, ready to attack them with an ice pick, stab out their eyes, leave them there screaming and bleeding, and end up in the prison for minors at San Juan de Aragón.

Did they survive?

I wish they had, so they would never see the world again and have to find another way to live, feeling themselves scorned, fucked, gone all to hell, assholes, sons of bitches.

Merlín was a mentally deficient boy. Not completely, but sufficiently so. Shaved head, the mischievous gaze of a happy imbecile, his mouth hanging open, snot dripping; the jailer who accompanied me explained that this boy was part of the bands of idiots criminal gangs used to commit offenses. They placed bombs in cars. They were a distraction during criminal acts. They served as decoys. They acted as false abductees. The smartest ones were spies. Almost all of them were given to the gangs by their families in exchange for money, and sometimes just to get rid of the runty little bastards.

Others, the amiable guard helping me to complete the course in forensic practice pointed out, had more talent but were born into the most absolute marginality, with lives close to those of dogs or pigs. Their only way out—he traced a wide arc with his arm and open hand—was crime or prostitution. He implied, to my amazement, that this black lake was in a way a place of seduction. Instead of a deadly fate, the kids who swarmed here, like phantoms, alone or arm in arm, all dressed in their sad caftans of coarse cloth, barefoot, scratching their shaved heads as if nits were their only consolation, picking at their companion's navel, scratching their balls and their armpits, blowing their nose with their hand, shitting and pissing at will, all together in the great underground cement pool in the obscene guts of the Federal District, all possessed a jailhouse destiny.

That was implied in the jailer's gaze, at once indifferent and obscure. Albertina said she had been kidnapped in a restaurant in Las Lomas, no less, when she went to the bathroom and disappeared while her parents looked for her and she, drugged, left the place in the arms of her kidnappers, except dressed as a boy, her curls cut off, her hair dyed black, and a pallor that did not leave her in the stupor of never knowing again who she was or who she had been, trained only to steal, to slip between security bars and end up behind prison bars, completely disoriented forever.

What do you want us to do?

I don't know how to get dressed by myself! screamed La Chuchita.

The boy with the scar on his back had been kidnapped in order to remove his kidney and sell it to the Gringos who require replacement organs. Thank your saints they didn't take both of them, asshole. He dedicated himself to finding who kidnapped him, drugged him, and operated on him. Since he didn't find them, he decided to cross the border and go from hospital to hospital destroying with a colorful cane from Apizaco the jars where other people's kidneys were resting. Broken glass, spilled fluids, kidneys that the boy picked up, cooked, and ate, wrapped in tortillas, like great Gringo tacos devoured by a vengeful Mexican. He was expelled from California, contrary to the United States policy of detaining Mexicans, especially those suspected of not speaking English. Catarino—that was his name—turned out to be too dangerous, even behind the bars of Alcatraz: He was capable of eating them all, like Hannibal Lecter.

Justice triumphed.

"Do you know how to swim?" said the jailer, whose face I looked at for the first time, having been so attentive to the small juvenile hell in the cement swimming pool.

He didn't give me time to answer.

Four streams of water came from the top of the sides of the tank-prison, splashing against the bodies and heads of the children and young people trapped in this pit, in the midst of shouting that was savage, happy, agonizing, surprising, under this downpour of rough, muddy liquids, channeled here from a dead river that emerged into life to subdue the children and young people who rapidly were floating, waving their arms, moving their heads, shouting, crying. The agitation of that small prison sea obliged me to swim, fully dressed, as the water rose, and I noted, in the confusion, that while some children swam, others, the smaller ones, it's true, sank, were trapped, and drowned with a howl at once personal and collective.

"This is how we force them to bathe," said the guard.

"And those who don't know how to swim?"

"This is how we control the excess penal population."

"What do you have to say about it?"

"I say too bad for them."

"Are you a demographer, Señor?"

Who offers up Mexico's prayers at the foot of the altar to its children?

DEAR SURVIVORS: I would be lying if I told you that the departure of my friend Jericó condemned me to irremediable solitude. I've mentioned that his absence coincided with the years of my university studies, culminating in the guardianship of Don Antonio Sanginés and my ghastly visit to the juvenile pit at San Juan de Aragón in the name of "forensic practice."

I haven't lied. I've omitted. I should remedy the fault. In my spirit, I tried to associate the absence of Jericó with a willed, ideal solitude, which reality took care of proving false as soon as I said goodbye to my friend in the airport. I can deceive the living. Who among all of (or the few of) you can disprove what I'm recounting here? Everything I've said may be pure invention on my part. You, Señor, Señora, Señorita who read me, there is no proof I'm telling you the truth. There isn't even proof I exist outside of these pages. You can believe me if I declare that my sex life, without the usual company of Jericó, was a desert without salt or even sand: an emptiness comparable to the children's pit, so deep, desolate, and cruel, a Sahara of cement . . . Imagine, if you wish, that I looked for and found the nurse Elvira Ríos, that I became her lover even though she was married, that I didn't become her lover because she was married, that she turned me down because she had sex only with the sick to console them, and I seemed as healthy as socialist realism in a poster from the Stalinist era whose pop art was on display, at the time, in the Palacio de Bellas Artes. You can deny it if I tell you I went back to the brothel on Avenida Durango a few more times to fuck the whore with the veiled face and the bee on her buttock. The truth? A lie? I didn't know her name. She was gone, she had left, "retired," according to the chaste expression of the madam and whoremistress Doña Evarista Almonte, alias La Hetara.

I could, then, deceive discreet readers and still ask them, as an act of faith in me, my life, my book, to believe that in the very act of saying goodbye to Jericó in Terminal One of the Mexico City Airport, in the midst of the infernal din characteristic of that elephantiastic building that extends in all directions, exits, entrances, cafés, restaurants, liquor stores, sarapes, trinkets, mariachi hats, books and magazines, pharmacies, silverware shops, sweets shops, sports shoes, baby clothes, and the life you live from day to day, like a lottery ticket, my country, admitting and expelling thousands of national and foreign tourists, the curious, pickpockets, cabdrivers, porters, police, customs officials, airline employees, in uniform, out of uniform, until in that enormous bowl of oats a second, simultaneously local and foreign city was formed, and I encountered an accident that changed my life.

In an instant a clamor was added to the aforementioned din, which I'll tell you about now. That's what happens at the airport, everyone's city: You think you're there for one thing and it turns out you were there for something very different. You think you know the direction, the route of your destination within the belly of the aerial ogre, and suddenly the unexpected erupts without requesting permission. You think you have everything with you, and in an instant madness takes the place reserved for reason.

The fact is I was walking calmly though sadly back to the Metro that would take me to my neighborhood, when a person fell into my arms. I don't say man, I don't say woman, because this individual was all leather—at least that's what I felt as I embraced without wishing to the person whose face was hidden behind goggles—or rather, aviator glasses that came down from the leather helmet covering the head of the person who kicked, embraced me in order to escape the police who were holding her, and screamed so they would know her sex. A woman's piercing voice shouted insults, called the police pricks, pigs, bums, dogs, half-breeds, brutes, sons of the original great whore, first among whores, Mother Evarista, Matildona in person (the name sounded familiar), bastards of all bastardom and of bastardly bastardhood, to make a long story short.

I embraced her. The police had their hands on her back.

"Let her go, please," I said, carried away by an instinct for sympathy.

"Do you know her?"

"She's my wife."

"Well, take better care of her, young man."

"Lock her up in La Castañeda," said the oldest and most outdated of the policemen.

"My colleague meant to say she's crazy."

"What did she do?" I summoned the courage to ask while the woman clutched at me as if I were a pillar in a storm.

"She wanted to take off in her own small plane on the runway reserved for the Er Franz flight."

Which was my friend Jericó's flight to Paris.

"What happened?"

"We stopped her in time."

"We confiscated the plane."

"Aren't you going to charge her?"

"I'm telling you we confiscated the plane."

I'm not sure if the policeman winked when he said this. His eyes with no cornea, the eyes of an idol, did not move, his lips traced an unwanted complicity. I did not have enough money for a "taste," and bribery repelled me morally though not philosophically. They made my life easier. All they wanted was to get rid of the woman, and the gods of the Aztec Subterranean, Airport stop, had sent me. I couldn't imagine, as the Untouchables turned their backs on me, the fate of the requisitioned plane, the tribal division of spoils.

"My name's Lucha Zapata."

I embraced her and moved away through the crowd at the air marketplace. I exchanged glances with another woman walking behind a young porter who made gallant gestures, as if pushing a cart of luggage in an airport were the most glamorous piece of acting imaginable. I didn't know why this modern, young, nimble, elegant woman who moved like a panther, like an animal restlessly tracking the porter, looked at me with such fleeting and intense interest.

"My name's Lucha Zapata," my companion repeated. "Take me with you."

I stopped looking at the elegant girl. I was conquered by minimal solidarity.

THE ENTIRE NEIGHBORHOOD of San Juan de Aragón, at least from Oceanía to Río Consulado, had been razed in a joint action of the City and the Federation in order to erect right there, in the heart of the capital and a few blocks from the lawless district of Ciudad Neza, the largest penitentiary in the republic. It was an act of defiance: The law would not go to distant wastelands where new prison cities with their own regulations are formed. It was a provocation:

The law would be installed in the center of the center, within reach, so criminals would know once and for all that they are not a race apart but citizens of prison, with ears that hear the movement of traffic, with noses that smell the aroma of frying food, with hands that touch the walls of the nation's ha-ha history, with feet a few meters from extinct rivers and the dead lagoon of México-Tenochtitlán.

I understood, continuing my pragmatic forensics course, that minors were kept between life and death in the great subterranean pool, left to the accident of death by water or a Tarzanesque survival. Now I learned that older criminals were confined on the upper floor, with devices that meticulously picked up the sounds of the city outside, a true metropolis of liberties and joy compared to the Dantesque city of sorrow—the *cittá dolente*—that awaited me on the upper floor, where it was difficult to hear the voices of the convicts over the snare of urban sounds, horns, motors, the squeal of tires, insults, the shouts of vendors, the silences of beggars, offers of sex, sighs of love, childish songs, school choruses, kneeling prayers, all amplified by perverse loudspeakers intent on torturing the prisoners with the memory of freedom.

I armed myself with courage to complete not only the requirements of the university course—"forensic practice"—but also to honor the decision of my respected teacher Sanginés. The upper prison of San Juan de Aragón, above the children's pool, was a large space on one floor. "Here nobody empties chamber pots down on us," said the unsmiling guard who was my guide now, but on whose shoulders a polished and repolished cleanliness shone with a faint perfume of shit.

Siboney Peralta was a Cuban mulatto about thirty years old with long hair arranged in twisted braids, naked to his navel with the clear intention not only to display his musculature but to frighten or forestall with the power of his biceps, the profound throb of his pectorals, and the menacing hunger of his guts. He wore no shoes and his trousers were rags wrapped around an indistinct sex that could just as easily have been a long hose or a little knob. His crime was not one of passion. It was, according to Siboney, an enigma, a mystery, chico.

"A small mystery?"

"No, very big, chico."

Siboney didn't know why he was in prison. He loved music, so much it turned his head, he said, flexing all his muscles, to the point where he couldn't help doing what the music said.

"I'm a child of the bolero, compay."

Siboney obeyed the bolero. If the words said "Look at me" and the woman didn't look at him, Siboney filled with holy rage and strangled her. If the song indicated "Tell me if you love me as I adore you" and the woman didn't turn around to look at him, the least she received was a Siboneyera beating. If he asked her at a distance if she had a thought for him and if at a distance she remained silent, the mulatto attacked with chairs, windows, plates, flowerpots, what he found at hand in the silent universe of his desire.

"And knowing your trouble, can't you control it?" I asked uncertainly.

Siboney bellowed with laughter that meant it isn't my trouble, it's my joy, my pleasure. What is? I told myself it was nothing less than believing in the words of songs, as I at this moment believe in what I am writing and transmitting to you, curious reader, with all the unpunished fatality of Siboney Peralta strangling the innocent women who did not take his songs literally.

Brillantinas and Gomas were placed in the same cell with the perverse intention of having them argue over the jars of brilliantine and envelopes of gum tragacanth that were the criminal obsession of the pair. Each one, not yet knowing the other, robbed pharmacies and beauty salons to obtain the scarcer brilliantines and ancient envelopes of gum for the hair that was their uncontrolled and uncontrollable fetish. The jailer explained to me that the original intention of the penitentiary's authorities was to bring together the two rivals to argue about the object of their desires until they annihilated each other over a jar of pomade. This was, he added, the guiding principle of the prison of San Juan de Aragón: to provoke the convicts into killing one another, thereby reducing the prison population.

"Each time one dies, one less mouth to feed, Licenciado," using the formal title for a lawyer.

"I'm not—"

"Licenciado."

He looked at me with his sewer eyes.

"Otherwise you wouldn't be here."

However, Gomas and Brillantinas agreed not to argue but to co-exist peacefully, smearing repulsive unguents on their hair.

"Can you suggest a way to have them kill each other?"

"Shave their heads," I said in an evil humor.

The jailer had a good laugh. "They'd put brilliantine on their balls and under their armpits, Licen."

Speaking of licenciados, I was introduced into the cell of the attorney Jenaro Ruvalcaba, whom I knew by name as a penologist of some fame in the Faculty of Law. When he saw me come in he stood and did his best to smooth his prison uniform: gray short-sleeved shirt and trousers far too big for the licenciado's small stature.

"He says he's committed no crime," the jailer remarked with a wink.

"It's true," Jenaro said calmly.

"So you say," the guard replied, mocking him.

Jenaro shrugged. I knew right away that asking him why are you here, what crime are you accused of, meant entering a labyrinth, with no exit, of excuses and injustices. Jenaro himself must have understood this—he was a slim, blond man about forty years old—when he sat down on the cot and patted it gently, inviting me to have a seat.

He said very calmly that the prison was filled with querulous, stupid people who want their freedom but wouldn't know what to do on the outside. Resignation? No, adaptation, said Jenaro. The punishment of prison, my young friend (that's me) consists in separating you from the world and then one of two things happens: either you die of despair or you invent new relationships inside what the Gringos call the Big House, which is what it is, after all, a house, a different kind of home but yours as much as the one you left.

"How do you manage?" I asked from behind my mask of a disciplined student.

"I accept what prison gives me." Ruvalcaba shrugged.

He saw the query in my eyes.

"Once you disregard what you shouldn't do," he continued, "in order not to be humiliated."

He anticipated my question.

"For example: Don't accept visitors. They come because they have to. They're always looking at their watch, they want to get away as soon as they can."

"In Mexico we have conjugal visits."

His smile was somewhere between cynical and bitter.

"You can be certain your wife has already found a lover—"

"Yes, but in any case she comes to—"

Jenaro raised his voice but grumbled.

"They'll both betray you so you'll stay in prison."

Crazed, he shouted and stood, clutching at his head with both hands, tearing at his ears, closing his eyes.

He came at me, arms flailing. The guard clubbed him on the back of his neck and the licenciado fell, weeping, on the cot.

El Negro España and La Pérfida Albión were two homosexuals incarcerated in San Juan de Aragón for the crime of solicitation exacerbated by robbery and murder. The institutional powers had not obliged them to reestablish their undesired masculinities. On the contrary, both had at their disposal makeup, tweezers, rouge, false eyelashes, and lipstick, which allowed them to feel comfortable and at the same time serve as a vice-ridden and contemptible example for the guards, who are all . . .

"Full-fledged hypocrites," said El Negro España, applying a false beauty spot to his cheek and adjusting his expensive comb.

He pointed at it. "I got this when I went to the Feria in Sevilla."

"Years ago," murmured La Pérfida Albión, an Englishman, I supposed, colorless, with very short hair, whose only mark of identity was the portrait of Queen Elizabeth stuck to his chest.

The flamenco dancer said that at first they had wanted to put them in separate cells in the hope the "normals" would beat them to a pulp. Except that just the opposite occurred. The most macho prisoners succumbed to the charms of La Negra España and La Pérfida Albión when they shouted "Lover," and though they called them, when they caressed, "Priscila" or "Encarnación," that only excited the men more, for which reason, the Englishman interjected, the authorities were resigned to putting them together again so they'd "do harm" only to each other.

They burst into laughter, caressing each other without shame, La Pérfida crooning arias from Madrid operettas in honor of La Negra, and La Negra, to please La Pérfida, singing tunes from Gilbert and Sullivan.

"Who protects us?" they sang together.

"We protect ourselves on our own," they signed off.

Ventanas, whose name came from his predilection for robbing by liberating windows, laughed a great deal when I asked him the reason for his incarceration. He had no teeth.

"I gave my teeth to the public welfare. I love philanthropy. I go even further, boy. I not only love all men, I love their possessions. For that you don't need teeth."

He guffawed between showers of saliva and thunderous coughs. He must have been sixty. He looked as if he were a hundred, and his hands did not tremble. He moved his fingers constantly, with the artfulness of a pianist.

He realized what he was doing.

"They called me Chopin. I would answer: Chofuckyomama."

This was his story:

"There are thieves who don't know how to get out of the house they're robbing. I was always very aware that the problem wasn't only getting in but getting away with no noise, no trace, not even a smell. And for that you have to work alone or with kids under ten so they can squeeze between the bars and open the windows for you."

He gave a distorted belly laugh, like the impossible music of a piano with no keys or only the black ones, so great was the depth of his throat, made even deeper by his lack of teeth.

"I always worked alone, for years and years, not carrying unnecessary baggage, light as one of those birds they call Phoeniz, and even if you burn them they're born again. Except they never burned me. What can you do?"

He sighed with breath like a squall. He was a solitary thief. Until the ailments of age obliged him to hire a boy of twenty to facilitate matters.

"Yes, he was agile, young, and an asshole. He knew how to get in. He didn't know how to get out, Señor Licenciado. He couldn't find the exit. After such a nice, clean entrance. After such an efficient robbery, the idiot got confused, he lost his way and led me from here to there and from there to here until the alarms went off, the lights went on, and the two of us were standing there, our spirits naked, surrounded by the police of Pedregal de San Angel, cursing the Esparza family and their damn security system."

"And your young accomplice?"

"I killed him in the paddy wagon on the way to prison."

"How?"

He raised his hands and let them fall on an imaginary nape of the neck.

I set down these facts because they had a decisive influence on how I saw society, the nation, and its people.

LUCHA ZAPATA. WAS it an announcement or a call? A proposal or a memory? *Mein Kampf, Mi lucha* or Lucha of mine? Lucha Zapata tonight at the Arena México. There was nothing of the fighter in her, I told myself when I rescued the presumed aviator and put her in a taxi, tremulous and diminished, curled up against me in a gesture that was not childlike. It was a declaration: Protect me.

From what?

From myself.

Words were not necessary to understand what she wanted. Her utterly helpless gaze, her radical lack of protection, delivered her into my hands. Not to my charity, because on the basis of compassion only the transient is constructed, to which is added resentment. Perhaps pity, only a little, the mercy that has been the emotional weapon of Christianity and the stage setting for the irresistible melodrama of Calvary. Was Lucha Zapata wearing a cross that hung between her breasts? The impenetrable leather top prevented certainty and condemned me to guesses. Everything I've said ought to convince your excellencies my readers that I have never once abused sentimentality. Instead, I've tried to be simple, direct, reducing myself from the beginning to this double visiting card: a decapitated head and a naked, unprotected skin. This, someone wrote a long time ago, is not serious: Tragedy is forbidden to the modern world. For us everything turns into melodrama, soap opera, newspaper serials, cowboy movies. The success of westerns (the modern epic, Alfonso Reyes would say, the saga of the plains, no longer of the sea) is the direct simplicity with which the spectator distinguishes Good from Evil. Evil wears black. Good wears white. The villain has a mustache. The hero is clean-shaven. The good guy brushes his teeth. The bad guy spits foul breath. The hero looks straight at you. The bad guy squints out of the corner of his eye.

The readings of the Greek classics that Jericó and I did as boys impressed on us a certain idea of tragedy as a conflict of values, not an opposition of virtues. Both Antigone and Creon are right. She has the values of the family. He has those of society. The law of the family demands the burial of the dead, the law of the state forbids it.

"Then," Jericó remarked, "tragic balance isn't quite as just as you say."

I asked him why.

"Because the law of the family will survive while the law of the city is temporary and revocable, isn't it?"

I recalled all this in the rattletrap taxi that drove the "rescued" woman and me to a destination I didn't know.

"Where to, chief?"

Where to? It was enough to look outside the car at the vast desert of the Anillo Periférico, the outer beltway that foreshadows the funeral that awaits us if we don't choose to turn ourselves into ashes first. Sacrificed after all, we die on the cement perimeter that reflects and celebrates a new city that has shed its old skin, its lacustrian sensuality, its igneous sacredness, displaced first by another beauty, baroque, name of the pearl beyond price, the misshapen jewel of the unborn oyster that Mexico City ostentatiously displays in its second foundation of volcanic rock, marble, smiling angels and demons even more jovial as if to compensate for the tears of blood (this isn't a bolero) of its tortured Christs in adjoining chapels so that the altar will be occupied by the tears that are pearls of his mother the Virgin who floats above the horns of the Iberian bull, our sacred animal. Sacred and for that reason, necessarily, syllogistically, sacrificial. Patient tombs and banished waters opening in avenues of pepper tree and willow, ascending mountains of pine and snow, proclaiming itself that region where the air is clear. Until it lands here, on the Periférico, an indecent sausage of funereal cement, scaffold and grave of two million broken-down taxis, materialist trucks, secondhand Volkswagens, insulting Alfa Romeos losing their way in the great urban tunnel, buses invisible under clusters of passenger flies, at once stoic and desperate, hanging any way they can from the armpits of the conveyance.

How was so much naked ugliness adorned? With advertisements. Commercial announcements were the only decoration on the Periférico. A world of gratifications, if not within reach, then within view of the consumer. A succession of images of desire, because none of them corresponded to the physical reality or economic possibility or even the psychic makeup of residents of the capital. The Periférico where I drove that night in a taxi with a defenseless and, I believe, valiant woman, her arms around my chest, looking out of the corner of my eye at a succession of invariably blond women used for everything: They advertise beer, cars, underwear, bathing suits, condominiums on the coast, films, audiovisual devices. Advertisements. Waiting for the uncommon but fatal catastrophe: One day, a small plane crashed into a vehicle filled with purebred horses. Nobody remembers the pilots. Only in advertisements of seaside vacations and sales in distant residential districts did the Mexican family appear, a happy grouping of the father in shirtsleeves, the modest, neat little wife, and two children—male and female—rosy-cheeked, smiling, happy to have found paradise in Satellite City, a guarded prison they will never leave, not in the advertisement and not in life . . .

Where would I go with my solitary companion? To the high-floor apartment on Praga? Didn't she have her own place?

I asked her.

She curled up more and more into my chest, not speaking.

She smelled of leather. Of alcohol. Of burned pot.

I raised her goggles and everything became concentrated, the taxi driving us, the speeding tomb of cement, the fixed, successive smiles of my compatriots happy because they had a terrific house in Colonia Lindavista, beach vacations without light or water, noisy cereals at breakfast, underwear that guaranteed sexual ecstasy, where? where? on the mattress, the mattresses that made the fortune of the Esparza family and built a huge residence in Pedregal, the stony and glassy mansion of mattresses . . . At this moment of enemy voices, visual offenses, commercial distractions, and cemented realities, I was the human mattress of the woman who, at the intersection where we finally left the Periférico, murmured her name in my ear:

"Lucha Zapata."

She looked at me with eyes so transparent and so clouded at the same time, so ravaged by age, declaring themselves as young as I wished, as old as I desired, that the fragility of the body embracing mine was transformed, by the art of sudden affection, into my own body of a (relatively) vigorous young man of twenty-four. I'm trying to say that whatever her fragilities and my strengths, at that moment in the taxi she got under my skin through the sorcery of her gaze and I got under hers, I confess, through the not very magical temptation of touching her breasts and finding there an immediate responsive promise, as if the nipples I caressed that night in the darkness of the damn dilapidated taxi had been waiting for me a long time and were, from now on, mine alone no matter how many other hands had caressed them before.

How could I find out about Lucha Zapata's past? Should I even try? Was it forbidden to me? Wasn't she demanding it: Find out about my past? Or was she affirming, in her extreme helplessness, in the worshipful abandonment of a little street dog, take care of me, you, whatever your name is, I'm exhausted, take me wherever you like, save me today and I promise to save you tomorrow.

I carried her like a rag doll up the stairs. Her head sheathed in the aviator helmet rested on my chest. Her swooning bird's arm hung inertly around my neck. Her jacketed torso smelled of damp.

Her damaged legs hung from my arms. Her shoes were falling off. I did nothing to retrieve them. It was urgent for me to carry her upstairs, lay her down, care for her, protect her.

The shoes would still be there tomorrow. It was Sunday.

MIGUEL APARECIDO LOOKED me up and down, hiding a smile that was not quite contemptuous but not indifferent either. I responded with my own gaze, meant to be bolder than his, among other reasons because I would leave the prison of San Juan de Aragón and lose myself in the tumult of the city and my occupations, while he—Miguel Aparecido—would remain here with his strange blue-black eyes flecked with yellow framing a look of violence tempered by melancholy, as if his life before prison was so turbulent that now he could compensate for it only with a kind of sadness that still shunned compassion. His bushy eyebrows joined in a scowl that would have been diabolical if his eyes had not provided a ray of light. The brightness I detected in him had to do with the way he stood, upright, without a trace of deference or, what is worse, defiance as a disguise for rancor. There were no external signs in this man of dejection or impatience. Only a way of standing that was serene though on the offensive, leaning forward. All this marked by his virile, square-jawed face, shaved too meticulously— I'm not a prisoner, it proclaimed—and with a light olive skin typical, my forgettable overseer María Egipciaca would say, of "a decent person." He was, however, a confirmed criminal. Appearances, my teacher Sanginés would add, deceive. Above all if, as in the case of Miguel Aparecido, the resemblance is to the actor Gael García Bernal and the singer Erwin Schrott.

Miguel Aparecido's nose seemed to sniff at me when I was admitted to his cell. I want to believe that a nose so straight and slender and therefore so immobile had to display some alert, impatient, defiant movement, everything the prisoner's almost Roman profile, similar to statues in a history textbook, did not betray, I don't know if in volitional defense or as a simple expression of his own nature. I played, when I met him, with the prisoner's Roman appearance, accentuated by the barely dissimulated smile of willful lips that wanted, it seemed at the time, to complete the quasi-imperial distinction of graying hair, combed forward but curly in the back.

Professor Sanginés had warned me: Miguel Aparecido is a strong man. Don't underestimate him.

I learned this when he gave me his hand in the Roman style, clasping my forearm and displaying a naked power that ran from his hand to his shoulder, where a kind of red toga hung that moved me to imagine he was a madman who had been locked in the prison for a very long time. In his personal lunatic asylum he was perhaps the Emperor Augustus. I still didn't know if in our national lunatic asylum he would behave like Caesar or like Caligula.

"Twenty years," Sanginés had told me.

"For what reason, Maestro?"

"Murder."

"Is it a life sentence?"

"In principle, yes. But Miguel Aparecido has been released twice: for good conduct the first time, in an amnesty the second. On both occasions he refused to leave prison."

"Why? How did he manage that?"

"The first time he organized a riot. The second, it was by his own wish."

"I repeat. Why?"

"That's why he's an interesting individual. Ask him."

Ask him. As if it were that easy to oppose my small humanity as a law student, small fornicator in brothels, small companion of boys perhaps smaller than me, small pupil of priests who may have been perverse, small hanger-on in a house of other people's mysteries I didn't understand, small slave of a tyrannical government, this small "I" confronting all the concentrated, powerful, iron strength (untouchable body, a gaze of such savage serenity it obliged me to lower my eyes and avoid his touch) of the imprisoned man who was saying to me now:

"How do you know who is guilty?"

I didn't know how to respond. He looked at me without mercy or irony. He was impenetrable.

"Do the law codes tell you?"

"We live under written law," I replied with my confused pedantry.

"And we die by the law of habit," the prisoner added, observing me constantly.

"One thing is true: The fucked-up thing is that they put you here and separate you from the world. Then you have to invent your own world, and the world requires connections to others," he continued.

"That's the fucked-up thing," he said, and smiled for the first time.

He was giving me a small class. He invited me to sit beside him on the cot. I was afraid to lose the effect of his terrible gaze. I observed him out of the corner of my eye. I believe he knew why Sanginés had sent me here. He owed the professor something. He didn't want to defraud him. He didn't want me to leave with hands as empty as my poor vacant head, scorned from the very beginning by the criminal.

"You have to invent new connections for yourself. That's fucked up," he repeated without looking at me.

"Does anybody protect you?" I dared to address him informally, using *tú* and taking advantage of our not looking in each other's eyes.

His answer surprised me:

"The first thing you learn here is to protect yourself on your own. There are people in prison who wouldn't know what to do on the outside."

I told him I didn't understand. If some convicts didn't know what to do out of prison, why did he stay here since he undoubtedly knew what to do on the outside?

He smiled. "They're whining, stupid people, without direction."

"Who?"

"Think," he murmured severely.

"Your prison companions," I insisted on gaining audacity's ground. "The others."

He turned to look at me and his eyes told me he had no friends here, no companions. And therefore? His arrogance did not permit him to praise himself. That he was different seemed obvious to me. That he was superior perhaps was his secret. He was open with me, frank. I'm certain his relationship with Sanginés included an inviolable pact: If I send you someone, Miguel Aparecido, talk, speak to him, don't leave him hungry. Remember. You owe me something.

Why did he commit another crime to stay in prison? Why did he refuse amnesty?

He didn't answer me directly. With a paraphrase that revealed the interior of his vast conspiracy to remain imprisoned, in spite of friendships and good conduct, without allowing me to understand the heart of the matter: Why did Miguel Aparecido want to remain imprisoned? For how long? Was there some reason that kept him from desiring freedom?

He said the first time they imprison you (he did not say, the distracted reader should note, "they imprisoned me"), anger explodes in your chest. You are blinded by a longing to take your revenge on the person who put you here (who put him here, wasn't it the law, was it an individual?). Then rage gives way to astonishment at finding yourself here, at knowing you are here, knowing (or believing, lying to yourself?) that you are innocent. This is the moment when you give up or begin to grow. You learn to create a scab, to cover the open wound with a mental or physical scab. If you don't, you go all to hell, you're defeated, surrounded as you are, you know? by the great wail of prison—he looked directly at me, with an infernal vision of desire in his eyes—the wails of the fistfighters, the shouts of the pitiless, the silence of the tortured. And the debilitating sound of the city, out there.

"There was a reporter here. A real bastard, very rebellious. He threatened: 'When I get out of here I'll denounce you all, you bunch of assholes. You'll see. As soon as I get out.' They broke his hands. 'Let's see what you write now, you son of a bitch.' It didn't occur to them that when he got out he could dictate with broken hands. The jailers are in jail, you know? It doesn't occur to them that there's life outside these walls. They really think the world ends here. And it's true. They don't read what an ex-con may write. It doesn't matter to them. They go on with their routine. The prison warden perhaps reads or receives complaints. I'll bet you, your name's Josué? (my name's Josué) that if he doesn't file them away, even when he acknowledges their receipt, he does nothing, what's called absolutely nothing, you understand me, asshole? Nothing."

He gave a sudden guffaw, as if freed of a commitment to himself not to express extreme emotions. If not a statue he was a stoic, I thought then, when I still didn't know the mystery of Miguel Aparecido's crimes.

It was his opinion that, as a young attorney, I ought to understand the rule of justice: Everybody's for sale, everybody can be bought. Sell the torturer, sell the pickpocket. No matter how clean he is when he arrives, the next one will also steal, also torture.

"Remind the prof of that, let's see what he tells you."

He took a deep breath, as if he were concluding. But that wasn't the case. He inhaled in order to go on. He was paying, I was convinced, a debt he owed the professor. It would take me some time to find out what Sanginés had done for this prisoner, strange in his serenity, vigorous in his determination to continue here and not obtain his freedom. Why?

"A man was tortured here and the idiot threatened to inform on the torturer when he got out of prison."

He paused so I would look at him and perhaps (I was beginning to observe) so I would admire him. He seemed to forget that I already knew what he was telling me. (What does prison do to one's memory?)

"The torturer simply told him: You'll never get out, asshole."

He looked at me with those eyes I've mentioned, blue-black with flashes of the plumage of a canary imprisoned in a liquid cage.

"He never got out."

I left and don't know if I really heard or imagined, along the eternal corridor that led away from Miguel Aparecido, the horrible chorus of curses, anathemas, and fulminations that descended from the forbidden heaven of San Juan de Aragón down to the pool of the cursed children. In my bones I felt something I didn't want to feel: the fury of failure, resentment like a sickness, anger like a probable salvation, and the final words Miguel Aparecido said to me.

"How do you know who is guilty? Above all, how do you know if you're innocent?"

I LEFT THE question unresolved. Had Miguel Aparecido performed a play for only one spectator: myself? If that was true, did he do it with the complicity of Antonio Sanginés? What united the prisoner and the professor beyond the relationship of accused-defender? Was my visit to the cells of the prison merely a part of my course in forensic practice, prepared by my professor with a dramatic, almost operatic example of perverse criminality? Because, after all, what keeps Miguel Aparecido imprisoned? Only his desire to remain behind bars? Or a secret maneuver, part of a web of interests I wouldn't dare to imagine because I lacked both data and experience?

I could not permit these circumstances to distance me from an immediate obligation, which was to look after the woman who had fallen so accidentally into my arms at the airport.

I tended to her the best I could. She was a doll without will, dependent on me. The incident on the airfield had wiped her out, as if in the decision to take control of a small plane and compete for a runway with the Air France jet she had abandoned that portion of will we all accumulate and portion out in installments until we die. Lucha Zapata was exhausted because she had left on the runway all the energy her spirit had possessed until then. Now on account of simply passing by, I was obliged to undress her, bathe her, lay her down in Jericó's bed, offer her a meal she barely tasted and vomited up before the food reached her stomach.

How to describe her?

She was a bird. A wounded bird who happened to nest in my garret. Which bird? We live in a country of birds. Two hundred sixty species in the Yucatec lagoons of Río Lagartos. Almost seven hundred species embalmed in the Saltillo museum. They are part of the great tropical coasts of the country and ascend like eagles to the highest peaks. They survive, who knows how, the deadly smoke of the city. That is to say, I had plenty to choose from when I determined a resemblance between them and Lucha Zapata. She was like a pink (tending to red) flamingo in a fishing village in Yucatán, a bird withdrawn into itself and its sacred, almost sepulchral silence. Noise must be avoided: A motor, for example, is a resonant catastrophe that obliges the bird to fly away. Silence is required to see it. And if I kept a single bird, it was in spite of the physical appearance of the woman who lay in Jericó's bed.

Lucha Zapata was a flamingo. Which is a bird, the dictionary says, with "very long bill, neck, and legs, white plumage on neck, chest, and abdomen, and intense red on head, tail, feet, back, and bill." But this woman was small, withdrawn, lying in a fetal position in bed, and her arms were injured, pecked at as if other birds, raptors, had constantly assaulted her throughout her life. There was, in spite of everything, something vibrant in the small body I had seen in extreme action, struggling with the police after an audacious, frustrated attempt to fly. Did she even know how to pilot a plane? Had she managed only to climb into the machine and drive it down the runway as if it were an automobile? Did she even get it out of the hangar?

I didn't dare ask her anything because between us loomed an invisible barrier that was in no way perverse. It was an untroubled boundary where, in implicit fashion, I offered her protection and she was grateful for it. Her nakedness was pathetic and at the same time natural and devout. What I mean is that Lucha Zapata was not embarrassed at her nakedness because she was without sin that needed to be forgiven. She lay in Jericó's bed like a newborn, needing care and affection, completely removed from a lust she did not offer or expect from me, as I did not expect it from her.

Why do I compare her to a flamingo? She was not pink. Her extremities were not long. Her tints, however, were reddish, for the hair on her head and her pubis shone like a bird's plumage. And if the body is our carnal plumage, hers was as pale as an early dawn, as wounded as a precipitate night. Lucha Zapata's pale skin was pecked from head to toe. Red wounds glistened on her arms and legs, especially on her wrists and ankles.

She opened her eyes and looked at me looking at her.

I knew, and she told me without words, that her wounds were caused by no one but herself.

Why, in spite of everything, do I compare her to what she was not: a flamingo lost in a distant Mayan lagoon? Because of the fright in her. Not a common, ordinary fear but a vocation for solitude that withdraws from contact, including the visual contact of another person's gaze, too often guilty of unhealthy curiosity and offensive prejudice.

Lucha Zapata looked at me and did not see evil in my eyes.

She simply extended her hand to take mine and said Dress me, Savior, pick me up and take me back to my house. My things are there. My medicines. Hurry. It's urgent.

What was I to do, compassionate readers, except satisfy the desires of this helpless woman who from now on—my head and heart told me so, even my respiration, the involuntary panting with which I picked up the defeated body wrapped in a sarape—would be my responsibility? I carried her down to Calle de Praga, hailed a taxi, and repeated the address she had just given to me with a sigh: "Cerrada de Chimalpopoca beside the Metro in Colonia de los Doctores."

I became accustomed to having two addresses. One on Calle de Praga, where punctually every month I received the check that allowed me to live without determining who sent it to me or asking at the bank for the name of a person who undoubtedly did not wish to be known or have the bank reveal his or her identity. The other on Cerrada de Chimalpopoca: the modest, bare little house of my friend Lucha Zapata. An old entrance, a courtyard with dead flowers, in the rear an unfurnished retreat with mats on the floor, a Japanese eating table, a pillow or two, and a rod where half a dozen skirts and trousers were hanging. Behind the improvised closet a tiny bathroom with a tub and shower. A variety of pharmaceutical products. I recognized some names but didn't know most of them. The towels were very old.

"Stay. Don't leave me."

How could I abandon her, I who longed to be responsible for someone since I couldn't be responsible for unknown relatives (who had been, in my opinion, humiliatingly, generously, shamefully responsible for me), or occasional though respected teachers (Filopátcr, Sanginés), or transitory friends (Errol Esparza), or healers who were both generous and aloof (Elvira Ríos), much less jailers as odious as María Egipciaca? What remained? Jericó's friendship, firm and constant since the days of secondary school. But Jericó wasn't here.

And now this fragile woman, inert in bed one day and the next as vibrant as an unattached electrical cable. At first in the little house in Colonia de los Doctores (symbol of a lost city, generous and ordered in the name of medical science, with one-story buildings and discreet façades, and an occasional gray residence built of stone) Lucha Zapata lived with me regaining her strength. I was afraid that when she recovered her stamina she would undertake adventures like the battle in the airport, for which I did not feel qualified. But for the moment, delicate and sweet, sometimes shaping unassuming movements, lying on the mat with a blue pillow under her head, Lucha Zapata told me, recalling our encounter, that if she went to the airport, exposing herself to danger, it was because aviation teaches us to be fatalistic, which gives me a reason for living in spite of the fatality all around us.

I talked to her, sharing the gourd of yerba maté Lucha always had in her hand and expounding on the openings or bases she constantly supplied, ideas about the fated as opposed to the voluntary, the free, and the virtuous, a distinction that pleased her a great deal, and she would ask me to explain: What I want can be good or bad, I told her, but it expresses my will. Does that mean that whether it's good or evil, what I do is free? How do I make my freedom not only free but virtuous? Freedom for evil? Or is evil not free precisely because it is evil?

"Don't get all excited," Lucha said with a laugh. "Whatever you do, things are going to happen with or without you."

"And so?"

"Don't get all excited. Let life happen, Savior."

That's how she spoke to me, with affection and a dose of simpli-
fication that could not demolish my theoretical constructions but
solidified them even more. I mean to say, reader, that Lucha's "common sense" was necessary for my "theoretical sense" and both of
them joined, perhaps, in an "esthetic sense" that was nothing other
than the art of living: how one lives, why, and to what end. Big questions. Small realities. She, with a certain mystery, confronted my ab-
stractions and I, with fewer shadows, confronted her mysteries.

Because I had no doubt that in Lucha Zapata was a mystery she
did not guard zealously. She did not guard it: she canceled it. It was
not possible to penetrate, in conversation with Lucha, the veil of a
past revealed, perhaps, in the scars on her graceful, long-suffering
body, but never in reminiscence. Lucha did not refer to her past.
And I asked myself whether this wasn't the most eloquent way to
unveil it. I mean: Because of everything she did not say, I could
imagine whatever I wanted and create a biography of Lucha Zapata
for my own use. A piece of foolishness that, in view of the silent curtains of her nakedness, revealed her to my complete pleasure.

I believe she guessed my strategy because in the afternoons, seeing me deep in thought, she would say: "With women you never
know."

You never know . . . I was young and understood that youth consists of choosing what was at hand or deferring it in favor of the future. This reflection made no sense for Lucha for the simple reason
that when she erased the past from her life she also eliminated the
future and installed herself, as if on her mat, in an eternal present.
I knew this was how she lived now: letting herself be carried along
by the minute hand of life, by everything occurring in the present
moment, though with references to the immediate past (the incident on the airfield, her relationship with me, so important she gave
me the undeserved and somewhat absurd name of "Savior," "Salvador"), and timid incursions into the future ("What do you want to
eat, my Savior?").

When we were lying on the mat at dawn, I liked to ask her half-
captious questions to see if I could make her fall into remembering

or looking ahead. What other airports have you assaulted, Lucha? Toluca, Querétaro, Guanajuato, Aguascalientes? The airport of the sun, Savior, she would reply. Didn't you ever have a job, Lucha? I'm at leisure. I don't need to work. Don't you feel somehow excluded from society? I can invade society before society invades me. Do you feel an internal conflict, Lucha? I have a quarrel with the world. What do you reproach society for? I don't want to be a perpetual debtor. That's what you are in society. An eternal debtor.

My affection for Lucha Zapata, which by this time should be evident to the least clever reader, did not make me blind. She did everything I didn't like. She was, let us say, a poly-drug user. Tobacco, heroin, cocaine, alcohol. When I met her she had well-stocked hiding places, so it wasn't necessary to go out to buy anything. How had she obtained this treasure? The nugatory pact regarding the past kept me from asking what she wasn't going to tell me. On the other hand, I came to appreciate deeply her domestic simplicity, her physical helplessness, and the mystery of her spiritual complexity.

In this way two years passed . . .

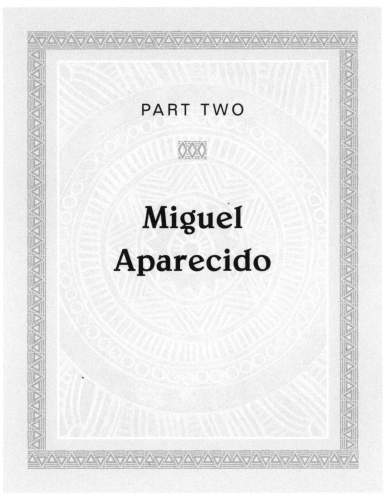

PART TWO

Miguel Aparecido

Once upon a time a man went down to hell and was received by a blond hostess wearing a miniskirt and a little blue cap with the English phrase WELCOME TO HELL. The hostess led the new arrival to a luxury suite with a king-size bed, marble bath, Jacuzzi, and a summer wardrobe for night and day, with labels from Madison Avenue, Calle Serrano, and Via Condotti, and sumptuous patent leather shoes, sandals, and moccasins. From there, the new arrival was led to a recreation area with an open bar and five-star restaurants along a tropical beach planted with palm trees, overflowing with stands of coconut palms and towel service.

"I was expecting something else," said the new arrival.

The hostess smiled and led him to a spot hidden in the luxuriant growth where there was a heavy iron door that the girl lifted up, allowing to escape a terrible sudden burst of flame and the vision of a lake of fire where thousands of naked creatures writhed as they were tortured by red devils with sharp-pointed tails who taunted the damned, piercing them with pitchforks and reminding them that this prison was eternal with no possible remission: the lake, the darkness, the site of "weeping and gnashing of teeth" (Matthew 25:30), the place of "the fire that never shall be quenched" (Mark 9:43). Whoever enters here does not leave, despite heretical theories of a final redemption of souls thanks to God's universal mercy. For if God is infinite love, eventually He has to pardon Lucifer and free the souls condemned to hell. Anathema, let it be anathema. To the devil with anyone who believes in God's mercy.

This is the hell for Catholics, said the hostess, closing the metal door.

It isn't true.

I, who am dead, attest to that.

What happens, then? You, readers caught in the web of my novelistic intrigue, will have to wait for the last page to find out. I, Josué, who live in another dimension, can continue the interrupted story and ask for the help of one of my new friends, Ezekiel, whom I found playing with a Spanish deck of cards in a place whose name I have forgotten and that is clearly not of this world. I asked him to move from solitaire to *tute,* he agreed, he lost, and as payment I requested (since dollars, euros, and pounds are not in circulation there) that he lend me a pair of wings so I could fly over the world and in this way go on with my suspended tale.

Ezekiel, who's a real pal (a good guy, but draped in togas, that is, sheets with Grecian borders like the ones James Purefoy wears on the television series *Rome*), asked to go with me because, he said, his territory had been ancient Jerusalem and he had never crossed the borders of Moab, Philistia, Tivia, and Sidon, all enemies of Israel, and the deserts that lead to Riblah, a city Yahweh promised to exterminate in order to demonstrate who was top dog in the Old Testament (in the New, Jesus Christ is the superstar).

Of course he wanted to see Mexico City, a place the most ancient chronicles don't mention, even though in questions of legends all of them end up resembling one another: Cities are founded, expand, grow, reach their high point, and fall into decadence because they were not faithful to the promise of their creation, because they wear themselves out in battles lost before they're started, because the horse was not shod in time, because the queen bee died and the caste of drones perished with her . . . Because the fly flew away.

Yes, I told my new friend the prophet Ezekiel, I'll take you to a city that goes out of its way to destroy itself but cannot succeed. It changes a great deal but never dies. Its foundation is peculiar: a lagoon (which has dried out), a rock (which was turned into a residential neighborhood), a nopal cactus (which is used to prepare lamb's quarters and stuffed chiles), an eagle (a species on the verge of extinction), and a serpent (the only thing that survives).

I shouldn't have said that. Ezekiel exclaimed that the serpent was the protagonist of paradise, the star of Eden, the most historic reptile in history, there are two thousand seven hundred species of serpents gathered, to simplify matters, into ten family groups, they crawl but listen, Josué, are you listening to me? the serpent is an animal that hears, it has auricular openings, eardrums, tympani, cochleae that sing and pick up the vibration of the earth: They know when there will be an earthquake, they count the shovels of earth at burials, they endure being covered over with asphalt superhighways, they survive everything and wait for us blinking, with eyes of glass. They don't taste with their tongues, those fuckers: They detect odors, serpents have a sense of smell, Josué, in their tongues, they swallow everything because they can extend their lower jaw and catch an eagle, yes, take revenge on the flying animal that has the criminal astuteness of the animal that crawls on the ground.

Ezekiel looked at me half amused and half amazed.

"They have a double penis. Hermipenes, they're called."

I didn't laugh. He became impatient.

"What am I good for?"

"For flying, Prophet."

I showed him—like this, with my hand raised and the cards fanned out—my winning hand: angel poker, four angels, four faces, four wings, faces of a man, a lion, a bull, an eagle, and the four wings with their four faces joined together as in a nervous fan ready to escape my hands, taking flight with Ezekiel clutching my heels, discovering that the marvelous wings of the cards not only had faces but men's hands to open the sky (which is a constellation of eyes, in case you didn't know) and let us be carried by a tempestuous wind until we flew over a valley smothered in mists of burnt-out gas, surrounded by eroded mountains. A place difficult to distinguish though I knew it all too well. A noisy receptacle of fiery arrows calling from the glowering sky we pierced with our wings. Ezekiel and I, the prophet growing more and more animated, in his element, a

lame biblical demon capable, I guessed, of raising the roofs of rotting tiles in Mexico Federal District Titlán de Tenoch Palaces city of
the besieged City Das Kapital of the Commonwealth, Res Publica,
public bull, Confined Bull, listening to the thundering voice of the
not very optimistic prophet Ezekiel, move away from the appearance
of your city,

> go beyond your face, Josué,
> scratch in the earth, my son,
> get to the lost place,
> scratch until you find the dirty sanctuary,
> sit on top of the scorpions,
> cook your impure bread on excrement,
> enter the sanctuary profaned by man,
> poverty, pestilence, and violence,
> observe the desolation of the temples,
> look at the corpses thrown at the feet of the idols,
> take it, Josué, take the roll of paper,
> eat the paper
> in order to recount the histories of rebel houses
> endure their faults
> prophesy with me against the mad-
> dened tribes of Mexico
> stop being the enemy of your own person
> for a moment, stop
> they'll put obstacles in your path
> wait
> your spirit rebels
> they are on their guard
> you endure, Josué
> close off the memory of the brothel of La Hetara
> (Durango between Sonora and Plaza Miravalle)
> close your eyes to the misery in the house of Esparza
> (somewhere between Coapa and Culhuacán)
> forget forever the house of María Egipciaca
> (Berlín between Hamburgo and Marsella)
> forget the solitude in the house of Lucha Zapata

(Chimalpopoca to the south of Río de la Loza)
forget the faults of the great house of Aragón
(beneath the Río Consulado)
anticipate the faults of the house of Monroy
(Santa Fe de los Remedios)
and above all, Josué, absolve the faults of the youthful days of Jericó . . .
(Praga between Reforma and Hamburgo).

Carried away by his prophetic passion (professional and innate in him), Ezekiel exclaimed they are rebel houses, founded on scorpions, they are thrones of dust, they will set obstacles before you, be on guard, endure the fault of the city, do not anticipate ruin and ignominy, rather live and let live but one day let them know the abominations of their parents, the names of the mobs, take out your roll of paper and write, Josué . . .

Ezekiel seized me by the back of my neck and then dropped me into the void.

I fell on my face.

I heard his voice: Lock yourself in your house.

I thought: I'm going to disobey you, Prophet.

I couldn't because my tongue cleaved to the roof of my mouth.

Then I heard the sound of wings, the great noise that moved away behind me, and though I was prostrate, I felt something that called itself spirit enter me as Ezekiel returned to heaven where prophets write, like novelists, the history of what could have been.

I had paper in my mouth. And I did not remember the face of the prophet.

I HAD PAPER and I had earth. I fell flat on my face where Ezekiel threw me: a gravestone. Blood ran from my lips onto the grave and washed off the writing. If the prophet commanded me "Write," present circumstances now told me "Read."

It took me some time to understand. The night was a dark fire like the aforementioned hell of the Catholics, though the light that fell where I lay foretold the coming dawn and the imminent sun urged me to be, for a few minutes, the thief of the night that the great poem of the world, written by the living for the dead but also by the dead for the living, confuses with sleep.

Look at me, readers, read with me as the dawn with its long-nailed fingers tears away the nocturnal veil and the wind of the plateau carries away the dust that covers the grave where I lie, face-down, scratching to read with difficulty the inscription that says, finally,

ANTIGUA CONCEPCIÓN

and under that, in smaller letters

Born and Died with No Date

The mystery of this stone was enough in itself. If that was the instruction of the dead woman, I immediately disputed it. The dry announcement on the grave of the so-called Antigua Concepción (was "Ancient Conception" a name, a title, an attribute, a promise, a memory?) woke in my spirit, agitated by the adventure with Ezekiel, a continuity of mystery. The prophet had placed the seed there . . . the "Antigua Concepción" made a tree grow in my chest. Who was it?

"Who are you?" I asked, lying there with no physical strength.

"How good that you've asked me," answered the voice of the grave. "I am Antigua Concepción."

My eyes showed not fear but an interrogating amazement for which she, Antigua Concepción, must have been grateful because she continued speaking from the depths of the earth.

I am Antigua Concepción.

I have waited in vain for someone to visit my grave.

No one comes here.

Do you know where you are?

No, I replied, except someplace in the city.

Then I won't tell you where you are. Promise.

I promise.

Keep my story to yourself. It is this. My name is Antigua Concepción because when I was born they baptized me Inmaculada Concepción de María but ended up calling me "Concha" and what is worse, "Conchita." Conchita, the name of a fake flamenco dancer, Concepción, the name of an afflicted virgin ignorant of who made her pregnant and when, we're almost in Pénjamo now! Its great variety of birds! Inmaculada is the name of a sanctified and blessed ass, bah! Concepción is worse, the name of a Paraguayan who has never seen the ocean, ha! a damn Concepcionista nun serving the Panchos (the holy Franciscans, not the trio of singers). Conceiving or saying ingenious stupidities. No dogmas for me, young man! I am etymologically a he-re-tic: I choose, not she choos-es, not is chos-en, and least of all now, at a depth of one me-ter.

She sighed and the earth seemed to tremble just a little.

From the time I was a little girl I rebelled against diminutives. "Diminutives diminish," I shouted, making a fuss, you won't call a Julio Julito or a Rafael Falito or my Concepción Conchita. Concha cunt, motherfucker! she exclaimed with a strange guffaw.

And "Antigua"?

At the age of twenty I already knew what I wanted to be. I had no aptitude other than mystery and more mystery than greatness.

I married and assumed my eternal form.

I stopped being Conchita.

I stopped being Concepción Martínez, a decent unmarried girl. I became Concepción Martínez de Monroy, a married woman.

I wore my hair pulled back in a severe style and put a nun's wimple on my head.

I dressed in a Carmelite habit.

I kept my key rings in the deep pockets of the habit.

I never had to wear underclothes again.

I sat on cottons.

No one saw my bodily forms again, and whoever imagined them was clearly mistaken.

I occupied a throne with no insignias.

With a hole in the seat my human necessities fell into a porcelain basin with the portrait of the president in power.

Don't ask. Whichever one you like least.

I was born in 1904, seven years before Don Francisco Madero, Apostle of the Revolution, became president and was betrayed and killed by the usurper Victoriano Huerta in 1913. Like Allende and the little traitor Pinochet with his faggot's voice. I was thirteen when the Constitution was proclaimed. Eighteen, when the president was General Alvaro Obregón, the one-handed man who lost his arm in Celaya beating the shit out of Pancho Villa, and nineteen when they treacherously killed Villa, and only fifteen when they treacherously killed Emiliano Zapata, and twenty-four when a right-winger dispatched Obregón with a bullet to the head as the general ate toasted tortillas in a restaurant in the southern part of the capital. More *totopos*! Those were his final, memorable words. I married my husband General Maximiliano Monroy because I knew they wouldn't kill him because he was one of the top dogs who invented the revolution, the ones who shot first and asked questions later.

My husband Don Maximiliano was a real Don Juan as a young man. I took advantage of his evil ways to become strong and independent, with no need of him. I barely knew him long enough to make a baby. He was thirty years older than me. I tell you he began as a womanizer and ended up pathetic. I didn't care. I'm just telling you about it. A person comes out of a revolution either very smart or damn stupid but never undamaged. My husband came out an absolute asshole. He took part in the last military uprising in 1936, I think just out of the habit of always being in revolt. I'm telling you, an absolute idiot. He didn't notice that times had changed, that the revolution was becoming an institution, that the guerrillas were getting down from their horses and into Cadillacs, that the only agrarian reform was the sale of residential lots in Las Lomas, that the freedom to work eventually meant unionized workers under the control of shameless leaders, that freedom of the press would be conferred by a paper monopoly operated by our compadre Artemio Cruz, heroic times, kid! If you don't concede you can't succeed, living and not playing the game is living in error, and if you don't appear in a photograph at a cocktail party, even one given by a shady character like Nazario Esparza, you're a lost cause, you're nobody, and if you don't marry your daughter in a squandering of floral, ecclesiastical, banquetish, photographic, and faggotish millions, then the girl is a whore and her father's poor and a poor politician is a *poor* politician, somebody dixit . . .

She heaved a sigh like an earthquake.

Once there were years, boy, of a vast, really vast displacement of fortunes, from the old patriarchal world of haciendas and peonage, from the usurpation of Benito Juárez's liberal victory by the personal dictatorship of Porfirio Díaz and the exploitation of the free market so the land would pass from the hands of the clergy into the hands of the huge landowners and for the original owners, the campesinos, a thumb to the nose and a go fuck your mother, my lad: here's your agrarian reform.

I was terrified. I mean, an obscene finger rose from the earth.

I'm telling you this so you'll know what's buried here with me: the history of the country, our past as incarnated in my husband General Maximiliano Monroy, an actor at every stage of this national melodrama, the civil war that lasted twenty years and cost us a million lives, not on the battlefield but in cantina shootouts, according to a really lovely gov, González Pedrero, ha!

A great guffaw came rumbling out of the depths of the earth and the finger returned to its place.

A million dead in a country of fourteen million inhabitants. How many of us are there now?

One hundred twenty million, I whispered into the grave as if it were the ear of the woman I loved. (Do I imagine myself telling the nurse Elvira Ríos listen, love me a lot, look, I'm one of a hundred twenty million Mexicans? Or the whore with the bee on her buttock, let yourself be fucked by a hundred twenty million Nahuatlacas? Or the defenseless Lucha Zapata just think, you're not alone, you're surrounded by a hundred twenty million citizens, my love?)

A hundred twenty million! exclaimed the voice from the grave. But what happened?

Health. Food. Sports. Education. I was going to say all that. It seemed like a sacrilege to introduce statistics into a conversation with death, though she soon refuted me: Death is the Queen of Statistics, though wars tend to overburden her accounting . . .

It is the country of betrayal, that's Mexico's worst account, Doña Antigua insisted. In 1910, Madero betrayed Don Porfirio, who thought he was president for life. In 1913, Huerta had Madero killed. In 1919, Carranza had Zapata killed. In 1920, Obregón had Carranza killed. In 1928, Calles pretended to be distracted while they murdered Obregón. Only General Lázaro Cárdenas put an end to the assassinations.

But he killed your husband, Señora.

He was executed for being an asshole, she said very pleasantly. Whoever gives the order . . . He deserved it . . .

But—

But nothing, fool, don't kid yourself. It has all been betrayal, lies, cruelty, and vengeance. You simply try to anticipate it. Follow my example. You have to create economic powers prior to the decisions of the government. And you have to fear yes-men. These are the two rules of Antigua Concepción. I have finished speaking. Become powerful on your own and to hell with flatterers. I have finished speaking.

But Concepción, Conchita, Antigua Concepción, had not finished speaking. Now she continued talking to tell me that her husband the general was a real revolutionary huckster who served Villa as easily as Obregón, Obregón as Carranza, Calles as Cárdenas, and when Don Lázaro ended insurrections through the power of institutions, General Maximiliano did not give up, he "rose up" on the border proclaiming the Plan of Matamoros, but he was the only dead Moor, strangled by a drunk and without a single bullet hole in a Texas cantina in Brownsville, where the stupid prick took refuge . . .

I didn't know if I should feel sorry for her because of these uxorial misfortunes. She didn't give me time. She was already on another track.

My husband the general was thirty years older than me. But he was a baby compared to me. All I had to do (you a young boy and I a young girl) was take a look at what was happening to make a decision: I would anticipate the future. I'd do first what would come later: Do you understand me, youngster? I had inherited haciendas in Michoacán and Jalisco. I divided them up among the peasants before the agrarian law demanded it or, more important, put it into practice. I told myself the country was going to emigrate from the provinces without will, impoverished by two decades of revolution, to the capital, the center. At the right time I bought empty lots in the Federal District, Morelos, and the State of Mexico, whose value has increased a thousandfold. And kid, I asked myself where they'd place the highways they'd need? I bought lots, level ground covered in huizache plants, mountains of pine, walls of basalt, whatever, because now it was important to get to the sea fast, to the borders, to the heart of the sierra in trucks filled with comestibles and combustibles that I organized into national fleets carburized for oil whose nationalization in 1938 I anticipated, when I was thirty years old, by acquiring strips of probable potential wealth in the Gulf, which had been mine, Mexican, since 1932 and that I later ceded, my lad, just think about it and get ready, to the government and Petróleos Mexicanos, along with my damn wedding ring to contribute to the cost of expropriation, a piece of jewelry I should have buried, if truth be told, in the grave of my by then deceased and decrepit husband General Don Maximiliano Monroy—R.I.P.

I believe she winked at me from the bottom of her grave.

Don't think I'm a cynic or an opportunist, she said. Everything I've told you was possible because thousands and thousands of people moved, the isolation ended that had been imposed by a geography of volcanoes and deserts, mountains and swamps, coasts strangled in mangroves, impassable cordilleras: It ended, children, women, and cows, trains, horses, and guerrillas moved, boy, in all directions, from Sonora to Yucatán, from Río Santiago to Río Usumacinta, from Nogales to Tapachula, from Gringolandia to Guatepeor, through dry fields and lost harvests, leaving orphans and widows strewn everywhere, creating new wealth beside eternal poverty, because you know, my little chick, only when fortunes change, only then do we recognize ourselves and know who we are . . .

I don't know if her buried gaze asked me: And what about today?

Today we're exploding as citizens of the Narconation, I declared. She had stopped at a point in the past. She didn't understand me.

Did you hear, dear readers, a sigh from the grave? Listen to it now. It seems it's not serious but, perhaps, humorous. It seems it isn't deep but, when it reaches the crust of the earth, superficial.

Antigua Concepción continued:

I anticipated the industrialization that could occur thanks to nationalized oil and the campesino labor freed by agrarian reform. But I no longer anticipate anybody because in 1958 Don Adolfo Ruiz Cortines left the presidency and I said to myself, this is the best president we've had, a mature man, severe but with a sense of humor, slyer than a spider, hidden behind an uncompromising, austere, penetrating mask with dark circles under the eyes to disguise the irony that is the artery of true intelligence, and above all, the head of a Greco-Roman wise man strangled by a bow tie with white polka dots, the president who could swallow a baked potato without making faces, the apparent cripple who walked the six years of the presidential high wire over the void and set the example of good sense, serenity, irony, and tolerance his country needs: We have more than enough inspired ideologues, ignorant ranchers, machos castrated by their harem of magpies, acrobats from the political circus, Machiavellis in huaraches, curly-haired Don Juans in Maseratis, ugly people who can't look at themselves in the mirror without declaring war on the world and going out to kill, and above all the thugs, the ones who rob our revolution of its legitimacy and hand us over, my little fool, to the madmen of democracy, *ay!*

I supposed her *ay!* expressed the unworthiness of democracy and her nostalgia for enlightened authoritarianism, but I said nothing. It was her business. She really was "Antigua."

She went on: You must remember, boy, that once there was a president who dispensed justice, heard complaints, received petitions. The Old King!

And now the exclamation was prolonged, plaintive, in the air for a period of time that Antigua Concepción interrupted with these words:

Look, that was when I retired to my front row seat and passed things on to my only child, Max Monroy.

She paused, satisfied.

I'm happy with him. As you'll see, he's like me though less folkloric. He anticipates events. He knows what has to be done before anybody else. He knows when to buy and how to sell. He's discreet. His life is not the object of writeups or gossip. He has never appeared in the magazine *¡Hola!* He has never been sponsor at the wedding of rock-and-rollers. He has never been fond of the sun. (He isn't albino!) He resembles the night. He lives in a tower in Santa Fe, to the west of the city. Find him. That's a good thing for you to do.

I believe she concluded:

Don't do any wishful thinking. Just try to anticipate catastrophes a little . . .

Later I would remember these words of Antigua Concepcion:

The state is a jealous work of art, enemy of the free individual and economic power. Remember what I've taught you: You have to create economic powers prior to the decisions of the government.

I HAVE MENTIONED, forgetful reader, that once a month an envelope with the previously mentioned check for my maintenance came to the mailbox of the building on Praga. I had become so accustomed to this punctuality that the favor no longer moved me. Whoever my obliging and invisible patron might be, time resolved two matters. Gratitude, if reiterated, would be unpleasant. And the donor, because unknown, proved to be agreeable, comfortable, and forgettable.

Except on this day, when I stopped at Praga to change my clothes, take a look around, and pick up the check on the usual date, the check wasn't in the box. Since it was a certified document, I wasn't alarmed. I simply didn't know where to go or whom to see to claim it. It occurred to me that if things became awkward, I could speak to Professor Sanginés.

I was thinking all this as I climbed the first thirty-nine (or was it forty) steps to our parrot cage and found the door open and the envelope with the check staring me in the face, held up by two hands I recognized immediately.

He had come back!

Enlightened or darkened by experience, the prodigal brother was here. The other Dioscuro, my twin, the other son of the swan, my companion on the great expedition of the Argos to Ponto Euxino to recover the Golden Fleece, sign and destiny of our lives, symbol of the soul in search of itself: of truth.

He dropped the check and embraced me, I don't know if with emotion but certainly with force. We were embracing our shared past. As well as the future that always united us, though time and distance might separate us. Paris, London, Florence, Rome, Naples, Vienna, Prague, Berlin, the postcards allowed me to follow the route of his travels, though his permanent residence was the Rue Poissonnière in the Deuxième Arrondissement in Paris.

Could he be carrying all those cities, all those addresses, in his young twenty-five-year-old gaze?

He was slimmer. The permanently plump cheeks of the childhood that is not completely resigned to abandoning our features had, in defeat, ceded his facial structure to a slender fiction of adolescence, as if time had a chisel that keeps sculpting the face we will eventually have and for which, at a certain point, we become responsible. He did not have a beard or mustache. And his head was shaved like an army recruit's. Perhaps because of that facial nudity his light eyes shone more than ever, playing the principal role in an appearance not distinguished by his snub nose or thin lips. A shaved skull. Brilliant eyes, the same but different, guardians of both a youthful past and a mature future.

He embraced me and I smelled the remembered sweat.

Jericó had come back.

"You look like a poor fool in an asylum," I told him.

"Punched in," he said in English, and immediately afterward, as if recalling and correcting: "It'll go like clockwork."

I CONFESS THAT the return of Jericó produced contrary feelings in me. After his absence, we were both entering our mid-twenties with

a separation that put our youthful friendship to the test. In principle this impinged on any other consideration, though he and
I—I imagined—were not strangers to the usury of time. The second
consideration, however, had to do with my closeness to Lucha Zapata and the daily, vital question of knowing where I would brush
my teeth, in the apartment on Praga, with him, or the little house in
Chimalpopoca, with her.

At first I didn't permit the choice between them to be a problem
that would interfere with my joy. Seeing Jericó again not only renewed my own youth but, in particular, rescued and prolonged it,
though with a bittersweet anticipation that I would also begin to
lose it. Until the moment of his departure, my friend was what you
already know because you read it here: the independent, audacious
boy who gave me my place in secondary school, saving me from
being the scapegoat of the gang of bastards who were going to feed
on me and my prominent nose as they would have taken advantage
of somebody who was cross-eyed or crippled. Jericó stood firm "in
the middle of the arena," obliged the "good-for-nothings," as Doña
María Egipciaca would have called them, to respect me. We initi-
ated the comradeship that now, after our separation, his return
would put to the test.

I admit as well that a series of ambivalent impressions followed
one another in my mind on the day I found my friend back in the
apartment on Praga. His physical appearance was different. I don't
know if it was better. Yes, he had lost some of the persistent baby fat
on his face. He looked more angular, more tense, more reserved. I
don't know if his shaved head suited him or not. I could lean toward
the side of fashion and accept it as one of the many ways of making
a statement with one's hair at the time: long manes, shaved heads,
multicolored locks, afros, Mohawks, Roman consuls, rebel dread-
locks, except that the combination of his shaved head and slender
face emphasized the strangeness of his naked gaze. His eyes, blue,
round, fixed, immeasurably enlarged by the nakedness of his entire
head, created a contradictory impression in me. I saw in those unprotected eyes an unusual innocence transformed with a mere blink
into a cynical, threatening, and wise gaze. I confess I marveled at

that instantaneous transition of a psychological profile, not only the next one but its opposite.

The strange thing (or is it reasonable?) is that his words when he returned to Mexico also blinked, passing from an ingenuousness that seemed out of place in the cynical, daring man I had known, to a gravity it took me a while to identify with the actual name of ambition. Could we reestablish our intimacy?

He recounted naïve things to me, for example that when he arrived at the Place de la Concorde he kneeled and kissed the ground. I laughed: As an act of freedom? Not only that, he replied: As an act of fidelity to the best in the Old World (I hid a nervous twitch of disapproval: Who would ever call Europe "the Old World"?) and above all, he continued, to France and the French ability to appropriate everything by redeeming the crime in culture.

"There's a Napoleon brandy. Can you imagine a Hitler brandy?"

I wasn't going to discuss the enormous difference between the "good" Bonapartist tyrant and the "bad" Nazi tyrant because in his tirade Jericó was already immersed in an amusing comparison of national European profiles and the clichés that went with them (the French have a sex life, the English have hot water bottles), leading to feverish amazement at having heard "all the languages we see at the movies" and the enumeration of Rue Lepique, Abbey Road, Via Frattina, Puerta del Sol, and above all the streets, the squares of Naples where, he said, he identified with the possibility of being corrupt, immoral, a killer, a thief, and a poet without consequences, as part of custom and perhaps the landscape of a liberty so habitual it leaves no trace of mortality, surviving, he said, in tradition.

"Why can't we be Neapolitans?" he exclaimed with a certain grandiloquence, appropriate to the friend who faced me with the arrogance of a Byron that I viewed as an antipoetic pose and, what is worse, as simple-minded, naïve, unworthy. Why are we, in Europe, nothing but Comanches, mariachis, or bullfighters?

He laughed, redeeming himself. "We ought to guard against being part of the national folklore."

This was Jericó, my old companion, passed through the sieve of an experience that he wanted, as I understood it, to share with me at a level of exaltation and camaraderie that would lead him to tear off his shirt, gesticulate, and assume the caricature of a bedazzlement that ought to end—I knew Jericó—with an excessive, ironic action, one that in a certain sense flagellated his own ego.

"On my knees in the Concorde," he repeated, kneeling in the middle of the living room with his arms stretched wide in an act at once grotesque and tender, and which I understood without understanding it, like a farewell to youth, a stripping away of the vestments of a tourist, the rustic skin that covers the traveler in transit, the soul of the "Argentine we all carry inside us": the superego.

Knowing Jericó, this display as part of his weaknesses did not fail to surprise me. Perhaps he wanted to indicate that beneath the appearance of return was a companion who had never left. Or, on the contrary, knowing it was impossible, he was asking for help in getting rid of distance and his experiences and returning to the point at which we had separated. We were the same but different. I had experienced studying at UNAM, the tutelage of Sanginés, the visit to San Juan de Aragón, the mysterious encounter with Miguel Aparecido, the strange, committed relationship with Lucha Zapata. What did Jericó have to offer, aside from the postcard he had just given me?

"Freedom," he said, as if he had read my thoughts.

"Freedom is kneeling down to give thanks in the Place de la Concorde?" I said, not very pleasantly.

He nodded, his eyes lowered.

"What shall we do?" he said then, and our life changed.

Jericó changed it as he himself, his physical attitude, his appearance changed in the next moment, when he let fly the issues he wanted to communicate after his prologue on the stage of touristic minimization and mental abandon.

What shall we do? he repeated. There are many possibilities for success. Which are yours and mine? Or rather, Josué, which success is worthy of you and me?

I wasn't going to answer with the reasons I've just given you, which can be summarized in the word "experience," for only on that basis did my expectations, though still vague, begin to take shape. I knew Jericó would not share much in the recounting of his European experiences, which (I was beginning to realize) he would never reveal beyond the brief tour he had just offered. His years of absence were going to be a mystery, and Jericó didn't even challenge me to penetrate it. There was in this attitude I've called Byronic a wager: The past has died and the future begins today. Make whatever guesses you like.

As a consequence, I changed my attitude. Instead of asking about his past, I proposed sharing our future.

"What do we want?" he repeated, and added: "What are we afraid of?"

He continued saying that he and I knew—or ought to know— what we could be or do. He recalled an earlier conversation about "not ever going to a *quinceañera,* a thé dansant, a baptism, the opening of restaurants, flower shops, supermarkets, bank branches, the celebration of university classes, beauty contests, or meetings at the Zócalo." Never being interested in the rock-and-roller Tarcisia who married the Russian millionaire Ulyanov, both of them barefoot, with Hawaiian leis around their necks and guests who welcomed the dawn dancing hip-hop on the sand at seven in the morning.

"Now, Jericó, how did they serve the stew to honor the father of the bride—"

"Who is a native of Sonora. Did you turn down the invitation?"

"No, Jericó, not at all, I'm not interested in being—"

"Not even if it's your own wedding?"

I smiled, or tried to. I remembered how I had admired Jericó's capacity for taking life very seriously.

I said I felt I had gone past those tests, didn't he? I refrained for the moment from mentioning Lucha Zapata, Miguel Aparecido, the children in the sinister pool at San Juan de Aragón. Perhaps Jericó responded indirectly, saying it wasn't enough not doing what we didn't do. Now we ought to decide what we were actually going to do. He stood and grasped my shoulders. He looked at me with his Delftware eyes. We didn't have, that was apparent, a talent for music, literature, tennis, water- or downhill skiing, racing cars, or directing films, we didn't have the soul of actuaries, accountants, real estate agents, porters, and all the sad people who accept their small destinies . . . he said.

"What do we have left?"

I told him to tell me. I didn't know.

"Politics, Josué. It's self-evident, brother. When you're no good as a street sweeper or a composer, when you can't write a book or direct a movie or open a door or sell socks, then you devote yourself to politics. It'll go like clockwork."

"That's what we're going to do?" I said, with false astonishment.

Jericó laughed and let go of my shoulders.

"Politics is the last resort of intelligence."

He winked. In Europe he had learned, he said, that the mission of the intellectual was to torment power with words.

"Then what do you want to do?" I asked.

"I don't know yet. Something huge. Give me time."

I thought without saying so that freedom is uncertainty. That is something I had learned.

He didn't read my thoughts:

"There can be many attempts at success. Which is worthy of you and me?"

I didn't know what to say. I was held back by another feeling. Above and beyond the words and attitudes, that morning of our reunion in the garret on Calle de Praga remains in my mind, especially now that I've died, as a moment of terror. Could we resume our intimacy, the common respiration that had joined us when we were young? Could we feel again the primary emotion of youth? Was everything we had lived only a prologue, a preparation for a goal we didn't really know yet how to define? Was our friendship the sole, poor shelter of our future?

Jericó embraced me and said in English, as if responding to all my questions, Let's hug it out, bitch.

STUNNED BY AERIAL excursions on the wings of the prophet Ezekiel and landings in the deep earth where Doña Antigua Concepción lies, exhausted by so much sky and so much history, disheartened by great promises, I walked very slowly toward Colonia Juárez and the apartment on Calle de Praga without knowing where I was coming from or the location of the secret grave that soon dissipated in the noise of engines, exhaust fumes, the ring-ring of bicycles, and thunder in the clouded sky, trying to leave behind the experience I had gained and concentrate on particular accidents, the personal inadequacies and small vices and virtues of men and women with their own names though lacking a historic surname.

Drunk on the chronological history of Antigua Concepción and inebriated by the undated apocalypse of the prophet Ezekiel, with infinite patience and humility I climbed the stairs of the house on Praga, prepared to focus my humanity again on Jericó's friendship and my care of Lucha. These were my priorities, soon dissolved by Jericó's urgent expression when he greeted me.

"Let's go to Pedregal. Errol's mother has died."

Years had gone by without our returning to the ultramodern mansion turned into a neobaroque mess by the dictatorial bad taste of Don Nazario Esparza. "Act as if you haven't seen anything" was Errol's recommendation to us, referring either to the arguments of his parents or the Transylvanian horror of his house. I remembered the lack of any initiative on our friend's part once he had provoked an altercation between his parents. Or perhaps I was misremembering. It had been six, seven years since I had seen my old classmate or visited his house.

Now, from the entrance door, black crepe announced the family's mourning. I thought the house had always been in mourning, locked with padlocks of avarice, lack of compassion, suspicion, meager love, scant serenity. Except that as I approached the coffin of Doña Estrellita de Esparza, with Jericó ahead of me, I felt that compassion and serenity, at least, had in fact inhabited this lugubrious mansion but were virtues that lived waiting for the death, and only in the submissive, preoccupied presence, of Doña Estrellita.

I looked at her corpse. Her waxen face had been blurred even more by the cold hand of Death, the Ashen-Faced, and caricatured by the rouge and lipstick the funeral director (or damned Don Nazario) had smeared on the grayish features. Doña Estrellita wore a hairdo that looked false, very 1940s, very Joan Crawford, high and full. Her ghostly hands rested on her chest. With a start, I realized the Señora had on her housewife's, maid's, and cook's apron, and this, I wanted to say to Jericó, this definitely was a final mockery by the sinister Don Nazario, prepared to send off his wife as maid to Eternity and celestial housewife. Don Nazario received without emotion or even the blink of an eye the condolences of his previously mentioned clientele, who expressed their sympathy and then dissolved again behind a veil of murmurs, inaudible conversations, and the passing of canapés, with the collective obsequiousness of a relative and the singularity of dissimilar manners and fashions, for those who had known him since his humble beginnings and those who acknowledged him at his present heights ranged from the owners of transient hotels to managers of hotel chains.

I looked at Doña Estrellita in order not to look at the crowd.

In spite of everything, the body continued to display a simulation of beatitude and the perpetual smile of someone going to a wedding of people she doesn't care about but who deserve courtesy. In death, Doña Estrella was confident in her boredom, and if she had lost the habit of crying, the fault was not hers. There was only one dissonant detail, because the apron was like a uniform. The Señora had a bright scarf tied around her neck.

Ruddy, tall, florid, Don Nazario received the customary condolences. I would have liked to avoid it. I couldn't escape the line of mourners. Jericó was ahead of me, his face composure itself though with a sarcastic line along his upper lip. Don Nazario extended his hand without glancing at me. I gave him mine without glancing at him. I looked for Errol.

"He isn't here," Jericó murmured.

"What do you think of that?" I asked.

"Were you expecting him to come?"

"To tell you the truth, yes," said my feelings and not me. "She was his mother . . ."

"Not me," Jericó declared over and above my opinion.

We made our way through the crowd of mourners. You could see it in their faces: No one loved this family. Not Don Nazario and not

Doña Estrella. Much less Errol, the dispensable rock-and-roller fag. They were all there out of obligation and necessity. They all owed something to Nazario Esparza. Don Nazario controlled them all. There was no love. No grief. No hope. What did we expect? my eyes asked Jericó as we walked through the crowd, all of them surrounded by the forest of funeral wreaths that turn Mexican funerals into a boon for florists. Become a florist and make your fortune: We are all passing through.

In the middle of the funeral forest I bumped into a woman and offered my excuses. Out of place, she was carrying a cigarette in one hand and a glass of champagne in the other. She bumped into me, the ash fell onto my lapel and a downpour of La Veuve onto my tie. The woman stopped and smiled. I made a useless effort to recognize her or to ask myself, Where have I seen her before? never addressing her directly, "Where have we seen each other?" because of a kind of tacit precept I couldn't explain to myself and that did not correspond to the amiability of the beautiful woman who approached like a panther, a predatory animal. A fake blonde, light tan touched with sun in her hair, and artificially moist lips.

"Listen," she ordered a waiter, "bring a drink for the Señor."

"Excuse me. This isn't the time," I said.

"A drink," she gave the order again, and the waiter inquired as if he hadn't heard her clearly:

"Pardon me, Señora?"

"A drink, I said. Go on."

The waiter didn't answer. He looked at me and Jericó, who was behind me now, understanding less than I did about the new scenario in the Esparza mansion.

The waiter said: "Welcome, Don Jericó, Don Josué. You're always welcome here."

And he went for the drinks ordered by the Señora, who already had champagne in her hand, a cigarette in her mouth, and the Chanel uniform of a black dress. She looked at us with a mix of charm and irony.

"Are you looking for Errol?" said this cunning woman.

We nodded.

"Look for him in a cheap cabaret on the streets of Santísima. He plays the piano there. It's your ass, Barrabás!"

She aimed an artificial laugh at us and, turning her back, hummed as she moved through the mourners, who instinctively made way for her, as if they already knew her and, what is more, respected her, and what is worse, feared her . . .

My friend and I looked at each other with unspoken questions. At a distance, Don Nazario was receiving condolences with his bottle-bottom eyes. From a distance, he smelled of vomit. From a distance, one could hear the jangle of his key ring.

We passed the wall of bodyguards protecting entrances and exits, recalling Doña Estrella thanks to a tacit memory: No one, except her son and the waiter, perhaps, remembered her for the many details that now, in her honor (and ours) we evoked as if we were sharing them with our pal Errol, the bald kid from secondary school.

She never laughed at jokes because she didn't understand them.

She believed everyone forgave her for her life.

Her husband had said once that as a young woman she was stupid but charming.

She guarded this phrase as if it were a treasure.

For the rest of it she always felt she was out of place.

She didn't understand the word "superfluous."

She didn't even know how to mistrust the maids (the opposite was obvious to us).

When she was reprimanded, she sang as if she were involved in something else.

"What do you think of papa's fortune?" "Very nice." "No, its origins." "Oh, son, don't be that way." "What way?" "Ungrateful. It's why we eat." "Shit." "Don't be vulgar. We owe everything to your father's efforts." "Efforts? Is that what they call crime now?" "What crime, son?" "Papa is a pimp, a *lenón*." "A *león*, a lion?" "No, a musician, John Lennon." "I don't understand." "Or a revolutionary, Lenin." "Son, you're making my head spin."

When we were on the street, cold and empty that night, Jericó asked:

"Listen, what does that red scarf mean that they put around her neck?"

I didn't know, and on Calle del Pedregal there were only long lines of luxury cars and bored chauffeurs.

WHEN JERICÓ RETURNED I didn't know whether to reveal to him my relationship with Lucha Zapata or keep it a secret. I opted for discretion. Ever since school, my friend and I had shared everything, ideas as well as whores, focusing on a fairly ascetic life of intensive studies and still unformed goals we didn't dare call ambitions. Castor and Pollux, the Dioscuri, sons of a god and a bird, two mortals worshiped as divinities, though they were not. Famous for their valor and skill. Exiled by Zeus to live alternate days in heaven and in hell.

The reader knows to what degree the fraternal union of Castor and Pollux, of Josué and Jericó, excluded many relationships common in boys our age. No family, no girlfriends, no friend except Errol and the shared teachings of Filopáter. Now, however, we were separated by years in which I acted without him and so could let myself be guided by Antonio Sanginés, penetrate the prison of San Juan de Aragón, interview the convicts, allow myself to be impressed by Miguel Aparecido's diabolical personality and, above all, take responsibility for Lucha Zapata.

I decided to keep to myself the existence of the red-haired woman who lived beside the Metro.

Telling Jericó about it would have put me at the disadvantage of letting him know my business without the reciprocity of learning almost anything about his. Because the superficial humor with which my friend recounted his European experience did not suit his conflictive, penetrating, bold, and ironic personality. I came to think that Jericó was lying to me, that perhaps he hadn't spent years in Europe, that someone else had sent the postcards in his name . . . How strange. All this came to mind because when he returned, as you remember, Jericó said a sentence in English that sounded strange to me,

Let's hug it out, bitch,

a sentence I didn't understand and couldn't translate, but that didn't fit into either European or Latin American culture. By elimination—I deduced, thinking like Filopáter—it could only be North American.

I didn't attribute too much importance to this, even though the matter remained suspended in my mind waiting for a clarification that would or would not come, because what Quixote says to Sancho about miracles—they rarely happen—can be transferred to mysteries—when they are revealed, they cease to exist—and I confess here and now that I wanted Jericó to have a truth hidden from me, since I had one hidden from him, and her name was Lucha Zapata.

I'm not ignoring the fact that Zapata's character put me to the test, at times making me want to leave her or at least share the burden and with whom but Jericó. I'm saying I kept the secret because not only my own dignity before my friend but the very essence of my relationship with her demanded it. This is another way of saying that in recent months, Lucha Zapata had come to depend more and more on me, and that had never happened to me before. Once I had depended on others. Now, a helpless woman, constricted into herself and emerging from that constriction only because of my presence (I thought then), depended on me for salvation.

I urged her to stop using drugs. She continued consuming narcotics until her hidden stash was used up. Then she drank more than usual. Except that alcohol did not completely replace the essential amphetamines. I felt she was approaching a critical point and decided to become strong for her and endure everything—her shouts, insults, depressions, collapses—in the name of her eventual health. In short: I took charge. And if I now summarize the things she said during this time, it is, perhaps, to announce the things she did. Except that these, in the end, refuse to remain under the rug (the mat, in the case of Lucha Zapata) and dominate the words, reducing them to the ashes of mere prattle.

"I want happiness for myself and for everybody," she would say in her moments of exaltation, as if she were stealing a plane again from a hangar in the international airport and was prepared to drop flyers on the city from the air, condemning all of us to joy.

"I can't tolerate poverty," she exclaimed immediately afterward. "It offends me that half my people are destitute, begging, stealing, without hope, exploited by the powerful, deceived by politicians, abandoned to the fatality of having always been and why not, tell me Josué, why not go on being destitute forever, tell me or I'll die right here . . ."

It was with this passion that Lucha Zapata evoked a past—that of our people, always oppressed—that she rarely applied to herself. Sometimes I set traps for her so she would talk about her life before our meeting. I never got her past—or almost never, actually—the evocation of our moment in the airport and her aerial view of a collective misfortune that, for her, was eternal, beyond time: Mexico had always been oppressed and would be so forever, inevitably . . .

"I want happiness for myself and for everybody. I can't tolerate poverty. What can I do, Savior?"

Sometimes she became violent and banged her head against the walls, as if she wanted to expel from her skull a brain that had been, she said, abducted. Why, by whom? I asked without receiving an answer other than a deep moan that was like hearing the protest of her lungs blackened by tobacco and drugs.

Then she would embrace me without defenses, like an old pillow, like a defeated ghost that knows it is divorced forever from a visible body, and say, "They threw me out because I use drugs, I'm an addict, if I had cancer they wouldn't throw me out, they'd take care of me, isn't that right, Savior?" She'd look at me with eyes so forsaken I simply held her even tighter, as if I feared that at those moments of extreme tenderness she'd leave me forever, freeing herself from life with a sigh that at the next moment would turn into a flare-up that burned my neck. I moved her away. She looked at me with intense hatred, accused me of keeping her locked up here, I'd open the door to the courtyard and invite her to go out, she called me horrible, an authoritarian type made in the image of power, a persecutor, an enemy and not a savior as she had believed.

"All of you, let me live my life!" she shouted in despair, tearing at her short hair and scratching her cheeks.

I stopped her by force, grasping her fists, bringing them up to my own face.

"Go on, Lucha, if you want to scratch, scratch me, go on . . ."

Then she would say Savior, don't be so bossy, and she would caress my cheeks and sing the usual song, "I'm a poor little deer that lives in the mountains and since I'm not very tame I don't come down to the water by day, by night little by little and in your arms, my darling."

I already knew that this song about the "poor little deer" was the code for love. In this way, Lucha would invite me to culminate the day's action, whatever it may have been, with an erotic moment that could be the quiet after a squall or the announcement of a coming storm, the gentle slope of peace recovered for a moment or a prelude to the tranquillity that, to be honest, she and I wanted to achieve and share without knowing exactly how to do it.

All of this occurred in the middle of her effort to stop using drugs and replace them with alcohol until I realized that tequila didn't give the same high as amphetamines, then she'd go back to drugs and discover, *ay, ay, ay,* that her hidden drugs were being consumed and tobacco and alcohol were no substitute and I was to blame for everything.

I knew very well that any person with Lucha Zapata would be "to blame" for a situation for which she was responsible. Asking her to take responsibility was like asking pears of an elm tree, as the unvanquished and sententious María Egipciaca would say. Lucha Zapata needed someone else to blame. Me, someone else, it didn't matter. But never herself. Herself, never. And I made note of her accusations and acts of violence for the simple reason that I've already indicated: I wanted to be responsible for a person.

Until the day she couldn't take any more.

But first she sang: "I'd like to be a fine pearl in your shiny earrings and nibble at your ear and kiss your cheeks."

———

I'LL SAY THAT Jericó never showed curiosity about my prolonged absences from the apartment we shared on Calle de Praga. It didn't surprise me and I didn't thank him for it. I didn't meddle in his life either.

I had my doubts.

How had Jericó traveled? What kind of passport did he have? Where was his passport? What was his name, after all?

Jericó what? I realized that deep-rooted gratitude for the protection the schoolyard champion gave the defenseless big-nosed kid kept me from seeing my friend in any light other than what is called in Roman law *amicus curiae.*

One of the great temptations when two people live together is rummaging through the affairs of the other. The temptation to open drawers, read personal diaries and correspondence, pry into closets, move like a cockroach under beds to see what the other has hidden under the mattress, in jacket pockets . . .

I don't need to tell you, you who are reading me and are all, without exception, decent people, that your author with the good memory Josué Nadal—I—never stooped to being a snoop. This did not stop me from cultivating certain doubts, all of them so unverifiable that they died before birth.

What was Jericó's last name?

Had he really spent four years in Europe, with Paris as his base?

Was his evocation of Europe a farce, theatrical and elementary? Kneeling on the Place de la Concorde, sure, not even Gene Kelly did that accompanied by George Gershwin's music, and if Jean Gabin or Jean-Paul Belmondo passed by, they didn't even blink.

Why didn't Jericó ever use those common expressions in ordinary French speech I knew only from old movies of the *nouvelle vague? Ça alors. A merveille. Quand même. Raison d'être. Savoir-faire. Laissez-faire. Franglais.*

Why, on the other hand, did North American sayings slip out? *Shove it. Amazing. Let's hug it out, bitch.*

And above all, unfamiliar allusions to youthful musicians— Justin Timberlake—or local television programs—*Entourage.* Let's hug it out, bitch.

I say I didn't inquire, but I suspected with no proof and no desire either to break the commitment to discretion, though I did consult the Entertainment section of *Reforma* to find out about Justin Timberlake and what *Entourage* was.

Other much more important concerns were set forth by Jericó with his customary mental speed and a certain childish audacity, firing them at me at times when I returned with no explanations from a night with Lucha Zapata: Who are we, Josué? How are we? Why are we? To what end are we? without obtaining more from me than an undulating smile and the urgent need to bathe, shave, make myself presentable after an exhausting session of guard duty at Cerrada de Chimalpopoca. I suspected that Jericó welcomed me with this salvo of abstract questions in order not to ask more concrete ones: Where are you coming from? Where did you spend the night? Why do you smell so strange?

The questions remained unresolved because of a new development.

It seems our garret, so bare at the beginning, was filling up with gadgets that came to our door in delivery trucks and then were carried up to our nest by dark men with strong backs and sparse mustaches.

Who sent us a laser fax machine, a television set with a 46 (or 52 or 70) inch screen? Who replaced our useless old black telephone with a white one from an Italian movie and then presented us with a couple of Sony Walkman portables and then—Creative Zen, Samsung YP-T9—others even more modern, with music, movies, calendars, and addresses? The last particularly interested me. What addresses did I have except for mine and Lucha Zapata's? It didn't take long for the light to go on. Or rather, the Sony Walkman with the name on the little screen of Maestro Antonio Sanginés and the phone numbers of his residence, his house in Coyoacán, and his offices on the Paseo de la Reforma.

Right there the message appeared that said:

I EXPECT YOU BOTH AT MY HOME ON JULY 2 AT 6:00 PM.

LIC. ANTONIO SANGINES.

I expect you both. Not I expect *you*. You *both*. Plural.

Now I waited for Jericó. He came in with his head high, laughing.

So then, once again, the two of us.

The maestro received us in his big old house in Coyoacán, surrounded as always by his noisy progeny, little children racing on tricycles, flying with arms spread, making engine noises, and eventually climbing on the professor's wingback chair, lying peacefully on his lap, or threatening a catastrophe from the top of the chair.

"Outside, boys," said Sanginés, laughing, and looked at Jericó and me when, in the same breath, he said:

"Come in, boys."

He wanted to position us immediately in what Roman law calls *capitis diminutio,* a kind of diminution of personality, due to the loss—Rudolph Sohm dixit—of the legal rule of freedom, of citizenship, or because of the minimal alteration of being expelled from the family.

More than enough for me. I was his student in the law faculty, he was my adviser in reading and my professional mentor. He sent me to do the famous "forensic practice" in the prison of San Juan de Aragón. He was directing my professional thesis. But Jericó? What relationship could he have with Sanginés? I tried to determine this in the form of greeting, always so revelatory in a country of embraces, pats, diminutives and augmentatives, remote suspicions, dissimulated gloating: Iberian America is also Italic America, a land of elegant appearances, the cult of the *bella figura,* and the memory of serial Machiavellianisms modulated to remember debts or forget grievances.

The fact is that Sanginés said only "Come in, boys," with an implicit "take a seat" in two leather chairs facing our host's wingback. We were simply two students subject to a certificate of proficiency examination.

The children left. The students sat down. I'll cut the message short: Sanginés believed we had completed an apprenticeship. With which I felt I was on the rungs of a medieval guild asking myself if this relationship was not, in fact, a transcription, though within the university, of the medievalism that is the watchword and perhaps the pride of Latin America, a continent that, unlike the United States of America, a nation with no antecedent more powerful than itself, did have a Middle Ages and as a consequence has—we have— from Mexico to Peru, mental categories that exclude a will not arbitrated by the Church or state. The Gringos are Pelagians without knowing it, descendants of the heretic who postulated individual freedom without the need for institutional filters, as opposed to his conqueror Augustine of Hippo, for whom grace was not individually achievable without the intervention of the Church. The North Americans, who don't have Pelagius or the Middle Ages, do have Luther, the Reformation, Puritanism, Calvinism, and all the heresy (I repeat: *choos-ing*) necessary to dictate with a very wide margin rules of conduct at the edge of institutions. We do not. Though the reader will note the constant benefit of Father Filopáter's lessons in preparatory school.

I believe Sanginés read my thoughts, because he immediately decided my destiny. I would finish the course of study (I needed only a year and a couple of classes I could pass in a proficiency exam) and conclude forensic practice in the prison of San Juan de Aragón.

"Begin to prepare your thesis. The subject is Machiavelli and the creation of the state," he pronounced, adding: "It is necessary for you to conclude your interview with Miguel Aparecido," before turning to Jericó and saying: "You have refused to follow a career. You believe experience is the best university. I am going to test you. Tomorrow go to the offices of the Presidency of the Republic in Los Pinos. They are expecting you."

And returning to me.

"And they are expecting you, Josué, in the office of Don Max Monroy in the building in Colonia—I should say the new city—of Santa Fe."

He sighed, as if longing for a modest city that could not exist again, rose to his feet, and brought the interview to an abrupt end, leaving me with a certain bad taste in my mouth; I didn't know whether to attribute it to an attitude unlike the normally amiable behavior of Professor Sanginés, or, more seriously, to a melancholy very similar to the sadness of goodbyes, as if a period in my life had just ended.

Jericó and I walked, looking for a taxi, toward Avenida Universidad, and were distracted as we crossed the Viveros de Coyoacán Park, breathing deeply, with no set purpose, because we were in one of the few lungs of an asphyxiated metropolis.

"What do you think?" he asked.

"Well," I shrugged. "I'll be doing the same things."

"No, the one who'll change is you. Max Monroy is a very powerful man."

"Bah. I may never even get to meet him."

Then I added: "Knowing you, Jericó, I think you'll not only get to meet the president—"

He interrupted: "He'll know me even if he doesn't see me," and added: "Look, hurry up and finish your degree. We're twenty-five years old. We can't go on waiting. We need a position. We can't give as an occupation 'I think' or 'I am.' We have to be and do."

I smiled in return. "One can always turn into a perpetually young old man, like Jelly Roll Morton, Compay Segundo, or Mick Jagger."

The reader will note that I wanted to test the connection I had suspected in Jericó with North American pop culture instead of a pretended French affiliation that, as I've already told you, seemed suspect to me. The problem is, if you talk about jazz and rock, of necessity you land in Anglo-American territory. France loves jazz but doesn't give it anything but love.

Jericó paid no attention to me. Who are we? What do we have? Name, occupation, status? Are we a vacant lot?

"Terrain vague," I said with my comic suspicions.

Jericó was unfazed. "A garbage dump of what could have been? A catalogue of debits and losses? Even the bottom of the barrel? So what's going on? I like it!"

"A hoarse-voiced basket where things accumulate?" I added, quoting Neruda but thinking of tasks I still had to do, not only the course of study in law, not only the mysterious prisoner Miguel

Aparecido, but in particular my unspeakable commitment to a woman who required protection, whom I could not leave alone, at large, helpless . . .

"Lucha Zapata" was the name on the tip of my tongue like a bird in an open cage who doesn't really know whether his well-being depends on flying away or remaining locked up and at the mercy of birdseed.

Jericó didn't go any further. There was in him, when we left the large Jardín de los Coyotes, a new, atypical reserve that undoubtedly had to do with the position Sanginés had just offered him and that now occupied our minds. Though in retrospect, I wondered if the maestro's unusual coldness was due to the unpublished presence of Jericó, which had skewed his behavior and evoked in my heart a dual feeling of nostalgia for the attention my teacher had previously paid me and reproach for his current manner.

Without saying goodbye, Jericó jumped on a moving bus with dangerous agility and I hailed a taxi to return to Lucha Zapata's house, undecided now as to my home and real address.

Unless, I smiled, it was the penitentiary where Miguel Aparecido—who knows to what end—was waiting for me.

"It's going like clockwork," Jericó shouted from the bus. *"Hug it out!"*

I NOTICED THAT Lucha Zapata was nervous, strange, different, and distant when I returned that night to the house on Cerrada Chimalpopoca next to the noisy Metro de los Doctores. She was involved in the ecstatic movements of preparing lunch, not looking at me as she cut the avocados in two, heated the tortillas, smeared them with the green flesh of a buttery fruit that relieves the acidity of Mexican corn. She knew I admired—and marveled at—this homemaking "professionalism" in my friend. She possessed a kind of domestic discipline contrary to the disorder of her life as an alcoholic and drug addict. She was an excellent cook and I arranged to have her cupboard always stocked with all the pleasures of the market that transform Mexican food into a gift of the gods for a country of beggars.

My mouth waters: jalapeño chile, habanero chile, saffron, jitomate, huitlacoche fungus, epazote tea, machaca dried beef, cochinita pork, chotes, chicharrón cracklings, oregano. I bought them at La Merced very early in the morning, assisted by a lively old woman with a straw-colored braid, Doña Medea Batalla. She appeared before me with her black cherry eyes and said: "Let me help you, Licenciado." "How do you know?" I said with a look. She touched one eye. "I know you all, Licenciado. You can spot a licenciado a mile away . . . just the way I can smell out villains."

I confined myself to placing produce in the basket. Lucha would transform it into blind mason's sauce, soup of corn ears and roasted chiles, uchepos or Michoacán corn tamales, Morelian enchiladas, enchiladas de plaza, and stuffed chayotes. I admired her concentration and skill, which contrasted so strongly with her life's disorder, wondering if asking her where she had learned to cook was the pretext for controverting the forgetfulness on which she insisted.

She defended herself. Her memory was locked away and her cuisine, she gave me to understand, was part of an atavistic, popular wisdom that wasn't taught. One is born, in Mexico, knowing how to cook. That was why I took pains to bring her the best produce, with the implicit hope that one day, eating well, she would remember something and live better.

It was a thin hope, not to mention a vain one.

"Did you bring beer?" she asked, standing, tottering.

"I forgot," I said, having just come from the interview with Sanginés and Jericó.

"Poor devil," she smiled with twisted lips. She laughed. "Beer makes you cold inside," she added for no reason.

I asked her to be calm, to lie down, what did she want? knowing that asking a person like her for "calm" was the same as telling her: You're crazy.

She said with sudden sweetness that she had a weakness for avocados. I told her I'd go out and buy a good supply right away. I regretted it. Lucha needed me there. She was helpless, a step away from death . . .

"What do you want from me?" she spoke from inside an internal cave.

I said nothing.

"My past. You're hungry for my past. You're a snoop," she said, reproaching me for what I wasn't, as my life with Jericó demonstrates. "A snoop. A meddler. You stick your big nose in."

She attacked my nose violently. It wasn't difficult for me to push her hand away. She fell onto the mat. She looked at me with immense sorrow and even greater resentment, not free of that great pretext for Mexican failure: feeling defeated, always being the loser, and obtaining salvation, perhaps, thanks to the blessing of defeat. We don't celebrate success except as a passing announcement of eventual defeat in everything.

"You see," she murmured. "You're the powerful one, the arbitrary one. You push me. You throw me to the floor. Do you see why I live the way I live? Because power is arbitrary, arbitrary, arbitrary . . ."

"Capricious," I said in a stupid eagerness to find synonyms for defeat.

"A caprice?" Lucha Zapata twisted what I said. "Do you think that living and dying is just a caprice?"

"I didn't say that." Clumsily I tried to apologize, standing while she knelt on the mat, looking up at me from the floor.

"Then what?" she asked in a voice at once defeated and victorious, ardent and dry.

I didn't say anything and she embraced my knees murmuring Love me Savior, I have only you, don't leave me, what do you need to love me more? what do you need to know I need you?

She looked at me as I believe one kneels and really looks at the "Savior," as she called me.

Did I want to know about her past? Like in the song, only if I got her what she needed, "Savior, I depend on you, I don't want to go out on the street, I'm here with you but you have to give me what I need, please, Savior, help me recover the good and leave the bad behind, first I need relief, then I swear I'll settle down, I'll be good, I won't hurt myself anymore, Savior, Salvador, go out and get me what I need and I swear I'll reform, understand that I have two I's like the cartoon El Señor Merengue, and the other I commands more than I do myself, what am I leaving behind? help me recover my soul, Savior, you know I'm good, don't think I have a taste for what's bad, don't think I like what's ugly, it's in spite of myself, I want to be good, look, I want to have a baby with you, Savior, make me a baby right now so I'm redeemed . . ."

She fell asleep. I already knew her sleep was a foretaste of death. I went out to get what she wanted. I came back. I watched over her. I spent the night watching. At six in the morning, Lucha Zapata woke, looked at me in anguish from the bare mat, and I soothed the entreaty in her eyes right away, giving her the injection and the syringe, helping her tie up her arm, watching her travel from hell to heaven and fall back to sleep.

I came back that night. She was sitting in one of those little Mexican chairs with a straw seat and brightly colored back, like a little girl being punished. I smiled at her. She looked up. A venomous sky struggled between her lids. She hugged herself with contained violence.

"You want me to repent just to give you pleasure," she spat at me. "You're like everybody else."

I caressed her head. She moved away contemptuously.

"You think you can control me?" She laughed. "Not even love controls me. Falling in love is submitting. I'm independent."

"No," I said without sadness. "You depend on drugs. You're a poor slave, Lucha, don't pretend to be independent. Don't make me laugh. You make me sad."

She let out an animal shout, the authentic howl of a wounded beast, arbitrary, arbitrary, she began to shout, you think habit can control, nothing controls me, where did you put my aviator helmet? only flying pacifies me, take me to the airport, give me a plane, let me fly like a free bird . . .

She stood and embraced me.

"Do it for your sweet mamacita."

"I don't know her."

"Then for charity."

"I don't have any."

"What do you have?"

"Love and compassion."

"Have compassion for yourself, asshole."

And the demon of consequences, what about him?

MY DISTINGUISHED READERS will say that going from Lucha Zapata's house to the prison of Miguel Aparecido was like passing from
one hell to another. Not at all. Compared to the house on Cerrada
de Chimalpopoca, the San Juan de Aragón prison was barely a purgatory.

I had the pass Professor Sanginés had given me. I went from
grating to grating until I reached Miguel Aparecido's cell. The prisoner stood when he saw me. He didn't smile, though in his face
I saw an unusual amiability. We exchanged glances before I went
into the cell. It was evident we wanted to please each other. What
did he want from me? I, from him, wanted only more information
for my thesis, though now that Sanginés had decided the topic—
Machiavelli and the creation of the state—I wondered what the Florentine thinker had to do with the Mexican prisoner.

It didn't take me long to find out.

Miguel Aparecido had a certain manner that really consisted of
a series of digressions, intended perhaps to educate me. His strong,
masculine figure, possessed of an aura of fatality together with an
appearance of will, stood as he received me, his arms crossed and
his sleeves rolled up, revealing arms covered with hair that was almost blond in the uncertain light of the cell, in contrast to the criminal's Gypsy air, olive skin, and his eyes: blue-black with yellow
flecks.

"He doesn't want to leave prison," Sanginés had told me. "The
day he completed his first sentence and left, he immediately committed a crime so he could return."

"Why?"

"I have no idea! I'm confused."

"Are you his attorney, Maestro?" I asked with a certain audacity.

"He has given me instructions to save him from freedom."

"Why?"

"Ask him."

I did, and Miguel Aparecido gave me an obscure smile.

"So, kid, why do I like prison? I could tell you things like this. Because I'm free of appearances. Here inside I don't have to pretend I'm what I'm not or that I'm what other people want me to be. Here I can laugh at all the conventions of courtesy, the how are things, how nice, at your disposal, at your service, let's make a date to get together, how's everybody at home, where are you going on vacation? how much did that beautiful watch cost? I'm not holding you up, am I?"

I laughed without wanting to and he became serious.

"Because I'm free of belonging to any class but especially the middle class we all aspire to. They want to be free, imagine. I want to be a prisoner."

"There are many classes in the middle class," I dared again. "Whom do you wish to be free of?"

He smiled. "Use *tú* with me or I'll kick your ass right here."

He said it in a savage tone. I didn't let myself be intimidated. I don't know what I had on my side. The assignment from Professor Sanginés. My differences with Jericó. The daily, fortifying trial of tending to Lucha Zapata. Or a recent confidence in my own superiority as a student, a free man, a citizen capable of confronting a recidivist criminal whose stake in the terrain of greatness was the decision to remain in prison. Forever? For how long?

Miguel Aparecido did not take long to return fire even before I could open the first document. He said I was very young but perhaps I hadn't fully understood something. What? That youth consists of daring. Growing old means losing one's audacity, he continued.

"What did you dare to do?" I asked, using *tú*, difficult with a person as forbidding as he was.

"I killed," he said with simplicity, aplomb, and finality.

I didn't dare to continue with a "why?" or a "whom?" which from the first had no answer. I concluded then and there that Miguel

Aparecido left this question hanging because answering it meant knowing the fatality of the plot and I—who had just moved from *usted* to *tú*—had a right only to the prolegomena.

"Do you know what's fucked up in prison?" he resumed. "Here you're not anything anymore. First, you're not anybody. You're separated from the world. You have to invent another world and then make a new relationship for yourself with a world that matters only if you've created it yourself, you know, boy?"

"Licenciado," I said with dignity.

He laughed. "Fine, Lic. You come here and first you ask yourself, who's protecting me? After a while, after humiliations, blows, lies, unkept promises, solitudes, tortures, punches, moans and you can't tell if they're from taking a shit or jerking off, the arrogance of the guards, the sadism of the other prisoners, you learn to protect yourself. How?"

He took me by the shoulders. I was afraid. He did it only to move me over and stare right into my eyes, not accepting any evasion in my gaze. If my life ended with my being smacked by the undertow on a Guerrero beach, I should add that in this scene with the ill-tempered Miguel Aparecido, I truly began to drown far beyond any previous circumstance in my life.

"Are you imprisoned unjustly?" said the classicist in my heart.

He replied that in a certain way yes, but in the long run, not really.

He read the serious questioning in my face.

"I'm here because of a great injustice," he said.

"But you're still here because you want to be," I added unemphatically.

He shook his head a little. "No. Because of my will."

"I don't understand."

He took a few steps in a circle. "First it makes you angry. You're suffocating."

He was timing his words to his turns around the cell, and these movements frightened me more than his words. He squared his jaw. His straight nose quivered.

"Then you're stunned at being here and surviving the initial hor-

ror and your permanent impotence, asshole . . . I mean, Licenciado." He smiled, looking at me. "Right after that you feel defeated,
absolutely fallen into misfortune."

He stopped and gave me a very ugly look.

"Finally you go back to anger, but this time in order to take your
revenge."

"On which people?" I said, about to fall into the trap of the
Count of Monte Cristo.

"On which *person,* asshole, just one person. Only one."

I looked at him expectantly. We both knew there were no premature answers and this would be the code of "honor" between us:
Nothing before its time.

As I had thought of Edmond Dantés earlier, now I tended
toward Doctor Mabuse, the prisoner who directs his crimes from a
Berlin cell. Is there anything new in these prison stories? Looking at
Miguel Aparecido, I told myself there was. The plots resemble one
another because they are part of the same destiny: lost freedom. In
prison, more than anywhere else, we realize there is no freedom because we live day by day, because our goals are futile, fragile, and in
the end unattainable, because death takes responsibility for cancel-
ing our contract and when we're dead we're not aware of what has
survived us, what has perished with us, and, at times, before us. It's
enough to walk down a busy street and attempt, in vain, to give transcendence to the lives passing by on their way to death, anticipating
it, trying to deny it, all subject to disappearing into a vast, collective
anonymity. Except the musician, the writer, the artist, the philosopher, the architect? Even them, how long will they endure? Who,
recognized today, will be unknown tomorrow? Who, ignored today,
will be discovered tomorrow? Few political and military figures survive. Who was Elizabeth I's chamberlain when Shakespeare was
writing, who the North American secretary of state at the time of
the obscure sailor and scrivener Herman Melville, who the secretary
general of the National Peasant Union when Juan Rulfo wrote *Pedro
Páramo? Eheu, eheu:* transient, I learned in the famous class on
Roman law: transience is our destiny but freedom is our ambition,
and it will take us a long time—I understood this in a flash looking

at the prisoner—to comprehend that the only freedom is the strug-gle for freedom.

Then why did this man refuse to be free, perpetuate his prison, and almost boast of being a prisoner? It was enough for me to look at him to understand that Miguel Aparecido did not deliver his truths just like that. It was enough to see how he looked at me to know I needed to respond with patience to his mystery, and this pawned a portion of my future and my own freedom to the life of this strange individual who finally, once the time periods imposed by life imprisonment were understood, told me something concrete and asked me for something explicit.

"You leave here for only three reasons. Because you die. Because you complete your sentence. Or because you escape."

If I looked at him in a questioning way, it was unintentional.

"And again, you escape only if you don't die, or because you're a badass for running away, or because you have powerful connec-tions," he continued. "Yesterday a convict left here only because of his connections. And that makes me very angry."

I believe that if the Devil exists, at that moment Miguel Apare-cido appeared to me as Lucifer, Satan, Mephistopheles, the Prince of Darkness enveloped in the shadows of an immense history of ac-cumulated vengeances, violent desires, delayed wishes, arbitrary destinies, and nights without light.

"The man and the woman who freed him unjustly must be pun-ished."

I still don't know how I survived that morning in the diabolical presence of Miguel Aparecido.

"Find your friend Errol Esparza. Tell him he ought to take his re-venge."

The order resounded for me in the vast hollowness of prison si-lences.

"He ought to take his revenge."

"On whom?"

"The man is Nazario Esparza. The woman is Sara Pérez, Sarape, she used to be a whore in La Hetara's house."

———

THE VENDETTA ORDERED by Miguel Aparecido was postponed because of other pressing matters. Sanginés sent Jericó to Los Pinos as a young aide in the presidential office. And me he directed to collaborate in the management of the powerful Max Monroy's enterprises, out toward Santa Fe, in a new border area of a troglodytic Mexico City.

The distances between remote neighborhoods of the capital can involve as much as two hours of travel. The distance from the apartment on Praga to Cerrada de Chimalpopoca and now to my unexpected destination of Santa Fe was the same as the distance from Rotterdam to The Hague and from The Hague to Amsterdam, without taking into account my visits to San Juan de Aragón prison.

What could I do? My bewilderment suggested a way out: another visit to the señora buried in the nameless grave, whose location I did not know, to ask her for advice. The dead don't have schedules. Unless eternity is the clock without hands where time melts.

I said these words to myself as I walked along Paseo de la Reforma, hesitant about my destination or destinations, when the sky darkened, the angel flew down from the top of the Columna de la Independencia, grasped me by the collar, rose up with a howl or sob or sigh—all at the same time—and taunted me as he asked, breaking my concentration:

"Do you know the sex of angels?"

I wanted to reply they have none, that's why they can be angels, except that the creature carrying me through the air silenced my words and spoke to me in a man's voice, and I recognized that voice, it belonged to my old friend Ezekiel, the prophet enveloped in a turbulent wind that flew me over castles and skyscrapers, magnificent slopes and bare hills, neighborhoods of mud and gardens of roses, stating his recommendations as we flew: be on your guard, don't fear them, speak to them even though they don't listen, fast, inform them a prophet will come among them, tell them to listen to the voices of the multitude, and I heard a great laugh when the prophet Ezekiel, who was also, in his free time and when he had a yen for transvestism, the Angel of Independence, let me go, and I saw that one of his feet gleamed but it was a calf's foot.

The storm steered my fall. A sudden ground blocked it. Green foliage softened it.

I fell on my face.

In front of me, once again the grave of

ANTIGUA CONCEPCIÓN

And the familiar voice:

Walk around my grave three times, Josué. Thank you for coming alone. We live in a guarded world. Nobody moves without a bodyguard. They say it's for security. Pure potatoes. It's pure fear. We live in fear. We tighten our asshole, to put it politely.

Her sigh made the earth tremble.

Not you, she continued. You're not afraid. That's why you come to see me alone. I'm grateful. Alone with your soul. Because even though you don't believe it, you have a soul, my boy. Take care of it. Don't trade it for a plate of lentils or bean soup.

"Señora," I said, "I'm going to work in the office of Max Monroy. Your son, Señora . . ."

I know that.

"Who told you?"

The earth trembles. It's her way of speaking. I receive messages each time it trembles.

"Ah!"

I suppressed my own astonishment and quickly added:

"What kinds of messages, Señora?"

That you're going to enter a new world, silly. Before, in the world I knew, it was the president of the republic who dispensed justice, listened to complaints, and received petitions, the old king! Once I came with my complaints and petitions to President Adolfo Ruiz Cortines, the last president. He didn't even look at me. All he said was: Don't bother me. Then, I answered, don't be president. He looked up and in his eyes drunk with the sun I saw what power was: a tiger's gaze that made you lower your eyes and feel fear and shame.

I believe at that moment the earth where the señora was buried was the enormous eye of a hurricane.

She must have read my mind.

Don't be an asshole, she said with the arrogant vulgarity I was already familiar with. If you're going to work with my son, be careful. Max Monroy is my heir. He's another breed of creature. Mine. Earlier millionaires are beggars beside Max Monroy. Look, I knew them all. They became rich thanks to the revolution, which raised them up from nothing, opening opportunities for them that had once been denied to those at the bottom. Federico Robles fought in Celaya with Obregón against Villa, and from then on One-arm pampered him, directing him into politics, and when politics became dangerous or stopped producing, he guided him into business, which was then virgin territory, or as Robles himself said—a strong but sentimental man who decided to build on desolate battlefields, and even to stain his conscience—one had to sacrifice ideals to build a country, to feel that one had a right to everything for having made the revolution, established the foundations of capitalism, created a stable middle class, and invented true Mexican power, which "consists," Federico Robles would say, "of nothing but grabbing the country by the back of the neck" and being "one big badass," and that same man, she declares, was capable of portraying a woman he loved, respecting her, loving her without raising her up or sinking her, offering her a sweet brutality, the strength that a woman—she, Hortensia Chacón—needed in order to love and deserve her life. This I know. Or the case of Artemio Cruz, another millionaire who came from nothing, from a miserable hovel, and made a fortune changing sides, moving at just the right time from one faction to another, betraying thousands to take over a newspaper and dedicate himself to making a fortune by serving the powerful man on duty at the time . . . who was, when all was said and done, himself, Artemio Cruz and no one else . . .

Another seismic sigh.

Ay! And yet he was a man, had loves, lost them, Artemio Cruz had a wound, kid, do you have any? I don't see scars on your body . . .

"Then what do you see, Señora?"

Ay, I see ignorance about yourself. You don't know who you are. You still don't know. Artemio Cruz had an open love wound and spent his life trying to close it. He failed. And it was his own fault he failed. That's all. He had a brave son. He lost him. On the other hand, that caliph of the northern border, Leonardo Barroso, that one has no excuse. He was a thug who never had a day of compassion, not even for his own impaired son, he took his wife away and prostituted her, are you listening to me? one Michelina Laborde, one of those little society whores sold to the highest bidder with no shame at all because in order to feel shame you have to have some smarts, just a little bit of brain, that's all, and these little society ninnies move their necks and you hear a marble rolling around though their eyes blink like calculators. Leonardo Barroso was a miserable asskisser to the Gringos, father of another cruel, misogynistic son, son and grandson of incest with the aforementioned Michelina but grandfather to a brave, astute, and perverse woman, María del Rosario Galván, whom you will suddenly meet in your new life. Generation after generation, degeneration!

I questioned in silence. She read the silence.

You know, my boy? Sometimes I feel . . . well, nostalgia for times gone by. Except we no longer have gold coins, like in the old days, to memorialize what we have lived. We have photos, we have movies, we have TV. That was our memory: photographable, filmable, archivable. Now everything has changed, and here comes the story of my son Max Monroy. The fruit doesn't fall far, etcetera. Except Max is no fruit. He's a trunk. He's like the Tree of Tule in Oaxaca, a gigantic cedar forty meters high and forty-two meters around and two thousand years old. And though Max Monroy is only in his eighties, it's as if he incarnated two millennia because he's so sharp and such a bad fucker though he's my son and that's the way he is because fortunately he inherited nothing from his father except the vague memory of a country destroyed by its own epic, kid, you can't live on that forever, I mean on an epic, and in Mexico the epic of the revolution justified everything, progress and backwardness, construction and corruption, peace and politics. Everything in the name of the revolution. Until the Tlatelolco Square massacre left the revolution stripped bare. Stripped bare but shitting blood, of course.

"How do you compete with an epic?"

The señora's voice trembled, and in it she did not hide a certain satisfaction with herself, about herself.

By moving ahead—she affirmed from the grave—as I did. I've already told you about that. I moved ahead of everything and that's why I could leave my son Max Monroy an independent fortune not subject to presidential favor or political changes. That exhausted my miserable husband. The general lived in a world of torments, tormented by insults, physical challenges, excessive praise, toadies, eventual guilt—when they were alone, do you think all the sons of bitches we've had in Mexico never felt guilty, do you think that?

Max Monroy, his invisible but indefatigable mother exclaimed from the grave, Max Monroy!

And then in a very low voice and jumbling together eras, dead dry fields, lost harvests, orphaned children, everyone to the mountains, always fleeing, children, women, cows, to the mountains, the mountains, the mountains . . . One day we had to be still, resigned, obedient . . . The nation was worn out. Or it was worn out by the marriage of indigence and injustice. Who knows?

The voice was fading.

The señora was lost in memories of what she wanted to forget.

It was all unpredictable . . .

"It still is, Señora," I dared to contribute.

Death, harvests, descendants . . .

"Do you want me to tell your son anything? A message?"

The sepulchral silence was followed by vast laughter.

Our souls hover like vampires . . .

When they cross the river, the dogs stay behind the soldiers . . .

The soldiers skinning goats, roasting pigs, it's over!

My tits swelled for a whole year.

To nurse my son.

Go on, three times around my grave.

———

I WOKE ON the mat in Lucha Zapata's house and looked, bewildered, at the light of dawn. My immediate memory did not hold the cemetery or the address or zip code of where I came from but only a nonexistent river on this desolate, dry, and stifled mesa. A river like a truncated finger pointing the way to the sea.

You, who already know my end, may think I'm inventing a posteriori the events of the past. I swear to you I'm not. And the reason is this: At dawn there was a recurrence of astonishing continuities between my hours at Antigua Concepción's grave and my waking in Lucha Zapata's house.

As if the voice of Max Monroy's dead mother continued in the voice of the living lover of Josué Nadal, who is myself, the narrator of this tale, Lucha Zapata, in a white nightgown, walked barefoot from the mat to the kitchen and back to the mat describing, evoking, as dazed as a sleepwalker, an encounter on an old forgotten street, sordid and dissolute. Lucha finds in a corner of the night (that's what she said, now these are her words, not mine) a man in rags and covered by newspapers. It is very dark. The man's eyes are very black and shining. Everything about him is exhausted except his gaze.

They look at each other. He gives his hand to Lucha. He stands without saying a word and leads her along the streets of the night. They stop in front of a lighted window. Inside people are holding a party. It is probably a family occasion. A girl of about eight or nine entertains the others by prancing about, telling jokes, and singing songs. Lucha seems charmed, she opens the door (which was already ajar) and goes in, moving toward the little girl who is the center of attention. Lucha approaches. The girl looks at her and retreats, farther and farther back, into a dark corner of the room.

When Lucha has her cornered, the girl sits down on a hard chair. She looks as if she were being punished. Lucha tells me the little girl is there, though in reality she is very far away. She hugs a stuffed bear and covers herself with her security blanket.

"Who are you?" the girl asks Lucha. "What are you doing here? We don't want you. Go away."

Lucha tries to say something but can't get the words out. Lucha doesn't understand the reason for the girl's rejection. She feels humiliated. She runs out. She trips over a white tricycle decorated with a flowered basket. She gets up and in the street she falls into the arms of the dark man who leads her far away.

The road descends abruptly. A gigantic night surrounds them, as irresistible as a carnival: Lucha allows her thoughts to carry her along, her thoughts carry her very far from the place where she is. The night is transforming her—she says, she tells me this morning—leading her to a world where her senses enjoy peace and sufficiency at the same time they are cruelly stirred, demanding more, always more . . .

Suddenly she addresses me. "You know, Savior? Pleasure is a little pride and another little bit of self-hatred. A feeling of desperation. Along with a childish sensation of eternal life . . ."

She says she was a member of a gang that protected her and gave her what she needed. She compared her earlier solitude and forgot the familial warmth. Now she was part of a gang.

She gave names: "Maxi Batalla. El Florido. El Tasajeado. El Cacomixtle. El Sabor de la Tierra."

They meant nothing to me. She knew that and went on.

"You become part of a legion of outsiders, of strange people or strangers, whatever you prefer. Your life belongs to no one. During the day you sleep."

One night—she continues—from that anonymous, faceless group, an individual emerges. A dark boy, tall and slim. She says that between the two of them a feeling is born of love, tenderness, and mutual appreciation. An attraction.

"I'm no longer a face in the nocturnal crowd, Josué."

I don't say anything. For the first time, she is remembering. I wouldn't interrupt her for anything in the world. I leave assembling the pieces of the puzzle for another time. I don't say she has met a man twice for the first time. Dreams have their own logic, and we don't understand it. She is also wrong to call a group "anonymous" whose names she "remembers."

"Yes."

She said that with him she felt totally free and open. He offered her a way out. Not a return to conventional values but a movement toward her own thoughtful, creative values.

"I wanted to be sincere with him. I wanted to return with him to the lighted window in the house."

Lucha Zapata opened her eyes and I realized that everything she had told me she had said without seeing.

"He understood. He understood where I was coming from. He understood how much of myself I had left behind and how much I owed to what I denied with so much rebellious zeal . . . One night, sleeping side by side, he woke and drew me to him. I don't know if it was dawn or dusk. But I did understand that after going with me to the lighted house, he was ready to be like me, do you understand? as much as he could. He made love to me and when I came I understood that with him I could reach a compromise. We wouldn't go back to the world I had left or the world where he found me. Together we would create our own world."

She said that was the concession. Together the two of them would leave the desolate city. That was Lucha's concession. His was to share with her one last night in the artificial paradise, evoking Baudelaire, "aflame with love of beauty, I cannot give my name to the abyss that will be my tomb," because what neither of them realized was that his body, which belonged to her sexually, no longer was hers organically.

"I tried to wake him," Lucha shouted on this morning. "I shook him, Savior. I touched him. He was the icy statue of death . . . And what did I do then, Savior? I abandoned him. I abandoned the corpse in the hotel room. I went down to the street. I fell into the center of the night wanting to die if that would bring him back."

I tried to get up from the mat to seize her waving arms and the hands that scratched at her eyes and she shouted to leave her alone, she had to tear off her own skin, her own identity, savage, blind, violent, searching for death—I gave her a tight embrace—courting death—I grasped her hands—closing the curtain of nothingness over any creative purpose that could deflect her from a life more and more and forever more reckless.

She hung from my neck.

"Savior, I'm the dead sweetheart of a living memory. There's no tomorrow tomorrow. You lose all sense of time. Each day is identical to the one that came before and the one that follows. What a fuckup, Savior!"

"If you want," I said to her, "don't put off your death anymore, Lucha Zapata."

"I'm not putting it off," she replied. "I'm speeding it up."

NO ONE WILL deny, Brother Angelo, my good intentions. I wanted to be an architect. I wanted to be a creator. I'm Venetian. I look at the tremulous light of Tiépolo. I embody it in the luminous architecture of Palladio. That light and this architecture populate the north of Italy: we have light and we have form. Being an architect after Palladio. Illuminating after Tiépolo. Brother Angelo: both things were denied me. I traveled from Venice to Rome—I was twenty years old—in the retinue of Francesco Vernier, ambassador of the city of Venice to the Pontiff. I looked at the eternity of its ruins. I looked at the fugacity of Rome in its papacy. The Pope dies. The court changes. Rome fills with new families clamoring for positions, favors, commissions. Eternal City? Fleeting, transitory city. Eternal City? Only the mute stone endures.

For that reason I wanted to be an architect, Brother. I saw the inert world and wanted to animate it with architecture. I wanted to create. The inertia of the world told me: No. There are enough works already from yesterday and today. Nobody needs another architect. Don't think about the works you won't be able to make. No? Ah! Then I'll think about the works I won't be able to make.

I did not find a Maecenas. Without a Maecenas nothing is done. And so I found a Maecenas. The city of Rome, asking me, Piranesi, Giovanni Battista Piranesi, I will be your Maecenas, I, Rome, with my ruins, my unknown corners, my scavenged garbage, my devastated sarcophagi, I offer myself to you, Piranesi, on the condition that you don't reveal my secrets, don't show me in the light of day but in the most obscure depths of mystery . . .

They demand, Why don't you study the nude more? Why do you

insist on depicting hunchbacks, the maimed, *cuadroni magagnazi, sponcherati storpi*? Why don't you show esthetic truth? Why?

Because I wager on esthetic infidelity. Even if it's ugly? No. Because it possesses another beauty. The beauty of the horrible? If horror is the condition for acceding to beauty that is unknown, latent, about to be born, if— Then do you scorn ancient beauty? No, I find the place that refuses to be ancient. And what place is that? Is there any place that doesn't age?

I gather together my guardians. Invoke my witnesses, Brother Angelo. Stone lions, looks. Stone bridges, sighs. Stone walls, confinement. Stone blocks, prisons.

I will introduce machines and chains, ropes and stairs, towers and banners, rotting crossbars and sickly palm trees into the space of the prison. A scenography. Invisible smoke. Deceptive sky. What do we breathe, Brother? What sky illumines us? Veils. There are the sky and the smoke. But they are uncertain, untouchable, part of the scene, passing distractions, theatrical illuminations: smoke and light for a prison with no entrances or exits, the perfect prison, the prison within the prison within the prison. A profusion of escapes: They lead nowhere. What enters stays here forever. What is alive dies. It becomes excrescence. And excrescence becomes ruin.

The world is a prison? The prison is a world?

The prison frees itself from itself in the earlier design of my stewardship? I, Giovanni Battista Piranesi, say this. Or is my own image the one that imprisons the prison?

There are no human beings here. But there is the human question regarding the origin of light. And if there is no light other than the question, the question becomes the negation of destiny, as somber as these prisons, sepulchral chambers of a heaven in eternal dispute. There are no human beings in the lost heaven. There are prisoners. The prisoner is you.

They poisoned me, Fra Angelo, the acids I use for etching. My art killed me. Will my prisons survive? I believe so. Why? Because they are the works I could not make: they are the ruins of the buildings I could not construct.

Still, I died with the ambition of designing a new universe. Except no one asked me to and I had to depart with one anguished question: How does one imprison life in order to destroy death?

I ask you, my brother Angelo Piranesi, because you are a Trappist monk and cannot speak.

NO DAD, NO mom, not even a little barking dog softened the guardian of my childhood and adolescence, Doña María Egipciaca, which signified my insignificance in the vast order of human relationships, beginning with the family. Destiny, if not virtue, later provided me with relationships that were fleeting (with the nurse Elvira Ríos), more or less permanent (with the tormented Lucha Zapata), and very vulgar and at the same time mysterious (as with the whore who had a bee tattooed on her buttock).

Now, the decision (apparently unappealable) of Maestro Antonio Sanginés led me to the doors of the Vasco de Quiroga building in the brand-new, prosperous district of Santa Fe, an old abandoned wasteland on the road to Toluca, full of sandy precipices and white chalk barrens, that overnight, driven by the great bursting heart of the Mexican metropolis, was flattened out first only to have erected immediately afterward, in a vast valley of cement and glass, vertical skyscrapers, horizontal supermarkets, underground parking garages, all of it always guarded by sentries of glass and cement that were like the raised eyeglasses of an imposing sun determined to avenge the challenge of a Scandinavian architecture made to admit the sun in a country—ours—where ancestral wisdom demands thick walls, long shadows, sounds of water, and hot coffee to combat the damaging effect of excessive sunlight.

The strange thing—I told myself as I approached the Vasco de Quiroga building—is that in Santa Fe the Spanish prelate of that name founded a utopia intended to protect the recently conquered indigenous population and offer them a society—another society—inspired in the ideas of Thomas More: a utopia of equality and fraternity but not liberty, since its rules were as strict and confining as those of any project that proposes to make us all equal.

In front of the building, the white statue of the prelate, standing and caressing the bowed head of an Indian child. Inside the building, an entrance watched over by classic bodyguards with shaved heads, white shirts, old bow ties, black suits and shoes, and jackets bulging with the unavoidable tools of the trade. The guards looked indifferently at the statue of the protector of the Indians without understanding anything, although, perhaps, they were certain that being gunmen who protected politicians, potentates, and even prelates in the Mexico of immense insecurity in the twenty-first century was a remunerated form of utopia. The truth is that behind the large black glasses of the guards and at the feet of their wardrobelike physical proportions, there was no reflection and no basis for any kind of utopia.

I complied with security requirements. I passed through the triumphal arches of universal suspicion. I rang for the elevator and got out on the twelfth floor of the building. A very short, very dark girl adorned, like an announcement of the loves of Pierrot and Columbine, with large glasses that had black-and-white frames, above whose glasses fell the light shower of the uniform hairdos of various secretaries, nurses, and saleswomen, which dance above the brows as if fleeing the skull, who said the often repeated "This way, Señor," and I followed the triumphal clicking of her heels (it announced her salvation from who knows what fate worse than death: I imagined her cornered, raped, beaten, hungry, why not? a toss of destiny's coin, heads or tails? was enough) with the fatal certainty I was walking behind the permitted spoils of war. One centimeter more and the señorita—

"Ensenada, at your service."

"Last name or first?"

"All that and more. I was born there, Señor," my small guide said pertly in the corridors of entrepreneurial power.

"Ensenada de Ensenada from Ensenada de . . ." I said with feigned astonishment.

She didn't like that. She opened a door and left me there, in the hands of the next woman, without even saying goodbye. I gave my name to woman number two, an affable matron with extensive concerns. She stood, opened a cedar door, and invited me into an aquarium.

I've spoken accurately. The lights of the office where I found myself swam, without betraying their origin, when they met the light that came in, filtered by aquamarine glass, and when both lights embraced—the invisible one inside and the filtered one outside—they created an atmosphere of subdued power. I don't know if the expression is stronger and less fortunate than the reality. What I mean is that the illumination in this office was a creation that took advantage of both natural and artificial light to create a visual space and could not be merely decorative, or even a symbol of an unemphatic function or power.

It did not take me long to understand that the space that received me had not been invented for me or anyone except the woman who got up from the easy chair located next to a revolving desk and who spent almost as many hours here as a fish in an aquarium. The office was hers, not mine. I felt like an intruder. She stood. I had a vague *paideia* of Hispano-Mexican courtesy: Women have no reason to stand when a man comes in.

The fact is that Asunta Jordán—which is how she introduced herself—was not an ordinary, run-of-the-mill woman but what the lights and their symbology had led me to realize. Not a woman with power or of power, though she was a powerful woman.

I knew beforehand that I was stepping onto the lands of the great Max Monroy, an octogenarian, strong, extremely rich, and the son of my ghostly friend Antigua Concepción who lay buried in a mysterious grave. But if at any moment I harbored the fantasy that my relationship with the mother assured me of immediate access to the son, Asunta Jordán now appeared, blocking the way, asking me courteously to have a seat and immediately and in vain initiating an instructive monologue, as if I, deep in this platonic cave where the lights of the real city were vague wavering shadows on the office ceiling, were paying attention to anything other than this woman of medium height, tending to tall, possessor of a vigorous, punctual,

professional body all of which I was disposed to guess at, beginning
with her black, fairly high-heeled shoes, with a low-cut vamp where
I could detect the beginning (the origin, the birth) of her breasts,
before ascending her crossed legs that she relaxed when (I believe)
she saw me looking at them with their flesh-colored stockings that
led to the skirt (which she instinctively pulled down, moving the
hand with a watch, a throbbing, silent pulse, to her thighs) and
jacket of the tailored dark blue pinstripe suit over a wine-colored
blouse. She wore pearls around her neck, a single diamond in each
ear, and then there was her head with the chin raised, as if that gesture announced the tranquil challenge of parted lips, darkened eyes,
alert nose, forehead without questions or answers, and short,
streaked, carefully casual hair.

I examined the reality and the mystery of this woman, realizing
immediately that the reality was a mystery and she guarded it jeal-
ously, as if anyone looking at her could believe the reality was
merely that: reality. Looking at Asunta Jordán for the first time, I
summarized my earlier experience with female matters by telling
myself that when people talk—and they talk a great deal—about the
"mystery" of a woman, in fact they are transferring to the female sex
a series of vices in order to emphasize the virtues of the male or, just
the opposite, attributing to the woman virtues that tacitly indicate
our masculine vices. Who, for example, keeps a secret better: they
or us? Who is more stoic in the pristine sense (Filopáter dixit) of
"living in harmony with nature," which lends itself to all interpretations because it supports all the vices and virtues that are in accord
with nature? And is there anything that nature excludes from its
kingdom, from mystic heights to moral depths, from saintliness to
sex?

I admit that in the presence of Asunta Jordán all this came to
mind not in a premeditated way but instantaneously, dissolving my
dual questioning into a single unitary affirmation: Asunta Jordán's
façade was one of duty, which accounted for her attire, her voice,
her position—despite her office of aquatic tides, more appropriate
to a siren than an executive secretary. Wasn't it all something more

than a concession to the senses, wasn't it an invitation more than a whim?

I stopped at her gaze hidden (like that of the guards) by dark glasses, which she suddenly removed, revealing eyes that would have been beautiful if they hadn't been so hard, inquisitive, imperious and that were—beautiful—in spite of everything I've said.

"You're not listening to me, Señor."

"No," I replied, "I was looking at you."

"Discipline yourself."

"I believe that looking at you carefully is the primary discipline in this place."

I don't know if she smiled or became angry. Her mouth allowed for any number of readings. Her deep black eyes betrayed the artificiality of her sun-streaked hair and solicited—I thought then—more intimate investigations.

LET NO ONE tell you I speak incessantly or don't listen to advice. Let that person search for balance. Bring a little harmony to the country. Give Mexico a triumphal air. And above all, not spend all his time, Mr. President, in demonizing his predecessor or doing favors for those who supported him.

Jericó told me that the President of the Republic, Don Valentín Pedro Carrera, received him in the formal office at Los Pinos with these concepts and asked him to have a seat in a chair conspicuously lower than the chief executive's as the president caressed with his long fingers the busts of the heroes—Hidalgo, Juárez, Madero—that adorned his vast, bare desk. In addition to heroes, there were a good number of telephones and behind Jericó's seat three television sets with the sound off but transmitting constant images.

He told Jericó he was always looking for new blood, for new ideas. Licenciado Sanginés had recommended Jericó as an intelligent, very cultured boy, educated abroad and with no political experience.

"Just as well," laughed the president. "Correct me in time, Jericó," he said with the heartiness of informal address immediately authorized by the difference in their ages: Valentín Pedro Carrera was close to fifty but said jokingly that "after forty-one you can't walk, you have to run."

"So you're very cultured, right? Well, take good care of me because I'm not. Don't hold back, correct me in time, don't let me talk about the Brazilian female novelist Doña Sara Mago or the Arabic female philosopher Rabina Tagora."

He guffawed again, as if wanting to ease tensions and put Jericó at his ease and receptive to what Mr. President Carrera intended to tell him.

"My philosophy, young man, is that there should be a rotation of individuals here, not classes. And it's necessary to rotate individuals because otherwise the classes become agitated seeing the same faces. Those at the bottom become agitated because the permanence of those at the top reminds them of the absence of those at the bottom. Those at the top become agitated because they're afraid a gerontocracy will perpetuate itself and the young will never get beyond subsecretary, or high-ranking official, or out-and-out mediocrity."

He narrowed his eyes until he looked like a Chinese-Aryan, since his Spanish features were crossbred with swarthy skin and both of them with an Asian gaze.

"I called you after talking to my old adviser Sanginés so you can give me a hand with a project I have in mind."

He smoothed his reddish, graying mustache.

"I'll explain my philosophy. The Mexican plateau is not only a geographical fact. It is a historical one. It is a flat height, or a high flatland, which allows us to look at the stature of time."

Jericó half-closed his eyes in order not to yawn. He expected a complete oratorical exercise. That did not happen.

"But to get to the point, Jero . . . May I call you that?"

What was "Jero" going to say except simply to nod his consent. He says he didn't feel intimidated and didn't stoop to "Whatever you like, Mr. President."

That individual proceeded to explain that man does not live by bread alone but also by festivals and illusions.

"You have to invent heroes and bequeath them," said Carrera as he caressed the innocent heads of the bronzed leading men of the nation. "You have to invent 'the year' of something that distracts people."

"No doubt," said Jericó, boldly. "People need distraction."

"There you go," the president continued. "Look." He caressed the three heads, one after the other. "For me Independence, Reform, and Revolution passed me in the night. I am a child of Democracy, I was elected and am accountable only to my electors. But I repeat, democracy does not live by ballot boxes alone, and here and in China memorable dates have to be created that give pride to the people, memory to amnesiacs, and a future to the dissatisfied."

He didn't say "I have finished speaking," but let's pretend he did. Jericó says he sent the chief executive a quietly interrogative look.

"Commemorative dates are born of unimportant dates," my friend ventured and realized, taking his measure, that the president did not like anyone to see him disconcerted.

"In other words," Carrera continued, "a president has to be a hedonometer."

Jericó feigned an idiotic face. Presidential vanity was restored.

"The pleasure, happiness, joy of the people must be measured. You're so cultured"—the tail end of irony appeared—"do you think a science of happiness exists? How much happiness does the average Mexican need? A lot, not much, none at all? Listen carefully. The voice of experience is talking to you, you can count on it!"

Though his gaze revealed the most perverse brutality.

"This country has always lived in miserable poverty. Always, a mass of the fucked and we, a minority of fuckers, are over them. And believe me, Jero, if we want it all to continue, we have to make the fucked believe that even though they're fucked they're happier than you and me."

His face became serene.

"In other words, my good Jero: I don't want Mexicans to be rich. I want them to be happy. Just look at the Gringos. Look at what prosperity has done for them! They work constantly, eat badly, you can bet they fuck in a hurry, a straight suburban quickie, they don't have vacations, they don't have social welfare, they retire at fifty and die beside a lawn mower. A lot of work, a lot of money, and not much satisfaction . . . Some happiness! In Mexico, at least, there's always been a certain, what shall I call it? pastoral well-being, you're happy with your tortilla here, your tequilas there . . ."

Once again the ogre.

"That's over, young man. Too much information, too many appetites, too much envy. Max Monroy with his handheld devices has brought information to the most remote corners. Once you could govern almost in secret, people believed in the annual report on September first, they believed that the more statistics there were, the happier they would be, but damn it all to hell, Jero! No more. People are informed and they don't conform and it's my job to fill in the gaps at the patriotic festival, the commemorative parade, the ceremonies that replace the imagination and appease their spirits, their thirst and hunger."

He gave Jericó a small, friendly slap.

"I need young blood. New people, with ideas, with education. Like you. Sanginés endorses you. That's more than enough for me. The good lic has never failed me, and if I'm here I owe it in great measure to Don Antonio Sanginés. Well, well," he said with a sigh. "This country is divided into cream, watery milk, yogurt, and the infamous dulce de leche. You choose."

He looked at Jericó as one looks at a man condemned to death who has just been pardoned.

"Think positively, my young collaborator. Think about the efficacy of the parade and the festival. A ceremony is the cloak of dignity everyone can place around their shoulders, hiding their rags. Bring me ideas. Let's celebrate sports and athletes, songs and singers, brands of beer, and national sweets, let's even celebrate ex-governors. Invent reputations, boy. Create museums and more museums. Parades and more parades. Lots of music, lots of trombones. Lots of 'Marcha Zacatecas.' And don't underestimate the political transcendence of what the assignment means. Ask yourself: Do people know their own interests? Max Monroy wants them to. I think they're not unaware of them, they just replace them with commemorations. In the long run, Monroy wants to transform luxury into necessity. He wants people to take for granted that they deserve what they once had to pay for. If he succeeds, Jero, power is over, undone by critical exigency. If wealth is transformed into necessity, power becomes unnecessary because people are satisfied only with what others don't have and power is satisfied only with what others already have. Otherwise tell me, what the hell are we promising?"

He stood and extended a robust hand. His rings hurt Jericó. The president stared at him. Like a tiger with its prey.

"Don't even imagine that I'm talking more than I should."

"No, Mr. President."

"If you repeat it, nobody will believe you but I'll make you pay."

"Of course, Mr. President."

"Don't even think you can begin your political career by beating me."

"If you think that, fire me."

The president gave a loud laugh, reverting to the familiar *tú*.

"Don't worry. I'll give you a pension. And something else."

"Tell me, Señor."

"Don't make a fool of me."

The telephone rang. The president walked over to answer it. He listened. Between silences he said:

"I won't forget what you're saying . . . Be sure to call my secretary . . . I hope we see each other again . . . Let's see when . . ."

"I don't know," Jericó said to me, "why each of those anodyne phrases sounded like a threat."

Especially when the president said goodbye to Jericó, asking him to be discreet, not to make a false move, and not to make himself noticeable.

"Be discreet, don't make any false moves, don't make yourself noticeable."

And Jericó simply thought, *What did we agree to?*

I'M A LOYAL man, Miguel Aparecido told me on the day I returned to the San Juan de Aragón prison, impelled by circumstances.

"I'm here because I want to be," he added, and I agreed because I already knew that.

His expression did not change. If he repeated this psalm, it was because he considered it necessary. Perhaps it was only a preamble.

"I'm here to serve a sentence imposed on me by life, not the law."

I made it clear I was listening attentively.

"I'm still here because of loyalty, I want you to understand this, Josué my friend. I'm still here by my own wish. Because if I were to leave here, I'd kill the person I should love the most."

"Should?" I dared to say.

He said no one obliged him to be here except himself. He said if he left here he would commit an unforgivable act. He spoke as if the penitentiary were his salvation. I believed him. Miguel Aparecido was a sincere man. A caged tiger with sleeves perpetually rolled up, stubbornly kneading his forearms covered with almost blond hair, as if they were the weapons of a solitary warrior afraid to be victorious in battle.

"I tell you this, Josué, so you can understand my dilemma. I'm here because I want to be. I like prison because prison protects me from myself. I like prison because here I have a world I understand and that understands me."

He gave me a capo's smile but didn't frighten me (if that was his intention) because I wasn't a prisoner or subject to any mafia. Because I, ladies and gentlemen, was free—or thought I was.

He only laughed. "Ask any prisoner. Talk to Negro España or Pérfida Albión. Consult with Siboney Peralta. You haven't done that, old friend? They're like a tomb. Don't go to any trouble. But if you talk to them on my behalf, they'll tell you the same thing I'm telling you. In the prison of San Juan de Aragón there's an interior empire and I'm its head. Nothing happens here, boy, that I don't know about, nothing I don't want or can't control. You should know: Even occasional riots are the work of my will alone."

He rubbed his hands over his face. It sounded like sandpaper. He was lying to me.

He said he could smell the air and when it became very heavy, a huge fight was needed to clear the atmosphere. When they're needed, he said, there are serious riots here, a chaos of broken chairs smashing against the walls, dining room tables in smithereens, scratches on metal doors, injured police, some even dead. Violations, abuses, sexual pleasures disguised as punishments, understand? Here we bite locks open.

Why was he lying to me?

"And then the smoke clears. A few ashes remain. But we are at peace again. Peace is necessary in a prison. Many innocents pass through here." He looked at me with a kind of religious passion that disturbed me. "They have to be respected. You've seen the children in the pool. Do you think they should have a life sentence? Well, I'll tell you that if this prison were like almost all the rest, I mean, concentration camps where jailers are the worst criminals, where police traffic in drugs and sex and are guiltier than the worst criminal, then I'd commit suicide, kid, because if there were chaos here it would be because I was powerless to establish the necessary order. Necessary, Josué, just that, no more and no less; the order that's indispensable so the San Juan de Aragón prison isn't heaven or hell, no, but just, and it's a lot, a fucking purgatory."

He was out of breath, which surprised me. In my opinion, Miguel Aparecido was a man of steel. Perhaps because in reality I didn't know who he was. Was he lying to me?

He took me by the shoulders and looked at me as a tiger must look at its dying prey.

"When something happens here that slips out of my hands, it makes me furious."

He repeated it syllable by syllable.

"Fu-ri-ous."

He took a breath and told me that an individual turned up here, and at first Miguel did not attribute the slightest importance to him. Instead he laughed at him a little. He was a mariachi who then became a cop or vice versa, it doesn't matter, but he was a born crook. It seems this mariachi or cop or whatever he was took part in a

neighborhood disturbance a few years ago when the police themselves, charged with maintaining order, created disorder where
there had been none, because the people in the district governed
themselves and dealt with their own crimes without harming anyone. They gave a phenomenal beating to the cop or mariachi when
neighbors and the "guardians of law and order" faced one another
one tragic night when the police were sacrificed by the crowd,
burned, stripped, hung by the feet as a warning: Don't come back to
the neighborhood, we govern ourselves here. Well, it seems the
mariachi or cop or complete ass, his name was Maximiliano Batalla,
pretended to be mute and paralyzed just so his mama, a very clever
but sentimental old woman named Medea Batalla, would take care
of him, feed him, and take him in his wheelchair to pray to the Virgin of the Immaculate Conception.

"Go on, Maxi, sing, don't you see that Our Lady is asking you
to?"

"And Maxi sang," Miguel Aparecido continued. "He sang ran-
cheras so well he deceived his poor mama, passing himself off as
mute and crippled while his comrades-in-arts—mariachis and police and potheads and thugs—visited him, and Maxi organized them
for a series of urban crimes ranging from the innocence of stealing
mail from the United States because workers are sometimes so ignorant they send dollars in a letter, to attacking pregnant women to
rob them at intersections when there's a confusion of streetlights,
traffic police, and racing engines."

The Mariachi's Gang—as it came to be known—invaded commercial centers for the sheer pleasure of sowing panic, without
stealing anything. It permeated the city with an army of beggars
simply to put two things to the test: that nothing happens to a criminal disguised as a beggar but everyone believes beggars are criminals.

"It's a gamble," Miguel Aparecido said very seriously. "A risk," he
added almost as if he were saying a prayer. "The plain truth is that
the Mariachi's Gang alternated its serious crimes with sheer fooling
around, spreading confusion in the city, which was its intention."

Maxi's gang was organized to swindle migrants beyond the simple stealing of dollar bills in letters. They were very perverse. They organized residents of the neighborhoods where the workers came from to stone those who returned, because without them the districts no longer received dollars and in Mexico—I looked at Miguel when Miguel wasn't looking at me—the poor die without dollars from the migrants, the poor produce nothing . . .

"Except workers," I said.

"And grief," Miguel added.

"So then"—I wanted to speed up the story—"what did Maximiliano Batalla do that you couldn't forgive?"

"He killed," Miguel Aparecido said very serenely.

"Whom?"

"Señora Estrella Rosales de Esparza. Errol Esparza's mother. Nazario Esparza's wife."

Then Miguel Aparecido, as if it had no importance, moved on to other subjects or returned to earlier ones. I was stunned. I remembered Doña Estrellita's body laid out in the Pedregal house on the day of the wake. I remembered the sinister Don Nazario and knew him capable of anything. I evoked the new lady of the house and did not know what she was capable of. My truest, most tender memory was of Errol, our old buddy from secondary school, with his head like an egg. I repressed my feelings. I wanted to listen to the prisoner of San Juan de Aragón.

"Do you know what hope means?" he asked.

I said I didn't.

"You're right. Hope brings nothing but sorrow, trouble, and disappointment."

I thought I was going to see him being sentimental for the first time. I shouldn't have had false hopes.

"What would happen if you were to escape?" I dared to ask him.

"Here, chaos. Outside, who knows. Here, people wither. But if I weren't here, the streets would be filled with corpses."

"More? I don't follow."

"Don't look at the moon's ass, prick."

I was a law clerk. I was a young employee in the companies of Max Monroy. I was bold.

"I'd like to free you."

"Freedom is only the desire to be free."

"Free of what, Miguel?" I asked, I confess, with a feeling of growing tenderness toward this man who, without either one of us wanting it, was becoming my friend.

"Of the furies."

The fury of success. The fury of failure. The fury of sex. The fury of resentment. The fury of anger. The fury of love. All this passed through my head.

"Free, free."

With an impulse I would call fraternal, the prisoner and I embraced.

"The Mariachi has left here, free. Nazario Esparza's influence freed him. Maximiliano Batalla is a dangerous criminal. He shouldn't be walking around."

He sneezed.

"You know, Josué? Among the criminals in San Juan de Aragón, there aren't only thieves, there aren't only innocents, or kids who must be saved, or old men who die here or are killed by a violence I sometimes can't control. They fill the pool without letting me know. Some kids drown. My power has limits, boy."

The tiger looked at me.

"There are also killers."

He tried to look down. He couldn't.

"They're killers because they have no other recourse. I mean, if you examine the circumstances, you understand they were obliged to kill. They had no other way out. Crime was their destiny. I accept that. Others kill because they lose the ability to endure. I'm being frank. They put up with a boss, a wife, a crying baby, damn it, listen to me, what I'm telling you is terrifying, I know, laugh, Josué, you tolerate a bitch of a mother-in-law but one day you explode, no more, death urges them on: Kill and death itself appears just behind them. I understand the attraction and horror of crime. I live with crime every day. I don't dare condemn the man who kills because he has no other recourse. There are those who kill because they're hungry, don't forget that . . ."

His pause frightened me. His entire body quivered without weakness. That's what made me afraid.

"But not the gratuitous crime. The crime that doesn't involve you. The crime they pay you for. The crime of Judas. Not that. Absolutely not that."

He looked at me again.

"Maximiliano Batalla came here and I couldn't read his face. His face of a criminal on the payroll of a millionaire coward. I reproach myself for that, kid. I entrust you with it."

"How did you find out?"

"A prisoner came in who knew him. He told me. In the end I control everything. The Mariachi doesn't even control his own dick. He's an asshole. But a dangerous asshole. He has to be done away with."

Then Miguel Aparecido stripped away any shred of tenderness or serenity and presented himself to me as a true exterminating angel, filled with sacred rage, as if he were looking into an abyss where he did not recognize himself, as if obedience were lacking in the cosmos, as if a demon had been born in him who demanded form, only that, the form that would permit him to act.

"The criminal left without my permission."

He looked at me and changed suddenly, became imploring.

"Help me. You and your friends."

I felt exasperated.

"If you left here, you could take revenge yourself, Miguel. I don't know for what. You could take action."

And his final words that day were at once a defeat and a victory.

"I'm a loyal man only if I remain here. Forever."

THE SECRET OF Max Monroy—Asunta gave me a class as she sat backlit in her office aquarium, seated so her super-legs would distract me, her most reliable test—is knowing how to anticipate.

"Just like his mother," I said only to be meddlesome.

"What do you know about that?"

"What everybody knows, don't be so mysterious." I returned her smile. "History exists, you know?"

"Max was ahead of everybody."

Asunta proceeded to give me a class on what I already knew from the mouth of Antigua Concepción. Except that what was spontaneous and lively in Max Monroy's mother was, in the mouth of Asunta, Max Monroy's executive secretary, contrived and dull, as if Asunta were repeating a class for beginners: me.

I decided, however, to be a good pupil for her (I admit it), the most attractive woman I had ever met. Elvira Ríos, the whore with the bee, my current ball-and-chain, Lucha Zapata, paled in comparison with this woman-object, this beautiful thing, attractive, sophisticated, elegant, and supremely desirable, giving me little classes on the businessman's genius. I realized she was repeating a lesson she had memorized. I forgave her because she was good-looking.

What did Max Monroy do? asks an Asunta whose mind, I observe, bursts into flame when she mentions super-boss.

"What has Max Monroy's secret been?"

According to Asunta, there is not just one secret but rather a kind of constellation of truths. He was not the first, she tells me, to put the modern telephone within reach of everyone. He was the first to foresee a possible clogging of lines because of short supply and excess demand, opening the possibility of buy now pay later but on condition you sign up with us, the companies of Max Monroy.

"Why? Not only because Max Monroy offered in one package telephone, computer, Vodafone, O2, the entire package, Josué, but without deceptive contracts or onerous clauses. Max didn't care about hiding costs, he didn't want to exploit or add clauses in illegible print. Everything in big letters, understand? Instead of high prices and high utilities, he proposed low prices and constant utilities with a gesture of freedom, understand? Max Monroy is who he is because he respects the consumer's freedom, that's the difference. When Max asked the consumer to abandon networks established earlier, his offer was freedom. Max told each consumer: Choose your own basic monthly package. I'll give it to you at a fixed price. I'll permit you to use whatever you want from our network, films, telephone, information, whatever you like and the way you like it. Max addressed specific groups offering them a fixed price in exchange for a constellation of services, assuming the operating costs and subsidizing operations when necessary."

Asunta adjusted the navy blue pinstripe jacket that was her uniform, which must have moved her to say that Max Monroy was a great tailor.

I laughed.

She didn't: "A great tailor. Listen carefully. Max Monroy never offered the same communication service to everybody. He promised each client: 'This is for you alone. This is yours. It's your suit.' And he kept his promise. We offer each client individual tailoring."

I think she looked with critical coolness at my classic attire of gray suit and tie. She looked at me as one looks at a mouse. Her eyes requested, without saying anything, "More contrast, Josué, a red or yellow tie, a thinner belt or some striking suspenders, look handsome, Josué, when you take off your jacket to work or make love, don't dress like a bureaucrat at the Ministry of Finance when you come to the office, how do you usually dress at home? Look for a modern mix of elegance and comfort. Go on."

"*Sans façon,*" she said very quietly. "*Charm-casual.*"

"Excuse me?" I said, guessing at the mimetic talent of Asunta Jordán.

"Nothing. Max Monroy invented individual tailoring for each consumer and each consumer felt special and privileged when he used our services."

"Our?" I permitted myself a raised eyebrow.

"We're a big family," she had to say, disappointing me with the cliché and returning me, for an instant, to my old nostalgia for our philosophical talks with Father Filopáter.

"Other companies put on pressure. Competition is intense. Until now we've beaten the others because all our activity is always directed to as many sectors as we can manage, as many consumers as we can imagine. Our strategy is multisegmentary. Growth with utility. Just imagine. What do you think?"

Asunta's discourse kept fading until it turned into a distant echo. She continued speaking about Monroy, his enterprises, our companies. I became more and more lost in contemplation of her. Words were lost. Life as well. I don't know why at that moment, before this woman, for the first time, I had the sensation that until then childhood, adolescence, and young adulthood were like a long, slow river flowing with absolute certainty to the sea.

Now, looking at her as I embarked on this new occupation dictated by the lawyer Sanginés—and I didn't know then whether to thank or reproach him for his attentions and painstaking care toward me and Jericó—I felt that, far from rowing peacefully to the sea, I was moving upstream, against nature, in a cascade of short, abrupt movements, violating the laws that had so far ruled my existence in order to escape into a vital—or was it fatal?—velocity that moved backward but in reality flowed toward an unfortunate tomorrow, toward a growing brevity that, as it approached its origin physically and violently, was, in reality, announcing to me the brevity of my days as of today. We all come to know this. I learned it now.

Was Asunta the person who would, when she touched me, at least give sense and tranquillity to the "great event," Henry James's "important" thing: death? I don't know why I thought these things as I sat across from Asunta this morning in an office in Santa Fe. Did the feeling of fatality authorize another, apparently opposite one, the desire I began to feel in front of her?

Had my conversation with Miguel Aparecido the night before been prolonged into this morning of leaden sun? Against my will my mood darkened because of the mission the prisoner had charged me with: avenging the mother of our buddy Bald Errol Esparza.

I was silent. One does not speak of these things here, under pain of being irrelevant to Max Monroy's great entrepreneurial machine, because if I intuited anything with certainty it was that the entrepreneurial world into which Licenciado Sanginés had thrust me, taking me out of a childish, studentish, irksome, brothel-going, crepuscular semiseclusion in a middle class that had abandoned its values to let itself be carried along by the current—I was thinking of

Lucha—this "new world" excluded everything that was not self-referential: the enterprise as origin and purpose of all things.

And Antigua Concepción? I asked myself then. Was she a mad-woman or a super-magnate? Or both?

Asunta, as I have said, was sitting so I could not avoid an occasional, discreet glance at her legs. I began to believe it was on the basis of those extremely beautiful, long, depilated extremities, encased in flesh-colored stockings, silky to mortal eyes, that my feeling of passion was born.

I say passion. Not affection, or love, or gratitude, or responsibility, but passion, the freest, least bound of obligations, the most gratuitous. A feeling that flowed from Asunta's legs to my falsely distracted, deceptively discreet gaze . . .

The world is transformed by desire. While she continued to enumerate the companies of Max Monroy for which I would begin to work starting now, all the times of my life—past, present, future, along with the prestigious names of the emotion: memory and desire, recollection and premonition—engaged with one another now and in the person of this woman.

I thought that life goes by rapidly. I never had thought that before. Now I did, and associated fugacity with fear and fear with attraction. Never, I admitted, had a female attracted me as much as Asunta Jordán did at that moment. And the dangerous thing was that passion and the woman who provoked it were, without my permission, beginning to transform my own desire, which in some way was no longer mine but was not yet—would it ever be?—hers.

From now on—I already knew it—my entire future would reside in that question. Asunta was turning me, without wanting to, into an inflamed man. Careful, careful! I told myself, to no avail. I felt conquered by the attraction of this woman and at the same time, without wanting to, without realizing it, I knew my life with the helpless Lucha Zapata was coming to an end.

The attraction of Asunta Jordán was inexplicable. It was instantaneous. Mea culpa? Because while she seemed desirable to me, she also seemed tiresome.

———

WAS LUCHA ZAPATA a fortune-teller? I didn't say anything to her when I returned that night to Cerrada de Chimalpopoca. I found her dressed as an aviator again. I noticed her resemblance to the celebrated Amelia Earhart, the valiant Gringa lost forever in a flight without a compass over the South Pacific. I hadn't realized it. They were alike in something. Amelia Earhart was freckled and smiling, like those North American fields of wheat that laugh at the sun. She wore her hair very short, I suppose in order to fly better and set the aviator's helmet firmly on her head. She wore pants and a leather jacket.

Just like Lucha Zapata now.

"Take me to the airport."

I hailed a taxi and we both got in.

I let her talk.

"Don't ask me anything."

"No."

"Remember what I told you one day. In this society you're in perpetual debt. Whatever you do, you always end up losing. Society makes certain you feel guilty."

I didn't say what I was thinking. I didn't correct her or indicate that in my opinion people were what they did, not what they were obliged to do. She was who she was, I thought at that moment, through her own will, not because a cruel, perverse, villainous society had determined it.

"What will you choose, Savior?" she asked suddenly, as if to exorcise the implacable ugliness of the city crumbling along the length of its cement escarpments.

"It depends. Between what and what?"

"Between the immediate and what you leave for another day."

"I don't understand."

"Don't look outside. Look at me."

I looked at her.

"What do you see?"

I felt an unexpected desire to cry. I controlled myself.

"I see a woman who wants to fly again."

She squeezed my arm.

"Thank you, Savior. Do you know what I'm going to do?"

"No."

"I'm free and I can choose. A ranchera singer? A poet?"

"You decide."

"Do you know I've been invited to be on a reality show?"

"No. What's that?"

"You have to show the most humiliating aspect of your character. You ask to eat on your knees. You fall down drunk."

El Salto de Agua. Los Arcos de Belén. José María Izazaga. Ancient domes. Modern ruins. Nezahualcóyotl. La Candelaria.

"You pretend," Lucha Zapata continued. "Don't pretend. It's like living in a Nazi concentration camp. That's television. An Auschwitz for masochists. You deprive yourself. You animalize yourself. You eat rancid food. Your towels are smeared with shit. Your clothes are infested with bugs. They don't let you sleep. Ambulance sirens sound day and night."

She shouted: "They turn night into day!"

The driver didn't stop driving but turned to look at me.

"What's wrong? Is the señora all right?"

"It's nothing. She's just sad."

"Ah," the driver said with a sigh. "She's going on a trip."

He whistled some of "Beautiful, adored Mexico, I die far from you."

I calmed her. I caressed her.

"You know? In the United States they call women a 'number.' What's my number, do you think?"

"I don't know, Lucha."

It seemed useless to talk. She, dressed as an aviator, looked very tired, very disillusioned, like Dorothy Malone in 1950s films.

"I don't know how to reason anymore."

"Easy, Lucha, take it easy."

From Calzada Ignacio Zaragoza we drove onto the long avenue that leads to the airport.

"I don't want to end up a fly in a bar."

"A what?"

"A barfly, Savior," she said in English.

The driver whistled, "Let them say I'm sleeping and have them bring me here . . ."

We arrived. The lines of taxis and private cars made me think that heaven was far too small for so many passengers.

I helped her out.

She adjusted her helmet and goggles.

"Where shall I take you?"

"With women you never know." She smiled.

"Shall I wait for you to come back?" I said as if I hadn't heard her.

"Aviation teaches you to be fatalistic," she concluded, and began walking away alone, hugging herself, and she staggered a little. I moved forward to help her. She turned to look at me with a negative gesture and moved her fingers tenderly, saying goodbye.

She became lost in the crowd at the airport.

And once again, as in one of those dreams that recur and dissolve into oblivion only to be sketched out in the second repetition, my eyes met those of a woman walking behind a young porter whose movements were gallant, as if transporting luggage inside the airport were the ultimate glamorous theatrical act. This woman, modern, young, swift, elegant, with the movements of a panther, an animal of prey, worriedly followed the porter.

I looked at her just as before. Except this time I recognized her.

It was the new Señora Esparza. La Sarape. The hostess at the wake of Nazario Esparza's first wife. The successor to the mother of our old buddy Errol. But now, when I saw her again, I knew something thanks to the prisoner in San Juan de Aragón, Miguel Aparecido.

The woman was a killer.

It's possible I vacillated for an instant. It's possible that when I "vacillated" I lingered too long on the word that among Mexicans acquires the meaning of rowdiness, anarchy, mockery, disorder: *vacile* (fun), *vacilador* (carouser), *vacilón* (spree), a verbal avenue that leads directly to the plaza of "dissipation" and its side streets "dissolute" and "disorderly," which reduce the world to chaos, ridicule, and senselessness, leaving behind another paraphrase, "hazard," whose straight meaning is chance or risk but in recurrent Mexican speech is a play on words with double and triple meanings, don't fuck with my asshole, then don't be a freeloader, then don't jerk off so much, will you pass me the pan? pancho's fucking tonight, don't fuck around, no ticket no fucking, no fucking way, and fuck you very much, ay Sebastián! done, which tests street ingenuity because in the salons it is dangerous and can lead to violent quarrels, duels, and assassinations.

"Do you see that woman going into the bar? Well, in the old days she couldn't get enough of my dick."

"Listen, that's my wife."

"Ay, how she's grown . . ."

I've said all this so survivors can understand why I wasted precious minutes after seeing Nazario Esparza's second wife following a porter, knowing she had killed Errol's mother according to the more than reliable version of Miguel Aparecido in the San Juan de Aragón pen and being immediately obliged to stop her by force, drive out any fear the porter would defend his customer (why did something so improbable occur to me?), confront her, if not with facts then with my sheer physical strength (would it be superior to hers?), and take her to the security office in the airport, denounce her, bring justice to my pal Bald Errol and his dear deceased mama, all this crossed my mind at the same time that a mariachi band interposed itself between my vacillation and my haste, six characters dressed as charros, striped trousers and black jacket, silver buttons and six roof-size hats embroidered in waves of gold, hiding faces I didn't have the slightest desire to see, perhaps fearing I'd recognize the famous Maximiliano Batalla escaped or freed unjustly from the previously mentioned prison and the presumptive killer of the similarly cited Doña Estrella de Esparza . . .

The criminal Sara P. disappeared among the mariachis who advanced (as if their outfits and hats were not enough) with the resonant outrage of their instruments, far from their historical origins as wedding bands, *musique pour le mariage* of the occupation troops of the French, Austro-Hungarian, Czech, Belgian, Moravian, Lombard, and Triestine Empire who contracted matrimony with pretty Mexican girls to the sound of the marriage-mariachi and now were passing by, interfering with the justice of my desire to apprehend the presumed or proven criminal, made impossible by the stanzas bellowed out by the musical advance of the band as it sang:

Out walked the torero in
his canary and silver suit,
handsome, anointed, valiant
flaunting his great good looks

to welcome the slim man, smiling though melancholy, with a fresh scar on his cheek, his hair plastered with gum tragacanth, lifted high by the mob of admirers who carried him shouting "torero, torero" while the above-mentioned bullfighter seemed to doubt his own fame, scattering it with an airy wave of his hand as if he were prepared to die the next time, as if he were laughing sadly at the glory given him by the aficionados who carried him and the mariachis who now attempted to play an out-of-tune pasodoble while the bullfighter reluctantly waved and rather than celebrating a victory seemed to be bidding farewell to the world at the opportune time to the uncomprehending astonishment of the flocks of tourists, Gringo, Canadian, German, Scandinavian? tanned, immune to climate changes, who formed into groups of young people and old people who wanted to be young, in beach sandals, T-shirts with the names of hotels, clubs, places of origin, colleges, first, second, third, and no ages confused in the forced gaiety of having enjoyed vacations, coming from a country, the USA, miserly in granting them, fatiguing its workers with the challenge of crossing an interminable continent that extends from sea to shining sea, while the Europeans formed a line as if they were receiving a well-deserved prize and a summer consolation won, without their knowing it, by the French government of the Popular Front and Léon Blum (who was Léon Blum?) in 1936, when paid vacations were first granted.

I made my way through mariachis, tourists, fans and the torero, in an intuitive search for an oasis of peace, since the object of my persecution had disappeared forever in the cloud of rank food and tepid drinks emanating from the transient dining rooms like foul air that had never seen the sun: The immense tunnel of an airport identical to all the other airports on earth exuded sweat, grease, flatulence, evacuations from the strategically placed WCs, but everything made sanitary thanks to large, intermittent gusts of man- ufactured air with subtle fragrances of mint, camomile, and violet to receive and support the next stampede of schoolgirls going on a col- lective vacation, not yet identified by their diminutive bikinis but still by their navy blue jumpers, flat shoes, heavy stockings, straw hats with a ribbon, the emblem of the school recorded on their cardigans. They smelled of sweet childish perspiration, of mouths irrigated by bean soup, of teeth tempered by Adams gum. They made an infernal racket because of the clear obligation to show their joy at the prospect of a European vacation, for all their faces said "Paris" and none said "Cacahuamilpa."

This wave was followed by one of boys in soccer shirts who sang at the top of their lungs incomprehensible slogans, partisan codas older than they were, sicketybooms, bimbombams, rahrahrahs, re- minding me of secondary school, the start of my life of connection to Father Filopáter, Bald Errol Esparza, and my soul brother Jericó with no last name: The tumult of young people brought me closer to the past but I was established in the most present of present times when a group of boys grabbed me from behind, stripped off my jacket, and put me in one of the red shirts of the team, school, sect, league, union, alliance, federation, band, clan, tribe, order, brother- hood, guild, club, squad, firm, division, branch, chapter, and com- mon market of the strongest and fastest of nations: Club Youth, which is a kick in the ass and a delirium of the soul, believing you are immortal and knowing you are a badass, in possession of every- thing and owner of nothing, irrelevance of the passing, celebration of the moment, seminal potency, lost opportunities, rivers in the sand, ocean of the future, sirens that weep: I saw them and I saw myself, all the days of a youth that was dying, harassed, came back to me surrounded by a mariachi band, a melancholy torero, some young girls on vacation, some adolescents in soccer shirts, and a lost woman whose residence, however, I knew. It was enough to go to the house on Pedregal with an arrest warrant arranged by the lawyer Sanginés to have the shameless Nazario Esparza and his consecrated concubine shit volcanic rock.

On the other hand, I was captive to the huge crowds coming in and going out of an airport with only two runways for twenty million locals and who knows how many foreigners. I stopped counting. The useless anarchy defeated me. The secret tremor of self-destruction. The chaos that appeared with no exit, drowning me in its mere existence.

I wanted to urinate.

I went into the strategic bathroom, asking myself How did I get here?

I produced my usual kidney beer.

I washed my hands.

I looked in the mirror.

Was it me?

Behind me, someone was sitting on the toilet.

He hadn't closed the door.

His trousers eddied around his ankles.

His shirt covered his noble parts.

I looked at his face reflected in the mirror.

He looked at me with great melancholy.

It was the face of a sad clown.

He looked at me asking me without speaking: How do we respond to a senseless world?

It was the voice of a sick clown.

An undulating light fell on his head.

I felt ill.

I wanted to throw up.

I made a mistake.

I opened the door of a closet instead of the door to a stall.

I was stunned.

In the closet, a dark, good-looking young man, his pants around his ankles as if he were going to take a shit, was fucking a woman with her skirt bunched around her waist and her panties entangled in the high heels of her shoes.

She looked at me with a strange start, as if she were expecting to be caught and liked the idea of a third person seeing her fornicate.

She was a modern woman, young, with the attitude of an animal of prey, but she no longer had the elegance I had once attributed to her.

I looked at her buttock. She had a bee tattooed on it.

I took off the soccer club's red shirt.

WHEN WE ENTERED the house on Pedregal de San Angel together—Errol, Jericó, and I—we didn't know what awaited us.

Sara was detained there. I had the advantage over Jericó of having seen the bee on her buttock. I said nothing to him because at that moment there was a certain tension between us. And besides, "circumstances" push us to keep some secrets without really distrusting each other. I abandoned the house on Cerrada de Chimalpopoca, uninhabitable without the life I had shared with Lucha Zapata. I took the liberty of going and leaving the door open, as if chance would be the next inhabitant of the modest little house of the woman who had filled me with so much passion. Passion becomes diseased if it counts only on an empty house for commemoration, as if past love were a phantom. I decided that the intensity of my relationship with Lucha required a final act that would not be like a stage curtain. She had left. I was going. The house would remain open, as if summoning a new couple. As if the destiny of our "nest" was to call to future birds.

I don't know. Only when she left did I realize how much I needed her, how much I loved her. There was a certain cynical disloyalty in this feeling, since, with admitted ingenuousness, I had already decided to fall in love with the svelte, elegant Asunta Jordán. What I couldn't foresee is that the trio of women who concerned me would eventually join another ghost from a past in some sense remote, for between the ages of eighteen and twenty-five a galaxy intervenes.

"Operation Sara"—for it was an entire operation—implied deciding first between returning to the prison to speak with Miguel Aparecido so he could enlighten me, or consulting with the lawyer Sanginés so he could orient me, or looking for Errol in some cabaret in the center of the city, or consulting with Jericó since in our erotic life we had shared the whore with the bee on her buttock.

This last proposition was the most difficult. I've already recounted how my life with Lucha Zapata had moved me away from Jericó and the apartment on Calle de Praga. The situation seemed to suit both of us on the basis of this premise: Jericó didn't ask me about my constant absences and I didn't inquire into his activities when he returned to Mexico. Except now my absences had become presences. Without the house on the Cerrada (without Lucha), I returned to my normal life (in the apartment on Praga). Except now I was living again with a Jericó who had taken advantage of my absence to envelop his presence in a mystery that daily life threatened to dispel.

To the preceding I should add that I multiplied my activities as an employee of Max Monroy's company in Santa Fe and as a law clerk obliged to write a thesis on Machiavelli, while Jericó had entered the presidential residence of Los Pinos, where the president himself, in an act that could appear to me as unusual or irrelevant, had given my friend—he told me about it without moving a muscle in his face—the responsibility of organizing something like festivals, commemorations, and national entertainments for a "depoliticized" youth. Was it important? Was it trivial? As Jericó didn't ask about my activities, I didn't look into his. The fact is that the arrest of Nazario Esparza's second wife obliged us to locate our old comrade the formerly bald Errol who, according to the presumptive criminal, played drums in a dive in the oldest section of the city.

His having told me that he had gone into the president's office and received the assignment placed me in a circumstance of disloyalty. Jericó trusted me. And what was I going to tell him? My relationship with Lucha was mine alone, it was something almost sacred, it couldn't be talked about by me or pawed over by other people, not even my fraternal friend Jericó. Was I betraying him with my secret? Should I open up to him? Was I inviting him to betray me as well? In fact, Jericó had told me he was collaborating at Los Pinos, something I already knew because Sanginés had told us so, and he already knew I was working for Max Monroy. Jericó didn't know about Lucha Zapata. Now he didn't know about Asunta Jordán. I had two advantages over him in the persons of two women. Was I the disloyal partner in our old friendship? Or was he not telling me more than I knew about or more than I was hiding from him?

With this kind of suspicion I realized, thanks to small signs (attitudes, greetings, goodbyes, calculations that raised their heads then disappeared like small snakes in our shared domestic life), that our friendship was being muddied and I sincerely lamented it: Jericó was half of my life and his companionship was a way of expunging myself from my own past . . .

The incident in the airport and my decision to report the woman and the porter fornicating so happily in the men's bathroom in reality created the opportunity for me to reconcile with Jericó and avoid a break, and for the two of us together to reinitiate a search that meant, in the long run, reknotting a lasso, tying up a thread before it broke, and coming together at the point where we had left the story: the burial of Señora Esparza and Errol's truncated destiny.

"Where is Nazario Esparza?" was Don Antonio Sanginés's first and logical question when we told him about a case whose precedents he knew better than we did and possibly its consequences as well.

Although he didn't answer his own question, he did supply us with some antecedents. Sanginés had handled several matters for Esparza, especially the testamentary situation caused by the demise of Doña Estrellita, who had brought her own fortune to a marriage with a division of property and an inheritance provision between the surviving spouses, while the matrimonial contract with Señorita Sara Pérez Ubico provided for community property, that is, upon Don Nazario's death, his second wife would come into possession of two fortunes: her husband's and Doña Estrellita's.

"Don Nazario should take good care of himself," Sanginés said with a sigh, interlacing his fingers in front of his chin.

"The Mariachi Batalla is a killer," Miguel Aparecido told me in prison. "I don't know who put him in here and why I wasn't able to stop him."

He too carried his hands to his lips and from there to his nose.

"I can almost always smell out guys like that because of my network of informants, and then I can have them thrown out of here. I don't know how this one got away from me. Something didn't work right." Miguel Aparecido frowned. "What? Who? How?"

"Thrown out?" I remarked as if I suspected an impulse natural in the person I was studying for my thesis on Machiavelli.

"You understand me," Miguel Aparecido said with a sinister subtext. "The fact is that when he's free, Maximiliano Batalla can commit any excess. I already told you about his antecedents."

"What makes you think he acted in concert with Sara P.?"

"Who's the porter she was fucking?"

Who was the porter?

This was the least of the mysteries. It took Sanginés no time to learn that the false porter in the airport was Maximiliano Batalla: an opportune disguise that my discovery linked to Don Nazario Esparza's dishonest wife, implicated for that reason in Maxi's crimes.

Like a Pandora's box, the sum of events opened to reveal one mystery after another. Who had gotten Maximiliano Batalla out of prison? What, besides sex, joined Nazario's wife to the Mariachi Batalla? Were they accomplices? If so, in what, and why, and to what end?

These were the hypotheses spread before me by the legalistic mind of Antonio Sanginés, pursuing in an unexpected way my juridical education, overly practical until then, which implied, first of all, recovering our friend Errol Esparza and arriving together, as I announced at the beginning of this chapter, at his family's house in Pedregal de San Angel.

IN THE MEANTIME, based on the presumption of importance that is also a part of being young and of a certain natural impatience to know more, I suggested to my apparent boss and secret love, Asunta Jordán, that she talk to me about the great man himself, Max Monroy, without ever revealing—this was tacit proof of my discretion and the growing conviction that some things should not be known— that I had spoken to the tycoon's mother in the cemetery where the sainted señora lay buried.

"I understood about his businesses," I said to her one morning. "You don't need to expand on that. You can stop now."

She laughed. "You have no idea how Max Monroy expands."

"Tell me."

"From the beginning?"

"Why not?"

I knew Asunta was going to tell me what I already knew, boring me to death. But what is love for a woman but an obsession independent of the foolishness she may repeat like a broken record? I was resigned.

Asunta told me in English that Max Monroy was not a "self-made man" (I reflected on the fact that one does not talk about modern business without introducing Anglo-Saxonisms) but the heir to one volatile fortune and another durable one. His father, the general, had "carranzaed," as it was called in the time of official corruption in the era of revolutionary combat under the command of the chief executive Venustiano Carranza: He had stolen. But that was like stealing chickens in a henhouse without touching the rooster or disputing his control. A little ranch here, a little house there, a tame flock here, a rough herd there, since things were easy to obtain and just as easy to lose. On the other hand, Max's mother had a crystal ball and was always ahead of events. Always a step or two ahead of the law and the government, she was on good terms with the second and consolidated the first: communications, real estate, industries, banks, credit, construction companies, until she exhausted the possibilities of the small Mexican industrial revolution and the concomitant role of intermediary to invent companies out of nothing, receiving funds by using different names, and avoiding final solutions. Max Monroy's career has been an example of fluidity, Asunta added. He doesn't marry anything forever. He observes what's coming down the pike. He's ahead of everybody. He excludes no one. He's not a monopolist. On the contrary, he believes monopoly is the disease that kills capitalist development. This, says Max, is what beginning capitalists don't understand: They think they've invented hot water though they're often second generation and their parents are the ones who boiled it.

"Take a look at the list of Max Monroy's businesses, Josué. You'll see he hasn't monopolized anything. But he has moved everything forward."

He believes final solutions are almost always bad. They only postpone and deceive. On the other hand, partial solutions are much better. Among other reasons, because they don't pretend to be final.

"Didn't he ever take sides?"

"No. He told me: 'Asunta, life isn't a matter of sides or chronology. It's a question of knowing what forces are at play at any given moment. Good or bad. Knowing how to resist them, accept them, channel them.'

" 'Channel them, Max?'

" 'As a conclusion it's desirable. But no matter how much will and foresight you bring to an issue, dear lady, chance always plays a hand. Being prepared for the unexpected, welcoming fortune—good or bad—and inviting her to dinner, like Don Juan with the Comendador, that—'

" 'Don Juan went to hell, Max.'

" 'Who's to say he didn't arrive in hell and transform it to his image and likeness?'

" 'Perhaps he already was living his own hell in the world.'

" 'It's possible. People live, or invent, their heavens and hells on earth.' "

" 'Thy Heaven Doors are my Hell Gates,' wrote William Blake," I recited, and added, pretentiously: "It's poetry."

I winked at Asunta and immediately regretted it. She looked at me gravely. How did you fight this bull? Because she was a bull, not a cow. Or was she a clever ram that is a ewe?

"I don't believe Max Monroy reads poetry. But he knows very

well the gates of heaven and the walls of hell in the world of business."

I let Asunta know I was prepared to learn.

" 'The position of the stars is relative,' Max always tells me, and I think that's why he's never said 'Do this,' but only 'It would be better if . . . ' "

"Then you don't feel inferior or subject to him, like a simple employee of Max Monroy?"

If Asunta was offended by my words, she didn't show it. If she intended to be offended, she smiled back at me.

"I owe everything to Max Monroy."

She looked at me in a forbidding manner. I mean: Her eyes told me Go no further. Stop there. Still, I detected something in them that asked me to postpone, only postpone, the matter. She moved her body in a way that let me know her spirit's willingness to answer my questions, she was asking only for time, time for us to know each other better, to become more intimate . . . That's what I wanted to believe.

I mean: That's what I read in her posture, in her way of moving, turning away from me, looking at me out of the corner of her eye, sketching a sad smile that would give promise and grace to a bygone, serious tale.

"The interesting thing about Max Monroy is that even though he could have established himself at the top from the very beginning, he preferred to go step by step, almost like an apprentice to the guild of finance. He knew the danger facing him was to sit at a table prepared ahead of time, when the butler named Destiny orders: Eat."

Did Asunta smile?

"Instead, he went out to hunt the stag, butchered it himself, took out the innards, cooked the meat, served it, ate it, and placed the horns over the fireplace in the dining room. As if none of it really mattered."

Asunta said this with a kind of administrative sincerity that irritated me a good deal. As if her admiration for another man, even though he was her boss and she "owed him everything," took away from me the position, perhaps a small one, that I wanted to obtain.

"Doesn't Max Monroy ever make mistakes?" I asked, very stupidly.

"I'll tell you. I'll tell you the truth. It isn't that he makes or doesn't make mistakes. Max Monroy knows how to escape the demands of the moment and see farther than other people."

"He's perfect," I remarked, marinating my own attraction to Asunta in more and more stupidities.

She didn't take offense. She didn't even doubt my intentions, irritating me even further. Did this woman consider me incapable of an insult?

"He escapes the exigencies of the moment. He moves forward. You understand that, don't you?" she asked, and I realized that with her question she was telling me she knew what I was attempting and, incidentally, didn't care. Max Monroy anticipates.

Asunta looked at me seriously.

"He moves ahead of the times."

"And what happens if you change over time?"

"You're defeated, Josué. Time defeats you."

" 'Think, Asunta, of the speed of things. Just in my lifetime Mexico has moved from being an agricultural country to an industrialized one. Once the cycles were very slow. A cycle of centuries (Max likes alliterations, Josué) for the agricultural country. A dozen decades for the industrialized one. And now, Asunta, now . . .' "

An exceptional gesture: Max Monroy slams his fist into the open palm of his other hand.

" 'And now, Asunta, a time of speed, a global race without borders, without flags, without nations, to the world of technology and information. China, Japan, even India, even Russia . . .'—he didn't mention the United States, it would have been redundant—'The global world is a techno-informational world, and whoever doesn't get on the train in time will have to walk barefoot and arrive at his destination late.' "

"Or not travel," I commented.

"Or at least buy a pair of huaraches," she said with a smile.

" 'Asunta, there are things I don't say but that you know. Understand them and we'll get along very well. Let's work together. In Mexico, in all of Latin America, we mistake rhetoric for reality. Progress, democracy, justice. It's enough for us to say them to believe they're true. That's why we go from failure to failure. We indicate a goal for Mexico, Brazil, Argentina . . . We convince ourselves that with words, favorable laws, the ribbon cut, and immediate forgetfulness we've achieved what we said we wanted . . . We say words that mock reality. In the end, reality mocks our words.' "

"Max Monroy wins out over reality?"

"No, he anticipates reality. He admits no pretexts."

"Only texts," I stated clearly.

"What he doesn't admit is the madness of the simulations our governments and some entrepreneurs are so fond of."

Asunta was telling me that Max Monroy was everything Max Monroy distanced himself from, and what he distanced himself from was the illusion and daily practice of Latin American politics.

"He moves ahead of his times," the woman I desired said with irritating admiration.

"His times never defeat him?"

"How?" she said with feigned surprise. "Just watch my lips. Let's see, with what? Please, just tell me that."

With old age, I said, with death, I said, with rage, more magnetized by the desire to love Asunta than by the respect I owed Antigua Concepción, my radical interlocutor, that is, the root of my possible wisdom, my fortune, my destiny.

And in your mind, boy, do you think you can visit my grave with impunity?

"No, Señora, I don't think that, forgive me."

Then respect my son and don't rush things, asshole.

Was I the secret emissary of Antigua Concepción in the world her son Max inherited and strengthened? I asked myself about my part in this soap opera, and what disturbed me most was my carnal desire for a woman who bored me: Asunta Jordán.

———

I'M GOING TO let Sara Pérez speak, Sara P., Nazario Esparza's second wife. I confess her vocabulary offends me, though less than the facts the words ostentatiously display. Ostentatious: Sara P. takes pride in her virtues: The ones that stand out are vulgarity, cynicism, ignorance, perhaps black humor, possibly a hidden desire for seduction, I don't know . . .

First of all, I'll correct my previous affirmation. Jericó begged off accompanying us to the Esparzas' house. "I don't have time" was the message he sent to Sanginés and me. "The president's office is very demanding. Besides, I don't know what I can contribute . . . Sorry."

We couldn't find Errol. Sanginés sent a real expeditionary force to all the old nightclubs in the city and to the new ones in outlying neighborhoods, the tony ones and the dives: Our friend couldn't be found anywhere, he had vanished, the city was very large, the country larger still, the borders porous. Errol could have been in any city in the United States or Guatemala. You'd have to be a new Cabeza de Vaca to go out and find him. And in our century there was no El Dorado as there had been in the sixteenth, except for the name of some casino in Las Vegas.

In short: Only Sanginés and I showed up, escorted by the police and the court secretaries to hear Sara Pérez de Esparza's statement. She was seated on a kind of throne placed in the center of the reception room that I remembered in another time, presided over by the timid chastity of Esparza's first wife, Errol's mother, and now by the female I could not help associating, in retrospect, with an act of coarse sexuality in the closet of a men's room in the Benito Juárez International Airport; with a hurried walk, preceded by a porter and dressed like Judith on her way to Bethulia, "for a chat," along the immense, crowded corridors of that airport; with a sorrowful day in memory of her predecessor Doña Estrellita; with another walk through the airport on the day I ran into Lucha Zapata for the first time; and finally, with the night on which Jericó and I fucked this same woman in La Hetara's brothel.

But back then she wore a veil and I could identify her only by the bee tattooed on her buttock, which I saw again during the absurd scene in the airport bathroom.

Now, Sara Pérez de Esparza was seated on her semi-Gothic and pseudo-Versaillesque throne, appropriate to her strange mixture of omnivorous tastes, for I was beginning to think everything could be found in this woman, the worst and the best, the most vulgar and the most refined, the most desirable and the most repugnant, without passing through any nuance of common sense. Seated on her throne, scratching at her forearms with silvered nails as long as scimitars, dressed like a star in *La Dolce Vita* in 1960s palazzo pajamas, black and gold with dolphins swimming between her bosom and her back, between her knee and her coccyx: the strangely out-of-fashion outfit with a loose shirt to generously display her breasts, and wide sailor's pants. Barefoot, though she had rings on four toes of each foot, a brilliant little jewel encrusted in each small toe, and several slave bands around her ankles, matching the entire metallic orchestra sounding at her wrists and competing with the sepulchral silence of her heavy rings and everything contrasting with the bareness of her neck, as if Sara wanted nothing to distract from the attention due her décolletage, the pride she took in her tits, boobs, melons, jugs, knockers, who knows what she herself called those enormous, immobile tubercles that peeked out, fixed like a double gravestone where lay buried the natural sensuality of this artificial being, similar to a mechanical doll that had to be wound up each morning with a gold key: Sara P. had, mounted on top of her corporeal extravaganza, a relatively small head made larger by the curls of blond hair that ascended like mountain ranges to a smooth forehead, lifted for its crown of black pearls, giving the terrifying impression that the jewels were eating her hair, all of it to sanctify a rigid, tightened face, beautiful in a vulgar, obvious way, like a farewell sunset in the movies, like a garage calendar, like the picture of a soldier, a cabdriver, a mechanic, or a teenage anarchist.

The firm gaze fixed, the full mouth like a paralyzed cherry. The uncontrollable nose nervous. Ears buried by the heavy weight of tricolored earrings: strange, obvious, unpleasant pendants in the colors of the national flag. For the first time I saw her up close, in detail.

She was a camouflaged woman. Smells. Wrinkles. Laughter. Everything was controlled, rigid, remade as if by enchantment.

She spoke, and from the beginning I sensed her words were at once the first and final ones of her life. Both a baptismal and sepulchral discourse.

Doña Hetara, the madam of the bordello on Durango, ministered to the tastes of her clients and the fortunes of her girls. She wasn't one of those brothel owners who simply run a business with whores. Much abused, Doña Hetara. Lots of bluster. Nothing of the fool about her. She would always say: Di-ver-si-fy. And so she managed not only a whorehouse but a nuns' school where Doña Hetara, who was very charitable, sent the old hookers to dress as religious and pretend to educate the young hookers who were looking for husbands. Because basically there is no whore who does not aspire to matrimony. It infuriates them that men don't call them "women" but "broads." Being a "broad" is being a whore, trash, tamale wrapper, *mole* pot. Being a "woman" is being a girlfriend who can become a wife and mother.

After a period of time to toughen her up in the brothel on Calle de Durango, Sara was sent to the aforementioned nuns' school to be refined, and there Don Nazario Esparza met her, for he was always on the lookout for new sensations and fresh meat for his "insatiable appetite" or, in other words, what good were all the furniture stores, hotels, movie houses, and commercial centers, what good were beds if he couldn't use them to have fun with a good *"broad"*?

"Don't trouble yourself, Don Nazario. Search no further, I'll take care of everything. Don't torture yourself. Take it slow. Buy into the idea that you're still a great lover. You're in great shape, that's the truth. A real cocksman."

And so the millionaire was seduced by the convent girl Sarita, who lived in a monastery where her parents had abandoned her.

"They abandoned her, Señora?"

"Let's say they made a present of her."

"Haven't they seen her again?"

"Don't worry, Don Nazario. We demanded a tidy sum for accepting the present and didn't let them see her again. Sarita is all alone. She'll have only you, Señor."

According to what he himself said and his son Errol told us.

You and a motley band of mariachis, thieves, bums, crazies, drug addicts, pimps, bongo players, and all those she hadn't met but imagined, for more men passed through her head than there were in an army, those who had fucked her and those who would have fucked her if they had known the tricks lodged in the well-disposed body of Sara P. Like a beautiful butterfly that could turn into a caterpillar of pleasure, imitate to perfection the manners of the upper class, and engage in all the wicked lower-class vices. I saw her as a funereal hostess on the day of Doña Estrellita's obsequies, she was refined but sham refined, something was out of place in her gestures, her dress, above all in the way she gave orders and treated the servants, the arrogant contempt, the lack of courtesy, the essential bad upbringing of Sara P. exposed with a disdain that assimilated her into what the stupid woman believed she despised.

Of course Sara came to the mansion on Pedregal with her virginity intact, and Don Nazario enjoyed the privilege of deflowering her. She was a Scotch tape virgin, astutely fabricated by the false nuns of the dissolute convent, who restored maidenheads as easily as they cooked *mole*. How could Don Nazario know? He hadn't fornicated with a virgin in his whole damn life except for the chaste but narrow Señora Estrellita, who had a psychic padlock between her legs, and since Sarita gave him that unheard-of pleasure, from then on he became a slave to his wife the false nun. Nazario, who was a Roman emperor accustomed to tossing coins into the crowd. Nazario, who demanded to be the center of attention. Nazario of the choleric temperament and blind rage. Transformed into a poodle, a lapdog, a plaything of the whorish, sensual, voracious, impassive Sarita: the pontiff vanquished by the unaccustomed lechery of the false priestess who gradually bared her soul, provoked lust, vomited filthy words, demanded animal positions, *Make me the lioness, Nazario, make me what all men like, tiger, not just you, enjoy my cunt, I want to enjoy it, I want everybody to enjoy it, the mariachi, the porter, the cabdriver, the potter: Shape me, Nazario, like I was your flowerpot.*

Did this repel Don Nazario? Did he care when she said she was giving him what everybody liked, not just her husband? She laughed at him, telling him about sexual experiences that she said were only imaginary and now she was demanding them of the increasingly dazed, distracted old man, bewildered by so much excitement, so much novelty, not realizing that she, even in their closest intimacy, saw him from a distance, scornfully, as if she were reading him, as if he were the day before yesterday's newspaper or an advertisement on the Periférico. But she didn't realize she wasn't humiliating him. She merely excited him more and more, fired his imagination. Esparza saw Sara in every conceivable position, imagined her fornicating with other men, enjoyed this vicarious sex more and more.

She hated him—she says—but he held her as if she were a dog. Eventually he desired his penis to be always inside her. She felt like castrating him. She told him that the more lovers who enjoyed her, the more semen he'd have stored up inside. Imagine, Nazario, imagine me fucking men you've never met.

"I'm just telling you. Whores: You take them by the ass, they're the cheapest. If they sit on top of the man, they're more expensive."

Except, at the same time, her marriage to the ridiculous old man made her more and more afraid. She started seeing herself as she wasn't, greedy, uncultured, spectral. She fervently desired the death of the man who loved, her, desired her, and at the same time kept her cornered by luxury and ambition.

That was when Nazario did her the favor of becoming paralyzed following an energetic sixty-nine. The old man became overly excited and was left half-rigid with a hemiplegia that kept him from speaking beyond a milky-rice mewling. Then she felt again the temptation to castrate him and even put his flaccid penis in his mouth. But she had a better idea. Gradually she scaled a policy of humiliations that began by parading bare-breasted in front of the paralyzed man. Then confused him by walking past his idiot's gaze, dressed in mourning one day, for a cocktail party the next, finally as a nurse, taking him out in the wheelchair to the Pedregal courtyard without shade so he'd roast a little, hours and hours in the sun to see if he dies of sunstroke, and Nazario Esparza encased in wool pajamas and a plaid bathrobe, without shoes, trying to avoid the direct gaze of the sun and observe how his yellowish toenails were growing . . .

Alone? Sara laughed a long while, at times with the manners of a modest señorita, at other times with whorish guffaws, what the hell, I brought into the house all the men I only mentioned before, mariachis, bums, my buddies the towel boys from the brothel who brought me warm cloths after lovemaking, bongo players who played tropical music while I danced for the rigid old man, pimps who did everything for him, cooked and served the food. They took the useless old thing out in the midday sun of the damn central plain, like a roast pig, though she pampered him too, put him in the bed and toyed with him, said into his ear Go on, do the nasty to me, whispered Mummies are so tender, and if he stretched out his trembling fingers she slapped him and said Quiet, poison and then stripped and made love with the Mariachi before the astonished, desperate, illogical gaze of Nazario Esparza, who signaled wildly for her to get into bed with him.

"In your bed, Nazario? In your bed all you do is piss."

It culminated, she recounts, with what she calls "everybody gets to fuck her." The entire cast of servants and parasites who gathered in the house in Pedregal staged the collective violation of Sara P. in front of Esparza. She exaggerated her poses, her screams of pleasure, her orders to action, she even exaggerated the fakery with orgasms that echoed on the mummified face of Nazario Esparza like a mirage of life, a lost oasis of power, a desert resembling death.

Which came to him, she declared, in the middle of the last staged orgy. It was verified by the bongo player, who could gauge from a distance the beats of the tropical world. It was testified to by the pachuco who searched men who died suddenly in houses of prostitution. Nobody saw him die. Though the Mariachi, who was embracing Sara at the time, says he heard, as in a song of farewell, the words of "The Ship of Gold":

I'm leaving now . . . I've come just to say goodbye.
Goodbye woman . . . Goodbye, forever goodbye.

Is it true, or is it poetry?

Where was he buried? asked Sanginés, on whose face a displeasure appeared that contrasted, I must admit, with my own fascination: the rocambolesque, surreal, indescribable tale of this woman stripped of any moral notion, enamored of her mere presence on earth, possessed of incalculable vanity, enveloped in an idiotic glory, with no more reality than that of her actions with no connection to one another, which only form a chain of servitudes that escape the individual's consciousness, all of it, in that instant, closed a stage of my youth that began in the brothel on Calle de Durango when together with Jericó we enjoyed the female with the bee tattooed on her buttock, and ended now, with the female seated on a prop throne, sex painted on her face so she would have a mouth and speak.

I THOUGHT, OVER the next few days, that my relationships with women never really concluded, they ended abruptly and lacked something that at my age was beginning to intrude as a necessity. Duration. A lasting relationship.

In preparatory school Jericó and I had read Bergson and because of that reading, the subject of duration reappeared at times in our conversations. Bergson makes a very clear distinction between duration we can measure and another kind that can't be captured with dates because it corresponds to the intimate flow of existence. What we have lived is indivisible. It contains the past as memory and announces the future as desire. But it is not past or future separate from the moment. Consequently each moment is new though each moment is the past of memory and longing for the future.

(One understands why Bergson's philosophy was the weapon of intellectuals at the Ateneo de la Juventud—José Vasconcelos, Alfonso Reyes, Antonio Caso—against the Comtean Positivism that had been transformed into the ideological mask of the Porfirio Díaz dictatorship: Everything is justified if in the end there is progress. At the Palace of Mining in Mexico City, a modern goddess, with the brilliance and opacity of leaded windows, is proclaimed a divinity of industry and commerce. She was the courtesan of the dictatorship.)

What does this movement of the moment contain that embraces what we were and what we will be? On the one hand, instinct. On the other, intelligence. People confronted by the creative act, confronted by Michelangelo or Rembrandt, Beethoven or Bach, Shakespeare or Cervantes, speak of inspiration. Wilde said that creation is ten percent inspiration and ninety percent perspiration. In other words, creating supposes work, and both Jericó and I believe the production of frustrated talents in Latin America is as great as the production of bananas because our geniuses are waiting for *inspiration* and wear out chairs waiting for it in cantinas and cafés. Ten percent, however, wait patiently beside the ninety that can appear, why not, in a bar or café, though it is better received in a room as empty as possible, with a pen, a typewriter, or a computer close at hand and a concentrated effort that otherwise can be made in an airplane, at a hotel, or on a beach. The text admits no pre-text.

Intention and intelligence. I believe my friend and I, in a long relationship begun in the schoolyard of a religious academy, did not need to pronounce those words to comprehend and live them. They weren't the only basis of our understanding, affirmed the day I went to live with him on Calle de Praga. Today, however, two or three days after hearing the damned (or was she blessed in her compassion?) Sara Pérez de Esparza, Jericó came into our shared apartment and said point-blank that the time had come for us to live apart.

I didn't change my expression. "I'll leave today."

Jericó had the grace to lower his head. "No. I'm the one who's leaving. You stay here. It's just"—he looked up—"I'll be traveling a lot around the country."

"And?"

"And I'll be receiving all kinds of visitors."

"You have an office."

"You understand what I'm saying."

I didn't want to linger over the obvious and think that Jericó needed to move to have greater erotic freedom. Perhaps he'd already had it while I was devoted to Lucha Zapata and now, without her, the promise of my constant presence had cost him a couple of "romances."

I realized there was something more when Jericó said abruptly, "Nothing obliges me to live against myself."

"Of course not," I agreed with gravity.

"Against my own nature."

It didn't even occur to me that my friend was going to reveal homosexual inclinations. Images return to my memory of the shared shower at school and, more provocatively, our eroticism with the woman who had the posterior bee. I also recalled what he said when he returned from his years of study in Europe, a trip planned with as much mystery as his return, a mystery deepened by a certain falsity I intuited—I didn't know, I only intuited—in the Parisian references of a young man who didn't know French argot but did use American slang, as he did now:

"Look, as Justin Timberlake sings: 'Daddy's on a mission to please.' Don't be offended."

"Of course not, Jericó. You and I have had the intelligence never to contradict each other, knowing that each of us has his own ideas."

"And his own life," my friend said exultantly.

I said that was true and looked at him without any expression, asking him rhetorically: "His own nature?"

I didn't say it trying to trap him, or with ill will, or deceitfully, but really wanting him to explain to me what "his own nature" was.

"We're not the same," he said in response to my tacit question. "The world changes and we change along with it. Do you remember what I said, right here, when I came back to Mexico? I asked you then, What do we have? A name, an occupation, status? Or are we a wasteland? A garbage dump of what might have been? A canceled register of debits and credits? Not even the bottom of the stewpot?"

I stopped him with a movement of my hand. "Take a breath, please."

"We need a position, Josué. We can't give as our occupation 'I think' or 'I am.'"

"We can turn into young old men, like some musicians, Compay Segundo or the Rolling Stones, why not? didn't I warn you?"

"Don't joke around. I'm serious. The time has come for us to apply ourselves to action. We have to act."

"Even though we betray our ideas?" I said with no mean-spirited intention.

He didn't take it badly. "Adapting ourselves to reality. Reality is going to demand things in line with our talents though opposed to our ideals."

"What are you going to do?"

"I'm going to do, I'm going to act in accordance with necessity and try, as far as possible, to maintain my ideals. What do you think?"

"And if your ideals are bad ones?"

"I'll be a politician, Josué. I'll try to make them less bad."

I smiled and told my friend we really were faithful to our Catholic education and the morality of the lesser evil when it's necessary to choose between two demons. Were we *Jesuits*?

"And besides, the Jesuit goes where the Pope orders him to, without protest, without delay."

"But that order was to save souls," I said with the irony his words provoked in me.

"And souls aren't saved passively," he replied with conviction. "You must have absolute faith in what you're doing. Your ends must be clear. Your actions, overpowering. A country isn't built without implacable acts. In Mexico we've lived too long on compromise. Compromise only delays action. Compromise is wishy-washy."

He was agitated, and I looked at him with distress, almost out of the corner of my eye.

He said that in every society there are the dominant and the dominated. The unbearable thing is not this but when the dominant don't know how to dominate, abandoning the dominated to a fatal or vegetative existence.

"One must dominate to improve everyone, Josué. Everyone. Do you agree?"

Smiling, I accused him of elitism. He answered that elites were indispensable. But it was necessary to unite them with the masses.

"A more mass-oriented elite," Jericó declared, moving like a caged animal around a place, ours until then, that he apparently was transforming now into a prison ready to be abandoned. "Do you think you're immortal?" he asked.

I laughed. "Not at all."

He waved his finger in my face. "Don't lie. When we're young we all think we're immortal. That's why we do what we do. We don't judge. We invent. We don't give or take advice. We do two things: We don't accept what's already been done. We renovate."

I laughed in spite of myself.

Me too—I said to myself—I think I'm going to live forever, I feel it in my soul though my head tells me otherwise.

"Do you think it's legitimate for the old to control everything, power, money, obedience? Do you?"

"Ask me that on the day I become old." I tried to be amiable with a friend whose belligerent face, so impassioned it changed color, distanced him from me by the minute.

Jericó realized I was looking at him and judging him. He tried to calm down. He made a sacrilegious joke.

"If you believe in the Immaculate Conception, why not believe in the Maculate Conception?"

"What do you mean?" I asked, a little shocked in spite of myself.

"Nothing, pal. Only that life offers us a million possibilities on every corner. Or rather, on every plaza."

His eyes were shining. He said to imagine a circular plaza—

"A *rond-point*?" I asked deliberately.

"Yes, a circle out of which, say, four or six avenues emerge—"

"Like the Place de l'Etoile in Paris."

"Ecole," he said enthusiastically. "The point is, which of the six avenues are you going to take? Because when you choose one, it's as if you've sacrificed the other five. And how do you know you've made the right choice?"

"You don't know," I murmured. "Except at the end of the avenue."

"And the bad thing is you can't go back to the starting point."

"To the original plaza. La Concorde," I said with a smile and, unintentionally, with irony.

He kept looking at me. With affection. With defiance. With an unspoken plea: Understand me. Love me. And if you love and understand me, don't try to find out any more.

There was a silence. Then Jericó began to pack his things and the conversation resumed its usual colloquial tone. I helped him pack. He told me to keep his records. And his books? Those too. But then he looked at me in a strange way I didn't understand. The books were mine. And him, what was he going to read from now on?

"Let's be baroque," he said with a laugh, shrugging his shoulders, as if that definition would transform the history of Mexico and the Mexicans into chicken soup.

"Or let's be daring," I said. "Why not?"

"Why not?" he repeated with a light laugh. "Life is getting away from us."

"And to hell with the consequences." I considered the unpleasant scene to be over. I touched my friend's shoulder.

I offered to help him carry down the two suitcases.

He refused.

I PROPOSED SHOWING indifference to beauty, health, and fortune. I wanted to transform my indifference into something distant from vice and virtue. I was afraid to fall into solitude, suicide, or the law. I wanted, in short, to avoid the passions, considering them a sickness of the soul.

The deafening failure of these, my new intentions (my doubt), had to do with the mere presence of Asunta Jordán. From nine to two, from six to nine, from the afternoon to midnight, I was never far from her during my period of initiation in the offices of the Vasco de Quiroga building in the Santa Fe district. The building itself consisted of twelve floors for work and another two for the residence of the president of the enterprise, Max Monroy, in addition to a flat roof for the helicopter.

"And you?" I asked Asunta with a mixture of boldness and stupidity. "What floor do you live on?"

She looked at me with her eyes of an overcast sea.

"Repeat what you just said," she ordered.

"Why?" I said, more fool me.

"So you'll realize your stupidity."

I admitted it. This woman, with whom I had fallen in love, was educating me. She led me through the twelve permitted floors, from the entrance on the Plaza Vasco de Quiroga, greeting the guards, the concierge, the elevator operators, and from there to the second, third, and fourth floors, where female secretaries had abandoned typing and stenography for the tape recorder and the computer, where male secretaries signed or initialed correspondence with a flourish and also dictated it, where file clerks transferred the old, dusty correspondence of a company founded by Max Monroy's mother (my secret interlocutor in a nameless graveyard) almost ninety years ago onto tapes, diskettes, and now iPods, blogs, memory sticks, USB drives, external disks, and from there to the fifth floor, where an army of accountants was at work, to the sixth, offices of the lawyers in the service of the enterprise, to the seventh, from which Max Monroy's cultural concerns—opera, ballet, art editions—radiated outward, to the eighth, a space dedicated to invention, to the ninth and tenth, the floors where practical ideas were devised for modern technologies.

On the eleventh floor I worked with Asunta Jordán and an entire executive army, one floor below the thirteenth and fourteenth floors inhabited, as far as my imagination could tell, by Bluebeard and his disposable women.

Was Asunta one of them?

"You're not a seminarian or a tutor," she said as if she could sense in me a hero of a nineteenth-century novel as embodied by Gérard Philipe. "You're not an ordinary run-of-the-mill employee because you were sent here by Licenciado Sanginés, whom Max Monroy loves and respects. And you're not socially inferior, though you're not actually socially superior either."

She looked me over from head to toe.

"You have to dress better. And something else, Josué. It's better not to have been born than to be ill bred, do you understand? Society rewards good manners. Appearances. Speaking well. Good form. Form is part of our power, even if we're surrounded by fools or perhaps for that very reason."

She elaborated—from floor to floor—speaking about the Mexican cultivation of form.

"We're the Italians of America, more than the Argentines," she said in the elevator, "because we were a viceroyalty and above all because we descended from the Aztecs, not from boats."

"An old joke," I dared to say. Asunta seemed to be repeating something she had learned.

She laughed, as if in approval. "Since you're none of that, it's right for you to learn to be what you're going to be."

"And what I want to be?"

"From now on, that's no longer different from what you're going to be."

To that effect—I suppose—Asunta took me to social functions she considered obligatory, in other offices and hotels, with powerful and sometimes pretentious people with a yearning for elegance, a subject that awakened in Asunta's gaze and facial expression a series of reflections that she communicated to me in a very quiet voice, both of us surrounded by the rapid sound of the social hive, as she tasted the glass of champagne in which she only wet her lips without ever drinking from it: When she set down the glass, the level of the drink was always the same.

"What is luxury?" she would ask me on those occasions.

Surrounded by clothes, aromas, poses, strategies, Hispanic canapés and Indian servers, I didn't know how to answer.

"Luxury is having what you don't need," she declared, her eyes hidden behind her raised glass. "Luxury is poetry: saying what you feel and think, without paying attention to the consequences. But luxury is also change. Styles change. Tastes change. Luxury tries to move ahead or at least catch up with style, creating and inviting it . . ."

She spoke of luxury not as if she had invented it but because she was inaugurating it.

" 'Luxury does not know that style and death are sisters,' " I said, citing Leopardi and testing her.

"It's possible." Asunta's expression did not change, and I recalled old conversations with Jericó and Filopáter.

"And because style is change, it affects our business. What do we offer the consumer? The most modern, the most advanced, at times the most useless, because tell me, if you already have a black telephone, why do you want a white one? I'll tell you: Because choosing between two phones today is choosing among a hundred phones tomorrow. Do you see? Luxury creates necessity, necessity creates luxury, and we produce and win. There is no. end to it! There's no reason for it ever to end! Ha!"

She didn't say these words as an exclamation. Her behavior at these social events was very distinctive. She knew she was looked at and even guessed at. Over and above the conversations, the clink of glasses, the scent of lotions and perfumes, the taste of sausages and quesadillas, Asunta Jordán circulated in a kind of light, as if a theatrical spot were following her, always looking for the best angle, making her hair shine, resting like an insolent bee on her plump red lips à la Joan Crawford, hot or cold? That was the question others asked as they watched her go by, does Asunta Jordán kiss hot or cold? murmuring in secret to Josué, exciting the curiosity of the guests, Ask yourself, Josué, who's looking at you, where are they looking at you from? Ask yourself but don't look at anybody, act in public as if you had a secret and wanted them to guess what it is.

She offered no opening. She let them look at her. She imposed silence as she passed. And if she held my arm, it was as if I were a cane, a walking puppet, a theatrical prop. She needed me to circulate through the reception with no need to speak with anyone, exciting everyone's curiosity each time she said something to me in a quiet voice, smiling or very, very serious. I was her support. A straight man.

In the real world (for me these excursions into society were almost imaginary) Asunta brought me up to date on my duties with rapid efficiency. There existed a national and global market of young people between twenty and thirty-five, Generation Y, given this name because they succeeded Generation X, who were now past forty and even though everybody adjusts to the customary until they fear that the newest thing will bite them, the twenty-year-olds are the primary target of consumer advertising. They want to make their debut. They want to be different. They want brand-new objects. They need technologies they can control immediately and that are (at least in their youthful imaginations) forbidden to "the older generation."

The notable thing—Asunta continued—is that in the developed world each generation of the young is smaller than the one before because of the decline in population. New families, more divorce, more homosexual couples, fewer children. On the other hand, in the world of poverty—ours, the Mexican world, Josué, don't kid yourself—the population increases but so does poverty. How can we combine demography and consumption? This is the problem set forth by Max Monroy, and your job, my young friend, is to solve it. How to increase consumption in an impoverished population?

"By making them less impoverished," I dared to remark.

"And how do we do that?" the queen bee insisted.

I opened my eyes to think clearly. "By taking the initiative? By opening limited credit for them and giving them short-term cards? By educating. Preparing. Communicating."

"Communicating," she moved ahead. "Letting them know they can live better, that they deserve credit, cards, consumption, just like the rich . . ."

I tried to look intelligent. She moved ahead of me like an Alfa Romeo passing a Ford.

"And how do we do that?" she said again.

Asunta was enthusiastic, dazzling me because I desired her, but I understand now that to have her I would have to respect her for what she was, an executive woman, an arm in the enterprises of Max Monroy that, like the goddess Kali, has as many arms as it has needs.

I was content with two, ready to love, caress, strangle me. She looked at me, confusing my desire with ambition. They're not the same thing.

"I'll tell you how," and she snapped her fingers, on the offensive. "Move ahead. Give them the medium of communication. Send an army of our employees from village to village, settlement to settlement. Bring in trucks loaded with handheld devices. Like tire salesmen did when the first highways and cars were promoted by Doña Concha, Max's mother, in the 1920s. Like the Christian missionaries did, so long ago, when they brought the Gospel to the conquered Indians. Now, Josué, we're going to bring in the medium of communication, the tiny device, call it Creative Zen, YP-Tq, LGs, whatever you like, the toy, show it to the poorest campesino, the most isolated Indian, the illiterate and the semiliterate, who by touching this button can express their desires and by pressing the other receive a concrete response, not dead promises but the living announcement: Tomorrow we'll install what you asked for, we'll give you a cellphone, an iPod so you can hear already programmed music, we know your tastes, an iPhone so you can communicate with your friends, and by God, Josué, break the isolation in which your, our, compatriots live, and once you give them the devices free of charge you'll see how demand is born, credit is given, a habit is created . . ."

"And generations will be in debt to us," I said with healthy skepticism.

"And so?" She managed to smile despite herself. "You and I will be dead."

"And while we're alive?" I said, not expecting a reply, since Asunta Jordán's program seemed to run out in this life, not the next.

Still, when I thought this, it occurred to me that at the age of eighty-three, Max Monroy had already considered the future, had already made a will. Who would be his heirs? What would Asunta obtain in Max's will, if in fact Max left her anything? And to whom else could Max leave his fortune? I laughed to myself. Public welfare. The National Lottery. An old age home. His own business, recapitalizing it. His loyal collaborator Asunta Jordán?

I digress.

———

I OUGHT TO have imagined, oh woe is me, that in a fashion parallel to my technosentimental education at the hands of the beautiful, crepuscular Asunta Jordán in the fiefdoms of Max Monroy, my old friend Jericó must have been receiving political instruction at the hacienda of our joker president.

Maestro Don Antonio Sanginés informed me that Jericó was still working in the presidential offices at Los Pinos. One night he invited me to supper at his mansion in San Angel, and after the previously mentioned patrol of children—they were already in their pajamas—he sent them away and sat me down to a meal not only of dishes of food but of biographies, as if, since he was the conductor of the destinies allotted to me and Jericó, it was now time for him to turn to a new function: the president's biography.

"How much do you know about President Valentín Pedro Carrera?" he asked before attacking a consommé with sherry.

"Very little," I replied, my spoon at rest. "What I read in the papers."

"I'll tell you about him. So you'll know where and with whom your friend Jericó is working: Valentín Pedro Carrera won the presidential election with the invaluable assistance of his wife, Clara Carranza. In the pre-election debates, each candidate boasted of his marvelous family life. The children were a delight"—Sanginés's eyes gleamed, and from the top floor we could still hear the prenocturnal tumult of his youngsters—"his wife was the ideal woman, a loving mother, a disinterested colleague, a First Lady because she was already his first companion (relatives had to be hidden)."

All the candidates fulfilled these well-known formalities. But only Valentín Pedro Carrera could swallow with difficulty, suppress a fat tear, take out a large colored handkerchief, blow his nose vigorously, and announce:

"My wife, Clara Carranza, is dying of cancer."

At that instant, our current leader won the election.

Who will vote, perhaps not for the candidate but no doubt for the health, agony, and probable death of Doña Clara, elevated to a combined sainthood and martyrology by that television moment when her husband dared say what no one knew and, if they did, had kept hidden in the old closets of discretion?

The candidate is married to a heroic, stoic, Catholic woman who may very well die before the election—vote for widower Carrera—after the election—what will happen first, the funeral or the inauguration?—during the ceremony—how brave Doña Clara was, she got out of her bed to support her husband when he rendered his affirmation that he would protect the Constitution and the laws emanating thereof!—or in the first months of the new government—she clutches at life, she doesn't die so as not to discourage the president—or when, at last, the señora gave up the ghost and Valentín Pedro Carrera transformed personal grief into national mourning. There was no church without a requiem, no avenue without posters with photographs of the transient First Lady, no office without a black bow in the window, no barracks without its flag at half-mast, no private residence without its crepe.

Virtuous, intelligent, charitable, devoted, loyal, what virtue did not come to rest, like a pigeon on a statue, on the spiritual eaves of Doña Clara Carranza de Carrera? What sorrow was not drawn on the distressed though ecstatic face of the commander in chief of the nation? What Mexican did not weep seeing on TV the repeated images of a saintly life dedicated to doing good and dying better?

A stupid woman, ignorant, foolish, and ugly, from whom unpleasant odors emanated. A strange, unintelligible woman because of her mania for always speaking in profile. A spur, however, to a mediocre, neurotic man like Valentín Pedro Carrera.

"What memories do you have, you dummy?" she would say at the private dinners Sanginés attended.

"I have a longing to be a nobody again," he would respond.

"Don't kid yourself. You are a nobody. Nobody, nobody!" the lady would begin to shriek.

"You're dying," he would reply.

"Nobody, nobody!"

Sanginés explained the obvious. The lust for power leads us to hide defects, feign virtues, exalt an ideal life, put on the little masks of happiness, seriousness, concern for the people, and always find, if not the phrases then the appropriate attitudes. The fact is that Valentín Pedro Carrera exploited his wife, and she allowed herself to be exploited because she knew she would not have another opportunity to feel famous, useful, and even loved.

Neither one was sincere, and this confirms that in order to achieve power, a lack of sincerity is indispensable.

"Valentín Pedro Carrera was elected on a corpse."

"Nothing new, Maestro," I interrupted. "It was the rule in Mexico: Huerta kills Madero, Carranza overthrows Huerta, Obregón eliminates Carranza, Carranza ascends on the corpse of Obregón, etcetera," I repeated like a parakeet.

"A bloodless etcetera: the principle of nonreelection saves us from succession by assassination, though not from ungrateful successions of heirs who in the end owe power to their predecessor." Sanginés finally tasted his cold consommé.

"The obligation to liquidate the predecessor who gave power to his successor," I completed the thought.

"Rules of the Hereditary Republic."

Sanginés smiled before continuing, having tasted with that spoonful my elementary political knowledge due, as you all know, to the secret information Antigua Concepción gave me in a nameless graveyard.

Many jokes were made about the presidential couple. Doña Clara loves the president and the president loves himself. They have that in common. And the black humor was profitable. In La Merced they sold dolls of the president run through with pins by his wife, with the legend: *You die first.*

Which is what really happened. Without the amulet of his dying wife, and as the memory of Clara Carranza, the martyr of Los Pinos, and the concomitant sorrow of Valentín Pedro Carrera began to fade, he was left without his saving grace, which consisted of living through the agony of waiting. At times you could say the president would have wanted to live the agony of Doña Clarita himself, make certain she continued to suffer, continued to serve him politically and not constantly threaten him:

"Valentín Pedro, I'm going to kill myself!"

"Why, my love, what for . . ."

"The fact," Sanginés continued, putting aside the consommé, "is that the weaknesses of Valentín Pedro Carrera wasted no time in appearing, like cracks in a wall of sand. Issues came up that required the decision of the executive. Promulgating and executing laws. Appointing officials. Naming army officers. Conducting foreign policy. Granting pardons and privileges and authorizing exemptions and import duties. Carrera let them slide. At most, he passed them on to his ministers of state. When he didn't, the ministers acted in his name. At times what one minister did contradicted what another said, or vice versa."

"We're negotiating."

"Enough negotiations. We must be firm."

"We have an agreement with the union."

"Enough coddling of the union."

"Oil is a possession of the state."

"Oil has to be opened to private initiative."

"The state is the philanthropic ogre."

"Private initiative lacks initiative."

"There will be a highway from Papasquiaro to Tangamandapio."

"Let them travel by burro."

"Let us collaborate with our good neighbors."

"They're the neighbors. We're the good ones."

"Between Mexico and the United States, the desert."

The truth, Sanginés continued, is that the president made the mistake of forming a cabinet composed only of friends or people of his generation. This formula had fatal results. Friends became enemies, each one protecting his small plot of power. The generational idea did not always get along with the functional one. Being from a generation is not a virtue: it is a date. And you don't play with dates, because none possesses intrinsic virtues beyond its presence—no matter how fleeting—on the calendar.

"Dead leaves!" Sanginés exclaimed when the servant came in carrying a platter of rice with fried bananas, and as he offered it to me, he said respectfully:

"Good evening, Señor Josué."

I looked up and recognized the old waiter from Errol Esparza's house who had been fired by the second and now overthrown wife, Señora Sarita Pérez.

"Hilarión!" I recognized him. "How nice!"

He said nothing. He leaned over. I served myself. I looked at Sanginés out of the corner of my eye. As if nothing had happened. The servant withdrew.

"Rumors began to circulate," my host went on. "The president does not preside. He inaugurates public works. He makes vague remarks. He smiles with a face more florid than a carnation. The unfailing evil tongues begin to speak of a cursed term. They even insinuate, in the second year of the government, that longevity in office is fatal to the reputation of the leader."

"And to his health as well."

Guided by a mad compass, Carrera dipped his big toe into foreign policy, the traditional refuge of a president of Mexico without a domestic policy. It turned out badly. The North Americans increased the armed guards along the northern border with increasing deaths of migrant workers. The Guatemalans opened the southern border for an invasion of Mexico by Central American workers. All that was left for the president to do was to stroll through the Davos Forum dressed as an Eskimo and give a speech at the General Assembly of the United Nations attended by no one except the delegates from Black Africa, who are very courteous.

" 'It was an unlucky moment for me when Clarita died!' " the president exclaimed one night.

" 'What you need is for half your cabinet to die,' " I dared to tell him. " 'Their incompetence reflects on you, Mr. President.' "

" 'What do you advise, Sanginés?' " he asked me with a desolate expression.

" 'New blood,' " I said. "The result"—and he liquidated the last fried plantain without making a sound—"is Jericó's presence in the office of the president."

"What a good idea," I said with sincerity but no conviction, trying to guess at the hidden intentions of Don Antonio Sanginés, a truly astute puppeteer and know-it-all, I realized at that moment, in our lives. Jericó's and mine.

"Shall I tell you what your friend has done at Los Pinos."

It wasn't a question. In any event, I agreed.

"He brought together functions scattered among various secretaries at the suggestion of the president. Appointments, the need to render accounts, consult with the executive before taking action, meet in a council of ministers presided over by Valentín Pedro Carrera, make periodic reports. And as for the president, to move ahead of the ministers in relationships with unions, management, universities, the fourth estate, the governors, the congress: Day after day Jericó took charge of everything, establishing a network of presidential control that made each leader or sector of activity understand that their responsibility was to the head of state, and that the other members of the cabinet were not autonomous agents or authorized voices but merely confidential employees of the president from whom he could withdraw his confidence at any moment just as he could grant it to them for a specific period of time."

"Mr. President," Jericó would say to him, "remember that as the opposition you could be pure. Now, in power, you have to learn to be less pure."

"To dirty my hands?"

"No, Señor. To make compromises."

"I was elected by the hope of our citizens."

"Now it is time for you to pass from the electoral light into the shadow of experience."

"Boy, you talk like an eager priest."

"I talk so you'll understand me."

"What do you want me to understand?"

"That I'm here to serve you and that I serve you by strengthening you."

"How?"

Once the immediate official apparatus was set in motion, Jericó asked the president for authority to attend to an absolutely key matter.

"What can that be, young man?"

"Youth, old man," Jericó dared to reply, and he understood what would happen, what could be, if the president of the republic, in that small detail ("Youth, old man") acknowledged the power of his young aide-de-camp and opened to the action Jericó was offering to him with enormously compromising words: "I'm doing it for you, Mr. President. I'm doing it for the good of the country."

"Doing what, kid?"

"What I'm proposing, Señor," said Jericó, reverting to respect.

"IF WE'RE GOING to spend time together," Asunta said to me one lazy afternoon, "it's better if I tell you about my life. I want you to know who I am because I told you about it, instead of having rumors coming up here from ten stories down."

"And what obliges me to believe you?" I said with a touch of irony, just to protect myself from the dark surge of her gaze and respiration filled with vague nocturnal perfumes that were beginning to surround us. I liked this woman. She bored me, she frightened me, and I liked her.

The truth is that before talking about herself, Asunta talked to me about Max Monroy and I, more fool me, did not realize right away that this was her way of telling me, Look, Josué, this is who I am, the woman who talks to you about Max Monroy is the woman who talks to you about herself. You can hold on to the certainty I talked only about him and you'd be wrong. I'm letting you know in time. I don't know any other way to tell you about my life than to tell you about my life with the man who determines my life.

"Max Monroy: You, who are writing a thesis on Machiavelli under my direction," Maestro Sanginés said to me, "know that the end does not always justify the means. Max Monroy decided from the very beginning that the way to obtain the best ends is to forget about them and act as if the means were the ends. Thanks to this philosophy, he strengthened his own business to the maximum. A man of means, Max valued ends, convinced they were as separate from means as day is from night. He distrusted ultimate solutions:

They're always bad, he says, because they classify you forever and close the doors of renovation to you. Even worse: If the ultimate solution fails, you have to begin all over again. On the other hand, if a means doesn't produce results, you have at hand a repertoire of other means that aren't ultimate but partial, as disposable as a Kleenex. Though if you're successful, they appear as ends. This is what Max Monroy rejects. Never ends. He never celebrates the success of an end but rather the viability of a means. Listen carefully to this, Josué. Everything Max Monroy accomplishes is only a means to achieving the next means, never an end. He says the word END serves only to conclude a film, turn up the lights, and ask the audience, courteously, to withdraw with no need to pick up the bottles of Coca-Cola or carry to the trashcan the popcorn scattered on the floor."

"The Max Monroy film, Josué, ignores the word END. In this way, you understand, he never admits failure. Some endeavors are successful. Others are not. He abandons these in time. Sometimes he finds himself obliged to proclaim victory after a failure: a program that did not succeed with the public, an innovation that was soon surpassed by the competition. Max changes the subject, he does not refer to what happened, he goes on to the next topic. In this way he leaves no rancor behind him. No one thinks he is the loser. No one considers himself the winner. But the cash register does not stop ringing," Asunta said to me the other day.

"Monroy is famous for having said that thanks to him we abandoned the abacus. He walked new ground just to open even newer ground. What I mean is that he's careful to have his successes not be failures paid for in exchange for success. Max is seen as an invulnerable entrepreneur who has to be stopped or eliminated. He navigates in silence over the waters of fortune. He is a master of the silent accomplishment, the stealthy success. He accepts his power. He tries not to allow envy to turn into idle conversation or an airplane without a motor destined to wander from airport to airport," Antonio Sanginés confirmed on another night.

(I thought of my afflicted and dearly loved Lucha Zapata. My

sincere though distrustful Asunta Jordán continued her discourse
while her eyes gleamed even more, as if to keep at a distance approaching night.)

"Max Monroy is like the serpent. He coils around himself. He is
a self-sufficient circle. When he looks out from the top floor of this
building, he acknowledges that the city's danger surrounds us. At
the same time, he listens to the sound of the street and says that
traffic is the music of business."

"Capitalism's symphony?"

Asunta laughed. Did she say it? Did Sanginés? Did I say it to myself? The discourse on Monroy in my head is unitary, like a fan that
has one piece of cloth and many ribs. "To talk about capitalism is to
think something can replace it. Max calls it one-worldism, globalization, internationalism. It's a question of a planetary phenomenon,
corrected if possible by social enlightenment. Max has always been
ahead of his time. He acknowledges that in Mexico there are
classes, abysmal differences between poor and rich. His utopia—
we're in the district of Tata Vasco and Thomas More, remember?—
is for there to be increasingly fewer differences and for us to become
a single river, with constant tides and a single current flowing to
the sea, if not with greater equality, at least with greater opportunities. In this he differs from conventional politicians. Max wants to
create the need in order to create the agency. Politicians create the
agency and forget about the need. It's what Max opposes in our
president."

(They tell me that with Jericó transformed into a presidential
adviser?)

"Because this is what happens, Josué," Asunta, Sanginés, and I
myself continued in identical reflections without divisions, attracted by the personality of Max Monroy: "Max asks those who believe the world is already made what needs to be done, and moves
ahead by doing it. His daily slogan is *Never think there's nothing left
to do*. Ask yourselves how much you've done and how much you
found done or allowed to be done. That, Max clenches his fist, is
what needs to be done."

"And with people, Asunta? Is Max Monroy the machine you've

described? Doesn't he deal with human beings? Does he live shut away like an eagle without wings up there in his aerie?"

I myself, Sanginés, and Asunta laughed again, as if my questions were tickling us. "Max Monroy knows how to use masks. They say he has a lifelong poker face. He knows how to pretend. He approaches, threatening. He becomes cordial again. But anyone who saw him threatening does not forget the threat. He knows the price of silence. He wounds no one without making that person believe that he himself will close the wound. And sometimes, if it suits him, he lets it be known that the wound will never close. He doesn't flatter anyone. And he doesn't allow himself to be flattered. He says the flatterer, the fawner, puts the intelligence of the flattered person to sleep. Max does favors when necessary. But he tells me constantly that for each favor he'll have one ingrate and a hundred enemies. He doesn't say a word about business. Let the politicians talk. Let them make compromises. Let them make mistakes. Max Monroy, zipper-mouthed. Max Monroy, close-mouthed."

"Doesn't he feel guilty for anything?"

"He says the angels will take care of discussing his vices and virtues. Why try to anticipate heaven?" said the collective voice about Max.

"Doesn't he ever ask for anything? Deference? Privileges?"

"Respect. That's what he gave me," said Asunta, opening her eyes wide and looking straight at me. "You asked about me? I answered with Max? Do you know who I am thanks to Max? Can you imagine me, Josué, my little Josué, before Max? Can you imagine a girl from the dry province, from the thorny north, with parents who wanted to turn her into a completely useless, completely supported girl, what could I be? Can you see me trapped in a family governed by three unbearable rules? 'We don't talk about that. Errors are not corrected. We don't regret anything, child.' Not anything? Where did my parents come up with the idea that everything they did was allowed, knowing they didn't do anything worth disallowing? The north, the desert, the emptiness, the highways going nowhere, the mountains in the distance, the desert close at hand, the ocean a pious lie, the weather always undecided between suffocation and dawn. A desert husband. Quick, we don't want the girl left behind with us. Is he the best? No. Is he the worst? Not that either. Who is he? He sells cars. Buses. Trucks. Is he in love? Is he calculating? Do we have more than he does? Does he have more than we do? Where did Tomás González come from? Where did Asunta López Jordán come from? Who's better, the Gonzálezes or the Lópezes? Who presumes what, just tell me that? Who boasts of their cactus, their desert, their rock, their paving stone or tortilla, just tell us that? Why does he presume so much, what is the presumptuous man presumptuous about? Why on your wedding night does he show you his penis and say, Baby, let me introduce you to King Kong, from now on he's going to sleep with us? Why is he presumptuous about everything except you? Why does he talk about you, Asunta López Jordán, as his ball and chain? Why does he presume with his friends that you take care of the house but he is a macho who needs broads livelier and sexier than you, Ernestina and Amapola and Cross-eyed Malva and Sweetass, all the whores of the north plus some from Arizona and Texas when he goes, as they say, to buy spare parts, sure, damn it, is that what they call it now? Why do you begin to pester him too, Asunta López de González, why do you tell him shave, you scratch when you make love to me, use deodorant, play golf, do something, stick King Kong in his cage?

"The gorilla's cage," Asunta Jordán said to me with no other commentary, "and I a pneumatic doll . . . pneumatic, but thanks to my neura attentive, alert, and for that reason dangerous: attentive, alert thanks to the horror of my husband and my family, convinced that these virtues of mine, in provincial society, were defects, I was dangerous, but perhaps in another society being violent and unpredictable was a virtue. In my town I unleashed negative reactions. When Max Monroy came fifteen years ago for the opening of the automotive factory, and I went to the reception afterward with my husband, Max Monroy looked out and saw a flock of contented women and a herd of presumptuous men and saw one woman who was discontented, that was me, and humiliated, that was me, and proud, that was me, and different, that was me, and that same night I left with him and here I am."

"You were saying that a woman is a luxury."

"No. A trophy."

"Why?"

"Because she's inconvenient. Where do you put an Oscar? He takes me away. For saying the wrong thing. For not wanting to make a good impression."

"Max Monroy saw that in you?"

"That's why he's Max Monroy."

(She stopped, alone in the middle of the dance floor. Her husband, Tomás, had gone off without saying goodbye. Couples danced. Families sat on three sides of the floor. The orchestra animated the entire nation from the fourth side. Couples danced. She stopped alone in the center of the floor. She didn't look at anyone. She didn't know if anyone was looking at her. She didn't care anymore. Then Max Monroy approached and took her by the waist and hand without saying a word.)

MY AGREEABLE (though disturbing) work in the Santa Fe office was interrupted (and it wouldn't be the last time) by Licenciado Antonio Sanginés. I wondered if my debt to the professor would be eternal. The heretics cited by another professor, Filopáter, said that the final proof of God's mercy would be forgiving all the damned and emptying out hell in one stroke. Not that my debt to Sanginés was hellish. On the contrary. I'm a grateful man. I was (and am) very conscious of everything I owed the maestro. Still, I couldn't help asking myself: How long will I be paying my debts—studies, thesis direction, meals at Coyoacán, admittance to the Prison of San Juan de Aragón, interviews with the prisoner Miguel Aparecido, even news about the destiny of my friend Jericó in the offices of the presidency—to Professor and Licenciado Don Antonio Sanginés?

A question without an immediate response, which still obliged me, no doubt because I did not have an answer, to suspend my work in the Vasco de Quiroga office and at the side of my platonic love Asunta Jordán and ask myself: Where was Sanginés's strategy leading with respect to the San Juan de Aragón Prison and the prisoner Miguel Aparecido? What, in essence, did Sanginés want when he opened the cell blocks of the penitentiary to me with a master key? Because I went into the prison and was made to feel right at home, with all kinds of facilities and even special considerations like this: Leaving me alone in the cell with Miguel Aparecido, a strong man focused on a personal resolve whose origin and fate I did not know: to remain imprisoned even though he completed his sentence; and if he ever was released, to commit a new crime that would keep him in prison.

A new crime. What was the first crime, the original crime, the offense Miguel Aparecido wanted to pay for eternally, since the ultimate solution of this enigma was to die in prison? Still, was this conclusion of mine, so easy and melodramatic, correct? Did a final point exist that would conclude Miguel's punishment in Miguel's mind, allowing him finally to leave his cell? Knowing this meant knowing everything. From the beginning. The origin of the story. The resolution of the mysteries I've been stitching together here and the conversion of mystery into destiny. Truths the prisoner did not seem disposed to reveal.

Least of all today. I went into the cell. His back was turned. The high, distant barred light drew lines on his body that were not part of his gray uniform: It was as if only the sun wore the striped uniform of the old prisons.

I went in and Miguel did not turn to look at me. It would have been better for me if he had. Because when he did, he revealed the face of a terrifying beast. His hair was wild, his cheeks scratched, his eyes as red as an ominous sunset, his nose wounded, his lips and teeth bloody.

"For God's sake, Miguel . . ."

I walked forward to embrace him, with a natural instinct to provide relief. He did not want help. He repulsed me brutally. I looked away, knowing he looked at me without affection.

Then something inside me said, "Don't look away. Look directly at him. Look at him as if you've seen him before. Like a vulnerable, bewildered human being in pain who rejects your affection only because he needs it, because he has no other support but you, just you, my poor Josué, double of himself."

I thought this and felt what we all know but never say aloud, because it is both a mystery and self-evident. I looked at Miguel Aparecido and saw myself reflected in him not as in a mirror but only in a question: We are body, we are soul, and we will never know how flesh and spirit are joined.

I looked at the unaffectionate eyes of Miguel Aparecido, feverish with the terror of the day, and for an instant I saw myself in them . . . I saw that both of us, I a free man, he a prisoner, were concerned with the same dilemma: Did we all deserve to be punished for the crime of a single man? Could the soul be saved if the body wasn't saved too? Could our body commit offenses without punishing the soul? Could the soul sin and the body remain free of transgression?

When I say I saw all this in Miguel Aparecido's gaze, I mean I was seeing it in the reflection that returned to my eyes from his. I recalled Filopáter and his reading of Saint Augustine: Sooner or later, human misery always requires the solace, the relief, the consolation religion offers through the promise of the resurrection of the flesh and the world with the promise of freedom in this life. Looking again (I don't know if for the first time) at Miguel Aparecido this afternoon, I thought religion and freedom resemble each other inasmuch as they believe in the unbelievable: the resurrection of the flesh or the autonomy of the individual. Perhaps the second is the greater mystery. Because we cannot know if we are going to be resurrected, we accept the secret of faith. But knowing we can be free, the absence of freedom opens before us an entire hand of anguished possibilities: to struggle for freedom or to renounce it; to act or abstain; to dirty one's hands or use gloves . . . If we choose one card, we sacrifice the rest. In life there is no change in cards. If you get four aces, you fucking win. If you get a weak hand, you're fucked. Though at times you win the game and save your life with a pair of fives. You play the hand you're dealt, and if you think you can ask for a different one, you're mistaken. Whoever deals the cards does it only once. We have to play the weak or winning hand destiny gave us.

Did I see in this man wounded both externally and internally the fatality of an existence I really had not known until now? Miguel Aparecido appeared (so to speak) to me like a strange but always serene being, master of a secret and comfortable with his own mystery, jealous of what he kept hidden in his bosom, intolerant when he was offered freedom, enigmatic when he decided to be a prisoner.

This was my idea of the man. I looked at what I saw before me when I entered the cell.

The earlier Miguel was not the present one and I could no longer wager on the truth. Was Miguel the severe, fatalistic man of yesterday? Or was he the destructive, beaten animal of today?

It is strange how, when a human being is set loose from acquired habits and customary masks are removed, barbaric feelings spring up, not in the usual sense of savagery or atrocity, but in the fuller meaning of existing earlier than convention, limits, and above all, the idea of the person. That was this Miguel Aparecido, a man earlier than himself, as if everything the world (and I) knew about him was a great deception, pure appearance, the skin of a phantom whose concealed body and soul belonged to someone else. This man.

Looking at him with great intensity, I thought of his decisive words. He counted on the loyalty of the other prisoners. Brillantinas and Gomas. Ventanas. Siboney Peralta. El Negro España and La Pérfida Albión. Then he had told me, boy, nothing happens here that I don't know about, and nothing I don't want to or can't control.

"Know this: even unexpected riots are the work of my will."

He had told me earlier he could smell the air and when the atmosphere in the prison became very heavy, a great internal fight was needed to clear the air. There were serious riots here when necessary, and then peace returned. Because peace, he said, was a necessity in prison.

"Many innocents come through here. They have to be respected."

I had seen the children in the swimming pool. They shouldn't be in prison forever.

"But if chaos did exist here, that would be because I am powerless to assure the order indispensable for the San Juan de Aragón Prison not to be heaven or hell but, and it's saying a lot, a goddamn purgatory."

On that occasion he had taken me by the shoulders, looking at me as if he were a tiger.

"When something happens here that slips through my fingers, it makes me furious."

Furious. The riot of broken chairs banging against the walls. The tables in the dining room smashed to pieces. Injured, dying, dead police. Padlocks first filed, then opened. Filed clean away.

Maximiliano Batalla. The Mariachi's Band. Brillantinas and Gomas. Ventanas. Siboney Peralta, who strangles and sings. Even La Pérfida Albión and El Negro España. Above all Sara P., the widow of Nazario Esparza and killer, along with Maxi Batalla, of Doña Estrella de Esparza, Errol's mama . . .

All of them. All of them. They escaped San Juan de Aragón. This time Miguel Aparecido did not provoke or control the riot. Maxi and Sara learned the lesson, they unleashed the barely contained fury of the criminal population, got the prisoners together, organized the riot, wreaked destruction, escaped.

"Who?" I asked, enraged by him, like him, Miguel Aparecido.

He looked at me like a dead man who has not lost the hope of resurrection.

"You, Josué."

No, I shook my head, astonished, not me.

"You, Josué, you have to find out what happened. How Maxi Batalla and Sara the whore were able to organize the escape. Why my allies abandoned me. Who organized them, who helped them, who opened the doors for them?"

He looked at me in an enlightened, perverse way, passing on to me the obligation that he, from prison, could not carry out, granting him a kind of vengeful halo with the desire to deceive me, make me believe that if I discovered the truth outside these walls it would also reveal the truth that remained here, confined, not so much inside the walls of the prison as inside the walls of Miguel Aparecido's head.

I could not see the weakness of the tiger that looked at me with the dissatisfaction of not having eaten because it had not killed. I could not see that the real menace of Miguel Aparecido consisted in telling the truth.

I understood only that it was not the flight of Sara P. and the Mariachi, or even—and this was worse—of Brillantinas and Gomas, Siboney and Ventanas, Albión and España that drove me mad, but the collapse of my illusion: Miguel was not, as he believed, the overseer of the penitentiary, the top dog, the sheikh. That is what infuriated him: the collapse of his jailhouse authority. The loss of the kingdom created by the sacrifice of his freedom. Being the head of the interior empire of the prison.

"I'm here because I want to be.

"I'm the head.

"When something happens here that slips through my fingers, I become furious.

"Fu-ri-ous."

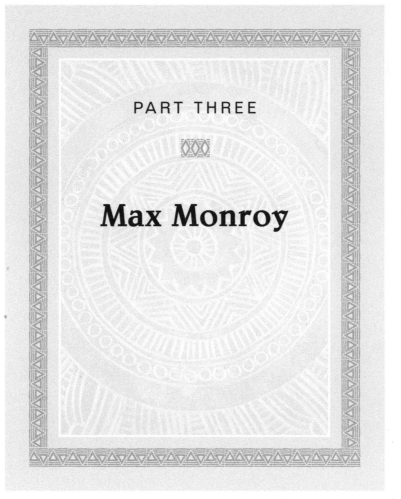

PART THREE

Max Monroy

A year went by following the events I have narrated so far. Perhaps things occurred in all the chapters of my life. I didn't return to Antigua Concepción in the nameless burial ground. I never
heard from my increasingly sentimentalized Lucha Zapata, who
flew away with the fugacity of a bird with a damaged wing. I had
completely forgotten about my sinister jailer María Egipciaca. I
knew that Elvira Ríos, my nurse, was barely a decisive though fleeting traffic accident. Doña Estrellita de Esparza lay buried, her despicable husband Don Nazario had been roasted alive in his own
courtyard by the very incarnation of immorality, the vile and ridiculous Sara P., the Lady Macbeth of Mariachiland imprisoned after a
macabre, imbecilic confession in the San Juan de Aragón Prison together with her *partenaire* in mischief, the immortal Mariachi Maxi,
who escaped with this same Sarape and an entire gang of criminals,
to the rage and despair of the presumptive capo of the penitentiary,
my friend Miguel Aparecido, mocked by a band of thugs and thrown
into a physical and moral anguish whose dimensions (I guessed) I
would never know, no matter how, from his eyes of a caged tiger, a
secret would peer out, veiled with difficulty by his bluish eyelids. Licenciado Antonio Sanginés, source of so much news and guidance
in my life, had absented himself (for the moment) and the truth is
that none of what I've just said mattered to me very much for a simple reason.

I was in love.

I could fail in sincerity with you, patient readers, both absent and present (present if you are kind enough to read me, absent if you do not and at times even when you do), and tell you whatever I feel like. In the course of a year, twelve months, three hundred sixty-five days, eight thousand seven hundred sixty hours, five hundred twenty-five thousand six hundred minutes, thirty-one million five hundred thirty-six thousand seconds, what can't an individual do, especially if he is author and protagonist of a novel dictated from and for death? What action is forbidden to him in my tale? What lie does not overcome my memory? What recollection of the past, what desire for the future? Don't you see: I persist, to my own despair (and, with luck, to yours), I am here, writing away, desiring the past at the same time I remember the future.

Desiring the past.

Remembering the future.

This, I assure you, is the paradox of death. Except that you have to die to know it.

What I want to say now is that for an entire year, dedicated to working in the offices of Max Monroy in the noble (but resurrected) region of Santa Fe, ancient seat of the Renaissance utopia of Fray Vasco de Quiroga in New Spain, I too was reborn. Reborn to love. I fell madly in love with Asunta Jordán. And from this fact my story hangs.

I have already recounted the experience of my training to be worth something in the business empire of Max Monroy. At first, desiring to show my energy and goodwill, I ran (two steps at a time) from floor to floor. Gradually I learned the lessons of the business, its phrasing, its designations: verbs, adjectives, and especially adverbs, not only endless but without end: The suffix "-ly," I realized very quickly, was not used in these offices. One said "recent" but not "recently"; "patient" without "-ly" and "original," "definitive," "occasional," or "formal" with no lymology at all. But don't think the elimination of the ending was the death of adverbial agency—rather, it was its elevation to the level of the implicit. By eliminating the adverb, all its protagonistic quality was given to the verb: to define, occasion, form, patient, and if not "to recent," then at least to bring everything to a today pregnant with tomorrow and sterilized and free of useless, nostalgic yesterdays, mere commemorations.

"Yesterday" did not register on the office calendars. It was as if Monroy's power expanded to turn to ash the pages of the past, convincing everyone that everything was today (and never the rhetorical *today-today-today* of an incinerated past), only the today of today, the instant with all its promises of the future so a well-made today would disappear in a fog denser than any forgetting.

And therefore everything was innovation in this business. And innovation consists in constantly expanding what was done today to what is done tomorrow. The miniaturized blog would end up hidden in a woman's handbag. Personal cameras transformed us all into instant paparazzi. MySpace, mySimon, and Deal Pilot pages allow us to compare prices, products, and possibilities instantly, and the multiplications of acronyms and headings—KDDI, XAML (the Facebook entry), ebXML, Oracle, Novell—would in the end be deciphered, like the Egyptian name of RosettaNet, into a single designation.

Everything, a great paradox, was destined to accentuate the greatest privacy as it transformed us all into public personages. Once we had entered the blogosphere, who could ever be an enigma again? If our lives are being filmed, what secrets can we keep? Was this the greatest challenge of Max Monroy and his industries? To strip us to the point where our essential privacy would be revealed and protected?

Was this a paradoxical invasion of private life intended to isolate and protect the most secret part of ourselves, the part that could resist any public notification? Our souls? Or would this combination of innovations and mysteries go into the public, popular sphere, guaranteeing each citizen direct access to the information once reserved to governments and managed by elites?

In short, was Max Monroy the emblem of the most inflexible authoritarianism or the most expansive democracy?

It would not take long to find out.

Everything is known. Everything is seen. There will be no more closets, much less skeletons in them. We ought to take the best possible care of the remains of our private life, invaded by the eye of the camera that is today—the camera—the Grand Inquisitor. And what does Dostoyevsky's Grand Inquisitor do? He protects faith with what offends it. Uses the weapons of the most material power to defend the most spiritual: faith.

Faith—I remembered the old talks with Father Filopáter—consists in saying and thinking: "It is true because it is incredible." Then can there be a faith that proposes being credible thanks to the natural existence of objects that prove it? But doesn't this faith subscribe to the concept of progress as a guarantee of universal life? We constantly move forward, nothing can stop us, human development is inevitable and ascendant. Even though a crematorium oven, a concentration camp, an Auschwitz, a Gulag, an Abu Ghraib, a Guantánamo, demonstrate the opposite . . . How I longed, in moments of doubt like this, to count on the voice of Father Filopáter and recover, in dialogue with him, my youthful camaraderie with my brother Jericó! To be again the Dioscuri, Castor and Pollux, the founding brothers, two luminous phantoms that gave victory to the Roman Republic in the battle of Lake Regillus.

A limited hero, as I've said, who at first, filled with the professional ardor of the novice, ran up and down stairs. Eventually I decided to take the elevator. Only to the twelfth floor, as I've stated, since the two top floors were prohibited. There, as in fairy tales, resided the Ogre, perhaps a benevolent Bluebeard who, having eliminated his earlier women (how many "broads" in a decade, or on average, did a man past eighty come into contact with? what's the ratio? what's the compensation?) resided, or dwelled, though I don't believe he had "settled," with a single woman and she was my own beloved enemy, Asunta Jordán.

Professional relationships can begin coldly and end with warmth, or at least congeniality. They can also begin cordially and end with hatred—or indifference. In any case, seeing each other's masks every day is something paid for one way or the other. My relationship with Asunta had no temperature. It was exemplary in its tepidness. Neither hot nor cold. She had the obvious mission of demonstrating and explaining to me the functioning of the great corporate elephant called, impersonally, "Max Monroy," with the purpose, no doubt, of preparing me to carry out functions: as a lowly nut and bolt, a perpetual stepping-stone, a midlevel official or, finally, as a chief, a functionary, a dignitary? Asunta's expressionless face gave me no answer.

Except that her perfect representation of the professional woman, her "official" permanent façade, without openings or windows (let's not even speak of doors), excited my curiosity. And since my curiosity turned out to be inseparable from my desire, inseparable in turn from my erotic will to possess Asunta Jordán, no matter how, I took the first step toward the forbidden.

During work hours I penetrated the darkness of Asunta's bedroom.

Nothing impeded me except the command of fables: Do not enter. But is there anything in a fairy tale that inflames more curiosity than a prohibition, anything more encouraging to the decision to violate the secret and break the imaginary lock than the warning: If you enter you will be punished? If you enter you will not come out again? If you enter you will be a cold corpse if things go well for you, an eternal prisoner if they go badly?

I called up some excuse to leave at twelve noon. I went up to the thirteenth floor, where Asunta Jordán had her rooms. I passed from the light of the living room to the darkness of the bedroom. I noticed there were no windows, as if the sleeping beauty of my dreams did not leave a single chink open to the curiosity of others, including the solar orb. I avoided looking at the bed. King-size, a marvelous size for a queen, queen-size. My eyes, my sense of smell, my desire, led me to the even darker area of clothing hung according to the seasons—touch allowed me to caress cottons, silks, cashmere, furs, and if I raised my hand a little, I touched hats of felt and straw, of mink and fox, baseball caps, visors, the unmistakable texture of a Panama, picture hats (from every wedding except hers and mine . . . *ay* . . .). None of that interested me. My fingers guided my eyes, and my eyes guided my sense of smell. At last my avid nose (long, pointed, my gentle readers will remember) came upon the perfume it was searching for.

I opened the drawer where Asunta Jordán's underthings were arranged. Dazzled, I closed my eyes and gave myself up first of all to the voluptuosity of smell, though my avid hands did not resist the desire to touch what I smelled, and in the combat between my nose and my hands, there was a delightful mixing of the aroma of lavender and the lace on panties, the scent of petals and breast cups, drops of anonymous perfumes and panties with Asunta's name, silk camisoles and padded bras, thongs, bikinis, all the forms of interior-exteriority that was my only possible approximation to the body of my beloved, perhaps more powerful than the nakedness that not only eluded me but did not even invite me, did not even forbid me. Lace, nylon, silk. Half-slips. Garter belts.

And so the interdiction flew over my excited approach to the drawers where Asunta's intimate apparel lay in innocent demise. I believe at that moment my physical and mental exaltation was so huge that I began to desire this erotic consummation and not another, not a physical one, which undoubtedly would be less intense than the approach, essentially modest though mentally vehement and shameless, violating Asunta's intimacy to incorporate it not into my own intimacy but into the vast territory of nameless desire.

I learned in that secret, sacred instant that desire moves us farther from and closer to obtaining the object of desire. I learned that we desire what we do not have and when we obtain it, just for ourselves, we desire to dominate what we have, deprive it of its freedom, and subject it to the laws of our ambition.

I closed my eyes. I breathed deeply. I closed the drawers, fearing to possess Asunta beyond this secret violation of intimacy. Fearful, above all, of myself, of my own desire and the limits or lack of limits that only desire could show me by inviting me, as it did at this moment, to be content with the objects I touched and smelled or take the step beyond the place where they intertwine and complicate the subjects of desire.

Asunta's maid suddenly turned on the lights in the room.

"And what do you think you're doing up here?"

———

WHAT HAVE I left in the inkwell? I mean, regarding my relationship with Jericó. Who defended me against the bullies at school, beginning with Errol Esparza in his earlier incarnation. Who took me in when I lost my orphan's home with María Egipciaca (and much more). Jericó taught me to drive a car. He opened my ears to the classical music he collected in the attic on Praga. He opened my eyes to reproductions of the great paintings of the past he assembled on postcards. He pushed me to examine the philosophical seeds planted by Filopáter in our flowerpots. He extended our joint readings to Dickens and Dostoyevsky, Balzac and Beckett. He even taught me to dance, though with a warning at once ironic and forbidding.

One night he invited me to a cabaret, and instead of leading me into the dance hall he took me to a kind of office from which you could observe the couples dancing but not hear the music. I was disconcerted for a minute. Then I suffered an attack of laughter watching the poses, the contortions, the senseless, graceless comedy of couples captured in an aquarium by dancing they obviously deemed charming, gallant, sophisticated, sensual, liberated, and libertine: heads gyrating, eyes closed dreamily or open in false amazement, hands shaking as if to throw or catch invisible balls, shoulders in grotesque calisthenics, legs freed of all control, halfway between prayer and defecation. And the feet, cockroaches in shoes to avoid death by Flit, two-toned men's shoes, cowboy boots, pointy-toed stiletto heels for the women, an occasional tennis shoe, all given over to the silent dance, the grotesque ritual of bodies deceiving themselves, feigning elegance, sensuality, good humor, which, stripped of accompanying sounds, reduced the dancers to a macabre imitation of an anticipated dance of death.

I thought that friendship was something fundamentally indecipherable. Pride, generosity, tenderness, accepted inadequacies, quiet reserves, the courage memory keeps acquiring—or the bitter absolution of its loss: everything united as in a chorus at once present and very distant, more eloquent in memory than in actuality, though with each gleam it brings the announcement of a future as unpredictable as a pistol going off at a piano concert.

"Let's be independent," Jericó fired at me. "Let's not have opinions imposed on us."

If the words surprised me, it was because they contained a tacit truth in our relationship. We had always been independent, I replied to my friend. He said I hadn't: I had lived in a mansion like the prisoner of a tyrannical nanny and saved myself by coming to live with him.

"And you?" I asked. "Have you always been independent?"

Jericó looked at me with a kind of compassionate tenderness.

"Don't ask me a question you could answer or be quiet about yourself, old pal. We're independent? First ask yourself: Who has supported us for as long as we can remember?"

I interrupted him. "Lawyers. Licenciado Sanginés, the—"

He interrupted me: "Were they sent? All of them, servants, sent by someone else?"

"Physically or morally?" I attempted to lighten the unusual conversation; we hadn't seen each other for more than a year, and this meeting in our old den on Calle de Praga was taking place on his initiative.

He ignored me. "We've assumed we have no past, that we live in the present, that the lawyers will provide and if we ask indiscreet questions, we'll break the spell and wake up no longer princes in the bedroom but frogs in the ditch . . . and with no way out."

I told him he was right. We had never inquired beyond the immediate situation. We received a monthly check. At times Sanginés led us to the doors of a mystery, but he never opened them. It was as if the two of us—Jericó, Josué—feared knowing more than we already knew: nothing. I suggested, before the ironic gaze of my friend, that perhaps our negligence had been our salvation. What or who would have answered our questions: Who are we, where do we come from, who are our parents, who supports us?

"Who supports us, Jericó?" I looked at him as if he were a mirror. "Are we innocent pimps? Are we better than La Hetara on Durango or the whore with the bee on her buttock?"

He remained silent, refusing to be surprised by my brusque remarks.

"Do you remember Father Filopáter when we were at school?"

I nodded. Of course.

Jericó said, after looking at the floor, that we had never under-stood—he spoke for the two of us—whether Filopáter pretended to be a false heretic to make faith palatable, like the false unbeliever who takes us down the path that leads to belief.

"Because Filopáter did two things, Josué. On one hand, he made us see the mindlessness of religion in the light of reason. But he also revealed the foolishness of reason in the light of faith."

"Reason compromises faith and faith compromises reason," I added without thinking too much about it, almost as a fatal, exact conclusion, that is, as dogma.

"Dogma." Jericó read my mind. We were Castor and Pollux again, the mystic twins, the Dioscuri. The inseparable pair.

"Listen, who decides that a dogma is a dogma?" I asked, step-ping back from the abyss of fraternity.

"Authority."

"Force?"

"If you think so."

I didn't know where or by what route he wanted to take me. I said force isn't enough. Force requires authority to be forceful.

"And authority without force?" Jericó asked.

"Is morality," I took a risk with my words.

"And morality?"

"I won't tell you it's certainty, because then morality and faith would be the same."

"Then, morality can be uncertain."

"Yes. I believe the only certainty is uncertainty."

"Why?"

"If you agree, Jericó, I'll only ask you not to feel superior or in-ferior. Feel equal."

"Do you remember when we were young we'd ask ourselves: What invalidates a man, what strips him of value?"

I nodded.

"Answer me now," he said with a certain pugnacity.

"You and I are each embarked on his attempt at success. I sincerely think we haven't defined ourselves yet. We're always someone else because we're always in the process of becoming."

"I have." Jericó intensified the conflict another degree.

"I haven't." I shrugged. "I don't believe you, bro."

"Do you want me to prove it to you?"

I looked at him with as much spirit (adverse, perverse, diverse?) as he showed looking at me.

"Sure, of course. I'll envy you because I'm not as sure as you are. It'll do me good."

I waited for him to speak. We understood each other too well. He hesitated for an instant. Then he observed, smiling this time, that to be coherent, he would respond with actions, not words. I returned the smile and folded my arms. It was a spontaneous gesture but it indicated a certain permanence on my part at this time and in this place we had shared since we were nineteen years old.

"Don't stop when you're halfway there," he said suddenly.

"You make the path as you walk, says the song."

"You understand me."

"Because I'm sitting here and you're over there. All we have to do is change places and all the truth we've just said collapses, goes all to hell, becomes doubt.

"And also memory," I insisted. "Let's remember where we were before."

"Though we don't know where we'll be afterward."

"We can predict."

"And if we're struck by lightning?"

"We live or we die," I said with a smile.

"We survive." He looked at me with eyes half closed and then opened wide as if by orders of an internal sergeant.

"Alive or dead?" I hesitated.

"Alive or dead, we're only survivors. Always."

I shook my head.

"We have no father," said Jericó.

"And?"

"If we did, we'd grow up to honor him so he'd be proud of us."

"And since we don't . . ."

"We can exist for ourselves."

"On condition we honor ourselves?" I smiled.

"Don't get lost when you're halfway there."

I detected a certain internal disturbance in my friend when he repeated: "Halfway there. There's more. Something more than you and me. Our country. Our nation."

I laughed out loud. I told him he didn't have to justify his job, his position at Los Pinos. I wanted to liven and lighten the situation.

"It all depends," I said. "What's the objective?"

"To be superior to all those who challenge us." He took another breath.

"Wouldn't it be enough just to be equal?"

"You're joking. I don't want them to say about us: They're like everybody else, they're the usual ones, the customary ones, the ones in the crowd. Agreed?"

I said probably, if my friend's words indicated that self-improvement was necessary, of course . . . Agreed . . .

"Are we different, you and I?" I said after Jericó's obstinate silence.

"What do you mean?"

"I mean you and I didn't have to survive. We always had food on the table."

"Like everybody else? Do you think I did?"

I took a step I hadn't wanted to take: "I suspect you did."

In that suspicion were summarized the doubts you already know about regarding the character called just "Jericó," with no last name, not even the past afforded me by the house on Berlín, the care of María Egipciaca, and the nurse Elvira Ríos, before my destiny and Jericó's converged like two rivers of fire, Castor and Pollux. I was Josué Nadal.

Jericó, without family names, who traveled without a name on his passport, who perhaps traveled without a passport, who perhaps—everything my affection for him had hidden was now suddenly revealed—had not been in France or the United States or anywhere except the hiding place of his soul . . . And wasn't it enough, I exclaimed to myself, to have a soul where you could take refuge? Wasn't that sufficient?

"Alive or dead . . . Survivors."

At this moment, when I heard these words, I felt that a stage in our lives (and consequently in our friendship) had closed forever. I understood that from now on he and I would have to be responsible for our own lives, breaking the fraternal pact that until then not only had united us but allowed us to live without asking ourselves questions about the past, as if, being friends, it was enough for us say and do things together to complement the absences of our earlier life.

It was as if life had begun when he and I became friends in the schoolyard. It was as if, when we stopped being friends, a barefoot death had begun to approach us.

"MAX MONROY," Asunta Jordán tells me tonight, "has two rules of conduct. The first is never to respond to an attack. Because there are so many, you know? You can't be as prominent as he is without being attacked, above all in a country where it's difficult to forgive success. Lift your head, Josué, and they immediately assault you and, if they can, decapitate you."

"Rancors in this country are very old and very deep," I remarked, and added Socratically, because I didn't want to disagree with her: "Mexico is a country where everything turns out badly. There's a reason we celebrate the defeated and despise the victorious."

"Even though we stay with our idols. If you become an idol, an idol of the ranchera, the bolero, the soap opera, sports, your life is pardoned," Asunta said with her style of popular humor.

"Idolatry here is very old." I smiled, continuing my adulatory tactic. "We believe in God but we worship idols."

Asunta shook off this ideological confetti with an elegant movement of her head. "But the fact of not responding to an attack is a terrible weapon. You don't give the attacker a moment of untroubled sleep. Why doesn't Max respond? When does Max respond? How does Max respond—if he does respond? What weapons will Max use to respond?

"In this way," Asunta continued, "Max doesn't need to do anything to answer those who assault him. The fact of not doing anything provokes terror and in the end defeats the attacker, who doesn't understand why he isn't answered, then doubts the efficacy or ferocity of the attack, immediately feels completely worthless because he doesn't deserve a response, and in the end aggression and aggressor are forgotten and Max Monroy goes on, as cheerful . . ."

"As Johnnie Walker." I laughed then.

She wasn't too happy with this joke. Asunta was already embarking on the second example she wanted to give to complete the picture of Max Monroy's conduct. A rancorous cloud passed over her gaze, evoking, without looking at me, those who tried to become famous by attacking the fame of Max Monroy. Lesson learned: They succeeded only in increasing it. They were forgotten.

"And the second case?"

Asunta came back as if from a dream.

"Max Monroy is a cautious man." She smiled with a certain bitter nostalgia that did not escape my attention. The second example was that Max, who naturally is a cautious man, becomes even more cautious when he receives an improper or unexpected favor.

"Improper?"

If Asunta hesitated it was only for a second. Then she said: As improper as having imprisoned a dangerous man only as a favor to the great Max Monroy.

I searched in vain for a rictus of laughter, an ironic intention, an angry emphasis in Asunta's voice, her gaze, her posture. She had spoken as a statue would speak—if a statue could speak.

"Favors are paid for, I think," I continued so our talk would not die, as it could have died, right there, since I was trying to tie up loose ends and bring together what I knew with what I didn't know . . .

"Favors have a price, and then we realize the mistake it is to grant them and go mad trying to find an action to wipe out the obligation we have acquired to the person who did us the favor," she went on. "Do you see?"

"Death?" I asked with the innocent face I have practiced most in front of the mirror.

"Death?" she replied with an incredulous affirmation on the point of becoming a question.

"Death," she continued calmly, though with a certain pleading tone.

"Whose?" I didn't let her go.

Perhaps she hesitated for a moment. Then she said: "The death of the one who did us the favor."

"Improper?"

Or unexpected. Unexpected?

"The one who did the favor died."

"The advantages of being old," I said with an erotic calculation doomed, I knew beforehand, to fail. She did not appear to understand. On the contrary, she stressed that Max Monroy was a self-made man, but only in part. He inherited a great deal (I remained silent about my relationship, valid only if secret, with Max's mother, Antigua Concepción.)

If she spoke like his mother Doña Conchita (with reason she changed her name, refusing the diminutive in exchange for voluntary antiquity) she would say: Agrarian reform benefited him as much as it did his mother. It was the end of the old haciendas as big as all of Benelux. It took two days by train to travel the lands of William Randolph Hearst in Chihuahua and Sonora. "Citizen Kane," I interjected, and she continued, not understanding the allusion. She repeated the lesson: "Thirty-five percent of Mexico's territory in the hands of Gringos. The hacienda was broken, the system of communal lands was created—all for all, sure—agrarian law was violated, now small properties were accumulated and campesino lands stolen to construct hotels on the beaches, the campesinos didn't receive a thank you, or a whiskey, or a swim in the kidney-shaped pools, but most fled to the cities, above all 'dissipated and painted' Mexico City and the new industrial sectors created by the expropriation of the petroleum industry. Max's good fortune: first, agrarian repartition; second, the system of communal lands; third, small farmsteads; fourth, communal landowners without credit or machinery, subject to the law of the market, without protection or even a five-centavo piece, and fifth—lucky five—the campesino flight to industry, creation of a domestic market, saturation in demand, inequality, unemployment, the flight of labor to the United States, money returned by workers to their old communities, the explosion of cheap consumerism."

"And Monroy taking advantage of it all?"

"He isn't a thief." Asunta looked at me without affection. "He has today's money just as he had yesterday's. He has built a fortune on the earlier one, his mother's. He has multiplied Doña Conchita's goods" (please: Antigua Concepción, more respect for the dead!), "imposed very severe rules of discipline, justice, independence, knows the gulf that separates reputation from personality, protects the second, scorns the first, is implacable in getting rid of incompetents at the highest levels, occupies the center of the center, governs himself in order to govern others better, does not overstimulate the public . . ."

"And all of this for what?" I interrupted her because her exaltation of Max was beginning not only to annoy me but, in particular, to make me jealous. It fell upon me to learn about Max Monroy through the love of his dear dead mama. I was irritated by the admiration, as repetitive as a record, as unrestrained as an orgasm, of this woman who was more and more awful and perhaps, for that reason, more and more desired. Or, just the opposite . . .

"Why?" she said, disconcerted.

"Or for whom," I said, not daring to throw up to her the lack of sincerity: Everything she had said to me seemed learned, like a lesson that had to be memorized and repeated by the loyal servant of Max Monroy.

She went on as if she hadn't heard me. "Max controls demand with what supply can provide," she said like a jukebox.

"For what, for whom?" I tossed a coin on the piano.

"It would have been enough for him to inherit, Josué, with no need to increase his inheritance . . ."

"For whom?" I said in my best bolero voice.

A tremor of anger fought in Asunta's body against the sorrow of a resignation that seemed too satisfied.

"For you?" I grabbed her shoulders. "Will you be the heir?"

"He has no descendants," she moaned, surprised, "he had no children . . ."

"He has a lover, what the hell . . ."

Asunta detached herself from my growing weakness. I thought desire would strengthen me. She was undermining me: the longing to love her. The longing, nothing more.

"What joins the two of you? He's an old man. What is it that joins you, Asunta?"

To my surprise she said that smell joined them. What smell? Many smells. Now, the strange smell of an old man, the smell of an animal in a cave. Earlier, the smell of the countryside, where we met. I laughed a lot. Perhaps all that joins us is the smell of cow, chicken, burro, and shit, she said, serious but with a good deal of humor.

She looked at me with a fixity suspended between love and defiance.

"Mexico poor and provincial, mediocre and envious, hostile . . ."

She threw her arms around my neck.

"I don't want to go back there. Not for anything in the world."

She told me this in a whisper. I looked at her. She wasn't smiling. This was serious. She took my hand. She looked at it. She said my hands were beautiful. I smiled. I wasn't going to enumerate the charms of Asunta.

"Please, understand me," she said. "I owe everything to Max Monroy. Before, my life was very frustrated. Now, I'm a guided force."

"Like a missile?" I said with misplaced humor, as if I hadn't guessed something more serious in her embrace.

She looked at me again.

"Please, don't distract me."

I woke before dawn. Everyone was asleep. I anticipated the surprise of waking beside Asunta Jordán. I already felt the suffering that awaited me as punishment for obtaining what I most desired. Now everyone else was sleeping. What is there outside?

THE SECOND ROYAL Tribunal of the City of Mexico met in 1531 and made it clear that enslavement of the Indians favors miners and *encomenderos,* the colonists who hold Indian labor. Yes, but at the expense of the Indians, disagrees Vasco de Quiroga, member of the Tribunal. The labor of the Indians is the sinew of the land, the Tribunal maintains. The prosperity of the land depends on respect for indigenous traditions, responds Quiroga, and he moves from words to deeds. He frees his slaves. He becomes a priest. He founds in Santa Fe—here, where you are, Josué—the Republic of the Hospice, dedicated to saving indigenous children by teaching them Castilian along with the Otomí language; to singing and officiating and also preaching Christianity to their parents, without discrediting the native sacred tradition, but fusing Christianity with innate religiosity; to celebrating, without candles, without consecration, the "Plain Mass" as a cordial invitation to shared spirituality. Quiroga evokes a time common to all, Spaniards and Indians: a Golden Age that renews the mythic spirit of the Otomís and also the faith of the early Christian church: The Indians, Quiroga writes, are simple, gentle, humble, obedient, they lack pride, ambition, and greed. They were not born to be slaves. They are rational beings. If some are vagabonds, they must be taught to work. And if some are indolent, it is because the fruits of this earth are offered too easily. Indians and Christians can be today what they were yesterday and in this way become what they will be tomorrow. From Santa Fe, Vasco de Quiroga expands to Michoacán and founds the Hospice of Santa Fe on the shores of Lake Pátzcuaro. He respects the Tarasco language as he teaches the Spanish language. He is inspired by Thomas More's *Utopia.* The Indians should organize communally, for they are adrift in societies shattered into a thousand pieces by the savage conquest that speeds like a lightning flash from the Gulf to the Pacific, from the land of the Otomís to the land of the Purépechas, from Oaxaca to Xalisco, today's history faster than yesterday's, tomorrow's history broken too if the Indians are not given a language and a roof, care and doctrine, work and dignity. Tata Vasco, Papa Quiroga, Father Vasco the Indians call him, and he gives them collective ownership of the land, a six-hour workday, assigning the fruits of their labor to the necessities of life. He forbids luxury. He organizes every four families under a Principal. Vasco de Quiroga, in whose shadow you work, Josué, teaches that social organization requires a practical economy, that the European world must learn to live in harmony with Indian customs. What will be born of this teaching and this mutual respect? Is it worth wagering that the simple life, work and education, will create a new Mexican community without conquerors or conquered but protected by liberty and law?

"Does happiness have a price?" you, Josué, ask of the statue of Fray Vasco de Quiroga, Tata Vasco, that you pass by every day.

"Yes," the friar affirms. "The Indians have to be recruited by force so they can learn to be happy . . ."

"And the reward?" you ask Tata Vasco.

"Christian rebirth."

"And the method?"

"Using tradition to . . ."

"To dominate?"

Fray Vasco doesn't hear you. There was a drought in Michoacán. Quiroga strikes a rock with his staff. Water pours out of the stone when the crook of the bishop's crosier touches it. Is the miracle enough for you, Josué? Do you need something more than a miracle?

The savage soldiers of Nuño de Guzmán the conquistador come down from Xalisco, burn villages, take prisoners, demand tributes, spices, labor, give themselves extensive and abundant lands and water. Utopia isn't good for a race of porters and vassals, Utopia doesn't allow forced labor in the mines or company stores on the haciendas. Silver, cattle, seized lands, alcohol for weddings and funerals: The Indian flees the utopia of Tata Vasco, subjugated by the swords and horses of Nuño de Guzmán, takes refuge on the *latifundios:* It's the lesser of two evils . . . What can we do.

Every morning Josué questions the statue of Fray Vasco de Quiroga, Tata Vasco, in the district of Santa Fe in México, D.F.

"I am the father of your culture," Tata Vasco tells Josué one day.

Josué wonders if his mission consists in maintaining or changing it.

"GO ON, ANDALE, *ándale*."

Order, greeting and farewell, communication, familiarity and alienation, this Mexican verbal expression lends itself to as many interpretations as its national insularity permits: No one outside Mexico says *"ándale,"* and a Mexican reveals himself when he says it, the lawyer Antonio Sanginés told me one winter night in his house in the Coyoacán district.

This time, the garland of mischievous children was not climbing around his neck, and on the maestro's face I observed a seriousness at once customary and unusual. I mean, he almost always was very serious. Except this time—I read it in his face—he was serious only for me. And this *only for me* excluded the other person with whom I had visited Sanginés on previous occasions. My old buddy Jericó.

"How long has it been since you've seen each other?"

"A year."

"Ándale."

As usual, Sanginés the pedagogue began by evoking a series of allusions to his dealings with President Valentín Pedro Carrera. He prized his role as court adviser to the powerful: in government and in business. He knew them both, in the office building in Santa Fe and in the political encampment at Los Pinos. This is how he defined it, with complete simplicity.

While Max Monroy presided over a permanent empire in Santa Fe, at Los Pinos Valentín Pedro Carrera was the transient foreman of a six-year-long ranch. The occupier of the presidency knew he was temporary. The head of the firm aspired to permanence. How did these two powers get along?

Sanginés did not have to tell me. He valued being the intermediary between the political executive and the business executive, between Valentín Pedro Carrera and Max Monroy. Confirming this, Sanginés looked at me without blinking, his chin resting on his hands, and enumerated—yes, enumerated—his recommendations to President Carrera, like a local Machiavelli (I wouldn't say a neighborhood Florentine, no, I wouldn't say that, because after all, Maestro Sanginés had directed my professional thesis on the diabolical Niccolò):

Don't exaggerate expectations.

Don't attempt to lengthen the six-year term or seek reelection.

Longevity in office is fatal to one's reputation.

Remember that presidents begin in the light of hope and end in the shadow of experience.

In opposition, purity.

In power, compromise.

Prepare yourself in time to leave office, Mr. President.

You will be seen as a good president only if you know how to be a good ex-president.

Pause. I never saw a more bitter expression on Antonio's face than at that moment.

Exaggerate.

Lengthen.

Illuminate the nation.

Don't commit to anything.

Remain in office.

Don't leave.

I'm here.

Ándale, Jericó, *ándale.*

I suspected that Sanginés felt very bitter, that in the past year Jericó had taken possession of the presidential ear, reducing Sanginés to the most absolute marginality.

Why had he called me now?

With the habitual circumlocution of a lawyer from New Spain, Antonio Sanginés launched into a narrative that occupied us for a good part of the night. He evoked. He reproduced. He accelerated. He lingered.

"The times of the hero are over," Jericó told Carrera (just as

Sanginés had told Carrera). A revolutionary state legitimizes itself. Washington, Lincoln, Lenin, Mao, Castro, Madero—Carranza—Obregón—Calles—Cárdenas. Even Tlatelolco and delegitimization by way of crimes against the pure, simple movement that ought to accompany the revolutionary state to accredit it as such. Halt the movement of the state: The movement of society supplants it. The United States is master of silent renovation: Its most reactionary groups appropriate rebellion. The Daughters of the American Revolution are a group of ultraconservative old women who still use pince-nez and wear chokers and color their hair sky blue.

"The times of the hero are over. Government, state, and revolution are no longer the same. The old revolutionary state has lost all legitimacy. You have to give new legality to the new reality," declaimed Jericó.

"Count on me," Sanginés told the president.

"I'll take care of it," Jericó told Carrera and added: "In your name, of course."

Something unites us, Sanginés said with a sigh, something unites your friend Jericó and me. We have exercised more power the more distance we have maintained from power. Except my distance, compared to Jericó's, was disinterested.

He said he advised keeping watch over the country.

"And Jericó?" I asked.

He looked at me sadly but did not respond. Still, there can be no doubt that the detail illuminates the life. Just as a small dog enlivens the stiff portrait of an aristocrat, a gesture by Sanginés spoke volumes to me about his thinking. The most banal gesture: taking a crumb of bread and transforming it into a ball that, finally, in an unusual act for a man so well bred, he tossed to the floor and flattened with his shoe.

Only then did he resume speaking.

"I've always known Valentín Pedro Carrera. I'll summarize his career for you. He was a young idealist. He ran his presidential campaign while his wife was sick. Cynicism or compassion? He made the electorate cry. Doña Clarita died soon after Carrera won the election. She died in time. Carrera got a second wind thanks to grief and solitude. Except that grief ends and solitude doesn't. Then the fires spring up: arbitrariness, abuse of power, a kind of revenge against the destiny that raised him so high just to strip him of what power gives in abundance—appearance, the use of appearing, the abuse of being present . . . My advice, Josué, was born of a desire to control these extremes and employ the affliction of power to benefit power . . ."

I didn't know what Sanginés was drinking from an empty cup.

"I believe I have discovered the great flaw in power. The powerful man does not want to know what is done in his name. The great secular criminal, an Al Capone, knows and orders everything. But even the most fearsome tyrant opens the floodgates of a violence he himself cannot control. Who assassinated Mateotti, the last opposition deputy who served as a democratic excuse for Mussolini, leaving him no option other than dictatorship? Did Himmler itemize the concentration camp horror beyond Hitler's insane, abstract desire, concentrating it into mountains of suitcases, hair, eyeglasses, dentures, and broken dolls in Auschwitz? Did Stalin do anything other than follow the tyrannical desire of the revolutionary who died in time, Lenin the lay saint, I understand him better than his democratic followers, Bukharin, Kamenev . . . ? Not Trotsky, who was as hard as Stalin, but to his misfortune an educated man . . ."

My attentive gaze was a question: And Valentín Pedro Carrera?

Sanginés told me anecdotes. Carrera is a man in love with his own words. He can speak without stopping for hours. It is absolutely necessary to interrupt him from time to time. To help him. So he can take a breath. So he can have a drink. We all knew that this president needed official interrupters. We presidential lackeys took turns interrupting him.

"What gives? Do they think everything they say is interesting? Or are they afraid to be quiet and give someone else the floor? Are they afraid of being contradicted? What happens?" I asked with intense ingenuousness.

"I tell you, it's an art knowing how to interrupt the president. Jericó's acumen consists in never interrupting. Carrera realized it:

'You never interrupt me, Jericó. Thank you for that. But tell me why.' "

Sanginés was present. Jericó, he says, did not respond. Why was Sanginés there? What would Jericó have said to Carrera in the absence of a witness?

"The president is garrulous. I'm telling you because he told me. He also is master of a kind of pedantic indecisiveness. I mean, he is not an indecisive man like Hamlet, who weighs and tests his options. His indecision is a kind of farce. It's a way of saying, paradoxically, I have the power not to make any decision at all and to say whatever occurs to me."

I repeat: Sanginés's cup was empty.

"That was Jericó's astuteness, I realize it now. He knew Carrera did not act out of pure vanity and arrogance. On both counts Jericó acted for him. Carrera did and did not realize it, and he thanked Jericó for relieving him of an unwanted responsibility: Making decisions is the queen bee of power; it can also be its dead fly of feigned meekness."

What did the president want? The impossible: "Give me easy solutions to difficult problems."

"*Ça n'existe pas,*" Sanginés murmured. "Jericó's wickedness . . ."

I raised my eyebrows. Sanginés sighed. He made it clear that he knew what he was talking about, that his was not the voice of a resentful man removed from the favors of power. He wanted to remain a loyal counselor. Not to mention a responsible citizen. I let my eyebrows drop. I accused myself of sentimentality. Because I owed a great deal to Sanginés. Because of my old friendship with Jericó. Because I was still, by comparison, an innocent . . .

"Think technical. Talk agrarian. Long live liberty. Down with equality. Count on me. Don't trust too many counselors. You prepare the *mole,* too many cooks spoil the sauce. Send your enemies to distant embassies. And your friends too."

With these and similar words, Jericó was insinuating himself into the president's confidence, alarming him at times ("You've taken the wolf by the ears, you can't let him go but you can't hold him forever either"), encouraging him at others ("Don't worry too much, equality is the most unequal thing that exists"), cutting him off on occasions (the classic symbolic knife slitting his throat), warning him on others (the no less classic eye opened by the right index finger on the lid), elaborating justifications ("politics can be soft, interests are always hard"). The president gave him simple tasks. Read the papers, Jericó. Keep me informed. At night I'll read whatever seems important.

"What did your pal do?" Sanginés asked rhetorically. "What do you think?"

He gave me an ugly look. I gave him a beatific one.

"He selected items from the press. He cut out whatever suited him whenever it suited him. News of general tranquillity and happiness and prosperity under the leadership of Valentín Pedro Carrera: A president becomes more and more isolated and eventually believes only what he wishes to believe and what his lackeys make him believe—"

I interrupted. "Jericó . . . I think that . . . he's . . ."

"The complete courtier, Josué. Don't be deceived."

"And you, Maestro?" I tried to irritate him.

"I repeat: a loyal counselor."

Ándale, ándale, ándale.

"DON'T OPEN YOUR mouth. Don't say anything."

And I who had my romantic phrases prepared, my sentimental allusions derived from a potpourri of musical boleros, recollections of Amado Nervo, dialogues from North American movies (Don't let's ask for the moon. We have the stars), everything refined, nothing vulgar, though fearing my good manners would disappoint her in bed, perhaps she desired more brutal treatment, coarser words (you're my whore, whore, I adore your tight little cunt), no, I didn't dare, only pretty phrases, and as soon as I had said one, the first one, when I was on top of her, she came out with that brutal "Don't open your mouth. Don't say anything."

I proceeded in silence. I came, censuring my mouth, the mouth

I wasn't to open, obeying her categorical instructions. And I'm not complaining. She gave me everything, except words. I was left in doubt. Are words intrusive in love? Or is love without words only partial, incomplete in its sentimental formulation? I shouldn't think that. She had given me everything. She had permitted me everything. As if in her, in this act, lay the culmination of half-complete loves with the nurse Elvira Ríos, tormented ones with Lucha Zapata, venal ones with the whore with the bee who ended up married to Errol Esparza's father, jailed as the presumed killer of Don Nazario, and escaped from prison despite the vigilance (unhealthy, obsessive, I now told myself) of Miguel Aparecido.

Asunta Jordán . . .

Preambles to love, Cupid's broken arrows that finally gave me the great pleasure of a complete sexual act, at once instinctive and calculated, demanding and permissive, natural and artificial, pure and perverse: What was there in the provincial body of Asunta Jordán that gathered everything into a single woman and a single act? Everything I've said and nothing. Nothing, in the sense that she expressed the words of the act, which did not encounter the verbal separation that I (that every man) wants to give it, though later he may repent of, or forget, the words he exclaimed, sighed, shouted when he came abundantly.

Were words necessary? Was Asunta telling me that the act was sufficient in itself, that words cheapened it because they were inferior to pleasure, verbal placebos, derivations of the bolero, of poetry, of the impossible analogy between the act and the language of love . . . ?

"Don't touch my face."

No. No. No. All the negations of the moment diluted the fiesta though the fiesta had been memorable and I was an imbecile who had no reason to complain. I did something wrong since, as satisfied as a god that creates love, the prohibition against speaking diminished the completeness of the act. I was mistaken. One could be mute from birth and enjoy the woman with no possibility of uttering a word. Why did I attempt to verbalize, give speech to the act that had culminated without the need for any words at all? And why did she forbid language in so categorical and severe a manner: Don't open your mouth. Don't say anything?

And why, silenced and confused, did I try to replace the forbidden word with an amatory and affectionate gesture? (The two things are not the same: The amatory is passion, affection is concession.) Or with good manners, gratitude, and why not, the brief prologue to seduction . . .

We know we have spent many hours together, at the office, at times in a café as a distraction from our obligations, often at working lunches, rarely at social dinners, more often at cocktail parties where she made her appearance as part of Max Monroy's power, the visible, tangible, desirable power of a man as famous as he is mysterious: A year in the office in Santa Fe and I still hadn't seen, not even glimpsed, the top dog, the chief, the bossman, the *qaid*.

Knowing she had constant access to him and all I knew about him I knew through her (and, in secret, through the informed, interred voice of Antigua Concepción, but this I could not repeat) . . . At the office, no one on the ten lower floors and the two top ones had met the chief executive, Max Monroy. I began to imagine he was a fiction created and maintained to make people believe in an untouchable power and to uphold the authority of the enterprise. I would have believed this if, from time to time, Asunta had not descended to the world of mortals to share with me something said or done by Monroy—his work a constant reference; his words a frequent one; his current life never mentioned.

My relationship with Asunta, therefore, had been purely professional. With the exception of my adventure in her boudoir, guessing at, touching, and smelling her underclothes, something only I and the maid who caught me in the act knew about. Had the servant told Asunta or was she so discreet—or fearful—that she kept quiet? I couldn't know and couldn't ask. If Asunta knew, she behaved as if she didn't, and in either case my sexual excitement increased: If she knew, how exciting it was to share that fact as a secret. If she didn't know, it was even more moving to have a sensation that made me solitary master of her underthings when they were not covering her body. And in any event—emotion, enthusiasm—what delight was produced in me by the memory of those bras, panties, garters, stockings, arranged like a small army of the libido in their ordered bureau drawers.

How could I approach her beyond our daily working relationship? By imagining her reality or realizing her imagination?

I tried to approach her by approaching those who worked in the Vasco de Quiroga building, as if the undesired origin of the desired woman would come alive in the origin of Monroy's employees in the Utopia building. As if on knowing them, I would see a lessened Asunta, still without power. As if, in my mean-spirited rancor, I desired to see her expelled from Olympus and returned to the mini-hell of anonymous work.

I WAS RESTING, my arms crossed above me and my hands forming a kind of pillow, when I heard footsteps on the stairs and identified them with Jericó. They were phantom steps that sent back to me an echo of my best friend and, perhaps, my best years. Everything was thrown into turmoil (for nostalgia should not last too long) by the sensation that Jericó not only had reached the apartment on Calle de Praga we once shared but was opening the door with the key we also had shared.

I felt a certain uneasiness: I was the one who lived here now, and this was the place I left to go to work at the San Juan de Aragón Prison or the Santa Fe offices. For the first time, I was the master of the house. Jericó's key going into the lock on the door was like a physical and spiritual violation. He came in and made himself right at home. He had told me, from the beginning, that the place needed his noise even though he shared it with me, the newcomer, the stone guest, the Tancredo of bullfighting.

"Wake up, Josué," he said from the door, raising his hand to his forehead in a kind of pseudomilitary salute.

"I am awake," I said reluctantly, looking at the advancing shadow out of the corner of my eye.

"Did you eat yet?" he persisted and didn't allow me to answer. "Because I ask you, pal, who digests better: the man who sleeps after a banquet or the one who goes out to hunt?"

I shrugged. Jericó was interrupting a daydream dedicated to Asunta, what she was like, how I could have her, would she love me again, or was our encounter only a passing quickie, informal, without consequences?

I was recalling and consecrating it, Asunta's body, and now Jericó proceeded with anatomical brutality: "Are you going out to hunt, are you coming home to sleep? How do you know?"

He poked my navel and drew a line between my ribs.

"By opening up your belly."

He laughed.

"There's the proof."

I emerged from my lethargy. I sat on the edge of the bed. Jericó prepared coffee. He had taken possession of something that, I told myself, offended, he had never left. I was the intruder. I was practically the vagrant.

"What do you want?" I said, longing to annoy him.

His expression didn't change: "I want you." He offered me a steaming cup of instant coffee.

"Why?"

He launched into a discourse that seemed interminable. Who were we? Two people shipwrecked from paternal authority. That's what makes us brothers. We lack a family. We didn't have an old man. We were abandoned, liberated, set adrift.

"Whatever you like."

"And?"

"That obliges us to know our internal limits. You realize that the majority of human beings never seriously ask themselves: Who am I? What are my limits? Why? Because family and society have marked out the path and boundaries for them. Here, kid, don't step off the path, look as far ahead as you like, but don't look right or left. Eyes fixed on the horizon we presented to you because we think about you, son, and want the best for you, don't think about anything, everything's been thought about in advance, my boy, it's for your own good, don't stray, don't venture anything, don't turn away from a destiny you don't deserve to know independently, why would you, boy, if we've already prepared it for you? We prepared the future for you the way you make a bed, here are the pillows, here are the covers, get in and sleep, baby, don't disturb the bed, after all, it took a lot for us to arrange it for you and have it ready so you can sleep peacefully, sleep and sleep and sleep, youngster, kid, baby, boy, son, and not worry about a thing."

He made a nasty face and then burst into laughter.

"Wake up, Josué, arise and walk!"

I told him I was listening. He didn't expect any words from me. He had brought his own speech and my job was to listen to him and not make a sound.

"I continue: You and I weren't born for domesticity. Consider your sexual life. From pillar to post, here a vagabond, there a whore, here a nurse, there a secretary . . ."

"I do better than you, a really solitary plainsman," I grumbled, angry that he knew what I thought he was unaware of.

"We have no friends," he said, somewhat disconcerted.

"Do you think we're part of a vanished civilization?"

"We're always obliged to correct the errors in our destiny, whatever it may have been, Josué. So it's more than the truth . . ."

"A different destiny? How?"

"By getting together with people. Organizing the people. Taking a bath with the masses, like the showers you and I used to take together, but now with millions of human beings who want to be redeemed."

"Won't they be redeemed better on their own?"

"No," Jericó almost shouted. "What's needed is the head, the leader!"

"The Duce, the Fuehrer," I said with a skeptical smile.

"The country is ripe," Jericó asserted, corrected his course, and returned to him and me.

"Yes, I swear to you, God's truth, only you, and only I, we weren't born to be husbands or fathers or even faithful lovers. You and I, Josué, were born for freedom, without ties, the road cleared to be and act without reporting to anyone, do you understand? We are free, old friend, free as the air, the rain, the sea, the birds!"

"Until a hunter shoots you, and you fall and become supper. Sure . . ."

"Risks," Jericó said with a laugh, "and the air can be disturbed by a cyclone, the rain can be stormy, the sea rough, and the bird, with luck, unconquered and flying toward freedom."

"An old bird, you mean," I said to harmonize with the jubilation of my old companion. I even sang: "Wounded bird of the dawn . . ."

"In other words, Josué, do you believe you and I have a special mission, since love, home, marriage are forbidden to us?"

"Friendship would be enough," I murmured with no desire to offend or even inquire.

He slammed one fist with the other. It was a gesture of action, of virtue, of energy, of a voluntary desire to lead. To lead me to him and himself to me as well.

He said the country was not advancing. Why? The president is weak. He hasn't governed with energy. We did everything halfway. You and I? No. Those who governed us. Everything halfway, everything mediocre. We though we were king of the world because we had oil. We sold it for a lot of money. With the profits, we bought nothing but trinkets. A luxury six-year term. We behaved like nouveaux riches. There was no "tomorrow." The price went down. Debts remained. A new horizon. Commerce. A quick treaty, to deck out another six-year term. Things are free to move about. Not people. Currency, stocks, objects move. Workers remain stationary, though they're needed in the USA. Come because we need you. But if you come, we'll kill you. Okay? Fair enough? Since then we simply fill in one hole before the next one opens. We're like the little Dutch boy in the story, his finger stuck in the hole in the dike to avoid the inevitable flood. But we only put our finger deep in our asshole. And it smells bad.

Theatrically, my friend Jericó pulled aside the curtain in the room to reveal, from our high perch, the omnipresent urban chaos of Mexico City, the great deep pyramid of Cementos Tolteca and Seguros América and Avenidas Cuauhtémoc, the fragmented pyramid sunk in primeval mud and asphyxiated in secondary air, the clogged traffic, the overflowing buses, the streets numerous but uncountable: the lines of workers at five in the morning waiting to go to their job and return at seven at night in order to return at five . . . Six hours for working. Eight for commuting. Life.

"Do you realize?" Jericó exploded and I saw him this way, now, in shirtsleeves, his shirt open to his navel, his hairless chest demanding the heroism of bronze, the childish cheeks, subtly stripped of baby fat, of a face consumed by the heroic gesture and the intense brilliance of his pale eyes.

Did I realize? he asked rhetorically, pointing down and into the distance, a country of more than a hundred million inhabitants that cannot provide work, food, or schooling to half the population, a country that does not know how to employ the millions of workers it needs to build highways, dams, schools, housing, hospitals, to preserve forests, enrich fields, construct factories, a country where hunger, ignorance, and unemployment lead to crime, a criminality that invades everything, the police are criminal, order disintegrates, Josué, the politicians are corrupt, the canoe has sprung a leak, we live in a Xochimilco with no Dolores del Río or Pedro Armendáriz or pigs to save us: The canals are filled with garbage, they were choked ·by filth, abandonment, thorns, the corpses of piglets, chicken bones, the remains of flowers . . .

He came up to me but didn't touch me.

"Josué. This year I've traveled the country from one end to the other. The president gave me the job of forming groups for celebrating fiestas. I betrayed him, Josué. I've gone from village to village to form combat groups, organizing immigrants who find no way out, campesinos ruined by the Free Trade Agreement, discontented workers, inciting all of them, my brother, to slowdowns, to boycotts, to stealing parts, to self-inflicted accidents, to arson and murder . . ."

I listened to him with a mixture of fascination and horror, and if one impelled me to distance him, the other led me to an embrace, a mixture that was idiotic but explicable of what in me refused and what in me desired. From village to village, he repeated, recruiting at funerals, churches, dances, barbecues . . .

"Following the orders of El Señor Presidente, you understand? preparing the festivities that matter to him so much in order to distract, deceive, put blinders on the mule, Josué, without realizing that here we have a gigantic force for action, a force of people who are fed up, forsaken, desperate, ready for anything . . ."

I asked without saying a word: Anything?

"For submission and abandonment, because that has been the rule for centuries," he continued, reading the question in my gaze. "For the festive deceit, which is what the president wants."

"And you?" I managed, finally, to squeeze in a word.

I didn't have to say what I was going to say.

And you?

"If you don't want to hear the answer, don't ask the question," said Jericó.

"DON'T TOUCH MY face." "Don't open your mouth." "Don't say anything." All these prohibitions from Asunta excited my imagination and I reproached myself, wondering if I could be so boorish that I was not satisfied with her sex but demanded of her a chatter that was, barely, a complement to my own "lyric poetry": the words that in my sentimental fictions corresponded to physical love. I felt in me a fountain of poetic chivalry that I wanted to accompany the *more bestiarium,* the animal custom that sex is, with a verbal reduction something like the musical accompaniment to a bolero, or the background music in a film . . . in any case, *more angelicarum.*

And Asunta asked for silence. She cut off my words and left me perplexed. I didn't know if the demand for silence was the condition of a promise: Be quiet and you'll see me again. Or a condemnation: Be quiet because you won't have me again. Was this the sublime coquetry of the woman, the doubt that left me hanging and allowed me to guess at the worst and the best, repeated delight or exile from pleasure, heaven with Asunta and hell without her?

I wanted to believe I was a ludic subject of the enchantress, that

I would return to her bed, her graces, her blessing, on a night when I least expected it. That, in a sense, she would put me to the test. That my virility had seduced her forever. That in secret she would tell herself, I want more, Josué, I want more, though her coquetry (or her discretion) moved her to circumspection in order to transform the wait into pleasure not only renewed but multiplied . . . It was enough for me to believe this in order to arm myself with patience and, with patience, to obtain many favors. The first, the gift of virtue. I deserved her love because I was faithful and knew, like an ancient knight, how to wait and not despair, stand vigil over the weapons of sex, respond calmly to the call of my lady. This idea of chaste love hampered my imagination for a few days. I launched into the reading and rereading of *Don Quixote,* above all reading aloud the passages of love and honor dedicated to Dulcinea.

I'll tell you, this mania did not last very long, because my flesh was impatient and my heart less strong than I had thought, so Asunta stopped being Dulcinea-Iseult-Heloise and became a base fetish, to the extent that her photograph at the head of my bed occupied a quasivirginal spot, and I say "quasi" because on a few nights I did not resist the temptation to masturbate looking at her face (upside down, it's true, given that my jerking off occurred while I was lying in bed and Asunta's image hung vertically, held up by a tack) and surrendering, in the end, to solitary pleasure, forgetting Asunta, reproaching myself for my weakness though repeating that line about "Things are known to Onan unknown to Don Juan."

Don Juan! I loved Mozart's opera though I was astounded that in it the seducer seduces no one: not the disdainful Doña Ana, or the peasant Zerlina, or his former lover Doña Elvira, bent now on revenge.

Stripped of literary, oneiric, onanist, fetishist, etcetera words and opportunities, what remained for me, I ask the reader, but to return to the attack, be brave, take the citadel by force? In other words, have the audacity to return at midnight to the Castle of Utopia, the palace inhabited by Asunta on the thirteenth floor, where one day I had ventured to contemplate and touch and smell my lady's underthings, risking ridicule at entering her bedchamber and taking her by dint of strength—or the success of being accepted because, ladies and gentlemen, this was what she secretly hoped for from me: audacity, risk, daring, boldness, all the synonyms you like to supplant and sustain the pure, simple desire of tasting the flesh and dominating the body of a woman named Asunta.

I had, thanks to my administrative duties in the company, master keys. I could go into Asunta's apartment and move around like a thief who has cased the terrain, even my beauty's bedroom. On the way I grew accustomed to the darkness, so when I reached the bedroom I was aware of Asunta's absence. The bed was perfectly made. No proof existed that she had slept here.

This simple fact unleashed in me a storm of jealousy and aberrant suppositions. If she wasn't here, where could she be gallivanting at one-thirty in the morning? I rejected the more obvious explanations. She was at a dinner. Why hadn't she told me about it? Because she had absolutely no obligation to let me know about her social activities. Had she gone on vacation? Impossible. I knew her schedule better than my own. Asunta was a workaholic who did not miss a single minute of her work schedule. Ah, the bathroom . . . Not there either. I opened the door and saw a dry, clean place free of humanity (or rather, the humanity I longed for). I had the sensation of how similar an empty bathroom was to a morgue. I lost my mind. No doubt Asunta was hiding under the bed to mock me. No. She went into her closet because, perversely, she liked to smell and feel herself enveloped by the clothing that once, when she was a little provincial wife, she could not have. Not at all. Behind a curtain, hiding from herself? Ridiculous.

What was left to explore? My exalted spirit, my jealousy coming in vague waves, my desire in tempestuous agitation, my loss of all common sense, were manifested in the uncontrollable movement of my body, the sweat that ran down my neck and armpits, the nerves roused in my arms and legs, the mute excitation of my sex, tense in secret repose, saving itself for the great fiesta of love waiting for me, I was certain, in some corner of this false utopia in Santa Fe.

"Max Monroy is a strong, secure man, Josué. So much so that

he never locks the door of his apartment, up on the fourteenth floor."

I knew that on the roof of the building there was a helicopter waiting for Max's orders and a wing for the services and rooms of his cooks, bodyguards, servants, and pilots. Also, I repeat, I knew his immense self-confidence (the vanity of the powerful man) kept open the doors of his apartment, which I now penetrated with the supreme audacity of a desire that drove away any feeling of danger as I blindly crossed what I supposed was a living room: The TV screens shone solitary in the night, as if they could not resign themselves to being turned off and would continue transmitting day and night commercial announcements, soap operas, political commentary, news, old movies, with an innocent longing, failed from the start, to find a conclusion.

I left out the dining room with its twelve chairs. The library with the gleaming backs of its books. The illuminated paintings of Zárraga, Soriano, and Zurbarán (I respected them as if they were a trio of singers). I dared to approach a door that announced repose and isolation.

I opened it.

They ignored me.

What I heard when I opened the door, Asunta's words of love for Max, readers must imagine . . .

I CLIMBED INTO the helicopter behind Asunta. She sat in the back of the craft, beside a shadow named Max Monroy. I had no time to greet him. I took a seat next to the pilot as the propellers made the sound of a hurricane and conversation—even the most elementary, like good morning—became impossible.

The helicopter made an alarming vertical ascent that seemed to pierce the sky and eternity for a vague instant before the low, dangerous, turbulent flight, difficult and problematic, that carried us from Santa Fe to Los Pinos, the offices of the honorable president of the republic Don Valentín Pedro Carrera, that is, to a bare, paved-over space surrounded by squat, reinforced buildings and protected, at the exit, by a blur of mastiffs howling so loudly they eclipsed—and almost demanded silence from—the helicopter's engines.

I got out before anyone else and saw Max Monroy for the first time. Asunta climbed down and offered her hand to the spectral being at the back of the craft who appeared before me like a shadow, perhaps because that is what Max Monroy had been—had always been—for me until then, so that his physical presence affected me as if my own soul had been revealed to me, as if this phantom, upon becoming corporeal, gave me a physical reality I had not known in myself before.

Asunta offered him her arm. Monroy refused with an energetic chivalry verging on rudeness. He walked along the pavement without looking at anyone but looking straight ahead, as if for him terrestrial accidents did not exist. Asunta was at his side, with a visible, irritating preoccupation very inferior to the serious—not to say severe—care the nurse Elvira Ríos had offered me. I walked behind the pair. Preceding all of us was an army officer—I couldn't read his rank—but I had eyes only for Max Monroy, dressed in black with a white shirt and a blue bow tie with white dots.

He walked upright, not saying a word. His head rested on his shoulders like a pumpkin on dark soil. He had no neck. His clothes were at once too short and too long, obliging me to wonder about his height. He wasn't tall. He wasn't short. He was as ambivalent as his attire, clothes that could seem stripped of personality if they hadn't been worn and therefore personalized by this precise human being who consequently seemed at that moment a man in disguise, but disguised as himself, as if he were crossing the stage of the great theater of the world knowing it was a theater, while the rest of us believed we were in and living with reality.

Knowing the world is a theater and giving it the advantage of knowing itself to be reality though we know it isn't . . . I wonder to this very day why, seeing Max climb out of the helicopter and advance along the landing strip with the firm though mortal step of a man in his eighties, my own clothing didn't make me laugh, along with the clothes of Asunta and the pilot who remained on the strip looking at us with a smile I chose to judge as skeptical. And the smile of the presidential guard ahead of us, leading the way. For in Monroy's body, his way of being and walking forward, I guessed at the multiple paradox of our knowing we were disguised not when we go to a carnival but when we dress every day to attend to our jobs, our loves, our diversions, our sorrows and joys. And when we see ourselves naked? Isn't this the primeval disguise, the toga of external skin that masks our organic dispersion of brain, bones, viscera, unattached muscles, like the contents of a shopping basket spilling out on the floor if not for the corporeal container?

The mastiffs barked. As Max approached, they maintained a silence of slavering lower jaws, allowed us to pass, retreated. No doubt the presidential guard walking ahead of us quieted them. It didn't fail to attract my attention, however, that Monroy had not, even for an instant, slowed his pace or looked at the dogs, moving forward at the speed he had settled on as if obstacles or dangers did not exist. Have I invented what I'm saying? Does it obey a reality and not my interpretation of reality? And wasn't this the dilemma Max Monroy had put in my hands: the eternal problem of knowing the line between reality and fantasy, or rather, between reality and a perception of reality? Was all of reality a fantasy in which a man like Max Monroy, in possession of the central character in the drama, assumes as true his own fantasy and leads the rest of us into being phantoms of a phantom, the cast that is secondary to the star of an *auto sacramental* pompously called *Life*?

In this state of mind, how could I not recall my youthful reading of Calderón de la Barca and his *Great Theater of the World*: The protagonist humanity waits impatiently behind the scenes until the supreme director of the drama, God himself, invents humankind and says: "Action! On stage!" But since "humanity" is an abstraction, what God really does is assign a role to each and every one of his creatures—Max Monroy, Asunta Jordán, Jericó, me . . . the entire extensive cast of this novel that well could be a short film of the superproducer God, Inc., L.L.P.

A preview. A trailer. But with a warning: The star is named Max Monroy. The rest are secondary roles and even extras. We who carry the spears. The ones in the chorus. The ones in the crowd.

Then who was this man who advanced between hidden weapons, silenced dogs, and a minimum escort: the officer, Asunta, and me? If he was a man in disguise, was the immense dignity with which he climbed the stairs to the president's office, his clenched jaw, his closed mouth with tight, invisible lips also a disguise? He walked forward and entered the office of the president, who was accompanied only by Jericó, not looking at Jericó and looking at the president with deep eyes, and when Valentín Pedro Carrera welcomed him and offered his hand, Max Monroy did not return the greeting, and when the president invited us to take a seat and he himself sat down, Max Monroy looked at him with that deep gaze filled with memory and foresight.

"Remain standing, Mr. President."

If Carrera was disconcerted, he hid it very well.

"As you choose. Do you prefer to speak standing?"

Monroy settled into a chair.

"No. I sit. You stand, Señor."

We looked at one another for a moment. Jericó looked at me and I at him. Asunta at the president and the president at Monroy. Max looked at no one. And not as proof of crushing pride but, on the contrary, as if it pained him to see and be seen, obliging me to realize, at that moment, why he never allowed himself to be seen. The gaze of others hurt him. It wounded him to see and be seen. His kingdom was one of absence. And yet, and this was the greatest paradox, his business was sight, sound, spectacle: He lived by what he was not; by what perhaps, repelled him.

For a moment I lost track of what was going on. Monroy was humiliating the president of the republic, whose only response as he remained standing before a seated Monroy was to order the officer who had brought us here:

"You may withdraw, Captain."

LEAVING BEHIND MY fraternal relationship with Jericó, a double movement impelled me both forward and back.

Forward: my fairly fleeting contact with other workers in the office of Max Monroy. Since I had grown up in the well-provided isolation of the house on Berlín, with no company other than the severe María Egipciaca and no friendships but those at school—Errol and Jericó—my contact with other young people had been, if not nonexistent, then barely sporadic. I don't know, vigilant readers, if when I have exercised the right of the narrator—an amiable authoritarian—to select the stellar scenes in my life, I have left in novelistic limbo the other persons who surrounded me at schools, in offices, on the streets.

I have already recounted the intense desires that carried me, at a given moment, from the house on Berlín to the apartment on Praga to the prison at San Juan de Aragón to the Cerrada de Chimalpopoca to the office of Max Monroy. But since I had been in that office for almost two years (and though my primary relationship was with Asunta Jordán and, through her, with a Max Monroy who assumed in my imagination the hazy trappings of a phantom), I could not fail to observe, though to a lesser degree than what I've said here, my colleagues at work and how I got along with them.

I should indicate here that my anxieties and concerns, enigmas and humiliations sought an outlet on two very distinct levels—contrary, I should say.

I spent some time ingratiating myself with my colleagues. Please remember that Jericó and I were brought up in a kind of hothouse, I with very little contact beyond the house on Berlín and my jailer María Egipciaca, and he in the enclosure of the garret on Praga. And this happened not because of a predetermined plan but in a natural way. I've already told how, at school, Jericó and I gravitated toward each other to the exclusion of the "high-spirited boys" more interested than Jericó and I in sports, tiresome jokes, and, in any case, family life, and we were soon connected by intellectual curiosity and the tutoring of Filopáter. We were closer to Nietzsche and Saint Thomas than to our classmates Pecas and Trompas, and our contact with the other teachers occurred only in class or when the innocent pervert Soler hefted our balls before we played sports.

Errol Esparza had been our only contact with a family life that, to judge by his, it was better not to have. Living domestically, as Errol did with Don Nazario and Doña Estrellita, was a hymn to the benefits of orphanhood. Though being an orphan may mean being abandoned to the expectation of recovering lost parents or a habitual resignation to never seeing them again.

I don't know if these ideas crossed the minds of those who one day compared themselves to Castor and Pollux, the mythical offspring of a queen and a swan. I lost sight of Jericó for years and still don't know for certain where he lived and what he did, since his memories of his time in France were patently illusory: There was no City of Light in his tale except as a reference so literary and cinematic that the contrast was obvious to the North American references he knew about. Jericó's Baedeker reached as far as the United States and did not cross the Atlantic. I came to this conclusion but never wanted to test it directly. As I've said, I didn't ask Jericó anything so he wouldn't ask me anything either.

On the other hand, a good deal had happened to me. Lucha Zapata and the little house in the district of Los Doctores. Miguel Aparecido and the penitentiary of San Juan de Aragón. I realized all this experience was in no way ordinary. Lucha was a lost, weak woman, while Miguel and the prison population were, by definition, marginal and eccentric beings. That gave rise to my decision to visit, floor by floor, office by office, the employees in the building on Plaza Vasco de Quiroga in the Santa Fe District, seat of Max Monroy's empire: Who were *the others*?

It was difficult to classify them. Except for the architects, who generally came from families with money and sometimes with a pedigree. The profession sheltered many scions of old, half-feudal nineteenth-century families who had disappeared with the revolution and were anxious to recover the stature they had lost by having their sons and grandsons follow a career "for decent people," which was the general view of architecture. You should note that the beach, country, and city houses of the new rich were the work of architects who were the children of the old rich (or the new poor). Those lodged in Monroy's offices were no exception. Their tailors had adorned them with elegantly cut suits, their shirts were discreet, rarely white, their ties had a foreign label, their shoes were Italian loafers, their hair was cut with a razor.

They were the exception. The lawyers in the company, the accountants, the secretaries, were the children of other lawyers, accountants, or secretaries, but their variety fascinated me: I visited them to learn about and be amazed at the upward mobility available to a part of our society. Drinking coffee, asking for a favor, receiving a report, going up and down the honeycomb of the Utopia building like a bumblebee, I met the son of the shopkeeper, the shoemaker, the mechanic, and the dentist, the daughter of the dressmaker, the receptionist, and the employee of the beauty salon and again the children of clerks at Sears, minor bureaucrats, and peddlers. Offspring of Ford, of Volkswagen of Mexico, of the Ceranoquistes of Guanajuato, of Millennium Perisur, of tourist agencies and hospitals, armed with Nivada watches and Gucci shoes, Arrow shirts and Ferragamo ties, driving their Toyotas bought with a down payment of three thousand pesos, taking their family on vacation in an Odyssey minivan, using credit from Scotiabank, celebrating festive occasions with a basket of imports from La Europea, they were men and women of all sizes: tall and short, fat and thin, blond, brunet, dark-skinned and chestnut-haired, no one younger than twenty-five or older than fifty: a young group, modern, stylish, embedded in the social life of national capitalism (sometimes neocolonial and often globalized), possessing generally good manners, though at times the women demonstrated a certain chewing-gum vulgarity in their fishnet stockings and high heels (like my never carefully considered Ensenada de Ensenada de Ensenada), most of them with a professional appearance, tailored suits, and severe hairstyles, as if copying the model of the principal Lady of the Enterprise, Asunta Jordán. And the men generally courteous, well-spoken, and even relishing their innate amiability, though as soon as they found themselves only with men they reverted to the vulgar language that certifies friendship among Mexican machos (among other reasons, in order to dispel any suspicion of homosexuality, above all in a country where greetings between men consist of an embrace, an unusual act for a Gringo and one repellent to an Englishman).

Let's say then that on the twelve floors permitted to me in the Utopia building, I tried to be a model of circumspection and affability, without any familiarity, cronyism, fake intimacies, or vulgar winking. On the other hand, my sentimental soul, wounded by Asunta's disdain, searched for the lowest, most falsely compensatory comfort: the return to the brothel of my adolescence, but this time only to be taken in and muddied up to my ears. I made a move toward the past in Hetara's house, where Jericó took me for the first time as a teenager and I fornicated with the woman with the bee on her buttock who one day reappeared as the second Señora de Esparza and then as the lover and partner of the gang leader Maxi Batalla, eventually becoming a prisoner and then a fugitive. Where were they now, she and the Mariachi? What surprises were they preparing for us?

I have left for the end my most laudatory thoughts about Max Monroy and his enterprise. I say this to purge myself of my sins and reappear before all of you in a dignified light. Many excellent young Mexicans, scholarship students, were educated in foreign universities. They attend centers of learning such as Harvard, MIT, Oxford, Cambridge, the Sorbonne, and Caltech. They acquire formidable scientific knowledge. They return to Mexico and cannot find a position. The large national firms import technology, they don't generate it. The young people educated in Europe and the United States stay and cannot find work or leave again.

I have to give Max Monroy credit—to give you the most complete version possible of what I saw and did in his company—for keeping young scientists and mathematicians educated abroad in Mexico. Monroy realized something: If we don't generate technology and science, we will always be at the tail end of civilization. He put Salvador Venegas, a graduate of Oxford, and José Bernardo Rosas, an alumnus of Cambridge, at the head of the technoscientific team, while Rodrigo Aguilar, who studied at the London School of Economics, coordinated the project dedicated not only to gathering and applying technologies but to inventing them.

The business team was guided by one norm: giving greater importance to research than to innovation. Venegas, Rosas, and Aguilar proposed taking the formative leap from computing and communications based on Max Planck's quantum theory. The unity of all things is called energy. The proof of energy is light. Light is emitted in discrete quantities. On the basis of this theory (science is a hypothesis not verified or denied by facts; literature is a fact that is verified without having to prove anything, I told myself), the young scientists apply thought to practice, perfecting a pocket simputer capable of immediately converting text to word and thereby giving information access to the rural, illiterate population of Mexico in accordance with Ortega y Gasset's exclamation when he interviewed an Andalusian campesino: "How erudite this illiterate man is!" Reducing the distances between economic vanguards and rearguards. Attacking an elite's monopoly of knowledge. Less bureaucratic statism. Less antisocial capitalism. More community organization. Less distance among the economic area, the popular will, and political control. Bringing technology to the agrarian world. Giving weapons to the poor. Julieta Campos's book *What Shall We Do with the Poor?* was something like the gospel of the intellectuals who worked in the Utopia building.

"What marching orders were we given?" Aguilar asked himself. "Activating citizen initiatives."

"Municipalities. Local solutions to local problems," Rosas added.

"Cooperation of urban universities with the rural interior," Aguilar continued.

"Putting an end to the nepotism, patrimonialism, and favoritism that have been the plagues of our national life," added Venegas.

The dark young scientist, focused, serious, and brilliant, concluded: "Either we create a model of orderly growth with local autonomy or fatally deepen the divide between the two Mexicos. Those who grow become rich and diversify. And those who remain behind remain as they have been for centuries, sometimes resigned, other times rebellious, and always disillusioned . . ."

I looked at the extensive series of buildings that continued the power of Max Monroy along the Plaza Vasco de Quiroga, the horizontal honeycomb of laboratories, factories, workshops, hospitals, garages, offices, and underground parking lots.

I thought again that Vasco de Quiroga established Thomas

More's Utopia in New Spain in 1532 in order to provide a refuge for Indians, orphans, the sick, and the old, only to give way later to a powder factory, a municipal garbage dump, and now, the modern utopia of business: the kingdom of Max Monroy, long, high, glass-enclosed . . . resistant to earthquakes? The nearby volcanoes seemed to both threaten and protect.

The reader will forgive my narrative sluggishness. If I pause at these persons and these considerations, it is because we need—you and I—a contrast—a positive one?—to the willful dramas, false affections, and frozen positions that occurred in the months following this, my year and some months of virtue and good fortune in the bosom of the small working community on Plaza Vasco de Quiroga.

Which I shall tell you about now.

I WANTED TO interrupt the account of the meeting between Max Monroy and President Valentín Pedro Carrera in the office at Los Pinos not for reasons of narrative suspense but in order to situate myself inside what José Gorostiza calls the site of the epidermis: "filled with myself, besieged in my epidermis by an ungraspable God who strangles me . . ."

The God strangling me was, in the long run, myself. Now, however, I was present at a duel between divinities, the supreme being of national politics and the civic deity of private enterprise. I've already recounted how Max Monroy came into the office of the president and how he ordered the head of the nation to remain standing while Monroy occupied a straight chair and sat in it even straighter than the chair itself. We have already seen how the president continued to stand and asked his aide to leave.

"Have a seat," Carrera said to Monroy.

"I will. Not you," replied Monroy.

"Pardon me?"

"This isn't a question of pardoning."

"Pardon me?"

"This is a question of listening to me carefully. While you're on your feet."

"On what?"

"On your feet, Mr. President."

I was ignorant of the reasons—long-standing debts, equally old loyalties, the age difference, dissimilar powers, unspeakable complexes, I don't know—that explain why the president of the republic obeyed the order to remain on his feet before a seated Max Monroy. The rest of us—Asunta, Jericó, and I—also remained standing while Monroy spoke to the head of state.

"It's better if we clarify where we stand right away, Mr. President."

"Of course, Monroy. I'm already standing," Carrera said with his peculiar humor.

"Well, let's hope you don't fall down."

"I would be at your feet . . ."

"I'm not a lady, Mr. President. I'm not even a gentleman."

"Then, you are . . . ?"

"A rival."

"In love?" said Carrera in a sarcastic, even vengeful tone, though without looking at Asunta, while Jericó and I observed each other, I uncertain as to my function in this soap opera, Jericó pensive and even cynical—it's not a contradiction—in his.

Both witnesses. Of the scene and, perhaps, of our own lives.

"Do you know, Mr. President? It took centuries to move from the ox to the horse and another long time to free the horse from the yoke and chest strap that choked him."

Did Monroy lick his lips, did he close his eyes?

"Only at the beginning of the last millennium before Christ, about nine hundred B.C., was the horse collar invented, freeing the animal from pain and increasing his strength."

"And?" interjected the president, perplexed or pretending to be perplexed behind a mask of seriousness.

"And we're at the point of staying with the ox or moving on to the horse and immediately deciding if we're going to mistreat the horse by choking him with a strap across the chest or free him thanks to a collar."

"And?"

"You must think, as Mexican political elites have always

thought, that in the end ability is measured with a peso sign, concluding that the rich are rich because they're better and the poor are poor because they're worse."

"You must be rich, Monroy." The president almost laughed out loud.

"I'm an old-style rich man," Monroy interrupted. "You're new rich, Mr. President."

"As your family was at the beginning." Carrera began to be defensive.

"Read my biography more carefully. Being at the top, I refused to begin at the top. Being at the top, I began at the bottom. Do you understand me?"

"I'm trying to, Don Max."

"I mean that ability isn't measured by a bank account."

"And?"

"From the ox to the horse, I tell you, and from the horse in a yoke to a liberated charger."

"Explain what you mean, I beg you."

"You, with your celebrations, want us to continue in the age of the ox because you treat us like oxen, Valentín Pedro. You think that with village fairs you'll put off discontent and even worse, bring us happiness. Do you really believe that? God's truth?"

Max Monroy's freezing gaze passed like a bolt of lightning from Carrera to Jericó, who tried to look back at the magnate. Jericó lowered his eyes immediately. How do you look at a tiger that in turn is looking at us?

"We are all responsible for the social unrest," Carrera ventured. "But our solutions conflict with one another. What's yours, Monroy?"

"Communicating with the people."

"Very lyrical," the president said with a smile, leaning against the edge of a table almost as an act of defiance.

"If you don't understand you're not only a fool, but perverse. Because your solution—governing by entertaining—only postpones well-being and perpetuates poverty. The curse of Mexico has been that with ten, or twenty, or seventy, or a hundred million inhabitants, half always live in poverty."

"What do you want, we're rabbits." Carrera repeated his irony, as if with sarcastic blows he could stop Max Monroy. "So then, distribute condoms."

"No, Mr. President. We stopped being agrarian barely half a century ago. We became industrialized and wasted time as if we could compete with the United States or Europe or Japan. We've remained behind in the technological revolution, and if I'm here speaking harshly to you, it's because at the end of my life I don't want us to come late to this banquet too, when it's time for dessert, or never."

The president sighed cynically. "To be bored, as they say . . . People want distractions, my dear Max!"

"No," Monroy responded energetically. "To inform, as they say. You've chosen national festivals, rodeos, cockfights, mariachis, cut paper banners, balloons, fried food stands to entertain and benumb. I've chosen information to liberate. That's what I've come to tell you. My goal is for every citizen of Mexico to have a device, only a handheld device to educate, orient, and allow communication with other citizens, to help them understand problems and resolve them, alone or with help, but eventually resolve them. How to plant crops better. How to harvest. What equipment is needed. What friends you can count on. How much credit you need. Where to get it. What employment is available. Campesinos. Indians. Manual laborers and white-collar workers, clerks, bureaucrats, technicians, professionals, administrators, professors, students, journalists, I want everyone to communicate with everyone else, Mr. President, I want each person to know his or her interests and how they coincide with the interests of the rest, how to act on the basis of those personal interests and the interests of society and not remain forever stranded in the ridiculous fiesta you are offering them, the eternal Mexican hat dance."

I believe Monroy took a breath. I did, of course.

"I've come here to notify you. That's why I came in person. I don't want you to find out what I'm doing through third parties, through newspapers, through malicious gossip. I'm here to face you, Mr. President. So you're not deceived. We're going to defend not only opposite interests but antagonistic methods. We'll see whom you can count on: I already have my people. I'm going to see that an increasing number of Mexicans have in hand the little device that will defend them and communicate with them so they act freely and to their own benefit, not a political elite's."

"Or an economic one," Valentín Pedro Carrera said with irritated sarcasm.

"No elite survives if it doesn't adapt to change, Mr. President. Don't be the head of a kingdom of mummies."

If Carrera looked sardonically at the defiant octogenarian who stood, refusing Asunta's hand, bowed to Carrera, and went to the door, Monroy was not aware of it, because he had already turned his back on the president.

I WON'T DENY that Asunta's diffidence—her disinterest, her lack of amorous confidence—was worse than her indifference—neither affection toward nor rejection of my person. Our relationship, after everything I've narrated, returned to a cold, professional channel, like a river that freezes but doesn't overflow its banks. Does the water run beneath the crust of ice? Having listened to the filthy words of love with which Asunta gave pleasure to Max Monroy, I knew not only that I could never aspire to that "melody" but that having heard it deprived me forever of my stupid romantic illusion. Asunta would never be mine "for sentimental reasons," in the words of an old fox-trot that Jericó sometimes hummed, for no apparent reason, while he was shaving.

Deprived of love with Asunta, witness to her sexual vulgarity in bed with Max, my spirit filled with a kind of wounded discontent. I knew what I wanted and now I recognized only what I would have wanted. And both resolved into a categorical negation of my illusions. Not Elvira, or Lucha, or finally Asunta would redeem me from lost loves and open up for me a reasonably permanent horizon, for no matter how much we think of ourselves as Don Juans, don't we aspire to a permanent, fruitful relationship with one woman? What is Don Juan essentially looking for but a constant woman, a long-term shelter of tenderness and peace?

My having thought Asunta Jordán was that woman is the greatest proof of my ingenuousness. I know there is a good deal of naïveté in me, and if Voltaire's subtitle is *Optimism,* I ought to assess my own great hopes by the experience of lost illusions.

What takes us from the loss of amorous illusion to the carnal consolation of the brothel? I don't know how to answer if I don't bear witness first to my plunge into the sexual pleasure of the famous house of La Hetara, where Jericó and I together fucked the whore with the bee on her buttock who ended up being the damned widow of Nazario Esparza, stepmother to Errol, and head of the criminal gang of the Mariachi Maxi. You, gentle readers, can imagine how my brush with those too-solid ghosts of evildoing brought me back to the brothel on Calle de Durango to explore the earth as in the biblical commandment, but also to explore the body, overcoming cowardice and the heart's dismay beneath the roof of sexual mercy that gives everything and asks for nothing.

I'm La Bebota, face of an angel, breasts of honey, hot kisses, ardent anal sex, I'm La Fimia, I give massages on the couch, I'm little and wild, I'll eat you up with kisses, I have a magnificent ass, I'm La Emperatriz, I like everything, you won't be sorry, the best ass, ask me for whatever you want, oral with no rubber, VIP level, I'm La Choli, a sexy little doll, an infernal butt, missionary with a deep throat, I'm La Reina, I raise your energies, I'm ardent and dominating, everything's fine with me, I'm stunning, dare to know me, down with timidity. I'll give you tail, get soft without fear, I'm La Lesbia, wet and clawing, look no further, sweet thing, I have no limits in bed, I'm Emérita, I came back with all my medals, you get everything with my rump sex, fantasies, sink into my breasts and enjoy without limits, I'm La Faria, only for the demanding, I don't give kisses on the mouth because I lose my head, I'm La Malavida, total goddess, I trade roles, double penetration and my name is Olalla, I'm a blond doll, hot and multiorgasmic, everything's fine by ass, I'm La Pancho Villa, because of my pistols, love among the cactus, I challenge you to extreme pleasure, shoot me, love, I'm La Lucyana, a real schoolgirl, I fuck in uniform, I already miss you, big boy, I'm La Ninón, new to the capital, perky little tail, horny, addicted to you, I'm La Covadonga, give me back my virginity, let's see if you can, I only accept demanding men, are you one?

Was I?

Could I close my eyes and see Asunta?

Could I open my eyes and feel her absence?

La Pancho Villa warned me:

"All the others come from Río de la Plata, Argentina exports all kinds of skin. Only I have an authentic Mexican ass. Come and find it. Ah! Sex goes with us and doesn't step aside."

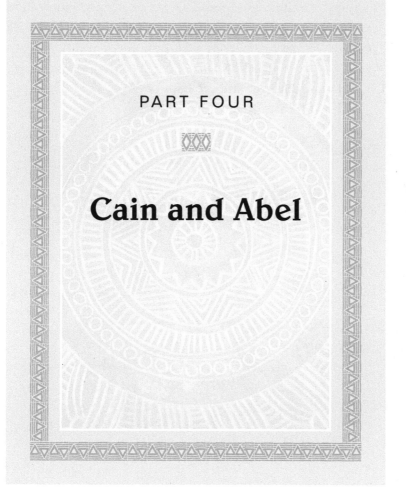

PART FOUR

Cain and Abel

Lunch, *la comida,* is a great ceremony in Mexico City. You could say it is the ceremony of the workday. In Spain and Spanish America it is called *almuerzo.* The verb is *almorzar.* In Mexico, it is *comer.* One eats *la comida* with an ancestral verbality that would be cannibalistic if it were not domesticated by a variety of foods that summarize the wealth of poverty. The food of destitution, Mexican cuisine transforms the poorest elements into exotic luxury recipes.

None is greater than the use of worms and fish eggs to create succulent dishes. That is why this afternoon (a respectable Mexican lunch does not begin until 2:30 in the afternoon or end before 6:00 P.M., at times with supper and cabaret extensions) I am sharing a table in the immortal Bellinghausen Restaurant on Calle de Londres, between Génova and Niza, with my old teacher Don Antonio Sanginés, enjoying maguey worms wrapped in hot tortillas plastered with guacamole and waiting for a dish of fried lamb's quarters in guajillo chile sauce.

I am going to contrast (because they complement each other) this lunch at three o'clock in the afternoon with the nocturnal meeting on the open terrace of the top floor of the Hotel Majestic facing the Zócalo, the Plaza de la Constitución, where traditional appetizers do not mitigate the acidic perfumes of tequila and rum, nor does the immensity of the Plaza diminish Jericó's presence.

Don Antonio Sanginés arrived punctually at the Bellinghausen. I got up from the table to greet him. I tried to be even more punctual than he was, in a country where P.M. means *puntualidad mexicana,* that is, a guaranteed, expected, and respected lack of punctuality. Some people, Sanginés first of all, followed by the presidents—the attorney because of good manners, the leaders because the general staff imposes *manu militari*—are always on time, and I had allowed myself to reserve a table for three in the hope Jericó would join us as stated in the invitation I left for him at Los Pinos. The end-of-year holidays were approaching, and something in the extremely formal and conventionally friendly spirit of the season led me to hope our teacher and his two students would get together to celebrate.

I hadn't seen Jericó since the tense meeting at Los Pinos between President Carrera and my bosses Max Monroy and Asunta Jordán, whom I had seen then for the first time since the nocturnal digressions I have already recounted, which left me in such poor standing with myself as a peeping tom, that is, an immoral and sexual unfortunate to the sound of a bolero. "Just One Time," like the widows whose groom dies on their wedding night. And so I appeared with my best wooden face, like a little monkey that does not see, hear, or say anything. I knew on that same night Jericó had made a date with me at the Hotel Majestic downtown. My spirit insisted on waiting for him at lunchtime, for the sake of resurrecting the most cordial memories and hopes that year after year throw us into the arms of Santa Claus and the Three Wise Men. "The Infant Jesus deeded you a stable," wrote López Velarde in *La suave patria.* And added, to qualify his irony: "and oil wells come from the Devil." I ought to tell you in advance I came to lunch with the first stanza, suspecting the second would be imposed at night.

"And Jericó?" I said innocently as I took my seat in the restaurant.

"This is about him," replied Sanginés. He remained silent, and after ordering the meal he grew more animated.

Days earlier the lawyer had been at a meeting in the presidential residence with Jericó and Valentín Pedro Carrera. While Sanginés advised prudence in response to Max Monroy's actions, Jericó invited him to retaliate against the businessman.

"I was looking for a point of agreement. The fiestas ordered by the president served a purpose."

"Circuses without bread," Jericó interrupted.

I went on. "Politics is a harmonizing of factors, a synthesis, the use of one sector's advantageous ideas by the other. We live in an increasingly pluralistic country. You must concede a little in order to gain something. The art of negotiation consists in coming to agreements, not out of courtesy but by taking into account the legitimate interests of the other sector."

"Following that course of action, the only thing you achieve is stripping the government of legitimacy," Jericó said petulantly.

"But the state gains legitimacy," countered Sanginés. "And if you had attended my classes at the university, you would know that governments are transitory and the state is permanent. That's the difference."

"Then we have to change the state," Jericó added.

"Why?" I asked with feigned innocence.

"So that everything will change," Jericó said, turning red.

"To what end, in what sense?" I insisted.

Jericó stopped addressing me. He turned to the president.

"The question is knowing what forces, good or bad, are at work at a given moment. How to resist them, accept them, channel them. Are you aware of those forces, Mr. President, do you believe they'll be content with the diversions of the carousel and the wheel of fortune you're offering them?"

"Ask yourself, I've asked Carrera," continued Sanginés, "how ready these forces are for compromise."

"Compromise, compromise!" Jericó exclaimed that night as we ate at the restaurant on the Hotel Majestic roof. "Compromise isn't possible anymore. President Carrera is a coward, a superficial man who squanders opportunities."

I smiled. "You're helping him, buddy, with your famous popular festivals."

He looked at me with a certain swaggering air and then burst into laughter.

"You believe that story?"

I said I didn't but apparently he did.

Jericó stretched his arm out from the table on the terrace toward the immense Zócalo of the capital.

"Do you see that plaza?" he asked rhetorically.

I said I did. He went on. "We've used it for everything, from human sacrifice to military parades to ice skating rinks to coups d'état. It's the plaza of a thousand uses. Any clown can fill it if he yells long and loud. That's the point."

I agreed again, without asking the tacit question: "And now?"

"Now," said Jericó in a tone I didn't recognize, "now look at what you don't want to see, Josué. Look at the adjoining streets. Look at Corregidora. Look at 20 de Noviembre. Look to the sides. Look at the Monte de Piedad. Look at the Central Post Office."

I tried to follow his urban guide. No, don't stop to look, don't distract me. Now look farther, at Correo Mayor, Academia, Jesús María, Loreto, Leona Vicario. What did I see?

"The same as always, Jericó. The streets you've mentioned."

"And the people, Josué, the people?"

"Well, passersby, pedestrians . . ."

"And the traffic, Josué, the traffic?"

"Well, focusing a little, it's very light, not many cars, a lot of trucks . . ."

"Now put it all together, Josué, put together the people scattered along the streets around the Zócalo, close off the plaza with the trucks, have armed guards climb down from the trucks, together with police and the people who are my people, Josué, do you understand what I'm saying? People placed by me at the four corners of the plaza, armed with pistols and studded clubs and brass knuckles and bludgeons, put them together with the people climbing down from the trucks armed with magnums, Uzis, and carbines. Look at the machine gun posts at the Monte de Piedad, City Hall, right here at the hotel. Try to listen to the cathedral bells. Don't you hear anything?"

I said I didn't, trying to penetrate the delirium of his discourse but insistent on humoring my enemy.

"They're mute. The tongues have been tied so they don't ring."

"Forever?" I wanted to follow his thread, as if he were a child, a madman.

"No. They'll ring again when we take power."

"We? Are there a lot?" I said with a wooden face, à la Buster Keaton, attempting serene impartiality in the face of my friend's intense, increasingly heated polemic.

"Yes," Jericó said feverishly. "A lot. A great many. And you? Can I count on you?" he said with passion.

"What about me, buddy?"

"With us or against us?"

"I told the president," Sanginés confided to me at lunch at the Bellinghausen, "that an ounce of prevention is worth a pound of cure."

"Let's see, Toño, who can do more, Monroy or me," the president said as if he were boasting.

"Don't be so sure the enemy's only outside the house."

"So there's an enemy on the inside?" Carrera raised his eyebrows. "My good licenciado, you are so suspicious. Don't torture yourself."

"Yes." I looked straight at him. "But that's not the problem."

"What can be worse?" Carrera seemed unconcerned, as he did in the good times.

"The enemy outside. The discontent to which Monroy referred, Mr. President."

"Aren't the fiestas enough to distract them?" Carrera asked, falling back into frivolity.

"The fiestas are turning into something else entirely."

"Into what, Sanginés? Don't be so mysterious."

"Into brigades. Into shock troops. Into threats to the established order."

"And what about Jericó?"

"He organized them."

"Jericó? Where? How?"

"From here, my amiable Don Valentín Pedro Carrera. From this office. Right under your nose."

"Who told you that?"

"Cherchez la femme."

"Don't hand me that French shit."

"Monroy came with his adviser, Asunta Jordán."

"A good-looking broad." Carrera licked his lips. "Raise her salary."

"She doesn't work for you."

"Ah! Still, a good-looking broad."

"I've brought you the answer."

"Whose answer?"

"Your answer, Mr. President. Your answer to Max Monroy and Asunta Jordán. A young woman, with fresh ideas, a graduate of the Sorbonne."

"Oh, those Frenchies. *Oh là là!*"

"We need help. The enemy has come in. Don't stay alone in the house with the viper. Because you can be very stubborn, but you should fear vipers."

Sanginés walked to the door. He opened it. A young woman came in, serious but amiable, elegant, beautiful, and with a gleam of power in her eyes, the swing of her hair, the severity of her tailored suit, the elegance of her shoes, and the flash of her legs.

"Mr. President, let me introduce your new assistant, Señorita María del Rosario Galván."

"Ahnshantay, Mamwahzel." Carrera bent to kiss her hand while still looking at her.

So I knew now what Sanginés knew about Jericó. And I resisted believing it, above all because I believed in the friendship that had joined my friend and me since we were in school.

THE CENTER OF Mexico City is like the country itself: A surface serves only to hide the previous one, which hides the one that follows. If the country is structured in ascending levels from the tropical coasts to the temperate zones to the high valleys and an unequal distribution of deserts, plains, and mountains, the city masks a vertical cut that carries it from the capricious modernities of our time to a copy of the boulevards and mansard roofs we inherited from the

Empress Carlotta of Belgium, "Carlotita" to her intimate friends, and from a flagrant colonial baroque to a Spanish city constructed on the ruins of the Aztec metropolis, Tenochtitlán. Mexico City, as if wanting to protect a mystery everyone knows, disguises itself in many ways: its cantinas, cabarets, brothels, parks, avenues, its luxury restaurants, popular eateries, churches, its mansions protected by high walls and electrified barbed wire, vast shantytowns and one-story hovels with flat roofs, its paint shops, grocery stores, car repair shops, its mothers wrapped in rebozos with a baby in their arms, child beggars, lottery ticket sellers, its armada of parrot-colored taxis, black armored vans, supply trucks carrying rods, bricks, bags of cement, roofs, and gratings for a capital in perpetual construction and reconstruction, the city forever unfinished, as if in this lack of a conclusion resided the virtue of permanence . . . Mexico City like a vast lunch box where the first dish is always the last. "Dry soup" or stew, wet soup, chicken *mole,* sweet potatoes . . .

And so I walked, ruminating and enumerating with a chaos that reflected the chaos of the city, looking for the streets Jericó had mentioned with mysterious emphasis during our encounter on the terrace of the Hotel Majestic. It was dark then, and lights beautified the empty space. Now it is noon, and I don't want the Historic Center to disguise itself anymore. I want to recognize the Calles de Correo Mayor, Academia, Jesús María, Corona, la Santísima and its bell tower that resembles a patriotic tiara, the Plaza de Santo Domingo and its temple sinking into the placenta of the old Indian lagoon, perhaps nostalgic for its canoes and canals and causeways that have disappeared forever: Mexico City is its own unburied, irrevocable phantom.

There were noble façades of *tezontle* and marble, large street doors of carved wood, jalousied windows, courtyards filled with flowers: I could see nothing. Sidewalk commerce hid street after street, twenty thousand vendors offered me radios, clothing, costume jewelry, even a television set was suddenly placed in front of my nose so I could see myself reflected in its silvery-gray surface: I thought, seeing my face both surprised and distant, that what the twenty thousand peddlers were selling here, the merchants guided by the long nose of the god that precedes them with a sheaf of staves and dollars, were all versions of my own life, of the faces I could have had, of the bodies that might have been mine, of the odors that might have emanated from my mouth, my armpits, my buttocks, my feet, and now were confused, were part of and emanations from the crowd that pushed me, offered me things, brushed me with charm, touched me with vulgarity, pushed and pulled me where? what was I looking for? the gang evoked by Jericó? could my less and less old friend—more and more my new nemesis—really believe he could mobilize this entire Hugoesque world of mischievous crime, survival by a wink, fierce independence when faced with the powers mocked here, subjected here to the simple law of survival? Could Jericó transform them into an army formulated to take power? Could Sanginés be right? Was I wandering here to confirm the truth? To find out whether Jericó was right or not, whether he believed he could control this hissing serpent slipping from street to street, market to market, favor to favor?

The thousand-headed hydra of Mexico City. In any event, if not a hydra an octopus, and Jericó believed the octopus had only one eye. It's enough to see it, knowing it isn't Medusa and can't petrify us with a glance, because the octopus isn't concerned with looking. It wants embraces. It has tentacles.

As if searching for respite, I walked through the crowd confirming that México D.F. has twenty-two million inhabitants, more than all of Central America, more than the Republic of Chile, along whose street I walked now toward the temple of Santo Domingo, protected by the Dominican priest Father Julián Pablo from postponable disasters and sometimes from ones that couldn't be postponed. I saved myself from the fake bullfighters who zigzagged with merchandise in their hands like assault weapons, and in Santo Domingo I encountered the resurrected profession of "evangelists," men and women sitting on low wooden chairs in front of old Remington typewriters, listening to the dictation of illiterate men and women who wanted to send to a distant village, to families in the countryside, the mountains, the provinces, their regrets, their words of love and sometimes of hate, which these clerks set down on paper and charge for; double if, as safety advises, the "evangelists" themselves are the ones who address the envelope and buy the stamp, promising to drop the letter in the mail.

"Sometimes, Josué, they give us the wrong address, or one that doesn't exist, the letter never arrives, and then things as sad as forgetting can happen, or as violent as wreaking vegeance on the scribe responsible for the letter's not reaching its destination—even if it didn't really have any destination at all.

"And what is destination, or destiny?" continued the voice I tried to locate, to recognize, in the row of people's scribes sitting in front of the old building of the Inquisition. "It isn't fate. It is simply disguised will. The final desire."

Then I was able to unite voice and eyes. A small man, bald but in a borrowed hairdo, his bones brittle and his hands energetic, white-skinned though tending to a yellowish pallor, for a couple of Band-Aids covered tiny cuts on one cheek and his neck, dressed in an old black suit with gray stripes, a shirt with a too-large collar unbuttoned at his throat and adorned by a wide, out-of-fashion tie that actually looked more like the covering for a defeated, emaciated chest, mortified by blows of contrition. Borrowed apparel. Secondhand clothes.

Our eyes met and I recognized old Father Filopáter, the guide of generous meticulousness during the early youth of Castor and Pollux, Josué and Jericó. I held back my tears, took Filopáter's hands, and was about to kiss them. I don't know what held me back. Shyness or distrust of his nails that in spite of being cut short showed signs of grime at the corners. Though this, perhaps, was due only to his work on an old typewriter and an apparently rebellious two-color ribbon, for when Filopáter pressed a key thoughtlessly, the entire ribbon unrolled into something resembling infinity.

"Maestro," I murmured.

"The maestro is you," he replied, smiling.

He accepted my invitation. We sat down in a café on Calle de

Brasil, Filopáter with his heavy typewriter (as big as his head) under his arm and eventually occupying a chair at our table, mute now but invited.

He looked at the typewriter. "Do you know? Each word you write strikes a blow against the Devil."

I wanted to laugh, amiably. He extended his hand and stopped me.

"As always, I listen to you with respect, Maestro."

I shouldn't call him that, he replied with a moment of annoyance. He was only a scribe and that, he said, was enough (he wanted to hurry on to two things) to explain his history. When we were served our coffee, he evoked Saint Peter, "If you cannot be pure, be careful," and concluded with the words of Saint Thomas, "Only virginity can make a man equal to an angel."

"What do you want to tell me, Father?"

He resigned himself to my calling him that as long as I forgot about "Maestro." He was about to sigh. He looked at me like someone picking up an old conversation. As if no calendars had intervened between today's and yesterday's words.

"I would like to have been a Trappist," he said with a smile. "The brothers of La Trappe can communicate only with feet or hands, gestures and whistles. On the other hand, look at me. If not a Trappist then trapped in the trammels of the word . . ."

"You taught us not to be afraid of words," I recalled with good intentions.

"But there are those who do fear the word, Josué, and I say this intentionally. Jesus said 'I am the Word' and he meant several things —"

"He meant that he was part of the Trinity," I recalled and repeated with a kind of red-faced enthusiasm, as if not only my youth depended on this memory but my farewell to it: The reencounter with our teacher indicated to me that a cycle was ending but the next one was slow in showing itself.

"I mean that the Trinity is God the Father, God the Son, and God the Holy Spirit . . . and the Word is an attribute of the Spirit but is shared in by the Father, the Son . . ."

I wanted to see admiration in Filopáter's eyes. I found only compassion. Because he knew what I meant, he was going to say the same thing, and we felt sorry for each other for knowing and saying it, as if we could be not only pre-Christians but true pagans, absent from faith in Christ because we were ignorant of it, but condemned to being absent even if we did know about it.

"The Trinity is a mystery," he began to speak again. "It cannot be known by reason. It is a revealed truth. It puts faith to the test. Either you believe, Josué, or you don't believe."

I wasn't going to tell him I had stopped believing because he knew I had never believed. That's why he immediately said: "The surprising thing is that, at the same time, the Trinity, the Word, transcends reason but is not at war with reason."

"The dogma of the Trinity is not incompatible with reason?" I asked, because I wanted to push Filopáter's words to a proposition that wasn't a conclusion but a confrontation. His current state told me clearly that something serious had occurred to make him abandon teaching, which had been his vocation since his youth, when he taught the Pizarro Leongómez brothers at the Javeriana in Bogotá and then, when the rough tides of Colombian politics washed him up in Mexico, he landed in our secondary school.

"No," he said with renewed energy. "It isn't. But that is the truth clerical intolerance can employ against a person if he attempts to reconcile the truth of faith and the reason of truth. It is not only easier"—did I detect an unusual disdain in the priest's voice?—"it is more cowardly. For as long as we maintain that faith is true though it may not be factual, you will be protected by a dogma that is a paradox we owe to Tertullian: 'It is certain because it is impossible.' A definition of faith . . ."

The coffee was bad, with milk it was worse. Filopáter sipped it almost as a sacrifice. He was Colombian.

"If you wager, on the other hand, on the rationality of faith, you expose yourself to the censure of those who prefer to deny reason to religion only because they wouldn't know how to explain their faith rationally, and therefore opt for a blind faith, an ignorant faith."

Filopáter became excited.

"No." He banged on the table and knocked over the glass bowl of sugar, spilling it. "One must sustain the mystery with reason and fortify reason with mystery. Faith does not exclude reason and reason does not destroy faith. Saying this exposes the dogmatic man, the passive man, the man who wants to impose a truth like the Inquisitors beneath whose walls you found me sitting this morning, or hides behind the wall denying the work of God—"

"What is it?" I asked with a certain impertinence. "The work of God, what is it?"

"The redemption of the world by means of the wearisome affirmation of human reason."

The glass sugar bowl had rolled off the table onto the floor, where it shattered, granulating the floor like a snowstorm that has lost its way in the tropics.

The owner of the café hurried over, alarmed, annoyed, a woman submissive to patrons.

"*Pro vitris fractis,*" Filopáter said solemnly. "Impose a surcharge for the broken glass, Señora."

MOVE LIKE TIGERS. Study the sites. They walk through public offices. They find out. Where are the telephone and telegraph installations? Which seem the places of least resistance? The Zócalo? The Paseo de la Reforma? The distant shantytowns, Los Remedios, Tulyehualco, San Miguel Tehuizco? The government ministries of state, post offices, private businesses, apartment houses? Study them all. Tell me which ones you like. Recruit in the penitentiaries. I, Jericó, will see to it that by my order Maxi Batalla, Sara Pérez, Siboney Peralta, Brillantinas, Gomas, and Ventanas are released, an order from the office of the president, signed by me, is enough, and the president will never know. Let the criminals join up with the laborers who can't get across the border; promise them good jobs in California; promise the unemployed in Mexico City, the unsatisfied workers, that they'll be rich and won't have to work; promise: promise the migrant workers thrown out of the United States, their families who will no longer receive dollars every month, those who can't find work in Mexico and see only a horizon of hunger: promise. Begin with work stoppages, slowdowns, stealing parts, voluntary accidents, intentional fires, until the city is set on fire and comes to a halt. You, Mariachi Maxi, go from business to business; you, Brillantinas, print up some fake passes; you, Siboney, go to funerals and see who you can recruit; you, Gomas, go from barbecue to barbecue, inventing rumors, the government is falling, there's repression, there are strikes, where? there? go on! arm and recruit impoverished young men, give them love, tell them now they'll have respect because of their pistols. Rancor. Rancor. Rancor is our weapon. Exalt rancor. Mexican resentment is the fertilizer of our movement. Ask each boy: Do you want to ruin somebody, do you want to take revenge on somebody, do you want to get what you deserve, what is denied to you by injustice, wickedness, envy, inequality, your parents, your bosses, these young millionaires, these corrupt politicians? Rancor. The damned tradition of rancor. The most constant Mexican tradition. Take the pistol I'm going to give you, take the Uzi, take the club, the bludgeon, the lasso, they're all good for attacking, make lists, boys, who do you want to ruin, who do you want to pay for their faults? Make lists! Find the places of least resistance, the most vulnerable, hospitals, pharmacies, commercial centers. Do you think we can take the airport? Ha-ha-ha, make yourselves invisible, don't look at one another until it's time for the attack, cut off the water, gas, electricity, isolate the districts in the city, isolate the center, the middle-class districts, the nameless ghost settlements where the city dies: feel united and don't give up. Personal vendettas allowed.

"Do you really believe the masses will follow you, Jericó?"

"Distinguish between rhetoric and reality. I have to invoke the masses to justify myself. I need only a shock corps to triumph. A small, determined group. All of that about a class in the vanguard is late-night Marxist rhetoric. If you wait for the masses to act, Josué, you'll wait till the cows come home."

Once again, his world of North American sayings and references surprised me. Wait till the cows come home. *Espera a que las vacas regresen.*

"All the people," I said to introduce an idea (let's see if it sticks). "The mass of workers."

"All the people are too much."

"Who then?"

"A small group," said Jericó, "a small, cold, violent group for in-surrectionary tactics."

"The mass of workers . . ."

"I don't need them!" Jericó exclaimed. "An assault group is enough. The assault group represents the mass of the dissatisfied. Do you realize that half a million workers have returned to Mexico from the United States and don't find anything but poverty and un-employment?"

"Detachments?"

"Armed. It's enough for me to say from Los Pinos: Distribute weapons to defend the chief of state."

I repressed my laughter. I transformed it into doubts. I managed to say: "They won't pay attention to you."

He turned red. Enraged. I saw something crazy in his eyes. As if saying to himself and saying to me, They are going to obey me.

"A few people," he said as if he were praying. "Limited terrain. Clear objectives, the vanguard forward, the masses back."

In the meantime, I should say that more than the insurrec-tionary tactics foreseen by Jericó, Jericó himself interested me, his evolution, his ambition. Should I have been surprised? Hadn't he been my first friend? Wasn't Jericó the one who gave me his hand in school, protecting me against the damned bullies? Wasn't Jericó the one who took me to his apartment when "the House of Usher" fell on Calle de Berlín? Wasn't he the one who introduced me to funda-mental readings? Didn't we argue together with Father Filopáter? Didn't we see each other naked in the shower? Didn't we fuck as a team the whore with the bee on her buttock? Weren't we Castor and Pollux, the Dioscuri, founders of cities, Argonauts equal to Jason and the archer Phalerus and Lynceus the lookout and Orpheus the poet, and the herald, son of Hermes, and the courier of Lapida who had been a woman and Atalanta of Calydon, who still was: Ar-gonauts plowing the seas in search—you Jericó and I Josué—of the Golden Fleece that hangs in a distant olive grove, guarded night and day by a sleepless dragon? I looked intently at Jericó, as if a direct gaze were still the guarantee of truth, the beacon of certitude, as if the most malicious men in the world had not understood—from the very beginning—that the direct gaze associated with frankness, humility, understanding, and friendship is the mask of falsehood, pride, intransigence, and enmity. I should have known it. I didn't want to know it. Until this very moment when I'm narrating what happened, I insisted on evoking our youth as students as the most valuable part of our past, the friendship that was the reason for being, the watchword, the birth certificate of the relationship between Josué and Jericó. A reality that had to be expressed thoroughly and to the very last moment—I told myself—under penalty of losing my soul.

My references to the ideas and images that united us were only a way of telling myself and telling Jericó: "Every friendship rests on a myth and represents it."

I asked: "In addition to the fleece, whom did the beast guard?" I answered myself: "A ghost. The specter of an exiled king whose return would bring peace to the kingdom.

"Recovering a ghost in order to sacrifice a republic," I murmured then, and Jericó simply asked me: "What was more interesting, recovering the fleece or bringing back the ghost?"

"Crowning a specter?"

I understand now that this question has hung over our destinies because Jericó and I were Castor and Pollux, part of the eternal expedition in search of desire and destiny, a mere pretext, however, for recovering a specter and bringing him back home.

"Did you see this?" I handed him the newspaper across the table.

"What?"

"What happened at the zoo."

"No."

"A tiger died after being attacked by four other tigers."

"Why?"

"They were hungry."

I pointed.

"They ate his entrails. Look."

Perhaps I just wanted to indicate that he and I became friends because of a *debt*. That brought us together. We established a lifetime alliance on the basis of that debt.

WILL VALENTÍN PEDRO Carrera go to Max Monroy's offices and residence in the Utopia building on the Plaza Vasco de Quiroga? Or would Max Monroy again go to the president's residence and office in Los Pinos?

"Let him come," advised the novice María del Rosario Galván.

"Why?" asked Carrera, prepared to admire the young woman's beauty in exchange for excusing her errors and disregarding her opinions.

"Well, because you are . . . the president . . ."

Carrera smiled. "Do you know what ancient kings did to exercise their rights?"

"No."

"Every year they went from village to village. They didn't ask the village to come to see them. They went to the village, do you understand what I'm saying, beautiful?"

"Of course." She attempted to recover her composure. "If the mountain doesn't come to Muhammad, Muhammad goes to the mountain."

"Exactly right, babe."

The president smiled indulgently and went to the neutral territory approved by his representatives and Max Monroy's. The Castle of Chapultepec, now the National Museum of History and the setting for Boy Heroes, Hapsburg Empires, and Porfirista Dictatorships. Monroy acceded to arriving first and viewing the tawny panorama of the city from the heights as if he were viewing nonexistence itself. Why pretend to be master of nothing when one was master of everything? On the other hand, the president came to the esplanade of the palace as if he were a boy hero about to throw himself into the void, wrapped in the flag. As if the throne of the dynasty that ruled Mexico the longest (more than two centuries)—the Hapsburgs—were waiting for him. As if he were prepared to govern for three decades because listen, María del Rosario, you have to come here thinking you're eternal, if not, you lose your six years the first day . . .

To see or not to see the arrival of the powerful entrepreneur Max Monroy? Act distracted, be surprised, greet each other, embrace?

"Ah!"

The embrace of the two men was recorded by cameras and microphones before Valentín Pedro Carrera and Max Monroy walked ten paces to distance themselves from publicity and bodyguards. María del Rosario Galván and Asunta Jordán, practically identical in their professional attire of tailored suit, dark stockings, and high heels, blocked the press and held off the guests.

"Truce, my dear Max?" The president's smile dissipated the capital's smog. "A meeting of two souls? *Primus inter pares*? Or pure show, my esteemed friend? An Embrace of Acatempan ending the wars of independence?"

"No, my dear president. Another battle." Monroy did not smile.

"If you divide you don't rule," Carrera reflected, trying to catch Monroy's eye.

"And if you rule by force, you divide but govern the parts."

"Each to his own philosophy." Carrera almost sighed. "The good thing is that when there's danger, we know how to come together."

"Understand it in terms of mutual convenience," Monroy said with great suavity.

"Does this mean I can count on you, Max?"

"You can always count." Monroy managed to smile. "What you don't understand, Valentín Pedro, is that my policies are part of your power. Except your power lasts six years. My policies do not occur every six years."

"And so?" the president said, halfway between amiable and falsely surprised.

"And so everything ends up contracting, understand that. The six-year term contracts. A life contracts. An era contracts."

"What?" Carrera exclaimed in surprise (or pretending to be surprised). "Look how my belly's growing and my hair's falling out. Don't kid me."

"Of course," Monroy continued, very calm. "With my policies I achieve what you're missing. If we stayed only with your policies, we'd stay with half-measures. You believe in circuses without the bread. I believe in bread with the circuses. I believe in information and try to communicate that to the majority. You believe in conspiracy reserved for a minority. That's why I believe that, in the long run, I can manage without you but you can't get along without me."

"Monroy, listen—"

"Don't interrupt. You and I never see each other. I'll use the occasion to say a person has to deserve my respect."

"And admiration?"

"For superstars."

"And esteem?"

"I'm a patient man. Everyone has gone. And those who remain ask me for favors. Our individual histories don't count. Who remembers President Lagos Cházaro? Who could have been Secretary of Finance under Generalísimo Santa Anna?"

What a strange look the politician directed at the businessman.

"We're part of the collective aggregate. Don't go around thinking anything else."

"What are you saying, Max?"

"Why am I telling you this? Well, we don't see each other very often."

Asunta—who tells me the preceding to the degree she heard something, guessed more, and read lips—says that Carrera sighed as if Monroy's words sealed a previously mentioned reality. The president wasn't going to change his policies of national distraction only because his official operative, Jericó, had betrayed him by taking advantage of the opportunity to find his own power base that turned out to be perfectly illusory, and Monroy would not abandon his of giving information media to citizens. The crisis perhaps demonstrated that the better informed the citizen, the fewer opportunities demagogic illusion would have.

"Or official carnivals?" asked Carrera, as if he had read (Asunta believes he did) Monroy's mind.

"Look, Mr. President: What you and I have in common is possible control of the real communication media in this day and age. Insurgents once believed that by taking the central telephone offices they would take power. Do you know something? My telephone operators are all blind. Blind, you understand? In this way they hear better. Nobody hears better than a blind man. On the other hand, a thousand eyes are in thousands of cellular devices, the mobile phones that replace television, radio, the press. I am giving all Mexicans, whether or not they can read and write, a message, a family, a past, an inheritance. They constitute the real national and international information network."

"You may be right," Carrera went on. "Just whistle once so the bird can hear you."

"You underestimate people." Monroy didn't bother to look at him. "It's your eternal error."

"When there's no paper, you clean yourself with whatever's at hand." Carrera made a vulgar gesture, like someone using a medieval *torche-cul*.

Monroy didn't look at him. "Just don't ignore what you need to survive."

Carrera raised his shoulders. "You see, it wasn't necessary to fire a single shot."

"The fact is the fortress was empty." Monroy threw cold water on his spirits.

"No, the truth is you're very clever. You just hide it." Carrera let his admiration for Max show. Max looked at Carrera with a flattering lie.

"This poor boy . . . your collaborator . . ."

"Don't fuck with me, Max." The president did not stop smiling. "We both win if you don't fuck around."

"Fine, your employee. His name is . . . ?"

"Jericó."

"Jericó." Monroy did not smile. "Who knows what old-fashioned manual he read."

(*Coup d'État: The Technique of Revolution* by Curzio Malaparte, murmured María del Rosario Galván at a distance: Napoleon, Trotsky, Pilsudski, Primo de Rivera, Mussolini . . .)

"Let's not be afraid of a gang insurrection like this one, Mr.

President, or an impossible revolution like earlier ones. You should be afraid of the tyrant who comes to power through the vote and turns into an elected dictator. That's the one to fear."

(I thought, of course, of Antigua Concepción, Max Monroy's mother, and her epic, revolutionary version of a history—was it buried along with her?)

"Dishonor," murmured Max Monroy.

"What?" The president heard only what he wanted to hear.

"Dishonor," Monroy repeated, and after pretending to admire the landscape: "Let's not engage in minor intrigues. Let's exercise irony."

"What?"

"Irony. Irony."

"I don't understand you."

"I mean it's very difficult under any circumstances to maintain power."

"Isn't that what I'm telling you?"

"You don't say."

An intolerant minority, Jericó told me, that's the key for coming to power, you have to energize the base with the example of an energetic minority, you have to favor the prejudices of the resentful, you have to demonize power: Saints don't know how to govern.

What did Jericó expect? The president, quite simply, made use of the army. Soldiers occupied highways, bridges, large houses, food depositories, munitions depositories, major intersections, banks: The army surrounded Jericó's followers as if they were mice in a trap. They prevented them from leaving, they gave them an ephemeral empire around the Zócalo that did not even interrupt the work of Filopáter and the other scribes on the Plaza de Santo Domingo. Fireworks, smoke, folk dances, an exceptional holiday, an obligatory alliance between Monroy and Carrera, as ephemeral as Jericó's frustrated rebellion.

The groups gathered together by Jericó were isolated in the center of the capital between the Zócalo and Minería, they never managed to communicate with the supposedly rebellious and certainly wronged masses, Jericó had operated on the basis of a fantastic ideology and a revocable power: the ideology decanted from his readings and his position inside the ogre's mouth: the office of the president.

Now I listened, thought, saw, and felt a profound sadness, as if Jericó's defeat were mine. As if the two of us had lived a great intellectual dream that, in order to exist, did not tolerate the test of reality. In the final analysis, were my friend and I barely hangers-on of anarchy, never makers of revolution? Did ideas we had read, heard, assimilated lose all value if we put them into practice? Was our confusion of ideas and life so great? Didn't those ideas resist the breath of life, collapsing like statues made of dust as soon as reality touched them? Were we becoming illusions?

The gang of the Mariachi and Sara P., Siboney Peralta, Brillantinas, Gomas, and Ventanas returned to the San Juan de Aragón Prison. Miguel Aparecido was waiting for them there.

The president withdrew first from the Castle, muttering to himself (Asunta heard him), "In the old days the hangman sold the boiled flesh of his victims," and Max, who followed seconds later, remarked to Asunta: "It's one thing to be based in reality. It's another to create reality."

And right after that: "Let's go, the sun's very strong and in the light of day one makes many mistakes."

The president simply sighed: "Making decisions is very boring. I swear . . ."

He was on his way out.

"MISERABLE OLD FOOL. Useless old bastard. Damn mummy."

Miguel Aparecido punched the wall of his cell, speaking in a wounded, vengeful tone of voice, sonorous and stifled, as if rather than words coming out of his mouth there were animals: insects, rodents, turkeys, grebes, bustards, and mandrakes, so intimate to his mind was the word and so desperate was it to find ways out, similes, survivals.

"Lock up a man whose hands are tied with a cat, then ask him to defend himself."

He looked at me with ferocity.

"He'll defend himself with his teeth. There's no other way."

What had disturbed him so much? He had won. The criminals released through Jericó's influence were back behind bars and I wouldn't guarantee their future. Jericó's transient power—his whim—had done something more than free a gang of bandits. It had violated the will of Miguel Aparecido, the master of the prison, the top dog, the big fucker inside these walls. Miguel felt mocked.

Still, there was something in his rage that went beyond Jericó, the flight from and return to prison of the criminals, the mockery of the very will of the man with the olive skin and yellow eyes and self-willed muscles, kept hard and flexible thanks to the discipline of imprisonment, as if the days and months and years of prison counted in a rogue's exercises, his knee flexions, air punches, arms extended in extremely hard flexion against prison walls, imaginary jump ropes, like a boxer who prepares for the big fight, overcoming through an act of will the noise of the city that filters through the corridors and catacombs of the prison.

He grabbed the newspaper. "Look," he said, poking at the image of Max Monroy and, in passing, that of the president. "Look."

I looked.

"Do you know he's never allowed his picture to be taken?"

"The president? He's always in the papers, on television, in displays . . . All that's left for him is to announce the lottery."

"Monroy," said Miguel, as if all the bitterness in the world were concentrated in that name. A yellowish saliva ran along the prisoner's lips. The tiger devoured by other bloodthirsty beasts in the Chapultepec zoo appeared, duplicated, in his eyes. "Monroy . . . motherfucker, at least he used to be discreet enough not to be photographed, the decency not to let himself be seen, the old bastard son of a bitch mother . . ."

I confess my discretion. Or my cowardice. I didn't jump to the defense of my old friend from the graveyard, the "bitch mother" of Max Monroy, Antigua Concepción.

"And worse, even worse," Miguel said syllable by syllable, "even worse is that son of the great bitch whore, Max Monroy's son."

"Who is he?" I said, innocent (but uneasy?).

This is the story Miguel Aparecido told me that afternoon in a cell in the San Juan de Aragón Prison, after going on a while longer in his diatribe, the asked-for explanation and the unasked-for one as well. I felt a strange emotion: Miguel Aparecido seemed like an hourglass anxious to empty the contents of one hour into another, though anguished by the fatal flight of time. The flight of time was the evasion in his narrative and if I was his privileged listener, at that moment I still did not know to what degree, so intense, so personal, Miguel's narration concerned me.

I thought at first he vacillated between emptiness and incoherence. I wanted to believe that at the end of the story both of us, he who was talking and I who was listening to him without saying a word, could find in ourselves something resembling compassion and from there pass on to comprehension. Now this was merely a desire (even an intention) of mine. Miguel Aparecido's discourse took another direction.

He said he was imprisoned by order of Max Monroy. He quickly cut me off: Of course judicial requirements had been met. Of course he had a trial. Of course testimony was heard and a sentence was announced. "Of course I was condemned to thirty years in prison for a crime I didn't commit . . . three decades of confinement starting at the age of twenty," he remembered, but in the voice of someone who, when recalling, also commemorates.

He looked at me with a defiant air. "I behaved well, Josué. I swear I made an effort. I intended to be the best inmate in the pen. Punctual, hardworking, obliging. All of it contrary to my own character: cleaning toilets, removing excrement, mopping up vomit . . . All of it to get out of here. Get out for only one purpose."

He was about to lower his eyes.

He didn't.

"To kill. I wanted to get out to murder Max Monroy. For having accused me falsely. Of attempted murder. Now I wanted to deserve the accusation. I got out. I prepared for the act, and now I was serious. I haunted the Utopia building. I imagined a thousand ways to eliminate the son of a bitch. Suddenly he intuited it, he didn't find out, he just smelled that something was going on because he knew

I was free. He had to have thought: What do I do to lock up this bastard again? Because he had to have realized that in this second round, either he'd kill me or I'd kill him . . ."

Miguel Aparecido was making a great effort to keep his gaze fixed on me, eyes wide open, as yellow as those of a canid race, Miguel-wolf with the jaw as strong as a padlock, arms and legs imprisoned but longing to get out and race toward his prey, but sad, afflicted by the confinement he had imposed on himself, he reveals to me now, he stopped prowling around the offices of Max Monroy, returned to prison, asked for the help of Antonio Sanginés, I want to go back to the pen, Licenciado, please have them take me back into jail, I beg you for your mother's sake, please, save me from the crime, I don't want to kill my father, if you really love Max Monroy return me to the pen, Lic, you can do it, you have influence, do me this favor, save me from sin by locking me up right away, accuse me of whatever you like, get me out of freedom, take away my desire to kill, save me from myself, put the chains of my freedom on me . . .

"I returned to prison, Josué. Sanginés invented some crime for me. I don't know which. I don't remember anymore. I think he revived the earlier sentence for reasons that escape me. Sanginés is a shyster. He knows all the tricks. He can resurrect the dead. He can get water from a stone. But he can't erase the memory you drag behind you whether you're free or in prison . . ."

SIBILA SARMIENTO WAS twelve years old when they decided she should be married. They all agreed that matrimony was very desirable but it would be better to wait for the girl to grow. For her first menstruation. For hair to grow under her arms. All of that. Sibila still played with dolls and sang children's songs. Matrimony was desired. It was also premature, said the girl's family.

The mother of the presumptive groom became enraged. An offer of marriage in the name of her son was not something you turned down. Marriage was not a question of hair or periods. It was an act of convenience. Sibila Sarmiento's family knew perfectly well that only the wedding of their children, right now, without delay, would join the names and properties of the Sarmientos and the Monroys and the great unity and productivity of their lands—Michoacán, Jalisco, Zacatecas—would triumph in hard cold liquidity before the law of the market and succession divided them into parcels, or an act of reiterated demagoguery gave them to the campesinos, transformed them into communal lands, and threw us all into poverty.

"Do you know the song? 'Just four *milpas* are left . . .' Well, unite the children so the lands can be united, and when the inevitable fragmentation comes we'll have something more than four cornfields left . . . After the storm . . ."

The squall was nothing less than the extension of the cities, urban sprawl, an exploding population, but Antigua Concepción persisted in her vocabulary at once revolutionary and feudal, agrarian and suspicious of the cities: She was crazy! She said another agrarian storm, recurrent in Mexico, was coming. They would declare null and void all appropriations of lands, water, and forests belonging to villages, settlements, congregations, or communities made by the previous power in violation of the law and abolished by the new power in confirmation of the law. She became confused. That's the bad thing about living so many years. And still, she had a witch's reasoning: She guessed with metaphors. The migrants were returning to Mexico and didn't find land or work. Gringo corn was wiping out the Mexican *milpa*. Villages were dying. Living in the past, Antigua Concepción prophesied the present. Like all prophets, she contradicted herself and became confused.

"The land would pass from few hands to fewer hands, passing through many hands, according to her," Sanginés explained. "Exempted was control exercised over no more than fifty hectares and for more than ten years. This reasoning was invoked by Señora Concepción, who was possessed by a kind of ravening madness in which past and future times, agrarian reform and the urban explosion, the place of inheritance and the will to begin again, mature sex and infantile sex were all mixed together: She imposed herself on her son because at heart she desired her son and wanted to castrate him by marrying him to a prepubescent child, incapable of giving or receiving satisfaction . . . Just to annoy . . ."

By uniting the Sarmiento and Monroy patrimonies, forty-nine

hectares were joined, those remaining were deeded to agrarian communities, one came out well with God and the Devil and offered an example of social solidarity by sacrificing something in order to save something, and the condition was the consolidation of protected lands through the marriage of a twelve-year-old girl, Sibila Sarmiento, and a forty-three-year-old man, Max Monroy, by means of matrimonial documents that could be disputed given the age of one contracting party but existed by virtue of the dishonesty of civil and ecclesiastical authorities in the desolate fields of central Mexico and, above and beyond everything else, even though one contracting party was a minor, the union of fortunes was consummated and the foresight of Doña Concepción, Antigua Concepción, proved correct: "I have what I want: The lands are ours and we can parcel them out; the marriage is theirs and let them arrange things the best they can. Get down to fucking, as they say."

"You didn't know my grandmother," said Miguel, and I didn't dare contradict him. "She was a witch, she had a pact with the Devil, she proposed something and achieved it, no matter who fell, she was insatiable, she never had enough money, if she had a lot she thought it was a little and wanted more, using every deception, the most sinister schemes, the most corrupt pacts as long as she not only preserved but augmented her power. And all of that with no reference to historical and political reality. She lived in her own time, the time of her making. Sibila Sarmiento was indispensable for mocking all the laws: childhood, marriageable age, agrarian law, even the personality of her son, in order to obtain what she wanted: another piece of earth. And I say 'earth' and not 'land' because each piece of land my damn grandmother acquired was for her the earth, the entire world, a universe embodied in every inch of earth, the earth was her flesh, it embodied her, and though I don't know where she was buried, I suspect, Josué, that for her the grave is another ranch she wants to own. And listen, never for her own benefit but for the sake of 'the revolution,' the entelechy she believed she was promoting by associating her desire with her destiny. That's how they were." I believe Miguel Aparecido sighed. "That's how they built our country. Telling themselves: If it's good for me, it's good for

Mexico. Tell me, what conscience isn't salved if this credo is repeated until you believe your own lie? Isn't this the great Mexican lie: I steal, I kill, I imprison, I amass a fortune, and I do it in the name of the country, my benefit is the nation's, and therefore the nation ought to thank me for my pillaging?"

Miguel Aparecido looked down, away from me, as I looked away from him during this discourse.

Miguel continued: "Her voracity went mad on this subject: acquiring properties, adding land, as if the secular tradition of basing one's fortune on owning land depended on this alone, as if she had already foreseen the moment when the great fortunes no longer depended on owning land but also on factories and now communications: This was," Miguel said in summary, "Max Monroy's conclusion. Not to be like his mother. To change the orientation of his wealth. Abandon the countryside and industry. Dedicate himself to communications. Build an empire of the future, far from the land and the factory, an almost impalpable universe barring his mother's way, a world of cellphones and the Internet that offered, instead of mudholes and smoke, videos, webs, music, games, and above all information along with the right to two hundred free messages and half an hour unlimited calling to each owner of a Monroy mobile."

And Sibila?

Imagine night falling on a face. Night fell on the face of Miguel Aparecido. He tried to rescue his account interrupted by all kinds of emotions, stammering and therefore unusual in him, even alien to the man I knew.

Sibila Sarmiento, a mother at fourteen. Deprived of her child at fifteen. Condemned to wander like a ghost, without understanding what had happened, through an abandoned ranch house stripped of furniture, in the care of absent servants who did not say a word to her. Did her husband, Max Monroy, understand what had happened? Or did he too absent himself from a situation that was nothing but the coarse, powerful whim of his mother, the monstrous old matriarch enamored of her own desire, her ability to show her own power at every opportunity so she would compare favorably to her husband the general, an irresolute womanizer, to believe she was ahead of events and mistress of the crystal ball, that reality did as she ordered because she did not endure reality, she created it, her caprice was law, the most capricious caprice, the most gratuitous cruelty, the least trustworthy desire, the most irrational reason: Now I'll take over the Sarmiento lands, now I'll marry my forty-year-old bachelor son to a twelve-year-old girl, now I'll declare the kid crazy and have her locked up at the Fray Bernardino because the poor idiot doesn't distinguish between the solitude of a ranch house and the helplessness of a lunatic asylum, rot there, imbecile, die there without realizing it, let's see who can do anything against the desire, the power, the caprice of a woman who has overcome every obstacle with the strength of her will, a female who rids herself of any unnecessary obligation; the child's mother to the funny farm; the child to the street, let him manage on his own, without help, let him become a little man without anybody's protection, let's see how he does, damn brat, if he has the right stuff he'll get ahead, if not, well then he can go to hell: all for you, Max, all so you can grow up and assert yourself without ballast, without family obligations, without children to take care of, without a wife to annoy you, nag at you, weigh you down, you'll be free, my son, you'll owe supreme thanks to the will of your magnificent mother Antigua Concepción, not Concha, not Conchita, no, but the mother of will, of whim, of caprice, of creation itself, of determination . . . The mistress of destiny. The overseer of chance.

"I made myself in the street, Josué. I grew up however I could. Perhaps I'm even grateful for being abandoned. I'm grateful for it but don't forgive it. I'll defend myself with my teeth."

I RETURNED WITH Father Filopáter to the Santo Domingo arcades. I wondered what brought me back. I guessed at some reasons: My interest in him and his ideas. The mystery surrounding his exclusion from teaching and from his religious order. Above all (because Filopáter was something like the final recollection of my youth), the memory of the moment when I learned to read, to think, to discuss my ideas, to feel, if not superior to then independent of the afflictions of childhood: subjection to a domineering housekeeper and especially ignorance of my origins. María Egipciaca was not my mother. My bones knew it. My head knew it when my confidence was withdrawn from the tyrannical housekeeper on Calle de Berlín. This did not resolve, of course, the enigma of my origins. But that mystery allowed me to uproot my life on the basis of an initiative determined by me, by my freedom.

Jericó was the symbol of my independence, of my promise of personal independence. But in the fraternal equation of Castor and Pollux, Father Filopáter, Trinitarian, intervened. He precipitated our intellectual curiosity, offered a port and a haven in what might have been aimless sailing regardless of the solidarity between the young navigators. If I had rediscovered Filopáter now, the event acquired an explanation: Jericó's distance returned me to the priest's proximity. Because if my friend and I had a "father" in common, it was this teacher at the Jalisco School, the priest who revealed to us the syntax of dialectic, the ludic element (in order not to be ridiculous) of ideological and even theoretical positions. To pit the philosophy of Saint Thomas against the thought of Nietzsche was an exercise, for Jericó and I were not Thomists or nihilists. The interesting thing is that Filopáter would find in Spinoza the equilibrium between dogma and rebellion, asking us, in a straightforward way, to be sure the ideology of knowledge did not precede knowledge itself, making it impossible.

"The truth is made manifest without manifestos, like light when it displaces dark. Light does not announce itself ideologically. Neither does thought. Only darkness keeps us from seeing."

Had Filopáter's position regarding dogma been what eventually excluded him from the religious community? Did the priest distance himself too much from the principles of faith in order to establish himself in the proofs of faith? These were the questions I asked myself when the chaotic or fatal events I have recorded here combined and broke the ties that until then had bound me to friendship (Jericó), sexual desire (Asunta), ambition (Max Monroy), and unspoiled charity (Miguel Aparecido).

What did I have left? The chance encounter with Filopáter appeared to me like a salvation, if by salvation you understand not a favorable judgment in the tribunal of eternity but the full realization of our human potential. To be what we are because we are what we were and what we will be. The question of transcendence beyond death is left hanging during the age of salvation on earth. Does the second determine the first? Does what happens to us after death depend on what we accomplish in life? Or ultimately, independent of our actions, is a final redemption valid when it is stimulated by confession, repentance, final awareness of the truth that pursued us from the beginning and which we believe only when we die?

Filopáter's reply (and perhaps the reason for his exclusion) was that each human being was granted individual value independent of belonging to a group, party, church, or social class. The individual inalienable being could, in fact, affiliate with a group, party, class, or church as long as this radical personal value was not lost. Was this what the religious order could not forgive in Filopáter: the stubborn affirmation of his person without discrediting his membership in the clergy, his refusal to hand his personality over to the herd, disappearing gratefully into the crowd of the city, the monastery, the party? He had been faithful to what he taught us. He was the favorite son of Baruch (Benoît, Benedetto, Benito, Bendito) Spinoza, excommunicated from Hebrew orthodoxy, irreducible to Christian orthodoxy, a heretic to both, convinced that faith is consumed in obedience and expands in justice.

Back at Santo Domingo and in conversation with Filopáter, I expected what he offered as we walked from the plaza to Calle de Donceles along República de Brasil, a continuation of our earlier talk, though part of my attention was devoted to crossing the crowded streets, keeping the good father from being run down by trucks, cars, bicycles, or peddlers' carts.

"I don't want you going around in circles about the reasons for my exclusion," he said then, and I understood that the miracle of his existence was not to die by being run down. "My crime was to maintain that Jesus is not a proxy for the Father. Jesus is God because he is incarnate and the Father does not tolerate that. Anathema, anathema!" Filopáter struck his emaciated chest, making the ancient tie fly up while I helped him cross the street. "And my conclusion,

Josué. If what I say is true, God appears only to the most unworthy of men."

"The most unbelieving?" I said, impelled by Filopáter's words.

"I don't believe in a totalitarian God. I believe in the self-contradictory God incarnated in Jesus. *Thou hast had my soul even unto death,* said Jesus the man in Gethsemane. And if he said *Father, why hast thou forsaken me,* what wouldn't he say to all of us? Men, why have you forsaken me? Don't you see I am only a helpless man, condemned, fatal, with no providence at all, just like you? Why don't you recognize yourselves in me? Why do you invent a Father and a Holy Spirit for me? Don't you see that in the Trinity I, the man, Jesus the Christ, disappear when made divine?"

When we finally walked through the large street door of number 815, Calle de Donceles, to a covered alleyway smelling of moss and rotting roots, Filopáter led me to a room at the rear of the crowded courtyard, avoiding with a glance I imagined as fearful the stairway that led to the residential floor, as if a ghost lived there.

Filopáter's room was in reality a workshop with tables prepared for precise work: grinding lenses. A table, two chairs, a cot, bare walls unadorned except for the crucifix over the bed. Since I looked longer than I should have at the bed, Filopáter took me by the arm and smiled.

"A woman doesn't fit in my bed. Imagine. Celibacy has been obligatory for priests since the Lateran Council of 1139, except that Henri, bishop of Liège in the thirteenth century, had sixty-one children. Fourteen in twenty-two months."

"A woman," I said just to say something, not imagining the consequences.

"Your woman," Filopáter said to my enormous surprise.

He saw the astonishment followed by incomprehension on my face; before my eyes passed the gaze of Asunta Jordán, in my ears the voice of the nurse Elvira Ríos, in my nose the smell of Señora Hetara's whores, but my sealed mouth did not pronounce the name Filopáter made himself responsible for saying:

"Lucha Zapata."

And then he murmured: "Perhaps the voice of Satan said to

Jesus on Calvary: 'If thou be God, save thyself and come down from the cross.' "

I WAS AFRAID as I walked up to the apartment on Calle de Praga. On each stair a false step threatened me. In each corner an enemy lurked. I went up slowly, accompanied by a legion of demons unleashed by the visit to Filopáter's hiding place in the center of the immense city. In the shadows, succubi adopted the intangible forms of women to seduce and condemn me. Worse were the incubi who offered themselves to me as satanic male lovers. And the horror of my ascent was that the incubi were men with the face of Asunta and the succubi women with Jericó's features, as if I wanted to erase from my vision Lucha Zapata's face, evoked by my visit with Filopáter on Calle de Donceles. Then I knew it was all a premonition.

I opened the door to the apartment nervously, hurriedly. I put the keys in my pocket and before I turned on the lights Jericó's voice asked me—ordered me—from the darkness: "No light. Don't turn on the light. Let's talk in the dark."

I accepted the invitation. Little by little, as usual, my eyes grew accustomed to the darkness, and Jericó's shadow was outlined with greater clarity.

But not much. The man, my friend, set aside an area of his own darkness that protected him from a world turned hostile. As if I didn't know. The arrest order had come from the office of the president with the fury reserved for a traitor.

From then on "Judas" would be the presidential term used to refer to Jericó, "Judas."

Now Jericó Iscariot was hiding in the most obvious and therefore most concealed place: our apartment on Calle de Praga.

"Do you remember Poe? We read him together. The purloined letter is in sight of everyone and therefore nobody sees it."

"You're taking a risk," I said with a reverberation of affection from my heart but not daring to say: Run away. I didn't want him, a fugitive, to feel expelled as well. What would I do except respect Jericó's desire, even knowing I might seem like his accomplice, his harborer?

"Get away. Don't compromise me."

I didn't dare say that.

He said it for me.

He saved me the grief.

"You know, old pal. We wanted so much in life, we read, studied, discussed so much, and ended up only being worth what you pay an informer."

I became angry. "I'm no Judas."

He became angry. "That's what they call me in the president's office."

"I had nothing to do . . ." I stammered. "I'm not a traitor. I don't work in the government."

"Then are you my accomplice?"

"I'm your friend. Not a traitor and not an accomplice."

I asked him without words to understand me. I didn't want to ask him to leave. Where would he go? He knew I wouldn't turn him in. He took advantage of our friendship. Did he sacrifice it? I rejected this idea, seeing Jericó cornered by shadows, failed in his illusory takeover of power, the act of an inopportune fascist fascination impossible in our time, the product of an imagination, as I now understood it, exalted by itself, by the past, by a feverish, perversely idealistic intelligence. My friend Jericó with no last name. Like kings. Like sultans. Like Asian dictators.

"Thanks, Monroy. Your monitoring has allowed us to keep an eye on all of Judas's preparations."

Max Monroy didn't tell the president that having access to all the strands of information was useful for something.

Valentín Pedro Carrera couldn't help making a joke.

"You kept the information till pretty late, Don Max. This Judas almost had his way and turned us into Christ, damn it."

Monroy shook his head, sunk deep into his shoulders.

"Nobody has his way anymore," he declared. "Everything's on file. There's no subversive movement that isn't known. If I was late in informing you, it's because most of these revolutions abort right away. They last as long as Indian summer. Why add to your worries, Mr. President? You have enough with preparations for your popular festivals."

The president did not respond to the blow. He owed Monroy too much. Monroy felt just a little embarrassed, as if he had abused his own power.

"When it's a question of serious matters, I'm at your disposal, Mr. President."

"I know, Don Max, I know and I appreciate it. Believe me."

Hadn't Jericó, dressed in shadows, known what I knew in Monroy's office thanks to Asunta's information?

"Were we in the wrong age?" I asked with no irony.

He went on as if he hadn't heard me. "Were we born in time or out of time?"

He said it was important for him to know that.

He evoked our childhood and early youth, both of us brought up without a family, without knowing our parents, without even knowing if we had parents, never knowing who supported us, paid for our schools, clothes, food . . .

"Because somebody supported us, Josué, and if we didn't find out who for the sake of convenience pure and simple, because it was totally awesome to receive everything and owe nothing, we didn't ask and nobody asked us either, our table was set, and did we deserve it, champ? Didn't the moment come to rebel against a destiny others had made for you and go out and create your own destiny?"

I didn't know what to say to him, except that his presence at that moment was for me like a tribute to the past he and I had shared. It was a way of telling him I had doubts about our friendship in the future. This was, after all, a moment of melancholy.

Jericó wasn't a fool. He grasped my words at once and adapted them to his own situation, he was here and was the friend I avoided in order not to harm him and he, now, was seizing his neck as the rebellious poet seized the swan "with deceitful plumage." Jericó wanted to twist his own neck, that was his dramatic vocation.

"Do you remember our first meeting, Josué? Remember it and then add on the facts of our relationship. Do you agree I was always the one who pushed you to act? Against school authority, against conventions of thought, against good manners, do you agree I always pushed you toward the path my life was opening for us?"

"It's possible," I replied, testing the shifting ground that spread before me.

"No," he said fiercely. "Not possible. True. That's how it was. I always went first, of course I did."

"To a point." I wanted to play along because I didn't want the stormy confrontation Jericó's gaze was sending out to me from the darkness.

"Believe it even if you don't believe it."

He laughed. I don't know if he laughed at the situation, at me, or at himself.

"You stopped, Josué. You didn't follow me to the end of the road."

"The fact is there was a cliff at the end of the road," I said with no desire to condemn him.

He took it differently. "You didn't have the courage to walk with me to the end of the road. You didn't cross the frontier with me, Josué. You didn't have the courage to explore the evil in yourself. Because both of us always knew that just as we did good, we could do evil. Even more: the 'better' we were, the less complete we would be. Each action in our lives means roads to the edge of the abyss. One precipice is good. The other is evil. Don't be confused, brother. You and I did not fall into good or evil. We simply walked along the street of ambiguity, both yes and no . . . A decision had to be made. There's a moment that demands definition from us. Does it depend on where we are, whom we're with, what influences us? Sure, I found myself at the center of political power. And from there, Jericó, my only option to be myself, to not turn into a puppet of power, was to oppose power with power, power of another kind, Jericó, the power of evil, because look, the power of good, where has it brought us? To a democracy that resembles a wheel with a mouse inside that runs and runs and doesn't get anywhere. And did I opt for a different action? And did that action lead to the stigma of evil? Reclaim it for me, if you like. Go on. *Ándale.*"

He breathed like a tiger. "Yes. That's what I did. Explored the evil in myself. I descended to the depths of my own evil and discovered that evil is the only valid enemy for a brave man. Evil as valor, do you understand? Evil as proof of your manhood."

I reacted with modest annoyance.

"I don't want the killing to go on, that's all. I don't want to smell more blood after the century we were born into, Jericó, the time of evil carried to the extreme of knowing itself as evil and celebrating evil as the great good of desire and destiny . . . It makes me sick, what about you, you bastard?"

(Before my open eyes passed the corpses in the trenches of the Marne and the camps of Auschwitz, in the blood-filled river of Stalingrad and the blood-filled jungle of Vietnam, the juvenile corpses of Tlatelolco and the victims in Chile and Argentina, the tortures of Abu Ghraib and the justifications, also corpselike, of Nazis and Communists, brutal soldiers and terrified presidents, Gringos maddened by the incomprehensible difference of not being like everyone else and French rationalists applying "the question" in Algeria: Now I told myself the probable summary of history is that we could analyze in detail and clarify the cultural modalities of the time but did not know how to avoid its evil. In the life of Jericó and Josué, how much was it worth to exalt the knowledge of good as a barricade against the preference for evil? Was our "culture" the dike against the Devil's flood? Without us, would we all have drowned in the sea of evil? Or, with or without us, would the evil of the time have been manifest in measures that did not matter in the light of just one little girl screaming naked, burned forever, on a path in the jungle of Indochina? Of one little Jewish boy forced out of the Warsaw ghetto with his hands raised, the star on his coat and his destiny in his eyes?)

"I don't want the killing to go on," I said then in a way that may seem irrelevant. Just then it was the only response dictated to me by the situation. "I want us to go on being Castor and Pollux, the brothers who were friends."

"Shall we be Cain and Abel, the brothers who were enemies?"

"That depends on you."

"You didn't have the courage. You didn't go with me," he insisted in a way that seemed desolate and lugubrious.

"I think you were wrong, Jericó. You misread the situation and acted accordingly. You acted badly."

"Badly? Something had to be done," he said in a tone of sudden modesty, fairly unexpected and chimerical in him.

"You can do something. You can't do everything," I responded with growing humility and blamed myself for treating a friend in a condescending way without meaning to. This was insulting. I was sure he didn't realize it. Was I wrong?

There was no time to reply. We clearly heard footsteps on the stairs. It was midnight, and in this building, aside from our apartment, there were only offices that closed at seven. For an instant I thought Jericó was going to hide in the closet. He moved. He stopped. He listened. I listened. We listened. The footsteps were ascending. They belonged to a woman. The click of high heels revealed that. Both of us, separated by a couple of meters, waited. There was nothing to do except, for an instant, separate as if only one would have to die, alone.

The door opened. Asunta Jordán looked at us as if the two meters of separation did not exist. She looked at us as if we were one, Castor and Pollux, fraternal twins, not Cain and Abel, the brothers who were enemies.

She turned off the flashlight in her hand. It wasn't necessary. The lights were on now. The purloined letter was in plain sight for everyone to see.

Outside, the Gothic statues of the Church of the Santo Niño de Praga did not give us their white smiles.

"I DIDN'T FINISH telling you," said Lucha Zapata in the letter she dictated to Filopáter that the priest handed to me now.

She didn't finish? She didn't even begin. And I never asked her: Tell me about your past. Not out of negligence. Out of love. Lucha Zapata gave me and asked for an affection in which memories were superfluous. This was how our relationship was established, without recollections but not amnesiac, because the absence of the past was a radical way of taking root in the present, love as the root of instant passion that remembers nothing and foresees nothing because it is self-sufficient.

This was the very mark of my relationship with Lucha Zapata, and if she was writing to me now she did so, I'm certain, in the name of chance and freedom. She did not betray herself. She was tossing a bottle into the sea. Would I read these pages? It would not depend so much on my desire as on my destiny. If I had not walked the streets of the Historic Center in search of clues to what Jericó was preparing (and wasn't this, no matter how I disguised it as official duty, a sickly form of disloyalty to a friend?) I would not have run into Father Filopáter on the Plaza de Santo Domingo. He could have rejected my approaching him. Out of a sense of decency. Because his new life was a break from his former one. Because I had no right to resurrect the past.

It didn't happen that way. He received me, recognized me, remembered me, led me to his poor lodgings at the rear of a poisonous garden on Calle de Donceles where Filopáter imitated the life of Spinoza, grinding lenses.

This matter could have ended there. If I hadn't seen my old teacher for eleven years, why wouldn't I have left him forever following our brief, accidental meeting? This is the question and no one is shielded from it. We met. We didn't meet. If we didn't meet, what things would not have happened? What opportunities would have been lost? What dangers avoided? But if we did meet, what things would happen? What opportunities would present themselves? What dangers would be realized?

Jericó was right: Perhaps we're always at a great crossroads, a circular plaza with avenues radiating from it, each one leading in turn to other plazas from which other avenues radiate. Six, thirty-six, two hundred sixteen, infinite plazas, infinite avenues for a finite life guaranteed a direction only by what we make with our hands, our ideas, our words, forms, colors, sounds, not what we do with sex, social relationships, family life: These evaporate and no one remembers anyone after the third or fourth generation. Who was your great-grandfather, what was the name of your great-great-grandfather, what face did your most remote ancestor have, the one who lived before photography, the one who wasn't lucky enough to be painted by Rubens or Velázquez? We are part of the distribution of the great collective forgetting, a telephone book with no numbers, a dictionary of blank pages where not even the fingerprints of those who turned them remain . . .

Why, then, did Lucha Zapata leave me this letter-confession in which she detailed her criminal life with individuals I came to know through the brothel life of my early youth, my visits to the Esparza house and the San Juan de Aragón Prison? Why did Lucha break the silence, the music of our love affair, with a criminal tale? Here Lucha Zapata appeared training in crime, first as one of the gangs of beggars, false blind men, cripples, the destitute, the incurable, whatever they desire, whatever destiny grants us. Lucha eating the bread of affliction on busy corners, from Avenida Masaryk to the road to the airport, her hand outstretched, reciting prayers, doggerel, God bless you, whatever Your Grace can spare, praise God, simulating bloody sores at the entrance to churches, hernias at the entrance to hospitals, fevers at the entrance to restaurants, allying herself in an ascending scale with thieves, thugs, pimps, houseboys who specialize in robbing houses, the pious who steal in churches, apostles who know how to use picklocks and open doors, bullfighters who steal from pedestrians in the light of day; hoodlums, paid killers, experts in knife fights, panderers, boys who work in brothels, aimless young people and old criminals as well who have no recourse but crime, old soldiers, ruined pensioners, those hounded by bankruptcy, late payments, overdue mortgages, devaluated currency, evaporated savings, discontinued jobs, nonexistent insurance, you see, Josué, how intertwined are virtue and destiny, chance and necessity, innocence and guilt in the legion of those who rob out of necessity because others, you know? need to steal or steal without need, as others kill for pleasure and others unnecessarily and others because they need to kill, are you charitable, do you understand, do you have enough charity to forgive if you know, Josué, or can you love only if you don't know? Can you love Lucha Zapata only if you know nothing about Lucha Zapata?

Yes, she was a vision, an aviator expelled from the airfield for attempting to steal a twin-engine plane from a hangar, a specter in a cap and goggles and leather jacket who fell by chance into my arms when I said goodbye to Jericó who was flying off to study in France and I saw Sara P. pass by preceded by a false porter who turned out to be the bandit and mariachi Maxi Batalla. Was this the truth? Everything else fiction? The mariachi wasn't beaten and mute as his poor mother thought but alive and well? Sara P. was part of the criminal gang organized by Jericó to attack power with violence because legality seemed useless to him and he confused revolutionary action with a police problem, which is what he received in return: disaster, flight, prison?

Everything eventually tied in a bundle that gathered up the threads of the plot in this chance encounter with Filopáter and the reading, even more fortuitous, of a letter Lucha Zapata wrote to me without losing hope I would read it one day? "You don't remember me" was the refrain of the letter. And again: "You gave me the pulse of happiness," and once again: "I had to suffer to love you."

A letter dictated to Filopáter by Lucha.

Why? What did she know?

Couldn't she write without needing an amanuensis?

Did Filopáter have to be the scribe of our destiny?

Or was this a way to confess what she never would have told me in person, since our dealings with each other, you remember, went beyond all reference to the past? But the element of chance prevailed over Lucha's desire. Perhaps I would never have walked through the Plaza de Santo Domingo. Perhaps I would never have seen Filopáter again. This was the point at which our desire— Lucha's and mine—and chance coincided. Dictating a letter to a public scribe in the hope I would find him and he would give me the letter to read. Like now, fulfilling a prophecy more than engaging in a coincidence, I did it, I read the letter.

At the beginning of everything, was there a kindergarten? Was there a hostile mother, embittered because youth is a seduction that doesn't last, because her daughter felt sad and solitary and wanted to expel the shadows and the mother told her Don't show your breasts and she told her mother I hate how you dress and they said things to each other like love is when things turn out well so the mother would return to her responsibility, didn't I tell you, didn't I say you could only live at your mother's side? And Lucha wanted to preserve a moment, just one, precisely the one when mother and daughter were admired together, at the same time, what a nice pair, they look like sisters, expelling the shadows, the threat, the deception, Didn't I tell you you could only live with your mother? before throwing herself out on the street, into voluntary beggary, crime, the company of Maxi Batalla and Sara P. and Siboney Peralta, Brillantinas and Gomas, the roguish and violent licenciado Jenaro Ruvalcaba of sad memory in this my course in criminality subject to the prison control of Miguel Aparecido but free, outside prison, free as a pack of hungry beasts, fangs sharpened, mouths slavering, eyes reddened by unwanted wakefulness, by Jericó's political ambition.

I was part of all this history. I knew the distribution of desire and also of destiny. I had loved this woman who saved herself from crime and punishment thanks to her chance encounter with me in the airport and thanks to our life together, uneven, a real roller coaster of emotions, alcohol and drugs, good food and better sex: What did I have to complain about if I knew how to avoid the vices and enjoy the virtues? What?

ASUNTA JORDÁN CAME into the apartment on Calle de Praga with all the authority of her bold gestures, imperiously clicking high heels, uniform of a high-level employee, ill-tempered face, eyes that managed to see my friend and me at the same time. She was peremptory and there was nothing to say. An armored car was waiting downstairs escorted by two more cars carrying armed people. I resigned myself. Jericó had a nervous reflex like that of a trapped animal. She played for a moment with my resignation and his fatal rebelliousness.

It wasn't what we feared. Jericó was protected by Max Monroy from the presidential decision to annihilate him. Judas. Jericó was driven to Max's building on Plaza Vasco de Quiroga, in the direction of Santa Fe. Asunta was in charge of the operation. Jericó, until he heard otherwise, would be hidden in an apartment in the Utopia building next to the one occupied by Asunta. I, with a bitter taste in my mouth, decided to remove myself, go to Filopáter's house, spend a week in that corner at the rear of the covered garden on Calle de Donceles and then return, perhaps purified, to the Santa Fe building. I read Lucha Zapata's letter.

On my return I entered a rarefied atmosphere.

Asunta received me in her office without looking up from the computer that distracted her.

"He's in the apartment on the thirteenth floor, next to mine. Take the keys."

She tossed me a key ring and I picked it up, trying to guess her intention. I didn't need keys. Max Monroy had a yen to live with open doors: "I have nothing to hide."

It was his best disguise, I had understood that. The fact that the probable presence of Jericó required keys and locked doors alarmed me as we may be alarmed by the presence in our house of a ferocious animal we feed so it will survive but that we keep locked up so it doesn't kill us.

I recalled the news item from the zoo. A tiger killed by the bites of other hungry tigers. Five tigers. Why was the devoured tiger attacked, why that tiger and not any of the four attackers? What united the aggressors against an animal of their own kind? Was it pure chance, the bad luck of the fifth tiger? Could the victim have been the killer of another tiger?

The image of a caged Jericó produced in me the memory of an invisible figure, mobile in the extreme, my friend, who came and went in the city and the world without explanation, without identity papers, without even a second name: just Jericó, the perfect symbiosis of desire and destiny, free as the wind, without family ties, without known loves. Almost, if he weren't so tangible in our familiarity, a phantom: my spectral brother, half of Castor and Pollux, the fraternal duality inconceivable in separation . . . Who had imprisoned the wind? Who had the free spirit under lock and key?

I knew the answer. Max Monroy. And the answer was added to the legion of questions I was asking myself at this time. What interest did Max Monroy have in rescuing Jericó and bringing him here, to the bosom of the large family, enterprise and home of Utopia? I imagined for a second it was all a ruse of Monroy's to defy the president, demonstrating where real power was to be found. Did Monroy plant Jericó in the offices at Los Pinos only so my friend would deceive the president, making him believe in a false loyalty and using the springboard of power to stage an unsuccessful, ridiculous coup, failed beforehand, as Monroy expected, proving to the president that he, Monroy, possessed the information leading to the crisis, and by possessing the information he possessed real power: calibrating the threat, letting ambushes pass when they had no future, suffocating rebellions in the cradle, and cutting off their heads if they arose? Had it all been Monroy's great masquerade for Carrera, a demonstration of where real power was to be found?

Or had Jericó's actions been independent of Monroy? Had my friend acted, unsuccessfully, on his own, caught up in a dead illusion of revolt, impossible in the modern world of information and power, omnipresent under all circumstances, Orwell's *1984* staged every day, without drama, without unnecessary symbols, without totalitarian cruelties, but disguised in the most absolute normality and accustomed to the technique of white-gloved castration?

Asunta Jordán did not look at me. Her complete attention was dedicated to reading the digital print, skipping the password, depending on two gigabytes of memory, connecting with the wireless net, showing me without even looking at me that the ideological world inhabited by poor Jericó was an illusion of the past, something as ancient as the pyramids.

"Older than a forest," Max Monroy said about himself.

But if Jericó was an agent removed from both Carrera's presidential and Monroy's entrepreneurial power, whom did he represent? Himself, only that? You are aware of the mutual respect my friend and I had for each other. He did not inquire into my personal life and I did not try to find out about his. The question that remained shrouded was, of course, Jericó's life during the obscure years of his absence. I acted in good faith. I loved my friend. I loved our old friendship. If he said he had been in France during that time, I believed him, no matter how false his French culture seemed to me and how conclusive his pop cultural references to the North American world. Did Jericó let slip Gringo exclamations intentionally—*Let's hug it out, bitch*—and never French ones? Did he want me to know I was deceived, did his old habit of playing with reality get the better of him, deceiving to amuse, masking to reveal? Did he want to seduce me, put me in the position of asking about him, transform him into my own mystery, transfer to Jericó the questions I did not ask myself? Did he know perhaps that my mysteries were nonexistent? Did he know what I've recounted here, everything you know: my affair with Lucha Zapata, my relationship with Miguel Aparecido, my employment in Max Monroy's enterprise, the recent revelation of Miguel Aparecido's relationship to Monroy, my secret talks with Monroy's mother, Doña Antigua Concepción, and finally my infatuation with Asunta Jordán, the pleasure of the night and the humiliation of the next morning, the fugacity of my pleasure with her, and Asunta's brazen, frightening giving of herself in her relationship of gratitude with the ancient tribal chief: Max Monroy?

Perhaps, with these questions, I disguised my own mystery, my origins prior to my life with María Egipciaca in the mansion on Berlín.

I felt I had voluntarily erased all memory before the age of seven, though I also think before that age we have no memory at all except what our parents tell us. I had no parents. Jericó, apparently, didn't either. I've already recounted how he and I would congratulate ourselves on not having a family if the family was like that of our friend Baldy Errol. This was one more disguise, perhaps the most sophistic of all. The fact is Jericó had no second name because he had renounced it. His example led me to mention only very occasionally the one I had in school, at the university, at work. Josué Nadal. Perhaps I rejected it to emulate Jericó. Perhaps a last name with no known ancestry made me uncomfortable. Perhaps he and I preferred to be Castor and Pollux, legendary brothers, without last names.

In this gigantic puzzle, where was Jericó? Who was Jericó? I had the anguished feeling, located in the pit of my stomach, that I absolutely did not know the person I thought I knew better than anyone: my brother Jericó, protector of the fraternity of Castor and Pollux, Argonauts destined for the same adventure. Retrieving the Golden Fleece . . .

The naked man, the animal that received me in the secret apartment in Utopia, was on all fours on a rumpled bed.

I remembered him in the same posture, defiant but smiling, sure of himself, master of a future as mysterious as it was certain, in La Hetara's whorehouse: Who knows what would happen, but it would happen for him, for Jericó, thanks to his desire and his destiny. And necessity? Could my friend exclude the necessary from the desired and the destined? I thought of him now as he was earlier, the day he announced his departure, moving like a caged animal around the space we shared, which had changed into a prison he was going to leave—without even imagining he would end up here, once more on all fours but this time really caged, shut in, a prisoner now as perhaps he always had been, of himself: Jericó under guard, mapping the prison of his bed.

His whitish body ended in a furious, disheveled head with bloodshot eyes, enraged lips, and murderous teeth, as if he had just devoured the tiger at the zoo. His body looked grotesque, elongated, in distorted perspective behind the blond head that encapsulated Jericó's entire person then, as if everything pulsating in him, guts and testicles, heart and skeleton, were concentrated in a monstrous, aggressive head that was intestines, balls, claws, and blood of the animal walking on the bed on all fours, fixed on me, taking pride in his verbal ferocity, his feverish dialect, there are men loved by many women, Josué you bastard, there are men no woman loves, but I love just one, you've had them all, I love only one, let me have her, damn it, let me have her or I swear I'll have you killed! Do you think you have a right to everything I didn't have? You're wrong, mother-fucker! I'll give you everything, like always, but let me have this woman, just one woman, why do you fuck with me, Josué you bas-tard, why don't you let me have the only woman I desire, the only woman who's made me feel like a man, the woman who captured me and mastered me and tore away from me mystery and the power to question, the woman who refuses to be mine because she says she's yours and Asunta rejects me saying she belongs to you, she can't be anybody else's, you bastard motherfucker, free her you son of a bitch, let her go for my balls, aren't we like brothers? Don't we share whores? Why do you want Asunta all to yourself, damn miser, stop stabbing yourself, fucking pig, fix yourself up, Okay, that's enough . . .

And he let out a savage shout:

"I'm going to kill you, you fucking pig, either you let me have that broad or I swear you'll be pushing up daisies!"

He said this in so horrible a way, on all fours, naked on the bed, his testicles bouncing between his legs, his face that of a ferocious animal, as if everything truly Jericó had come out to be depicted on the threatening face that no longer belonged to the valiant compan-ion Pollux but to the murderous brother Cain.

A naked Jericó slavered, in a bestial posture and concentrating on me, I realized, the frustrations so contrary to a life that took place on the stages of success, from school until today. Jericó the bold, the sharp, the triumphant, the protector, the mysterious, the one who didn't show his cards and won the game with a poker face, was showing his cards now and he had nothing: not even a miser-able pair of fives, not even when the lower numbers had been elim-inated. It was this naked feeling—physically, morally naked—that concentrated the hatred of my brother Cain against me, and when Asunta appeared behind Jericó's bed and I looked at her, I understood her perverse game. Whatever the motives of Max Monroy in saving Jericó from the president's vengeance and bringing him to the shelter of Utopia, Asunta's game, no matter how tangential to Monroy's intentions, was what had mortally wounded Jericó.

I looked at Asunta at the rear of the bedroom, her arms crossed over her chest, the executive figure disguising her origin as a provincial wife dominated by an unhappy macho, and I knew she was victorious, in possession of the plot. Subject to Max's design but independent of him: Asunta had made Jericó believe she was my lover, that in this building the only Utopia was the erotic satisfaction she and I gave each other and I, beyond the nurse Elvira Ríos and the abandoned Lucha Zapata, had fulfilled my sexual life in nights of ecstasy with Asunta Jordán. Fuck me!

Asunta told this to Jericó. In this way Jericó's treason was avenged, even though Monroy had been the author of his salvation, which still needed to be demonstrated.

None of it mattered.

My world collapsed with Jericó's murderous look. I didn't want to believe that behind our long and proven fraternal friendship, disdain was the mask of the hatred that was the real face of our relationship. Because concentrated hatred is what gleamed around the maw of a Jericó animalized by defeat, by Asunta's erotic disdain, by Monroy's probable deception, by the political triumph of President Carrera, by the humiliation of knowing that if not for Asunta's appearance in the apartment on Calle de Praga, he, Jericó, would have been a victim of the fugitive law, shot in the back as he tried to escape, or locked up in San Juan de Aragón with his miserable conspirators. Exposed to the implacable vengeance of Miguel Aparecido.

I feared for him.

I should have feared for myself.

SO YOU'RE GOING to write your thesis on me, Josué? What do you plan to say? Are you going to repeat the same clichés? Niccolò Machiavelli, calculating, hypocritical, the icy manipulator of the power he never wielded, only advised? Are you going to talk about my mainstays, necessity, virtue, fortune? Are you going to write that necessity is the stimulus for political action though in its name there is also betrayal and ambition? Are you going to repeat that virtue is a manifestation of free will though it can also be the mask of the hypocrite? And, finally, are you going to say that I compare fortune to feminine inconsistency, capricious and inconstant, concluding that the man who depends on it least endures longest?

Machiavelli the misogynist! Didn't I marry Marietta Corsini to obtain, in a single hymen, both virginity and fortune? Ah, Josué, don't repeat the tired phrases that pursue me from century to century. Be bolder. Have the audacity, my young friend, to penetrate my true biography, not the one by "serious" historians, no, but the one about my real, vulgar, crude, lustful existence: Niccolò Machiavelli says it aloud so everyone can hear: "I don't know anything that gives more happiness, doing it, thinking about it, than fornication. A man can philosophize all he wants, but this is the truth." That's what I wrote, and now I repeat it to you. Everybody understands it. Few say it. You can quote me. It irritates me that people are ignorant of my taste for women and sex. Let them be ignorant! What difference does it make! But if you're going to write truthfully about me, you'll repeat with me: Sweet, trifling, or weighty, sex creates a network of feelings without which, it seems to me, I could not be happy.

Look at them: One is named Gianna, another Lucrecia, still another La Tafani. I'll tell you something beyond their names: Desire responds only to nature, not morality. La Riccia was a prostitute well known all around Florence? That does not diminish in the least the pleasure she gave me. She was my lover for ten years. It didn't matter to her when my fortunes changed. She didn't change. Friends changed. She did not. And La Tafani? Charming, refined, noble, I can never praise her as she deserves. Love entangled me in her web. They were nets woven by Venus, my young friend, soft and sensitive . . . Until the day the nets harden and imprison you and you can't undo the knots and don't care about the punishment. Don't forget, Josué, all love is pardoned and pardonable if it gives you pleasure. I had relations with women and also with men. It was another time. Homosexuality was common in Florence.

In general, all my love had sweetness, because loved flesh gave me delight and because when I loved I forgot my troubles, so much so that I preferred the prison of love to having freedom, yes freedom, *ay!* granted to me.

I remember and savor all this because *The Prince,* the work you're studying on the instructions of your Professor Sanginés, was received in 1513 as the work of the Devil (Niccolò Machiavelli, Old Nick, the Demon, the double of Beelzebub, Belial, Azazel, Mephistopheles, Asmodeus, Satan, the Deva, the Cacodemon, the Evil One, the Tempter, and more familiarly, not only Old Nick but also Old Harry, Old Ned, the Dickens, Old Scratch, the Prince of Darkness), all because I brought light to the business of politics, deceived no one, told them this is the way things are, like it or not, it isn't a moral judgment of mine, these are our political realities, read me seriously, I am inspired not by darkness but by light, learn that a good government is in accord only with the nature of the time and a bad government is opposed to the spirit of the time, learn that old governments are secure and manageable and new governments dangerous because they displace the authorities of previous governments and leave their own followers dissatisfied because they thought with power they would obtain everything that can be given only with an eyedropper in the tension between the legitimacy of its origin, which in no way assures the legitimacy of its exercise . . .

Why go on? Politics is simply the public relationship among human beings. Freedom is the regularization of power. Men are mad and want to see the origin of power in sacred revelation, in nature, in race, in a social contract, in revolution, and in law. To them I say no. Power is simply the exercise of necessity, the mask of virtue, and the chance of fortune. Unbearable. Do you know, to restore my spirits, sometimes I return to the countryside and change clothes. I put on togas and medallions, gold sandals and laurel wreaths, and then, alone, I converse with the ancients, with the Greeks and Romans, my peers . . .

It is a great lie: a fiction. The truth is I need the city. I love the city, its works, its plazas, its stones, its markets, its bodies. The sweetness of a face allows me to forget my sorrows. The heat of sex invites me to leave my family, making them think I have died. Madness!

And still, here I am back in office, serving the Prince, remembering perhaps that love is mischievous and escapes from the liver, the eyes, the heart. Only the administration of the city—politics, the *polis*—saves me, Josué, from the suicidal ardor of sex and the onerous imagination of the historical past as I wait for my trip to hell, a much more amusing place than heaven.

Understand, then, my smile. Understand the portrait of me by Santi di Tito in the Palazzo Vecchio. Do you see now why I smile? Do you realize there are only two comparable smiles, the Giaconda's and mine? She was the Mona Lisa. Will I be the Mono Liso, Smooth Monkey? There is no risk. If you like, call me, in Mexican, Machiavelli, Chango Resbaloso, Slippery Monkey.

"JERICÓ'S MISTAKE," SANGINÉS remarked during this new lunch, now in the Danubio on the Calles de Uruguay, "consisted in believing a dissatisfied mass would follow a revolutionary vanguard. He didn't see two essential things: First, that the revolutionary masses are an invention of the revolutionary vanguard. Second, that when the masses have moved it's because they have reached the end of their patience. That doesn't happen here—or hasn't happened yet. Most people believe they can achieve a better situation. People make promises to themselves. People, if you like, deceive themselves. Go away. Fine. The worker goes as a migrant to California, Oregon, the Carolinas. Fine. But people see the ads and what they want is to be like that, like the ad. Have a car, their own house, go on vacation, whatever, fuck the 'Classy Blonde.' Have you seen, Josué, the faces of people when they come out of a movie, imitating— unconsciously, no doubt—the star they've just seen?"

"Nicole Kidman," I intervened just to say something, when I should have paid attention to the platter of shellfish the Danubio waiter had placed in front of me. "Errol Flynn," I added, unusual for me, in memory of Baldy, our friend, but also with a certain mockery, as if Sanginés were teaching me what I already knew and I, out of respect, was pretending I was still learning, as I did when I was his student at the law school.

"We have created a society," Sanginés continued while, as was his custom, he made little balls out of bread crumbs, "which for the most part wants to move up, have things, cars, women, clothes, sun, and if you press me, an education for the children, life insurance, social security, hospital and television insurance."

"Bread isn't enough," I tried to interject like a French monarch. "They want cake."

Sanginés smoothed the tablecloth as if to rid it of wrinkles or crumbs—and to avoid paying attention to me.

"There are also desperate ways out," he argued so as not to withdraw. "Go as a migrant worker to the United States, defy the guards' bullets, the barbed wire, the walls, the truck in which the coyotes can abandon you or leave you to suffocate . . ."

Did the restaurant tablecloth, white and bare, resemble a desert along the border? Were the salt and pepper shakers beacons that would guide the position of our dishes, already ordered, on their way, bean soup, ceviche, fillet of beef with mashed potatoes . . . ?

Sanginés looked at me somberly. He maintained a silence that prolonged unbearably the wait and increased hunger with no immediate hope of deliverance. Rarely have I seen him so pessimistic. He didn't want to look at me. He dared to look at me.

"The border is going to close. The United States, our Northern Wall, will be worse than the Berlin Wall. One was dictated by Communist ideology and Soviet paranoia. The wall that will run from the Pacific to the Gulf, from San Diego–Tijuana to Brownsville-Matamoros, is dictated by irrational racism. They need workers the North American market doesn't have. But they have to be kept out because they're dark, they're poor, they work hard, solve problems, and expose discrimination in mortal combat with necessity . . ."

I felt like wiping up my plate with a tortilla: Sanginés's words, which should have taken away my appetite, made me hungry.

"You also have to consider that Gringo businessmen pay low wages to migrant workers and don't want to pay high salaries to local labor," I argued, because Sanginés liked that.

He was served bean soup. I had ordered an Acapulcan ceviche. He dipped his large spoon. I used my small fork. We ate.

"That isn't the problem. The United States is being left behind. It has a workforce from the time of the Industrial Revolution. The smokestack cities are dying. Detroit, Pittsburgh are dying. Carnegie and Rockefeller died. Gates and BlackBerry were born. But the North Americans don't renounce the great industrial dream that founded them as a power. Chinese and Indians graduate from North American universities. Chicanos graduate."

"Except the Chinese go back to China and advance it and the Mexicans go back to Mexico and nobody even wants them, Maestro . . ."

Without meaning to I knocked over the saltshaker. Sanginés, cordial, put it back. I, without thinking twice, cupped my hand, gathered the spilled salt, and held it. I didn't know where to put it.

"Max Monroy understands this," I said without thinking. "Valentín Pedro Carrera doesn't. Max looks for long-term solutions. Carrera feels the six-year term concluding and wants to postpone the end with a swindle. His festivals, his jokes . . ."

Did Sanginés grimace? Or were the beans more bitter than he had expected? Like an idiot I emptied the salt on my ceviche. I ate without looking at him. If you begin by selecting fish, you end up with olives.

I said that he, Antonio Sanginés, was lawyer to them both, to Carrera and Monroy. I asked him to analyze them for me, the president and the magnate, the two poles of power in Mexico (and in Iberoamerica). He gave me a look that announced: I don't want to say the words of misfortune. I won't be the one . . .

Well, I interrupted, I was still preparing the professional thesis he himself had suggested, *Machiavelli and the Modern State,* so our talks were, in a way, like part of the course, weren't they?

I looked for his friendly, approving smile and didn't find it.

"We can all feel jealousy, hatred, or suspicion. The powerful man should eliminate jealousy, which leads him to want to be someone else, and in the end he becomes less than himself. He should avoid hatred, which clouds judgment and precipitates irreparable actions," Sanginés declaimed.

A bean was caught in his teeth that I only now suspected might be false. He extracted it and disposed of it carefully on the bread plate.

"But he should cultivate suspicion. Is it a defect? No, because without suspicion one doesn't gain political or economic power. The guileless man does not endure in the city of Pericles or in the city of Mercury."

"How long does the man endure who only suspects?"

"He would like to be eternal," Sanginés said with a smile.

"Even though he knows he isn't?" I returned the smile with an ironic gesture.

"A politician's capacity for self-deception is in-fi-nite. The politician believes he is indispensable and permanent. The moment arrives when power is like a car without brakes on a highway with no end. You're no longer concerned with putting on the brakes. You don't even care about steering. The vehicle has reached its own velocity—its cruising speed—and the powerful man believes that now nothing and no one can stop him."

"Except the law, Maestro. The principle of nonreelection."

"The nightmare of those who wanted to be reelected and couldn't."

"Couldn't? Or wouldn't?"

"They were not permitted to by a cabinet."

"Alvaro Obregón was assassinated for being reelected."

"Others were forbidden reelection by insurrectionist cabinets. Or a false belief that if one chose one's successor, he would be a docile puppet in the hands of his predecessor. What happened was just the opposite. Today's 'stand-in' destroyed yesterday's monarch because the new king had to demonstrate his independence from the one who named him his successor."

"Adventures of the Mexican six-year monarchy," I remarked, watching as our empty plates were withdrawn like ex-presidents.

Sanginés said he found it astonishing that the lesson had not been learned.

"From the first day, I advised Carrera: Imagine the last day. Remember that we are subject to the laws of contraction. The president wants to ignore political syneresis. We all say right now. He says maybe later, as if he were asking God: Holy God, give me six more years . . ."

"*Now,*" I said in English with a smile and a paleological intention, "*now now now.*"

"It's the terror of knowing there is an afterward." Sanginés received the thick, succulent fillet with an involuntary salivation of his mouth and a liquid gratitude in his eyes, as if this were his last meal. Or his first? Because in any event, he and I had never met to converse in so conclusive a manner, as if a chapter of our relationship were closing here and another one, perhaps, were beginning. I was no longer the inexperienced young law student. He was no longer the *magister* placed above the fray but a zealous, intriguing, influential gladiator, a boxing manager with a champion in each corner of the ring and, I saw it clearly, a sure bet: No matter who loses, Sanginés wins . . .

"He should not be underestimated," he said very seriously, though with a touch of arrogance. "I've seen him act up close. He possesses a tremendous instinct for survival. He really needs it, knowing as he knows (or should know) that a leader arrives with history and then leaves when history has left him behind or goes on without him. He refuses to know, however, that mistakes are paid for in the end. Or perhaps he knows and for that reason doesn't want to think about his exit."

He looked at me with intense melancholy.

"Don't judge him severely. He's not a superficial man. He just has a different idea of political destiny. He wants to create, Josué, politics with joy. It is his honor. It is his perdition. He carries in his genes the omnipotence of the Mexican monarch, Aztec, colonial, and republican. Everything that happened before, if it's good, ought to justify him. Nothing of what occurs afterward, if it's bad, concerns him. And if the good he did is not recognized, it's sheer ingratitude. He prefers evoking to naming. He sneezes with a smile and smiles sneezing, to deceive others . . . They are his masks: laughing, sneezing."

"Is he deceiving himself, Maestro?" I sopped up the mix of juice from the meat and mashed potatoes with a piece of bread.

I don't know if Sanginés sighed or if he did so only in my imagination. He said at times Valentín Pedro Carrera becomes lost in thought, joining his knotty hands at his forehead as if his head were hurting. At those moments he seemed old.

Sanginés looked at me intently.

"I believe he says something like 'too late, too late,' but reacts by taking out his portable, picking at keys, and consulting, or pretending to consult—"

"And Max Monroy?" I interrupted so Sanginés wouldn't fall into pure melancholy.

"Max Monroy." I don't know if Sanginés permitted himself a sigh. "Let's see, let's see . . . They're different. They're similar. I'll explain . . ."

He looked in vain for a dish that didn't come because he hadn't ordered it. He picked up an empty glass. He avoided looking at me. He looked at himself. He continued.

"Power wearies men, though in different ways. Carrera becomes exasperated at times and then I see his weariness. He has unacceptable outbursts. He says inconsequentially violent things. For example, when he passes the Diego Rivera frescoes in the Palace, 'You don't paint a mural with lukewarm water, Sanginés,' and when I sit down to work: 'We'll open a credit column for Our Lord Jesus Christ, because I'm going to fill out the debit column right now.' He tries to avoid violence but can be disparaging and even vulgar when he refers to 'the street pox.' He prefers the government to function in peace. But it's difficult for him to admit change. He prefers doing what he did: inventing popular festivals to entertain and distract people. Then he transformed the Zócalo into an ice skating rink. And then he opened children's pools in areas with no water. People were hurt in the rinks. They drowned in the pools. It didn't matter: Circuses without bread."

"Have a good time, kids," I added without too much sense, suspecting that by talking about the president, Sanginés avoided talking about Max Monroy.

Sanginés nodded. "When I tell him all this doesn't solve problems, Carrera replies: 'The country is very complex. Don't try to understand it.' In the face of that, Josué, I am left speechless. Injustice, intolerance, resignation? With these facts our leader makes his bed and night after night lies down with these paradigmatic words: 'Making decisions is boring.' "

"Does it console him to know that some day he'll be seen naked?"

"Naked? His skin is his gala outfit."

"I mean without memory."

Sanginés ordered an espresso and looked at me attentively.

Certainly it attracted his attention that I equated "nakedness" and "memory." I do realize that in my imagination memory is like a seal in which wax retains the image without any need to pour it. My conversation with Sanginés placed before me the dilemma of memory. Immediate memory: ordering an espresso and not remembering it. Intermediate memory: When all was said and done, would I keep it?

"A man without memory has only action as a weapon," said Sanginés.

"Did the president's patience come to an end?" I insisted.

"Your friend Jericó ended it for him."

He wasn't going to let me talk. And I didn't want to talk.

"Jericó tricked the president. He offered loyalty and gave him betrayal. This is what Carrera didn't forgive. Everything else I've told you this afternoon was left behind, it collapsed, and the president was left alone with only the black tongue of ingratitude, and of solitude, which is even more bitter."

The coffee tasted less bitter than his account. I felt that interrupting him was something worse than foolishness: it was lack of respect.

"He's clever. He realized that to crush Jericó the forces of law and order were not enough, though I can tell you he used them. Jericó gave the president the opportunity to demonstrate his social power, his ability to represent the nation. And for that he needed Max Monroy."

"Monroy doesn't like Carrera. I know, Maestro, I saw it myself. Monroy humiliated Carrera."

"What serious politician hasn't eaten shit, Josué? It's part of the profession! You eat toads and don't make faces. Bah! Carrera needed Monroy to demonstrate unity in the face of an attempted rebellion. Monroy needed Carrera to give the impression that without Monroy the republic can't be saved."

"A pact between thieves." I tried to be ironic.

Sanginés ignored me. He said I should understand Max Monroy. I said I had never underestimated him (including his sex life, which I had learned about and never would reveal out of respect for myself).

"It's difficult not to admire a man who never allows himself to be flattered. He knows the best men lose their way in flattery . . ."

He looked at me with something resembling sincerity: "In Mexico we have a word that is categorical, juicy, and insuperable: *lameculos*. The person who flatters to obtain favors. In my day we talked about the UFA. United Front of Asskissers. Today it would be the UFT, United Front of Traitors."

"And Monroy?" I said in order not to reveal I didn't know what he was talking about. The UFA! The Stone Age!

"Monroy."

"He can't bear a flatterer. It's his great strength in the midst of the national milieu of political, professional, and entrepreneurial asskissers."

"But . . ." I interrupted and didn't dare continue. The name and figure of Miguel Aparecido were on the tip of my tongue. Instead, I came up with a question: "And Jericó?"

"He's in a safe place," Sanginés answered without looking at me. He said it in a categorical, almost disagreeable way.

We left.

Outside the Danubio it was raining. Lottery sellers pursued us. Sanginés's driver got out of the Mercedes, offered us an umbrella, and opened the door.

"Where can I drop you, Josué?"

I didn't know how to answer.

Where did I live?

I got into the Mercedes like an automaton, removed from the intense activity of Mexico City. I lived in the Zona Rosa, transformed once more into the bohemian district, an oasis from the surrounding violence of the city and, in any case, from the latent menace that was more the rule than the exception. I tried to comfort myself with that idea . . .

What Sanginés and I talked about in the car is too important and I'll leave it for another time.

ASUNTA JORDÁN RECEIVED me again in her office and didn't raise her head. She reviewed papers. She signed letters. She initialed documents. She told me Jericó was "in a safe place." What does that mean? That he won't bother anyone anymore. Is he dead? I asked, getting right to the point. He's in a safe place. Did she mean he wouldn't cause any more trouble?

I tried to control conflicting impulses. In a safe place? What did the formula signify? I remembered it from my studies of law. Especially Roman law. The verb *recaudar* means to collect money. It also means to watch over or guard. And finally, to achieve what you want through entreaties. The scholarly tome says all this. To be in safety. Miguel Aparecido is, voluntarily, in his cell in San Juan de Aragón. Maxi Batalla and the shameless Sara P. are, against their will, in the same prison. Where is Jericó? A fraternal impulse that refused to die disturbed my breast. My friend Jericó. My brother Jericó. Castor and Pollux yesterday. Cain and Abel today. And the woman who knew everything didn't tell me anything. She reviewed papers, not as a way to disguise her feelings or distance herself from the situation but as part of the daily work of an office that had to function. The Utopia office on the Plaza Vasco de Quiroga in the extensive district of Santa Fe in an interminable Mexico City.

Asunta Jordán.

"Why did you make Jericó believe you and I were lovers?"

"Aren't we?" she said without raising her head from the papers.

"Only once." I tried to hide my bad feelings.

"But intense, wasn't it? Don't say it was a quickie, all right?"

She meant resign yourself: only once, but enough for a lifetime. Is that what she wanted to tell me? I don't know. She didn't want to say what she was thinking. Asunta told Jericó she was my lover because in that way . . .

"I told him I was yours alone and couldn't be his."

"In other words, you used me."

"If that's what you think."

"Whom do you love?" I asked insolently.

She looked at me at last and in her eyes I saw something like triumph in defeat, a victorious failure. Passing through Asunta's eyes were her provincial childhood, her marriage to the odious and despicable owner of King Kong, her fortuitous meeting with Max Monroy, and the simple, available nakedness of Asunta, the innocence with which she stood in the middle of the dance floor and waited for the inevitable, yes, but also for the evitable, what could be and what could not be. Waited for Max Monroy to approach, take her by the waist, and never let her go again.

I believe that in the most profound depths of Asunta's inner life, that instant defined everything. Max took her by the waist and the past became just that, a stony preterit, something that never happened. Max took her by the waist and she gave herself completely, without reservation, to what she desired most at that moment: a strong man, a protector who would shelter her from the miserable mediocrity of her destiny. But the woman I knew (and *ay!* knew only once, biblically) owed everything to Max Monroy, which humiliated her in a certain sense, made her inferior to herself, placed her in a situation of obligatory gratitude with Max but of obligatory dissatisfaction with herself, with her desire for independence.

At that moment I understood Monroy's intelligence. The man who saved her did not demand banal gratitude from her. It was he who demonstrated total confidence in Asunta. He didn't need to stress his age. He didn't need to ask Asunta to give him what he needed from her. Constant professional rigor and sporadic erotic rigor. I was witness to both. Was there something else? Of course. Max gave Asunta power and sex. He also gave her independence. He let her love whomever she liked, on two conditions. He was not to find out anything about it. She could love another man knowing she could count on Max Monroy's acceptance.

Jericó was one of many. But she knew Jericó had to be destroyed. And his destruction consisted in not only denying him sex but telling him her sex belonged to me, his brother Josué. In this way her obligation to Max and her personal freedom were satisfied, I understood it, but at the price of Jericó's mortal enmity toward me. Castor became Cain.

She knew he would hate me. Jericó said it, on all fours and naked like an animal, there on the bed: He had always given me everything, he preceded me in everything, ever since we met, first him, then me. With Asunta he was second, not first. How would his infinite vanity tolerate that? A vanity, I knew, identical to blindness. The moral, political, human blindness of Jericó . . . I saw it only now. I swear I never suspected it before. How many things does the most intimate friendship conceal?

"But that isn't true," I said with brutality. "You belong to Max Monroy."

She didn't look up. "I belong to myself. I belong only to Asunta Jordán. Ta-dum. Curtain."

It debilitated me, disconcerted me, infuriated me that she would say these things without looking at me, signing papers again, reviewing memos, marking dates on her calendar . . .

"And Monroy?" I asked with the blind vision of the coarse and bestial, compassionate and senile, artificial and devout love between Asunta and Max, buried in my obligatory silence, in my ridiculous sense of discretion . . .

That did oblige her to look at me again for an instant before returning to her papers. The look told me: "I belong to Monroy. I owe him everything. Besides, I'm like him. I'm also Max Monroy because

Max Monroy made me what I am. I'm Asunta Jordán because this is what Max Monroy decided and wanted. Max Monroy took me out of the provinces and raised me to where I am now. You may think an administrative job, no matter how privileged, in Max's huge organization, is minor in the general scheme of things, but learning to talk, to dress, to conduct myself with intelligence, coldness, and the necessary disdain . . . that's something you can never pay for."

She said it with a show of sincerity, though with a poorly disguised arrogance. She looked down. For her, being where she sat now was utopia, yes, the place of imaginary happiness, a satisfaction in the end comparative with respect to something earlier, which one left behind and to which one does not wish to return. Looking at her sitting there, immersed in her work, almost pretending I was not standing in front of her, made it difficult for me to separate Asunta's person from Asunta's function, and between the two, with the slim edge of a razor, I introduced the idea of happiness. Because when all was said and done, why did she work, why did this woman dress, style her hair, act, and lie except to maintain a position, yes, a position that assured her the minimum of happiness to which she had a right, above all comparatively. I thought of her history. The wife subjected to the vulgar, noisy machismo, hereditary and without direction, of a poor, unaware, difficult devil, her husband. Her destiny in the middle class of the arid society of the northern deserts. Mexico along the border, so smug about being the most prosperous part of the country, the industrial north, without Indians, without the extreme poverty of Chiapas or Oaxaca, bourgeois Mexico, self-satisfied in contrast to the outstretched hand of the beggar south. Mexico energetic and proud of it in contrast to the great devouring capital city, fat, dissipated, heavily made up, the urban gorilla of D.F. squashing the rest of the nation with its shameless buttocks . . .

But the same north from which Asunta came was south of the border with Yankee prosperity, it was "south of the border, down Mexico way," the wealth of the Mexican north was the poverty of the North American border. The passage of clandestine workers through Arizona and Texas. The barbed wire fence. The coyote's truck. The border guard's bullet. The maquila in Ciudad Juárez. The drug dealer from Tijuana to Laredo. Gangrene. Pus. What Sanginés always recalled when we got together.

And from all this, she extracted a semblance of happiness. And what was happiness? I asked myself this morning, standing in front of Asunta's desk, her own border facing the subordinate employee or the occasional lover. Was happiness an internal fact, a satisfaction, or was it an external fact, a possession? I didn't see in Asunta a semblance of bliss if by bliss one understands happiness. Was happiness synonymous with destiny? Perhaps. To a certain extent. But in Asunta Jordán I saw a destiny too dependent on things that weren't hers. For example, Max Monroy's desire, origin of Asunta Jordán's "happiness" in the sense of power, well-being. And inheritance? What would Max's will say about Asunta's destiny? And while we're on the subject, would Max remember his son Miguel Aparecido, the voluntary prisoner in San Juan de Aragón? Would he remember?

She told me once: "I have alert sleep. I also have dreamy wakefulness. You should know that. God's truth. Do you understand?"

"And what else?" I insisted so as not to give her the last word by giving it to her.

"Before I break my chains myself, Max frees me from them. But he gives me the keys so I have hope."

I looked at Asunta. Had she succeeded in uprooting desire and fear? Was this true happiness, not to desire, not to fear? Was this serenity? Or was it simply the disguise of a passivity that counts happiness as the absence of fear and the absence of desire? If ataraxia signified serenity, perhaps the price was passivity. Asunta's calm, I knew, I learned, was the result of a forced and forceful desire. It was a satisfaction that rewarded her for having overcome the mediocrity of her matrimonial past. It was also a dissatisfaction that in the name of gratitude to Max distanced itself from the free enjoyment of love chosen by her.

Did she love me?

She read my mind. "I hope you don't have any hopes, my poor Josué."

I said I didn't, lying.

"If I went to bed with you," she didn't look up, "it was because Max allowed me to. Max allows me sexual pleasure with young men. He knows the limitations of his, well, his third age. He lets me have pleasure. The pact with him is permanent. With the others, it's temporary."

It occurred to me there was certainty in her mind: Max knew about her loves, he permitted them, he respected them. Perhaps he even enjoyed them, as long as they didn't interfere with her professional relationship. Perhaps the proof of her love for Max consisted in being unfaithful to him, certain that for him this was part of love. I believe I understood, thinking about Max and Asunta, that loving each other a great deal and getting along well can lead to indifference and hatred. Max Monroy must tolerate Asunta's "betrayals" because he wants and needs them.

"*Solamente una vez,*" I managed to sing: "Only once," as if the words to a bolero could sublimate all our emotions.

"Exactly. Like in the song."

"And Jericó?"

"What about Jericó?"

Why did Asunta present herself to him as my lover, unleashing a mortal hatred that was, in the end, more than my lack of solidarity with his political project, the thing that ended our longstanding friendship?

"Why?"

She refused to look at me. This time I understood the reason. Before, she didn't look at me because she was haughty and powerful. Now her absent gaze was shameful and shamefaced. Then she had the courage to raise her head and look straight at me.

"I belong to Max Monroy. I owe him everything. It's shit to owe everything to one person. It's shit."

When I heard her say this, I knew Asunta was both happy and unhappy. Her passion disturbed me more than her indifference. With me, she made love with her eyes open.

That's why she didn't need to explain anything else to me. I understood Asunta lied to Jericó when she told him I was her lover, and to me when she told me only one night was mine to win, my God, I understood, it hurt me, it stripped my life bare to understand it, to gain a position of freedom before Max without harming Max but irreparably harming the ancient fraternity of Josué and Jericó, Castor and Pollux.

Cain and Abel.

Did Asunta realize what she had unleashed? Perhaps her egotism became confused with her true satisfaction, the cliff's edge of happiness to which she believed she had a right, even at the cost of a fratricidal war that in her eyes was, perhaps, barely a genteel war, one of those waged as if it were a game, with no real risk . . . And the abyss?

She didn't realize. I felt a kind of compassion for Asunta Jordán and a destiny she valued, perhaps, only by comparison. It was in reality a destiny, I thought then, that was despicable, deceptively liberated, in fact alienated.

"Who was your friend Jericó with before all this?"

"Who was he with?"

"Women."

"Whores. Only whores."

"The imbecile fell in love with me."

I didn't believe it and didn't interrupt her.

"He told me he was falling in love with a woman for the first time."

"What did you say to him?"

"You already know. That I belonged to you, Josué."

And immersed again in her papers, she added:

"You have nothing to worry about. We have him in a safe place."

I DON'T KNOW if memory is a form of incarnation. In any case, it must be a stimulus for the spirit that by means of recollection manages to revive. Though perhaps memory consists only in holding on to an instant and immediately returning movement to the moment. Is memory barely a scar? Is it the past I myself don't recognize? Though if I don't know it, how can I remember it? Is memory a mere simulation of recalling what we have already forgotten or, what's worse, have never lived?

I would have liked to give to memory the surname of imagination. Sanginés did not permit me to. In that slow trip from the Danubio on Calles de Uruguay to my cloistered garret on Calle de Praga, the lawyer said what he said because what occurred had occurred. The fraternity of Castor and Pollux had been transformed into the rivalry, the hatred of Cain and Abel. Passing memories, a different script, what was the difference, the profound difference, not the obvious, computable one?

I will try to reproduce, in my own words, from the scar of my memory, what Sanginés told me that afternoon when the rain made everything vanish like a sleeve of water on an immobile mirror.

I knew the history of Miguel Aparecido, which he himself recounted behind bars in San Juan de Aragón Prison along with terrible evocations of his grandmother, Antigua Concepción, that surfaced like an earthquake from the hidden grave where the not very venerable señora lay, creator of the Monroy fortune, despite her husband the general's violent frivolity, for the sake of her pampered son Max Monroy, whom the deceased manipulated as she chose, to the extreme of marrying him at the age of forty to an adolescent in order to appropriate the girl's lands, with no consideration at all of the feelings or desires of the innocent Sibila Sarmiento or of Max himself, unmarried until that moment through the power and grace of his mother's implacable will: will and destiny associated like a single figure in the mind of Antigua Concepción. She operated with both when she bought real estate with the Monroy fortune and passed it on to her son. The condition was that, he, Max, would submit to his mother's will in order to inherit. And if an intrusive, unpleasant, punishable, irritating, ungrateful necessity should filter down between them, the old matriarch in her Carmelite habit would bow before it with a gesture of repugnance, holding her nose, certain her son Max would thank her one day for the necessity in the name of his fortune.

The helpless Sibila Sarmiento locked away in an asylum, the son of Max and the madwoman abandoned to grow up fighting on the besieged, murderous streets of the capital: I travel with Sanginés through the city of the moon, if the moon had a city. Or better yet, if the moon were a city, it would not only be *like* this one. It would *be* this one. The dolorous city (malodorous city?) through which Antonio Sanginés's Mercedes drives me: the trip of postponed recollection, the expedition of memory as an unrenounceable past.

The Mercedes is driven by a chauffeur. Sanginés raises the glass that separates us from the driver and continues: "A moment arrived when the powerful matriarch decided her son Max could walk alone without maternal props, with his own destiny, freed of the necessity she assumed without thinking about it twice, though the third time she said to herself:

"In exchange for necessity I'll leave Max my desire and my destiny."

Desire and destiny, murmured Antonio Sanginés.

Max Monroy.

"He is master," Sanginés began his tale during our slow progress from the Historical Center to the Zona Rosa, "of a self-assurance that is in no way ostentatious. It is invisible. You saw him when he met with President Carrera in the Castle of Chapultepec. Where does it come from? He didn't inherit it from his mother, who was like a cross between the devouring Aztec goddess Coatlicue and the national patron saint, the Virgin of Guadalupe. He had to pass, however, through a period of becoming detached. Inheriting from his mother but distancing himself from her. Only the death of his mother Doña Conchita eventually allowed him to do that. Before then, like her, in order to prove himself to her—I tell you so you'll know—he allowed corruption. He had to submit to political chiefs and bosses, just as his mother had. He didn't kill them. He bought them. Energetically. Astutely. He knew they were for sale. He permitted them to steal but on the pretext that when they did—just listen to the national paradox—they were building, creating. He understood his mother's lesson: They had to be transformed into revolutionaries without a revolution. What are they afraid of? The middle class won the revolution just as they had in France and the United States. There is no revolution without the middle class and Mexico was no exception. The revolution that excludes the middle class is not a proletarian revolution. It is a dictatorship 'of the proletariat.' In Mexico, the heroes died young. The survivors grew old and became rich. Max Monroy bought, suggested, insinuated, threatened, and also built and knew where to walk. He guessed the future faster than the rest and deceived the rest by making them believe the present was the future."

How to know if Sanginés sighed when the rain turned into hail, striking the roof and windows of the car like the drum of God?

Political bosses. Governors. Entrepreneurs. How did Monroy win? By hating what they did but beating them at their own game. Before the boss of San Luis acted on his own, Max sent him an army general to take charge of the plaza "for your own security, Governor." When the cacique of Tabasco was preparing to buy legal decisions in the capital to build the highway fifty-fifty, Max got ahead of him by acquiring the construction company that gave the costly gov only twenty-five percent. Etcetera. I'll make it brief. In this way Max was transformed into an intermediary, a creator of coalitions (*non sanctas*, if you like) between the federal and local governments, keeping the lion's share, not only financially but politically. Becoming indispensable to everyone.

In order not to become lost in Sanginés's memory-filled account, was it the Academy de las Vizcaínas, a refuge for poor girls and rich widows, that obliged me to think of Esparza's two wives, Doña Estrellita the saint and the dirty whore Sara P., both from real or apocryphal convents like this one, whose oculi and pinnacles became invisible in the rainy twilight? Did I want to think about this, about them, because I was afraid, for no obvious reason, of what Professor Sanginés's words would reveal to me?

Didn't I want to think about another extension of prison, about the asylum where Sibila Sarmiento, the mother of Miguel Aparecido, had been locked away?

Sanginés continued. Broker. Agent. Intermediary, and his mother's heir. I imagined a young Max Monroy, hiding the public secret of his inherited fortune in order to act as an ambitious beginner: Wasn't this what the fearsome Concepción wanted, to have her son earn his inheritance from the bottom, with effort, compromising himself, getting dirty if need be, just like everyone else?

"He invented companies out of nothing," Sanginés continued. "For each one he received capital that he invested in other new companies. He shuffled the names of businesses. He justified himself by telling himself—telling me, Josué—the country of misery had to be left behind, Mexico's closed shop had to be broken, markets created, price fixing broken, communiqués communicated, modernity brought to the country."

Modernity opposed to the closed shop. Communicating. The wrinkled parchment of mountains and precipices, forests and deserts, valleys and volcanoes that with a blow of his fist Cortés the Conquistador described to Carlos the Emperor: A wrinkled parchment, that's what Mexico is. How to smooth it out?

"He was animated, Josué, by the dream and desire to found a collective kingdom together with a private empire. Is it possible?"

The capricious hail returned, like a purely nominal reality, to the Salto del Agua Fountain beside the Chapel of the Inmaculada Concepción, and I imagined a country filled with thirst as a condition of purity. A parchment country.

"I don't know, Maestro . . ."

He ignored me.

"A collective kingdom. A private empire. Ah! Impossible, my dear Josué, without the necessary final submission to political power. Except Max guessed what the change in Mexico would consist of: from a bourgeoisie dependent on the state to a state dependent on the bourgeoisie."

"Without realizing," I dared to interject, "that private empires are built on quicksand?"

I saw Sanginés smile. "You had to count on incalculable factors . . ."

"And fame? How did Monroy administer his fame?"

Now Sanginés burst into laughter. "A great reputation is worse than a bad one, which is better than no reputation at all. You must realize that Max Monroy opted for divine imitation. Like God, he is everywhere, and no one can see him."

I caught the double meaning of the phrase. I abstained from

commenting. I fought against the comfort of the Mercedes whose springs were putting me to sleep. I had said enough when I suggested Max didn't know that the foundations of all power are pure illusion. The emperor has no clothes. We are the ones who dress him. And then, when we demand that he return them, the monarch becomes angry: The clothes belong to him.

"Max Monroy," continued Sanginés, "realized something. His peers, adversaries, accomplices, subjects, did not read and were not thoroughly informed, they navigated by trusting in pure instinct. Max transformed Unamuno into a kind of personal Bible that gave him, like an aureole of the spirit, the tragic sense of life. From this repeated reading he drew certain conclusions that differentiate and guide him, Josué. The worst vices are purity and presumption. Sharing sorrows is no consolation. And the question is this: How can we master our passions without sacrificing them?"

Behind the blurred windows of the car, the equally blurred forbidden images returned of Max Monroy and Asunta Jordán joined in the darkness of sex, blacker than the darkness in the bedroom, and when I once again expelled this vision from my mind, Sanginés was commenting, as if he had read my indecent thoughts, that Max Monroy does not permit ambition and lust to impose on his reason.

"They can impose on his virtue. Not his reason."

I remarked with audacity that our desires are one thing and our loyalties something else entirely, evoking the figures of Asunta Jordán and Lucha Zapata side by side.

"He doesn't attempt to correct the errors of others," Sanginés said with a smile, "and he rejects well-known pleasures. Do you know something? Monroy has never gone to Aspen, where our wealthy feel they're from the first world because there's snow and they go skiing. He has never gone to Las Vegas, where our politicians return to chance what they seize from necessity."

"What makes him happy, then?" I said as if I didn't know, and emboldened, for no reason other than the severity of the words, by the name of Arcos de Belén that redeemed me from the anonymity of the nearby Plaza of Capitán Rodríguez M. beside the Registry Office. This enigma shifted my thoughts languorously: Who was Captain Rodríguez M., who could he have been to deserve his own plaza?

I don't believe Sanginés left his own question unanswered. He guessed it in my ignorance, and knowing it gave me a strange, quieter emotion. The lawyer went off on a tangent. He told me the penthouse occupied by Monroy in the Utopia building was the entrepreneur's own utopia, as far as possible from what he called "the damn streets," these same arteries along which Sanginés and I were now driving, the "damn" streets Monroy saw from above with those eyes of broken glass.

" 'I forget the names of the streets,' is what Max Monroy says from his vantage point. And it's true."

Sanginés took my hand and immediately let it go.

"He's beginning to be distracted. At times, I confess, he becomes incoherent . . ."

His words shocked me. "Why are you telling me this?"

"He says he no longer drinks because alcohol causes mental lapses and he doesn't want to neglect his life and legacy. Things like that."

"Asunta is his heir?" I asked, impertinent.

"He says old age is like a smuggler who puts ideas that aren't yours into your head. He says his organs get ahead of his death."

"Asunta is his heir?" I insisted.

I didn't want to see Sanginés's twisted smile.

"At times he's delirious. He says he's walking alone and naked and crazy through a large empty plaza. That's when Asunta protects him from himself."

"You haven't answered—"

"I heard him say to Asunta, 'Will you live without me?' "

"What did she say?" I asked avidly, as if, when Max died, Asunta would really be bequeathed to me.

"She says, 'Yes, but I won't be able to love again without you.' "

The car braked at a green light because the opposite light was also green and cars screeched to a halt, blowing impotent horns.

"The end of life is sudden and inexplicable," Sanginés managed to say over the noise.

"Of power or of force?" I said in a voice so quiet he perhaps didn't hear me, because he continued unperturbed.

"Believe me that one lives a final moment in which one's life slips away in taking more and more pills, not for relief, not even to survive, Josué, but just to urinate. Like a—"

"An animal," I interrupted brutally.

"The thing is . . . The thing . . ." murmured Sanginés as if he doubted what he would say next. "The thing is . . ."

He didn't look at me. He didn't want to look at me. I obstructed his gaze.

"Miguel Aparecido isn't an animal. He isn't a thing. He's the son of Max Monroy. Why don't you talk to me about that, Maestro? That abandonment, that irresponsibility, just tell me this: Doesn't that abandonment condemn Max Monroy's entire life, doesn't it disqualify him as a man and as a father?"

The noise of maddened car horns, police whistles, furious voices did not mitigate my own inflamed voice, as if, in the name of my friend Miguel Aparecido, I had acquired a recriminatory tone stronger than all the city's cacophony, the din that penetrated in dissipated form all the way to Miguel Aparecido's cell, as if México D.F. would not grant peace even to prisoners—or the dead.

He decided to look at me. I wish I had avoided that. Because in Antonio Sanginés's gaze, when he and I were enclosed in a car stopped at the intersection of Chapultepec and Bucareli, I saw my own postponed truth, my own destiny deflected and eventually recovered, the lost origin of a child who lived on Calle de Berlín in the care of a tyrannical governess . . .

Sanginés said calmly: "An entire life looking for one's own place, one's personal position. That's what Max says. And he adds: I don't want to give anything to anybody. Let them struggle. Let them stand on their own feet."

"Who?"

"His sons," said Sanginés with a certain repentant brutality.

"His son, Miguel Aparecido," I corrected him spontaneously.

"The hope that the courage and will demonstrated by him are repeated in his sons. That's what you mean."

"His son," I repeated. "That's what I mean—"

"Otherwise, the silver platter is the same as the silver bridge your enemy runs away on," he insisted.

"I've visited Miguel Aparecido. You know that, Maestro. You allowed me to enter the Aragón prison. I know Miguel's story. I know his father treated him with contempt and cruelty. I know Miguel left prison prepared to kill Monroy. I know he returned to prison in order not to do it, to distance himself from the temptation of parricide . . . I understand him, Don Antonio, I understand Miguel, I swear I do."

"Instead"—I don't know if Sanginés smiled or if the play of lights turned on suddenly along the avenue feigned the smile—"let the boys stand on their own feet. Let them know difficulties. Let them achieve happiness and power on their own. But don't let the destiny of Miguel Aparecido be repeated, the abandonment and crime determined by my powerful, invincible mother, Doña Concepción.

"Do not let it be repeated," Sanginés said two or three times. "Let my sons be formed alone but not forsaken. Let them count on everything, house, servants, monthly allowances, but not with the deadly cushioning of a rich father, not with lassitude, abandon, frivolity, the unfortunate security of not having to do anything in order to have everything. Let them have something in order to have something. I'll put them to the test. You send them the money each month, Licenciado. Let them lack for nothing. But not have too much of anything. I want their own life for my sons, without guilt or hatred . . ."

Clearly Sanginés, for the first time, confronted his emotion, abandoned the upright gravity of a discreet lawyer and prudent adviser, freed himself for a kind of catharsis that moved more quickly than the car when it left the traffic circle at Insurgentes to take Florencia to the Paseo de la Reforma.

I looked at him with amazement. He wanted to abandon discretion, gravity, not simply rein them in.

"He left them free, without the intolerable pressures and distorted affections of a mother," Sanginés said in his new emotional tessitura.

"He left them? Who?" I tried unsuccessfully to clarify. "Them . . . ? Who . . . ?"

"He left them free so they could be themselves and not a projection of Max Monroy . . ."

"Free? Who, Maestro? Who is it you're talking about?" I insisted, calmly.

"Let my sons not repeat my life . . ."

"My sons? Who, please? Who?"

"Let them create their life and not be content with inheriting it. Let them never believe there is nothing left to do . . ."

The Mercedes stopped in front of the apartment building on Calle de Praga. A feeling of malaise, of uneasiness, together with a humiliating sensation of having been used, impelled me out of the car.

"Goodbye, Maestro . . ."

Sanginés got out too. I took out the key and opened the door. Sanginés followed me, disturbed and nervous. I began to climb the stairs up to the top floor. Sanginés followed warily, impatiently, with something resembling pain. I didn't recognize him. I imagined his actions were driven by a duty perhaps not his own. Actions driven by someone else. Such was the nervous preoccupation of his behavior.

The stairway was dark. On my floor the light was not turned on. Everything was shadows and reflections of shadows, as if total darkness did not exist and our eyes, don't they eventually become accustomed to the blackness, in the end denying its dominion?

"He didn't want to leave them adrift in crime, like Miguel Aparecido," Sanginés said urgently.

I didn't reply. I began to walk up. He came behind me, like an unexpected ghost in need of the attention I denied him, perhaps because I feared what he was telling me now and could reveal to me later. But there was no later, the lawyer wanted to talk now, he pursued me from step to step, he didn't leave me alone, he wanted to snatch away my peace . . .

"They let Max Monroy into the asylum."

"The asylum?" I managed to say without stopping, compelled to reach the sanctuary of my garret, astonished by the lack of logical continuity in a man who taught the theory of the state with the precision of a Kelsen.

"He maintained the asylum, he gave them money."

"I understand." In spite of everything, I wanted to be courteous.

"They let him in. They left him alone with the woman."

"Who? With whom?"

"Sibila Sarmiento. Max Monroy."

I was going to stop. The name halted my movements but hurried my thoughts. Sibila Sarmiento, Max Monroy's young bride, locked away in the madhouse by the wickedness of Antigua Concepción.

"Miguel Aparecido's mother . . ." I murmured.

Sanginés took my arm. I wanted to pull away. He didn't let me.

"The mother of Jericó Monroy Sarmiento one year and of Josué Monroy Sarmiento the next."

"HE'S IN A safe place." The phrase repeated by Sanginés and Asunta regarding Jericó's destiny tormented me now. It referred to my brother. It brought up huge questions associated with memories of our first meeting at the Jalisco School, El Presbiterio . . . Was that encounter prepared beforehand too, wasn't it simple chance that brought my brother and me together? To what extent had Max Monroy's desire directed our lives? Beyond the monthly allowances each of us received without ever finding out where they came from. Who argues with good luck? Beyond the coincidences we didn't want to question because we took them as a natural part of friendship. Through my memory passed all the acts of a fraternity that, I knew now, were spontaneous in us but watched over and sponsored by third parties. And this was a violation of our freedom. We had been used by Max Monroy's feelings of guilt.

"Believe me, Josué, Max felt responsible for the destiny of

Miguel Aparecido, Miguel threatened him with death, Max knew the fault lay with Doña Concepción, he didn't want to blame her, he wanted to make himself responsible, and the way to take on the obligation was to take charge of you and Jericó, making certain you wouldn't lack necessities but that extravagance wouldn't make you slack, this was his moral intuition: You should be free, make your own lives, not feel grateful to him . . ."

Sanginés said this to me in the stairwell.

"Did he intend to reveal the truth to us one day?" I became confused and was angry with Sanginés. "Or was he going to die without telling us anything?"

I regretted my words. When I said them I understood I had associated fraternally with Jericó, and I knew if Sanginés revealed Max's secrets it was because Max had already exiled Jericó, as if he had tested us all our lives and only now Jericó's gigantic, crucial mistake gave me primogeniture. Jericó—it was the sentence without reason or absolution—had been put in a safe place . . . What did it mean? My uneasiness, at that moment, was physical.

There was an anxious pulse similar to a heartbeat in Sanginés's words. "Max allowed desire and luck to play freely in order to form destiny—"

"And necessity, Maestro? And damned necessity? Can there be desire or destiny without necessity?" I looked at him again without really making him out in the gloom, believing my words were now my only light.

"You didn't lack for anything . . ."

"Don't tell me that, please. I'm speaking of the necessity to know you are loved, needed, carnal, warm. Do you understand? Or don't you understand anything anymore? God damn!"

"You didn't lack for anything," Sanginés insisted as if he would continue, to the last moment, fulfilling his administrative function, denying the emotions revealed by his avid, nervous, anxious figure, I don't know, distant from what he was but also revealing what he was.

"And Jericó?" I stopped, photographed in front of myself like a being of lights and fugitive shadows.

"He's in a safe place," Sanginés repeated.

The phrase did not calm the vivid but painful memory of my fraternity with Jericó, the intense moments we had together, reading and discussing, assuming philosophical positions at the request of Father Filopáter. Jericó as Saint Augustine, I as Nietzsche, both led by the priest to the intelligence of Spinoza, transforming the will of God into the necessity of man. Were we, in the end, loyal to necessity in the name of will? Was this what my brother and I desired as a goal when we loved each other fraternally? Did our great rapport consist of this, associating necessity with will?

One scene after another passed through my mind. The two of us united at school. The two of us convinced not having a family was better than having a family like the Esparzas. We had signed a pact of comradeship. We felt the warm teenage satisfaction of discovering in friendship the best part of solitude. Together we made a plan for life that would bring us together forever.

"Maybe there will be, you know, separations, travel, broads. The important thing is to sign right now an alliance for the rest of our lives. Don't say no . . ."

For the rest of our lives. I remember those afternoons in the café after school and the other side of the coin gleams opaquely. An alliance for the rest of our lives, a plan for life to keep us together forever. But on that occasion, hadn't he proposed obligations all imposed by him? Do this, don't do the other, turn down frivolous social invitations. And you'll also despise "the herd of oxen." But let's also make a "selective, rigorous" plan for reading, for intellectual self-improvement.

That's how it was, and now I'm grateful for the discipline he and I imposed on ourselves and deplore the docility with which I followed him in other matters. Though I congratulate myself because, when we lived out our destinies, he and I respected our secrets, as if part of the complicity of friendship included discretion about one's private life. He didn't find out about Lucha Zapata and Miguel Aparecido, or I knew nothing about Jericó's life during his—how many were they?—years somewhere else. Europe, North America, the Border? Today I couldn't say. Today I'll never know if Jericó told me the truth. Today I know nothing about Jericó's identity except the blinding truth of my fraternal relationship with him. I couldn't blame him for anything. I had hidden as much about myself as he did. The terrible thing was to think that, "put in a safe place," Jericó would never be able to tell me what he didn't know about himself, what, perhaps, he would dare tell me if he knew, as I did, that we were brothers.

Understanding this filled me with rancor but also with sorrow. Once, when he had returned to Mexico, I wondered if we could take up again the intimacy, the shared respiration joining us when we were young. Was all we had lived merely an unrepeatable prologue? I insisted on thinking our friendship was the only shelter for our future.

It was hard and painful for me to think our entire life had resolved into terms of betrayal.

And too, as if to soften the pain, the moments returned of a strange attraction that did not lead to the encounter of bodies because a tacit, equally strange prohibition stopped us at the brink of desire in the shower at school, in the whore's bed, in our cohabitation in the garret on Praga . . .

Had friendship stopped at the border of a physical relationship subject to all the accidents of passion, jealousy, misunderstanding, and attribution of unproven intentions that torment yet attract lovers? In mysterious ways, the desire felt under the shower or in the brothel was subject to this mysterious prohibition, as strong as the desire itself. A desire that, seen from a distance, is the first passion, the passion for cohabitation and contiguity, while the incestuous desire is confused with these virtues and therefore prohibited with a strength that can deny fraternity itself . . .

What could we do then, he and I, except feel like forbidden gods? We had the permanent possibility of violating the commandment regarding a prohibition only the gods can transgress against without sin. Who prevented us? How easy it would be for me today, after everything that has happened, to imagine it was the "call of the blood" holding us back. The feeling in the deepest part of ourselves that we were brothers without ever knowing it . . . Or perhaps he and I had no reason to turn to incest, since incest between siblings is a rebellion against the parents (says Sigmund from the couch) and we did not have father or mother.

The truth, I tell myself now, is that time and circumstances moved us away from all temptation: When Jericó returned from his absence (Europe? the United States? the Border?), facts themselves gradually divided us, doubts began to appear, perhaps Jericó's Naples wasn't Naples, Italy, but Naples, Florida, and his Paris was in Texas . . . Elective affinities emerged first with cordiality, then with growing antagonism in our workplaces, in my slow apprenticeship in the Utopia tower while he ascended rapidly in the Palace of La Topía. I was an open book. Jericó was a message in code. Perhaps this was what I wanted. Wasn't my life a secret to everyone except me, and if it no longer was it's because now I'm telling and writing it. Perhaps Jericó, like me, is the author of a secret book like mine, the book I knew nothing about as he knew nothing of mine. The sum of secrets, however, did not abolish the remainder of evidence. Jericó had wielded a real influence on presidential power. He had felt authorized to go beyond the power granted him to the power he wanted to grant himself. He made a mistake. He thought he would deceive power but power deceived him. And when he found out about it, my poor friend, cornered by the reality his illusions disdained, the only recourse he found to save his personality was to fall in love with Asunta . . . He wanted to defeat me in the final territory of triumph, which is love. And even there, Asunta handed me the victory. She defeated Jericó by telling him she was my lover.

Why did she lie? What caused her to give the coup de grâce to the large animal, the living, palpitating thing beyond all logic, the carnal and cruel, aflame and affectionate thing that is friendship between two men? Two men who are brothers though they don't know it and move into fierce enmity perversely incited by Asunta Jordán: For the first time, my brother Jericó desired a woman and that woman, in order to humiliate and paralyze Jericó, declared she was my lover, awarding me a sexual laurel I did not deserve. Asunta presented to her Jehovah, Max Monroy, Abel-Josué's harvest and Cain-Jericó's, and since the terrestrial God preferred mine to his, Jericó the fratricide was prepared to kill me. I believe now the failure of his political insurrection, the way in which he deceived himself about the desire and the number of his followers, was identical to his blindness: Jericó could not distinguish between the reality of reality and the fiction of reality. Now I understand, finally, that this, the fiction, was imposed on reality because it came closest to my brother's fratricidal desire: His war perhaps was not against the world but against me. A latent war that had gone on forever, put off perhaps because Jericó's personality was stronger than mine, his triumphs more apparent, his capacity for intrigue greater, his alliance with the secret more covert: personality, success, imagination, mystery.

These were my brother's weapons, except he couldn't use them against me because . . . Why? Now as I enter San Juan de Aragón Prison thanks, once more, to the good offices of Licenciado Antonio Sanginés, now as I pass the cells from which they look at me like caged animals: the Cuban mulatto Siboney Peralta, the thieves Gomas and Brillantinas, the Mariachi, and Sara P., all of them behind bars, I look down, toward the swimming pool of imprisoned children, deficient Merlín with the shaved head, and Albertina who was a boy who was a girl, and the eloquent Ceferino guilty of being abandoned, and Chuchita looking at her tears in the mirror, and the girl Isaura dreaming about a volcano, and Félix the very sad happy boy, and right there Jericó and Josué passed like phantoms, and now I ask myself why, if we were so fraternal, so protected after all, so far from the ruined destinies of these children of Aragón, why weren't we Félix and Ceferino and Merlín, abandoned children, helpless like our brother Miguel Aparecido? In this strange prison counterpoint, the figure of Asunta Jordán abruptly appears in my head like a sudden revelation. Asunta, Asunta, she prevented the repetition of the biblical verdict and at the same time guaranteed it. Jericó, once Castor, did not kill me, his brother Pollux, because this time Cain did not kill Abel, I found out now, just today, thanks to her, thanks to the woman, thanks to Asunta Jordán who deflected the destiny of the deadly, ancient story: Jericó did not destroy Josué, Cain did not kill Abel thanks to the woman, the seer, the priestess, the enchantress emerged from a desert on the border between life and death, rescued from mediocre obscurity by a man who recognized in her, by simply taking her by the waist during a provincial dance, an earthly strength, the power that he, subject to the voracious whims of his mother, did not have: Would she, the woman desired, admired, feared, censured by me, be the author of my salvation? She condemned my enemy brother. She, on the pretext of saving him from Carrera's revenge, took him to the mansion of Utopia and exhibited him there to me, degraded him in my presence, in my presence put him naked on all fours and took away from him the fratricidal destiny of killing me on the pretext of jealousy . . .

Pre-text. Ah, then what will be the text?

IF I SEND you someone, Miguel Aparecido, tell, talk, don't leave him unfed. Remember.

He was the same. But different. The blue-black eyes flecked with yellow. A violent gaze tempered by melancholy. A sadness that rejected compassion. Very heavy eyebrows. A dark scowl and eyes flashing light. A virile face, square-jawed, carefully shaved. Light olive skin. An inquisitive nose, straight and thin. Graying hair, combed forward, curly in the back.

He was the same. But he was my brother.

Did he know? For how long? Did he not know? Why?

He shook hands in the Roman style, clasping my forearm and showing me once again a naked power that ran from his hand to his shoulder.

"Twenty years."

"Why?"

"Ask him."

How could I demand a reply to something that went beyond us and defined us? Children of the same father and mother. I saw Miguel Aparecido's face, immobile and defiant. I was troubled by the image of our father Max Monroy and his abominable droit de seigneur in the asylum. I imagined him at night, or by day, what difference did it make, going to the asylum to visit our mother Sibila Sarmiento. She was locked away. I don't know if she looked forward to Monroy's arrival as a possible salvation or as a confirmation of her sentence. Perhaps she knew only that this man, father of her three children, desired her with fury, stripped her without asking permission, gave in to the passion she inspired in him and that both of them, Max and Sibila, shared, she because even though in the fleeting moments of Max's visits, she felt loved and needed, free to see herself naked with pleasure, overcome by the passion of the man who tore at her hair and kissed her mouth and excited her nipples and caressed her pubis, clitoris, and buttocks with an irresistible force that freed her from this prison to which her own lover had condemned her, because Sibila Sarmiento was pleasure when captive and danger when free. And Max Monroy loving Sibila physically, freely, and not by order of his tyrannical mother, had no other way to take his revenge—with no filial unease—on damned Concepción.

Miguel Aparecido's tiger-eyes told me he understood. He asked me to accept that Sibila our mother won the love of Max our father. This was enough compensation for her imprisonment in the hospital. She could receive Max's love and be satisfied, almost grateful because she had the love of the world without its pitfalls. Eventually, receiving Max and making love to him was the same as being free without the dangers of life, the city, the world, which surrounded her like a gigantic threat dissipated only by the man's visits and then by successive months of waiting: the birth of a son, and much later another, and soon after that a third, and all at the same time.

Miguel Aparecido. Jericó. Josué.

The Immaculate Conception descended on Sibila Sarmiento's womb intermittently, unpredictably. For her—I imagine now—the instant was eternal, everything happened at the same time, there was no real time between the visits of the man who deflowered her at the age of twelve and the man who impregnated her after that, then again, and then a third time: I believe for her everything happened at the same moment, the act of love was always the same, the pregnancy a single one, the child the only one, not Miguel, not Jericó, not Josué, a single child being born forever, prepared to leave

the enclosure, the prison, the asylum, the womb, in the name of
Sibila Sarmiento. Born in a cell, and therefore worthy of freedom.
Born in misery and therefore destined for good fortune. Engendered
in impotence and therefore heirs to power.

My brother Miguel gave me his arm in the Roman fashion and
did not have to say anything. The fraternal pact was sealed. Pain was
another name for memory. We looked at each other with depth in
our eyes. What we had to say about the past had been said. It was
time for us to speak about the future. The syntony, in this regard,
was total.

There were a few minutes of silence.

We looked in each other's eyes.

Discord did not take long to break out.

He said he felt content that Brillantinas and Gomas, Siboney
Peralta, and the whole damn troop who accompanied Sara P. and
the Mariachi Maximiliano Batalla in their catastrophic attempt at
rebellion were back in prison.

I told him I had seen them in passing, behind bars, as I came to
see him now.

"Well, take a good look at them, my brother, because you won't
be seeing them again."

He looked at me in a way that meant I couldn't avoid the cold at
my back. At that moment I knew the gang of Sara P. and the Mariachi wouldn't leave jail except feetfirst.

"And Jericó?" I dared to say, abruptly.

"They were his people," replied Miguel Aparecido. "He got them
out of prison from the office of the presidency. He organized them.
They were his people."

He looked at me with those blue-black eyes I've mentioned, and
the yellow flecks acquired their own life of never-satisfied intelligence.

"He didn't calculate. He didn't realize. He had a half-baked idea
that if a vanguard acts, the masses will follow. He was wrong. He believed that by penetrating as he did the offices of power, he himself
could rise to power. Very smart, sure . . . It's your ass, Barrabás!"

I said it was an old sickness to believe power is contagious . . .

He didn't realize that power doesn't commit hara-kiri. Power protects itself.

"Understand what the public meeting of President Carrera and
the magnate Monroy in Chapultepec meant," Sanginés had said to
me. "Neither went to see the other for pleasure. They're rivals. But
each understands that the other has his own dynamite factory, and
dynamite factories have to be placed at a distance so they don't blow
one another up. Each part—Carrera, Monroy, power, business—has
a kind of veto over the other. They join together when they feel
threatened by a third exogenous force, a stranger to the inbreeding
of power. Power originates in power, not outside it, just as a cell
forms inside another. This is what Jericó didn't understand. He believed he could head a popular force that would carry him to the
top. He didn't understand that the movement of the people, when it
occurs, is necessary, not artificial, not a product of a messianic desire."

"Revolutions also create elites," I noted.

"Or elites head them."

"Though they also erupt from the people."

"Yes," Sanginés acknowledged. "The ruling classes have to be renewed in order not to be annihilated. They can do it peacefully, as
has occurred in Mexico. They can do it violently, as has also occurred in Mexico. The revolutionary knows when he can and when
he cannot. His political talent consists in that: when to and when
not to."

"If all of you knew that, I mean, Carrera as well as Monroy, why
didn't you let Jericó fade away all by himself with no followers except this gang of hoodlums imprisoned here? Why?"

Sanginés replied with the wisest of his smiles, the one I remembered from his classes at the law school, far from the awful grimace
that deformed his spirit when he followed me in the darkness up the
staircase on Praga. The smile I admired.

"I have confidence in both houses, the house of political power
and that of entrepreneurial power," he continued.

He closed his eyes blissfully. I already knew that.

"And do you know why they trust me?"

I didn't want to answer with some offensive joke.

"No."

"Because they know I possess all the information and don't trouble anyone with what I know."

"And what's that?" I wasn't pretending innocence: I was innocent.

He said in Mexico, in each Latin American country, rebellions are being forged day and night, in the hope of marking an *until here* and a *from now on* as, let's say, Bolívar or Castro did. He said he wouldn't go into the reasons why it was difficult for revolutions "like the ones in the old days" to occur again. Present-day power is more sophisticated, better informed, societies have higher expectations, the left is familiar with electoral routes, but the right will have to have its innate voraciousness limited from time to time by a little fear.

"It seemed to me, Josué, that Jericó's little adventure, so secondary, so minimal, so directed toward failure, ultimately so lacking in danger, offered me the opportunity to alert power without undue cost and give the right a shock. And in passing, to deflate the grotesque vision the extremely ambitious Jericó had acquired of himself."

Sanginés's smile was very offensive.

"He read Malaparte and Lenin. He felt like a little local Mussolini. Poor kid!"

"But in reality there was no danger," I insisted, moved, in spite of myself, by a feeling for Jericó that went beyond fraternity and simply called itself friendship.

Sanginés knew how to disguise his smiles. "Exactly. Because there wasn't, we could pretend there was."

"I don't understand, damn it."

Sanginés didn't celebrate his small logical triumph. "The greatest threats are fought in secret. The lesser ones should be denounced as a warning to the greater ones that we know what they want and control what they do. And to let the public know they are, at the same time, both threatened and safe."

I looked at Sanginés with unaccustomed fury.

"He's my brother, Maestro, he's worthy of a little respect—some compassion—a—"

Sanginés continued as if he had heard nothing.

"Carrera and Monroy may be rivals, but they won't be each other's victims. Stopping Jericó is effective proof of this. At the moment of danger, the two powers unite."

"He's my brother," I insisted.

And he was Monroy's son.

Sanginés looked at me with burning coldness.

"He was Cain."

Was Cain our brother? I wanted to ask Miguel Aparecido in the cell in Aragón and didn't dare. There was a prohibition in his blue-black gaze. If Jericó was Cain, he and I were not Abel.

"Was he Cain?" I insisted to Sanginés.

"He was your brother," the lawyer Sanginés agreed with salutary cruelty, telling me there was no better example than this to teach a probative lesson regarding the futility of rebellion and the cowardice of a response without balls. The winners were the Statesman and the Entrepreneur, like that, capitalized.

Cain and Abel.

I read this with vast, indescribable clarity in the gaze of my brother Miguel. We were not Abel. We hadn't saved ourselves skillfully from either the curse or the good fortune. We had assumed, without fully realizing it, the responsibility of caring for our brother. Wasn't Jericó our brother?

"He was Cain," said Miguel Aparecido.

I didn't have to ask for explanations. I remembered the curse Jericó had hurled at me from Asunta's bed, with a murderous look and a disdain revealed by the mask of hatred. Jericó naked on all fours, a captured animal, threatening me—I'm going to kill you, fucking cocksucker—slavering, frustrated. The concentrated hatred of my brother Cain. And my painful doubt: Had the hatred he showed me the last time always been inside Jericó? Did he "patronize" me when we were young, look down on me, despise my independence and my supposed sexual triumph with Asunta?

Was this the end of the story? No. I didn't know what had happened to Jericó. The question ate through my entire body like a restless acid concentrating in my heart only to flee my soul and remind me, my soul, that it was captive in a body.

I knew Miguel Aparecido's response before he gave it. It seemed to be the answer agreed on by all of them, by Sanginés, by Asunta, by Miguel.

"Where is Jericó? What has happened to Jericó?"

"He's been put in a safe place," Miguel Aparecido replied.

In spite of this definitive statement, I knew the story would never end.

I wanted to assuage my own fears by saying: Just like Sara and the Mariachi and Gomas and Siboney? Put in a safe place? All of them imprisoned? All of them at peace?

Then Miguel Aparecido looked at me with a strange mixture of contempt and compassion.

IN SPITE OF this categorical statement, I knew the story never ended.

"The worst one of all is walking around free," said Miguel Aparecido, and I didn't want to put a name to anyone I knew, because my spirit could not tolerate more guilt, more shame, more capitulation.

"Who?" I said in haste. "Everything's in—"

He cut me off with a forgotten name: Jenaro Ruvalcaba.

With an effort the scoundrel I met once during my first visits to the San Juan de Aragón Prison returned to my memory. Licenciado Jenaro Ruvalcaba was a criminal lawyer of scant renown. He received me courteously in his cell. He was agile and blond, about forty years old. He told me the prison population consisted of complaining, stupid people who didn't know what to do with freedom.

"And how do you manage?"

"I accept what prison gives me." He shrugged and proceeded to a reasonable analysis of how to behave in prison: Don't accept visitors who came out of obligation, doubt the fidelity of the conjugal visit . . .

"Both will betray you," he shouted suddenly.

"Who?"

"Your wife and her lover." He stood and put his hands to his head. "Traitors!"

He closed his eyes, pulled at his ears, and attacked me with his fists before the guard hit him with his club on the back of the neck and Ruvalcaba fell, weeping, on the cot.

"He's free?" I said to Miguel without hiding my terror, for this attorney was a proven menace.

"He'll never be free," remarked Miguel Aparecido. "He's the prisoner of himself."

Then he told me the following story.

Ruvalcaba did not lack talent. He was shaped by misfortune. A criminal gang kidnapped his father, his mother. They killed his father. They let her go, so she would suffer. The mother was a brave woman, and instead of sitting down to cry, she decided to educate her son Jenaro and give him a career as a criminal attorney so he would defend society against criminals like those who killed his father. Jenaro studied law and became a penologist. Except as he was preparing to defend the law he wanted to be a martyr to the law. He felt equal admiration and revulsion for both his father and those who killed him.

"The old prick, how could he let himself be kidnapped and murdered by that gang . . . ? Fuck me . . .

"My father was a brave man who let himself be killed so my mother could go free . . . Fuck me . . ."

And so between admiration and contempt the divided, schizoid character of Jenaro Ruvalcaba was formed, at once defender and violator of the law: a poisoned fruit constantly fragmenting into inimical pieces.

Miguel said to make a long story short, a division was created in Ruvalcaba's mind between the forbidden and the permitted, which eventually resolved into a situation worthy of farce. Ruvalcaba sublimated his psychological schism by molesting women. His vice consisted in boarding public transport—the Metro, buses, collective taxis—and harassing women. Don't ask me why he found in this activity the reconciliation of his contrary tendencies. The fact is his maniacal pleasure was to take the Metro or the bus and first look at women with an intensity that was troubling because more than any-thing else, it was intrusive. He leaned against the female passen-gers. He recriminated them if they gave him dirty looks. He put his hands on their hips. He pawed their buttocks. He went straight to the nipple with his fingers. At times it was furtive, at times aggres-sive. If they reproached him or complained about him, Ruvalcaba would say: "She's an old flirt. She led me on. I'm a criminal lawyer. I know about these things. Old women in heat! Frustrated old women! Let's see if anybody will do them a favor!"

Ruvalcaba derived supplementary delight when the women began to defend themselves. Some stuck him with pins, others with hairpins. A few had rings with a cutting edge. All of this excited Ru-valcaba: He saw it as a counterpart to his own actions, a recognition of his own audacity, an involuntary conspiracy between victim and aggressor. The women liked to have their buttocks touched, their pubis rubbed, their breasts caressed. They were his accomplices. His accomplices, he would repeat, excited, my accomplices.

"That was the reason," Miguel continued, "for his astonishment at the inauguration of what was called 'pink transport' only for women. The sign 'Ladies Only' excited him in the extreme. Ruval-caba disguised himself as a woman in order to ride on the Metro with impunity, causing a phenomenal disturbance when, made up and in a blond wig, he put his hand on a fat passenger and a com-motion began that led to a free-for-all, a brawl that ended at the Metro stop and the collective turning over of Jenaro Ruvalcaba to the police."

As the scoundrel was an attorney, he convinced the judge that his disguise had as its object to make certain the law was fully com-plied with and that women, if threatened, were capable of defend-ing themselves. The judge, because of machista prejudice, pardoned Ruvalcaba, but, feeling like a magistrate in a Cantinflas movie as guided by a play of Lope's, he ordered him exiled to the western part of the country, where the indiscreet and duplicitous Ruvalcaba lost no time in establishing an association with the owner of an avocado plantation, a front for a drug trafficking operation presided over by

Don Avocado himself, who was delighted to count on a shyster as skilled in deceptions as Lic. Jenaro.

From the plantation in Michoacán, Ruvalcaba performed great services for Don Avocado by supervising drug shipments, money laundering, loans, investments in transport, and the constant reconstruction of the plantation so it would continue to be viewed as an emporium of avocado trees and not a rat's market. Ruvalcaba took care of everything for Don Avocado: buying protection, relationships with Gringo buyers, the loading and unloading of high-speed launches, the acquisition of magnum revolvers and AR-15 assault rifles. He learned to kill. He shot numerous rivals of the drug dealer and developed a special liking for cutting off their heads after killing them.

He did everything until Don Avocado told him things were turning ugly since in this business there were plenty of snitches and especially assholes who wanted to rise at the expense of the powerful man in charge, you know, get out of my way and let me in . . .

"The upshot, my dear Jenarito, is that they have more on us than an old whore's fart, and if we want to continue in this business our only choice is to change our face, I mean, put a knife to our puss, I mean, the plastic surgeon is waiting for us."

"You change your face, Don Avocado, you're uglier than a fasting motherfucker, and don't mess with my movie-star profile. What would my dear mama say, God rest her soul?"

With these words Jenaro Ruvalcaba fled Michoacán and came back to Mexico City, where his deferred vice—putting his hand on women in Metro cars and buses—flourished in the most dangerous routine of collecting fares from and pinching women in collective taxis, counting at times on the complicity of the driver, at times running the risk that the driver would put him off because of his riders' protests, searching for farcical ways out disguised as a woman or a boy sailor from whose short pants charms peeked out that were hardly a child's.

Until the vengeance of Don Avocado extended from Michoacán to D.F. and, denounced as a murderer, a trafficker, and worst of all, a transvestite and pedophile, Jenaro Ruvalcaba ended up in the Aragón prison.

"Where I met him," I said with troubled innocence.

"And which he left thanks to the imprudence of our . . . Jericó," Miguel Aparecido said with a certain uneasiness, for he had not resigned himself to sharing fraternity with either Jericó or me. It was as if his singularity as the son of Max Monroy had been in some way violated by the truth, and although he had esteemed me earlier, he was not inclined to extend his affection to a man who like Jericó did not need (it was the tombstone Miguel Aparecido erected for him) to be a glutton of his own ego.

"You and I, on the other hand"—he embraced me—"we'll eat from the same plate."

And he pulled away from me.

"Take care, brother. Take care. Not everybody's in a safe place."

HOW LONG SINCE I had eaten at the home of Don Antonio Sanginés?

Now as I return to the mansion in Coyoacán, I'm doing so, of course, at my teacher's invitation and with the clear awareness that this time my brother Jericó would not be there and had not been invited. I didn't have the courage to ask about him. I knew the answer formulated ahead of time and transformed into a slogan:

"In a safe place . . ."

The ambiguity of the expression troubled me. It meant precaution and care: a verbal "alert" that referred to being secure or watched over. The disturbing thing about the words was their not saying clearly if someone "put in a safe place" was secure, yes, taken care of, that too, locked in, perhaps, cared for, perhaps, by whom? to what end? With an involuntary shudder I imagined my old friend, recent enemy, and everlasting brother Jericó Monroy Sarmiento handed over to the perfect custody of death, the security of the sepulchre, the precaution of eternity.

If this was what brought me back to Sanginés's colonial house filled with books, ornaments, and antique furniture, he did not seem ready to fall into the repetition—exceedingly banal—of "in a safe place." Soon the reason for his companionship appeared, and when I arrived, Sanginés led me to the breakfast area decorated in Pueblan tiles and came right to the point, saying, "The dream has ended."

The question surrounding my life authorized him to go on. The seventy years of moderate dictatorship in Mexico, beginning in 1930, had assured economic and social growth without democracy, but with security. Sanginés welcomed democracy. He lamented the lack of security because it identified democracy with crime . . .

He looked at me with a strange dreaminess that spoke clearly of Sanginés's decades of service as a professor of law, court adviser to presidents of the republic, member of the boards of directors of Monroy's private enterprises. An entire career based on judicious opinion and opportune warning, on objective counsel and advice, with no interest other than the reconciliation of public and private concerns on behalf of the nation.

He didn't need to say it. I knew it. His eyes communicated it to me. But the sour expression on his face not only gave the lie to all I've just said: It misdirected, disputed, and desired it in spite of regrets. In spite of what could be viewed as accommodation, opportunism, flattery, the counselor's vices stopped at the shore of the courtier to take on, in short, the adviser's virtues of objective intelligence and reason indispensable to the good governance of the individual and the state, business and society. There was nothing to apologize for. If I didn't know the rules of the game, it was time I learned them. If I didn't want to learn them, I'd be left out in the cold, adrift. I thought of Sanginés imploring, uncharacteristically pleading for comprehension of Monroy in the stairwell on Praga. This supper at his house, I understood immediately, erased that scene on the stairs. As if it hadn't occurred.

I understood all this because Sanginés communicated it to me indirectly, by means of expressions, qualities, and solicitations that undoubtedly summarized the long journey we had taken together, converging at a point in his long life and my short one.

I grew up, he said, in a society in which society was protected by official corruption. Today, he continued categorically but with a

trace of both criticism and resignation, society is protected by criminals. The history of Mexico is a long process of leaving behind
anarchy and dictatorship and reaching a democratic authoritarianism . . . He asked me, after a pause, to forgive the apparent contradiction: not so great if we appreciated the freedom of artists and
writers to savagely criticize its revolutionary governments. Diego
Rivera, right in the National Palace, describes a history presided
over by political hierarchs and corrupt, lying clerics. Orozco uses
the walls of the Supreme Court to paint a justice that laughs at the
law from the gaudily painted mouth of a whore. Azuela, in the middle of the revolutionary struggle, writes a novel about the revolution
as a stone rolling down an abyss, bare of ideology or purpose.
Guzmán tells of a revolution in power interested only in power, not
in revolution: They all order one another murdered in order to
continue in the presidency, the great cow that gives milk, dulce de
leche, cheese, a variety of butters, and security without democracy:
a comforting lowing.

"Today, Josué, the great drama of Mexico is that crime has replaced the state. Today the state dismantled by democracy cedes its
power to crime supported by democracy."

Perhaps I knew this, to a point. I had never admitted it with
Sanginés's painful clarity.

"Just yesterday," Sanginés continued, "a highway in the state of
Guerrero was blocked by uniformed criminals. Were they fake police? Or simply real police dedicated to crime? What happened on
that highway happens everywhere. The drivers of the blocked buses
and cars were brutally interrogated and pistol-whipped. The travelers were obliged to get out. Their cellphones were thrown onto a
garbage pile. Among the travelers were individuals working for the
criminals. Confusion reigned. It turns out some police believed in
good faith they were intercepting narcotics and counterfeit money.
They were soon disabused of that idea by their superiors and urged
to join the criminal gang or be stripped and stranded there as imbe-
ciles and assholes.

"Inexperienced police. Corrupt police. To whom do you turn?"

The prisons are full. There's no more room, he said, for the criminals.

"You saw San Juan de Aragón Prison. An agreement was reached there between jailhouse sadism and the minimal order guaranteed by Miguel Aparecido. That isn't the rule, Josué. The prisons in Mexico, Brazil, Colombia, Peru can't hold more criminals. They're released right away so new malefactors can come in. It's a never-ending story. Recidivist offenders. Detentions without a trial. Defense made impossible. Badly paid attorneys incapable of defending the innocent. Judges paralyzed by fear. Improvised judges. Courts incapable of functioning. False testimonies. No consistency. No consistency . . ." the lawyer lamented and almost exclaimed: "How long do you think Latin American democracy will last under these circumstances? How long will it take for the dictatorships to return, applauded by the people?"

I didn't recall hearing a sigh from Sanginés. Now I saw an air of fatality more than resignation in his sour expression.

"Pages and more pages." He made a large gesture, graceful at the end, with his hand. "We are drowning in paper—"

"And in blood." I dared to intervene for the first time.

"Papers soaked in blood," Sanginés intoned, almost like a priest singing the *requiem aeternam.*

"And do you prefer the law to be defiled by government and not crime?"

"I would like a little more pity," the licenciado said as if he hadn't heard me.

"For whom?" I prompted.

"For the poor and the ambitious who have lost their way and their faith in others. Especially for them."

I thought of Filopáter and his own forsaken priesthood. At that moment, the group of three little boys laughed behind the door of the tiled kitchen and Sanginés put on an astonished face. The children ran to him, climbed on his lap, his shoulders, mussed his hair, and they all laughed.

I realized, thanks to my prolonged absence, that these three children were still between four and seven years old. Just like the last time. Just like every time.

Sanginés caught the surprise in my gaze.

He laughed.

"Look, Josué: Every couple of years I renew my offspring. Three children I manage to rescue from the Aragón prison. You saw the subterranean pool where these poor kids play and sometimes are thrown into the water and sometimes swim and save themselves and sometimes drown, reducing the prison population . . ."

He saw the horror in my eyes. His begged me to understand the pity that allowed him, every two or three years, to save two or three children from the horror.

"And then?" I asked.

"Another destiny," he said summarily.

"And Jericó's destiny?" I dared to say angrily.

"In a safe place."

He took my hand. "I've never married. I appreciate your discretion. Have a good trip . . ."

"What?" I was surprised. "To where?"

"Aren't you going to Acapulco?" Sanginés feigned a not very credible surprise.

I DREAMED. AND in dreams, as everyone knows, figures enter and leave with no explicable order, voices are superimposed, and the words of one follow on the tail of another before beginning again, in a different tone, in another voice, other voices . . .

The space I inhabit (or that I only think or dream) is as transparent as water, as solid as a diamond. It is a frozen space, in every sense of the word: You have to move your arms vigorously to advance, you have to let yourself be carried by the current, to get anywhere you have to touch bottom knowing it doesn't exist . . . The near and the far succeed each other like a single reality and I don't know to whom to attribute the voices I haven't quite defined because they join in and vanish in the blink of an eye.

The voices speak in the peremptory tones of a lawyer or judge but dissipate with the advance of the whitish figure with the large, bald head sunk into his shoulders, similar to a self-portrait of Max Beckmann in which the light of the face barely reflects the external shadow that illuminates it: bald, with heavy eyelids and an inexplicable smile, Beckmann wants to reflect in his face the constant theme of his work: cruelty, the trenches and corpses of war, the erratic sadism of men against men. What does Max Monroy reflect?

At this moment in my dream, the self-portrait of Max Beckmann assumes the form of Max Monroy, fleeting, gray, slave to uncertain displacements, seized by a physical pain that has set him between movement and repose, possessed of a dignity in brutal contrast to the parrot chatter of the other fleeting figures in the dream, were they Asunta Jordán, Miguel Aparecido, Antigua Concepción affirming, interrogating me, discordant, accusatory, vulgar voices, so different from the quasi-ecclesiastical dignity of the gray figure of Max Monroy? asking me questions, blaming this man who had been revealed as my father, accusing him as if to tell me not to believe in him, not to approach him, no matter how the present dignity of the man and my oneiric proximity to his figure appeared to be the scenario of the encounter we both, father and son, required, interrupted by the voices.

Do you believe Max Monroy is a generous individual? Do you believe he visits his wife Sibila Sarmiento out of pure charity? Or because the measure of his sadism fills to overflowing when he fucks a prisoner, a woman with no will who is also the mother of his three sons? What do you think? Do you think that out of pure beneficence Max kept his other two sons, Jericó and you, at a distance, supposedly so you'd grow on your own, with only the help that was absolutely necessary, free of the burden of being the sons of Max Monroy, rich kids with a Jaguar and a plane, broads and travel, contempt and bribes, you and he making yourselves with your own efforts, your own talents? Do you believe that? No way! He did it because he's a miserable man, like an entomologist who puts his spiders down in the courtyard to run around just to see what they can think of to survive, to see if they save themselves by scurrying along the walls, to see if a shoe doesn't squash them, to see, to see . . . He plays, Max plays with destinies. And do you know why?

I'll tell you: Because that's how he takes his revenge on his dear old mother Antigua Concha, takes his revenge for how the old bitch manipulated him, imposed her will on him, handled him like a puppet at a fair, one of those from the old days with pink stockings and a bullfighter's costume that are still seen at village fiestas. I try to view Max Monroy's life like a long, very long revenge against his mother, the revenge he couldn't take while Doña Concepción was alive and filled the world with an imperious will, tall and strong and unpredictable like a gigantic wave made of skirts and scapularies and broken nails and the sandals of a feverish nun, Antigua Concepción: Who can endure being conceived not once and for all but all the time, conception after conception, born morning noon and night, the imposed obligation not only to love or even venerate his sainted mother but to obey her, you hear me? even in what she didn't command. Obliged to imagine what his sainted mother asked of him even when she wasn't asking anything. Do you believe when Antigua Concepción died Max Monroy freed himself of her influence? Well, don't go around thinking that. At times I surprise him muttering to himself, as if he were speaking to an invisible being. And when I spell out his words I know he's talking to her, he asks forgiveness for disobeying her, he admits she would have done things better or in another way or wouldn't have done anything at all, she would have known when to act and when to do nothing, letting the entourage pass without hearing the band, as hypocritical as a scorpion before it strikes and then Max Monroy behaves as if the insect had bitten him, except he differs from his mother in that she was a showy creature, as ostentatious as a band of clownish mariachis, and he, by way of contrast, is serene, calm to the point of perversity, astute, still, as if only in this way, as you have seen, he could differentiate himself from his mother without offending his parent's sainted memory, be himself without turning against her . . . "One makes haste slowly."

"Do you know where the señora is buried?" I asked with an air of innocence.

"Nobody knows," the voice of voices continued. "Not even Max.

He handed the body of Señora Concepción to a group of criminals he got out of prison with the promise to free them and told them to bury Concepción's corpse wherever they liked, but never to tell him about it . . . or anyone else. It goes without saying."

"What trust in—"

"None at all. Instead of freeing them, he abducted them. Nobody knows where they ended up. They were never heard from again. Just imagine."

"But Miguel's there, he's in prison . . ."

"Miguel Aparecido is the only person Max Monroy couldn't handle. Miguel Aparecido chose to remain locked in a cell in San Juan de Aragón as a precaution against his own desire to get out and murder his father, and his father accepted his release, or his imprisonment, as a compromise between two certainties: his and Miguel's. Max didn't liquidate Miguel and Miguel didn't annihilate Max. But Max served an infinite sentence, worse than death itself, and Miguel lived his life creating an empire inside prison."

"He didn't control the sadists who killed the children . . ."

"It was part of the compromise."

"What compromise?"

"Between Miguel and the authorities. I'll give you this in exchange for that. A swap."

"Are you telling me the jailers have the right to kill a few kids and Miguel has the right to save them?"

"He's the big boss."

"How do they choose?" I said with no horror in my oneiric voice, losing the order of the acts, the words attributable to Asunta, to Miguel, to Antigua Concepción, I don't know . . .

"They choose at random. Eagle or sun. Heads or tails. This one stays in prison. That one drowns in the pool. The ones who don't cross themselves are really lucky!"

"And the ones who know how to swim?" I said without much relevance.

"They're saved too."

The voice in my dream went on: "The worst criminals get away,

led by the Mariachi Maxi and the whore with the bee, the damned
Sara P. . . . Not everything turns out the way we want, isn't that
right?"

"They've been put in a safe place," the chorus repeated the
sacramental phrase.

"In a safe place?"

"They belong to Miguel. I don't guarantee their well-being."

"Just like my brother? Just like Jericó?"

"We don't talk about that."

"In a safe place? What? How? Isn't anybody going to—?"

"I can show you."

"What? Not in . . . ?"

The voices dissipated. They dissipated. Dissipated. They were
insignificant voices that bring dreams to distract us from what wants
to summon us and we can scarcely guess at.

On the other hand, the figure of Max Monroy advances toward
me, shoulders high, head sunk into his body, defiant, as if wanting
to tell me that insults, physical abuse, praise and blame did not even
graze a man of action who was also a solitary man: Action and solitude, solitude and action, joined, are never used up, said Monroy's
voice in the dream, the record of a man's motives is huge, there is
avarice, desire, rancor, rarely complete satisfaction, Josué, if you
fulfill a desire the desire engenders another desire and so on until
sorrows flourish because the sun did not come out and we cannot
understand that our desires are one thing and our loyalties something very different and in order to obtain what is desired you must
separate it from all loyalty immediately, my son, without harming
anyone. That is what those who detest, envy, or accuse me do not
understand: I did not have to harm anyone to be who I am . . .

He advances toward me preceded by that strange odor of an animal recently emerged from a cave that Asunta evoked one day.

"Being old does not mean having impunity," said the shade of
Monroy. "Or immunity."

In the logic of the dream, he launched into a list of his ailments
and the medicines he took to alleviate them. I'm old, he said, the old

feel threatened by the young. I'm ossifying. Go on, touch my bones. Go on. *Ándale.*

I didn't dare. Or I experienced the illogical transitions in the dream. Max Monroy was saying things separated by the oneiric instincts that dissolve the concretion of things, new enterprises disturb the old order, the old resist them, I create them, I am my own opposition . . .

"I admit that advanced age develops greater doses of cynicism, a measure of skepticism, a degree of pessimism. Why?"

I said I didn't know.

"You have to know how to say no."

"Ah."

"Being old does not mean having impunity. Or immunity," he repeated. "You have to know how to look deep into my eyes to know who I am. Who I was."

The voice resonated as if it were traveling the length of a gallery of mirrors.

He said his joints ached.

He said: "There are things I don't want to know."

I asked Asunta Jordán: "Why do you appear almost naked at parties and with me only in the dark?"

"Why is your penis so long?" I believe she asked him.

"To cool off my semen," responded Monroy.

"What does it mean to be put in a safe place? Wait just a minute . . ."

"And what does it mean to go to bed with Max, like you do, Asunta?"

"What do you know—"

"I've heard you."

"Have you seen us?"

"It was very dark. Don't fuck around."

"Black. It was black, you spying bastard!"

"Go on, don't play dumb, answer me."

"Don't be a busybody, I'm telling you. What a meddler you are!"

This reproof, which seemed to come from Asunta, in fact was directed at me by Antigua Concepción: I felt the outrage of her wrinkled hand weighed down with heavy rings, almost in the posture, rather than attacking me, of defending her son Max, who advanced like a ghost, white as chalk, surrounded by the tolling of deep bells, disconcerted, with eyes that said,

"I feel like sleeping . . ."

Max Monroy came toward me, expecting to be interrupted, wanting it, anticipating it.

The bell rang with a muffled sonority.

Max said to me: "What, who is it tolling for?"

I had the courage to respond: "Who stopped destiny?"

"Your stopping mine or my stopping yours?" he said in a voice desperate with unwanted concern before the entire dream vanished . . .

THOSE WHO HAVE accompanied me throughout this . . . What to call it? Agony? Mental anguish, aching passion? Those who accompany me (you, semblance, brother, hypocrite, etcetera) know my internal chats all strive to be dialogues with Your Graces, efforts of desperate appearance and agonizing reality to escape the site of my epidermis and tell you what I tell myself, without the certainty of truth, with the insecurity of doubt.

How was the person of Jericó, put "in a safe place," not going to return constantly to my soul as I walk slowly from the apartment on Praga to an uncertain destination? A pedestrian of the air, because while my feet trod the sidewalks of Varsovia, Estocolmo, and Amberes, my head had no compass. Or rather: North was Jericó, in more than one sense. The cardinal point of my life, the wind that cools it, pole star, guide, direction, and above all frontier, the limit of something more than territories, a frontier of exiles, distances, separations that the life of Jericó made irremediable . . .

Did our life end before our youth?

At what moment?

I loved and admired this man, my brother. Now I summarized my life with him in a question: Everything that happened to us, did it happen to us freely? Or, in the end, were we only a sum of fatalities? Did we rebel against particular destinies—masculine sex, or-phans, aspirants to intelligence, I'll say! translators of intellectual talent to practical life—We won't be doctors or mechanics, Josué, we'll be political men, we'll influence the life of the city . . . the city he described to me from the terrace of the Hotel Majestic, length-ening it with a gesture of his arm, denying we were puppets of fatal-ity, only to arrive, exhausted, at our destiny chosen as a compromise, as our personal will, to discover at the end of the road that all des-tiny is fatal, gets away from us, closes life like an iron door and says to us: This was your life, you have no other, and it wasn't what you wanted or imagined. How long will it take us to learn that no matter how much will we have, destiny cannot be foreseen, and insecurity is the real climate of life?

And in spite of everything, Jericó, wasn't there a certain equilib-rium, an ultimate harmony, an involuntary measure in all you and I did and said? Necessity on one side, chance on the other, they go beyond us and place us, eventually, on the crest of a wave, at the brink of death, conscious that if we don't know our destinies, at least we're conscious of having one . . .

How was our shared destiny revealed to the extent it was not shared but chosen by each of us on his own, knowing we were in-separable: Castor and Pollux, even before we knew we were broth-ers: Cain and Abel? And I don't know whether as boys we fought not against each other but against the necessity that seemed to impose itself on us. How did we lose our way? Judge me if you wish. I don't judge you. I merely confirm that gradually, in the apartment on Praga, seeing the Zócalo from the Hotel Majestic, gradually your face gave way to your mask only to reveal that your mask was your true face . . . We spoke of the tiger in the zoo devoured by the other four caged tigers. Why that tiger and not one of those that at-tacked it?

"Use force as if it were an animal you release so it can do harm and then return to its domestic enclosure."

You released it, Jericó. You couldn't control it. The tiger didn't return to the zoo. You turned yourself into the animal, my brother. You believed that from power you would defeat power and turn yourself into power. You told me: Be violent, be arrogant, they'll respect you in the end and even come to adore you. You believed it was enough to assign a destiny to the mass of people to have them follow you with no motive of their own, only because you were you and no one could resist you. And when you failed, you accused them of treason: the masses who ignored you, Max Monroy because he didn't consult with you, Valentín Pedro Carrera because he got ahead of you, Antonio Sanginés because he read you in time, Asunta because she preferred me.

I stopped on Calle de Génova, at the entrance to the tunnel that leads to the Glorieta de Insurgentes. The darkness of the urban cave gave me a sense of agony, that word in which accountability and death are associated as they laugh at us and mock our challenges, inspirations, powers . . .

What was the sin, Jericó? I go onto the plaza filled with young Mexicans disguised as what they are not in order to stop being what they are, and it comes to me like a revelation: your lack of interest in others, your inability to penetrate another's mind, your pride, Jericó, your rejection of those who are unwanted in the world, which is the immense majority of people. The mobocracy, you said once, the massocracy, the demodumbocracy, *la raza,* that *raza* incarnated now, when I penetrate the darkness of the tunnel, in a scuffle, a shove that joins my lips to other lips, a fortuitous kiss, unexpected, dry, unknown, accompanied by a smell I try to recognize, a stink, a sweat, something sticky, an incense of marijuana and bait, the urban smell of tortilla and gasoline . . .

Rapid, fleeting, the kiss that joins us separates us, the tunnel brightens with its own light and we see each other's faces, Errol Esparza and I, Josué once Nadal from Nada, now Monroy of a kingdom . . .

I EMBRACED ERROL, Baldy Esparza, as if he were my past, my adolescence, my precocious thought, everything I was with Jericó and that Errol returned to me now, in a diminished though nostalgic version, thanks to a fortuitous encounter on the Glorieta de Insurgentes.

What did he say to me? What did he show me? Where did he take me? He couldn't take me to the emo clubs because only young guys went there and not uptight ones like me, dressed to go to an office (a funeral, a wedding, a *quinceañera* dance, a baptism, everything forbidden by Jericó?), and on the plaza, congregating in silent groups, adolescent girls and boys with no gaze because they covered their eyes with bangs, wore extensions at the back of the neck, dressed in black, with self-inflicted wounds on their arms, drawings tattooed on their hands, very skinny, more dark than dark-skinned, sitting on the flower boxes, silent, abruptly moved to kiss, decorated with stars, perforated from head to foot, I felt impelled to look and avoid their gaze, suspicious of the danger and drawn by an unhealthy curiosity until Errol, my guide through this small parainferno or infereden, placed like a navel in the center of the city, said to me,

"They like it if you look at them."

A tribe of skinny dark bodies, stars, skulls, perforations, how could I not compare them to the tribes on the Zócalo that Jericó trusted to attack power and where Filopáter earned his living typing at Santo Domingo? Never, with Jericó, had I approached this universe where I was walking now guided by Errol, who had become the Virgil of the new Mexican tribe that he, in spite of his age—which was mine—seemed to know, perhaps because, skinny and long-haired, dressed in black, he didn't seem to be his age and had penetrated this group to the degree that he approached a girl and kissed her deeply and then her companion, who asked me:

"Do you smooch?"

I looked at Errol. He didn't return my look. The dark boy kissed me on the mouth and then asked if I had a vocation for suffering.

I tried to answer. "I don't know. I'm not like you."

"Don't stigmatize me," answered the boy.

"What did he mean?" I asked Errol.

That I shouldn't distinguish between reason and sentiment. They viewed me as a thinking type who controlled his feelings, Errol said, that's how they view every outsider. They wanted you to free your emotions. My emotions—wasn't I going over them again and again on my walk through the Zona Rosa? What other extreme,

what externalization of my emotions could I add to the internaliza-
tion I've narrated here? A generational abyss opened before me. At
that instant, on Insurgentes, with Errol, surrounded by the tribe of
emos, perhaps I stopped being young, the eternally young Josué, the
apprentice to life, graduated and moved a step away from retirement
by this Bedouin tribe of adolescents determined to separate from
me, from us, from the nation I have described, analyzed, and constantly evoked here, with Jericó and Sanginés, with Filopáter and
Miguel Aparecido. A secession.

Now, on the Glorieta de Insurgentes, at dusk on this Wednesday
of my life, I felt the country no longer belonged to me, it had been
appropriated by children between fifteen and twenty years old, millions of young Mexicans who didn't share my history and even denied my geography, creating a separate republic in this minimal
utopia on a plaza in Mexico City, another in Guadalajara, another in
Querétaro: the other nation, the threatening and threatened nation,
the rejected and rejecting country. It was no longer mine.

Did Errol read my gaze that afternoon as we strolled around the
sunken plaza of Insurgentes?

"They're only trying to substitute one pain for another. That's
why they cut their arms. That's why they pierce their ears."

Substitute one pain for another? I would have liked to tell my
friend I too had a tribal esthetic, had nonconformity, had depressions, couldn't stop falling in love (Lucha Zapata, Asunta Jordán)
and suffering. Was it only my esthetic that was distant, not my sen-
timents? This sudden need to identify with the young people on the
square was doomed, I knew, to failure. It had value on its own, I
thought, it had value as an effort at identification, even though
physically I could never be part of the new, ultimately romantic
nation of darkness longing to die in time, to save itself from maturity . . . from corruption . . .

They were romantics, I said to myself, and to Errol I said:
"They're romantics."

I sensed the personal excitement, the desire to leave the great
shadow of poverty and mediocrity and become visible, free the emotions forbidden by the family, religion, politics . . .

"Don't stigmatize me."

"What are they called?"

Darketos. Metaleros. Skatos. Raztecos. Dixies. They form groups, crews. They help each other. They defend themselves. They're grateful. They're emos.

Suddenly, the peace—passivity—of the emo world was shattered with a violence Errol himself didn't expect, and he took me by the shoulders to lead me off the Glorieta. The Génova, Puebla, and Oaxaca entrances were closed by the invasion of young men shouting assholes, fuckers, get them, throwing stones while the emos covered their faces and said—they didn't shout—equality, tolerance, respect, and offered their arms to be wounded by the aggression until the skateboarders took the initiative and chased the aggressors with their boards and a kind of peace returned followed by a slow nocturnal migration to other corners of a restless city that both was and was not mine.

"I want to kill Maxi Batalla and Sara P.," Errol said when we sat down to drink beers at a café on the Glorieta. "They killed my mother."

"Somebody got there first," I told him.

"Who? Who did?" There was slaver on my friend's lips.

"My brother Miguel Aparecido."

"Where? Who?"

"In the San Juan de Aragón Prison."

"What? He killed them?"

I didn't know how to answer him. I knew only that the Mariachi Maxi and the whore with the bee on her buttock were "in a safe place," and with that, perhaps, the history of my time closed and a new history opened, the history of the kids on the plaza who one day, I reminded Errol, would grow up and be clerks, businessmen, bureaucrats, fathers as rebellious as their own fathers had been, pachucos and tarzans, hippies and rebels without a cause, gangs and the unemployed, generation after generation of insurgents eventually tamed by society . . .

"Do you understand, Errol, why, if there are five tigers in a cage, four get together to kill just one?"

"No, old buddy, plain and simple, no."

We agreed to see each other again.

"YOU NEED A vacation," Asunta Jordán told me when I returned to the office on Santa Fe. "You look a wreck. It's time for a rest."

For the sake of my mental health, I rejected the idea of a conspiracy. Why did everyone want to send me on vacation? I looked in the mirror. "A wreck": vitiated, damaged. Ruined by evil companions? Their distribution in my life flashed through my mind: María Egipciaca, Elvira Ríos, Lucha Zapata, Filopáter, Max Monroy, Asunta herself, Jericó . . . Evil or good companions? Responsible for my being a "wreck"? I had enough honor left to say that I alone— and no one else—was responsible for the "damage."

I looked in the mirror. I seemed healthy. More or less. Why this insistence on sending me away for a rest?

"To Acapulco."

"Ah."

"Max Monroy has a nice house there. On the way to La Quebrada. Here are the keys."

She tossed them, with a contemptuous gesture though with a friendly smile, on the table.

It was a house on the way to La Quebrada, Asunta explained. It dated from the late 1930s, when Acapulco was a fishing village and there were only two hotels: La Marina, in the middle of town, and Hotel de La Quebrada, which came down from the hills and settled on a terrace where one could admire intrepid divers who waited for the right waves and then threw themselves into the narrow inlet of water between steep, craggy cliffs.

Now Acapulco had grown until it had millions of inhabitants, hundreds of hotels, restaurants, and condominiums, beaches polluted by the uncontrolled discharge from the aforementioned hotels, restaurants, and condominiums, and increasing sprawl to the south of the city, from Puerto Marqués to Revolcadero and even as far as Barra Vieja, in search of what Acapulco used to offer like a baptismal certificate: limpid water, tended beaches, paradise lost . . .

I arrived at Max Monroy's house at La Quebrada on a solitary Monday with one suitcase and the books I wanted to reread to see if one day I would present my lawyer's thesis, *Machiavelli and the Modern State*. Erskine Muir, who explains the Florentine by means of his time, the Italian city-states, Savonarola, the Borgias; or Jacques Heers, who sees a not very rigorous but passionate historian, poet, and author of courtly plays and carnival songs whose literary imagination was applied to reasons of state, making generations believe that carnival is serious and curiosity the law. Maurizio Piral, who questions the famous smile of Niccolò as the female author of the book Niccolò did not write: the book about life, its paradox, its uncertainty. A misinterpreted man, insists Michael White: his mental lucidity forgotten, his duplicity and ambition codified. Sebastián da Grazia sends Niccolò to the hell made up, of course, of his contemporaries. Franco Fido studies the paradox of an author who writes "The bible of his own enemies," from the transformation of Niccolò by Elizabethan dramatists into "Old Nick," the Devil in person, to his vulgar rhetorical invocation by Il Duce Mussolini. The Jesuits, the ignorant, Fichte: Who has not been concerned with the "most famous Italian in Europe," especially the Italians themselves, who reduced him to municipal, confessional, and academic boundaries?

All this was in my knapsack. The indispensable commentaries. Above all, those of the statesman speaking to Machiavelli power to power: Napolcon Bonaparte feels he is the Machiavellian incarnation of the New Prince as opposed to the Hereditary one, but is anxious to endure in power: to be succeeded, as the New Prince, by his descendants, who will be the Heirs . . .

I say all the preceding so the reader can know my good—magnificent—intentions when I withdrew to Acapulco loaded down with Machiavellian literature and with a touch of melancholy, an inevitable residue of my recent personal history, not imagining that the true Machiavellianism wasn't in my knapsack but waiting for me in the house at La Quebrada, which you reached by ascending the mountainous curves over the bay until you reached a rocky height and entered a mansion that rushed, with no distinction of style be-

yond a vague "Californian" from the 1930s, past the kitchens, bedrooms, and sitting rooms to the reward of a huge terrace overlook-
ing the Pacific Ocean and, farther down, the narrow private beach.
In its entirety, it was like one of those white porcelain dinner pails
my guardian María Egipciaca prepared for me with five little
stacked plates, from wet soup to dry soup to chicken to vegetables
to dessert . . . the works.

"Max Monroy built it for Sibila Sarmiento," Asunta Jordán told
me surprisingly when I reached the terrace and she came toward
me, highball in hand, barefoot, dressed in palazzo pajamas I knew
from rooting through her closet. Loose blouse. Wide pants. Black
with gold trim and edges.

She offered me the drink. I feigned casualness. She didn't tell
me too much. It wasn't the first surprise this woman had given me.
She looked at the ocean.

"But Sibila Sarmiento never got to live in it. Well, in fact, she
didn't even get to see it . . ."

She saw me. She didn't look at me. She saw me there: like a
thing. A necessary but awkward thing.

Asunta laughed in her fashion: "Max had illusions that one day
he'd be able to bring the mother of his three sons here, to Acapulco,
and offer her a quiet life by the ocean. Well. What a hope!"

Her gaze became cynical.

One more of Max's illusions. He imagined that one day Doña
Concha would free him from the maternal dictatorship to which she
kept him subjected.

"A man at once complicated and simple," she went on, "it's difficult for Max Monroy to digest. Everything takes him time. He
never belches, you know? There are things he doesn't want to know.
He doesn't want . . . And another thing. Between utility and revenge,
he always chooses the useful."

She raised her glass. She almost winked at me.

"I'm just the opposite . . ."

She laughed. "Then he strikes like a bolt of lightning."

She indicated that I should sit in a wicker chair. I remained standing. At least in this I could rebel against what I felt was the implicit dictatorship of Asunta Jordán. She didn't care.

"Max Monroy!" she exclaimed as if she were invoking the sunset. "A civilized man, right? A reasonable man, don't you think? He always asks for suggestions. He's open to suggestions. Ah, but not to criticism. Suggesting is one thing. Criticizing is another. Criticizing him means thinking he can't think for himself, that he requires orientation, another's opinion . . . False. The suggestions should stop halfway between two hateful extremes, Josué, my good Josué: flattery and criticism."

She told me she would criticize, for example, this useless, uninhabited house . . . a mansion for a ghost, for a madwoman. Or for a ghostly madwoman.

She smiled. "Imagine Sibila Sarmiento wandering here, not knowing where she is, not even looking at the ocean, distant from the moon and the sun, prisoner of nothingness or of a hope as crazy as she is. The hope Max will return and rescue her from the asylum. Or at least make her another son. Another heir!

"Thank me, Josué . . . I flew here to prepare the house for you so you'll be comfortable. It was sealed tight, as if with a cork. And in this heat? Air it all out, dust off the furniture, smooth out the sheets, put out towels and soap, just look, everything to receive you as you deserve . . ."

Who knows what she imagined in my gaze that obliged her to say: "Don't worry. All the servants have gone. We're alone. All, all alone."

She caressed my cheek. I didn't move.

She said not everything was ready.

"Look. The pool is empty and full of leaves and trash. There's an air of abandon in spite of all my efforts. The grass is uncut. The palm trees are gray. And Max always said things like 'I want to be buried here.' How curious, don't you think? To be buried in a place he never visited . . ."

"Nobody looks forward to the cemetery," I dared to say.

"How true!" the voice declared. "Didn't I always tell you? You're smart, you asshole Josué, you're really smart, good and smart."

And she threw the contents of the whiskey glass at my chest.

"Just don't get too smart."

I maintained my calm. I didn't even raise my hand to my chest. I looked, distracted, at the setting sun. She resumed the air of a tropical hostess.

"I don't want neighbors," Max had said.

She made a panoramic gesture.

"And he did it, Josué. There's nobody here. Only a high mountain and the open sea."

"And a beach down there," I added, not to leave anything out, and I sensed Asunta becoming uncomfortable.

"Don't expect anyone to stop there," she said in a rude tone.

I tried to be frivolous. "Your company's enough for me, Asunta. That's all I ask."

The shirt stuck to my chest.

"You can have champagne for breakfast," she said in a tone between diversion and menace. "In any case," she sighed and turned her back on the sea, "enjoy the luxury. And think of just one thing. Luxury is acquiring what you don't need. On the other hand, you need your life . . . Right?"

She laughed. Her soul was being laid bare, little by little. Not all at once, because I had been observing her since I first met her, disdainful and absent, walking through cocktail parties with her cellphone glued to her ear, imposing silence, not entering into conversation with anyone. I had to understand her as she was and for what she was. An attentive woman and for that reason dangerous. Because extreme attention can unleash violent, unexpected reactions: It's the price of being aware, of being overly aware.

If, like an adolescent, I fell in love one day with this woman and her visible attributes, if she ever had them, she had been losing them gradually until she played the sinister game of presenting herself as my lover to Jericó and driving my brother mad with the first great passion of his strange life of austerity without purpose, lust without enthusiasm, a lover without love. I knew Asunta's malice exceeded both my capacity for loving and Jericó's icy ambition. We were, in some way, pawns in a vast chess game that led to the solution, apparently ritualized, of "putting in a safe place."

"And Jericó?" I insisted. "In a safe place as well?"

"We don't speak of that."

"In a safe place? What? How? Isn't anybody going to tell me?"

"I can show you."

"What? Not in . . . ?"

"What it is to be put in a safe place? Wait just a little . . ."

"And what it is to go to bed with Max, like you?"

"What do you know—"

"I heard you."

"Did you see us?"

"It was very dark. Don't fuck around."

"Black. It was black, you spying bastard!"

"Go on, don't play around, answer me."

"Don't be a snoop, I'm telling you. Big nose!"

"All that not to go back to the hellhole in the desert, Asunta, the town in the north where you were nobody and put up with a macho, presumptuous, hateful husband? All that out of gratitude to the man who took you away from there and put you on your little peak of business and influence . . . ?"

"I would have left there with or without him," Asunta said, her face extremely tense.

"I don't doubt it. You have a lot of guts."

"I have smarts. I have a very clever brain. But Max was a stroke of luck that came to me. There would have been other opportunities."

"How can you trust in chance?"

"Necessity, not luck. I would have found the means to escape."

Mistress of the game? Even of the great Max Monroy? These questions teemed in my mind during this twilight facing the Mexican Pacific.

As if she had read my thoughts, she exclaimed: "Nobody blessed me. Nobody chose me. I made myself on my own. I think—"

"You're the creation of Max Monroy," I said, taking her by surprise.

"Nobody blessed me. I made myself on my own!" She grew angry.

"I can see you now, abandoned in Torreón without Max Monroy, damn dissatisfied provincial . . ."

I don't know if this defense of my father came from some corner of my soul, though I realized Asunta would come at me and scratch my eyes out . . . I restrained her. I lowered her arms. I obliged her to leave them hanging by her hips. I kissed her with some passion, some disdain; in any case, an uncontrollable mixture of my own feelings, which may not have been very different from the emotion any man can feel if he is embracing a beautiful woman, no matter how much of an enemy she may be, no matter how . . .

For a moment I suspended my reason and liberated my senses. We all have a heart that doesn't reason, and I didn't care that Asunta didn't respond to my omnivorous kisses, that her arms didn't embrace me, that I forgot myself before repenting of my actions, before thinking she was responsible and that in this entire situation—I felt this as I was chewing the lipstick on her lips—we had all been concealing the most secret secret of our souls . . .

Because a personal emotion let loose like an animal, even though it isn't returned, can abolish for an instant the customary hierarchies of love, power, and beauty. Why did Asunta let herself be kissed and groped without responding but allowing me to continue?

I moved her away, imagining she would say something. She said it.

"I have the bad habit of being admired," she informed me with a cynical, even happy air of self-sufficiency. "It's useful . . ."

"Sure. The bad thing is your appearance doesn't manage to disguise your real desires. I believe—"

"What are they?" She stopped me. "What are they? my desires?"

"Serving Max Monroy and being independent of Max Monroy. Impossible." I affirmed my own intelligence in the matter, I defended it as if it had been cornered.

"Max protects me from myself," was her reply. "He saves me from bad luck. From my bad luck, you're right, the misfortune of my previous life . . ."

"There are people who are like screens for other people. You're Max's screen. You don't exist." I spat the words at her with a kind of frivolous rage, as if wanting to bring the scene to an end, get away, conclude the farce, pick up my suitcase and my books and get away forever from the spider's web woven by Asunta around a man, Max Monroy, who had been revealed as my father and, I told myself confusedly, whom I ought to honor, know and honor, get close to instead of Machiavelli, damn it, what was I thinking of? I thanked her, Asunta Jordán, for shaking me, taking me out of the vast juvenile illusion that I could go on with my life as if nothing had happened, write my thesis, graduate . . . And then, and then?

I got out of this illusion by telling myself duty is independent of desire. Bad luck. But that's the way it is.

Who knows what Asunta read in my gaze. I saw her with a background of sudden madness.

"You're too intelligent to be loved," I told her as a logical consequence of my own thoughts. "What does Max Monroy think of that?"

She began to speak with unusual nervousness, as if the answers to my question were, all at the same time, an invocation to the sun to disappear immediately and leave us in the most profound darkness, yes, though they were also disconnected phrases, disguised words I had forgotten because eventually Asunta returned to her implacable, affirmative logic.

The madwoman Sarmiento was locked away forever in the asylum, she said, and the end of the day resonated in her voice.

Your brother Jericó has been put in a safe place, she said, and an armada of dark clouds announced the coming night.

Your brother Miguel Aparecido languishes in an Aragón cell and won't come out because he's afraid of killing his father Max Monroy.

"And Max Monroy, what about him?"

"I've already told you there are things Max Monroy doesn't want to know. He doesn't want to know he's going to die. Sanginés has prepared a will for him in which the heirs are Sibila Sarmiento, Miguel Aparecido, Jericó Monroy Sarmiento, and Josué Monroy Sarmiento . . ."

"And you, Asunta?" I asked without too much premeditation.

"I'm at the tail end," said the poor girl from the north, the provincial I saw now disguised as an important executive, without her palazzo pajamas, her omnipresent cellphone, the glass in her hand: I saw her in a little percale dress, flat shoes, permanent-waved hair, rouged face, porcelain earrings, and a gold tooth.

That's how I saw her and she knows I saw her that way.

My imagination had stripped her and returned her to the desert.

"And you, Asunta?"

"Don't you dare mock me," she said with icy fury. "I'm always at the tail end. I inherit only a handout."

"And do you want to inherit it all?"

"Because I deserve it all. Because no one has done as much as I have for Max Monroy."

"What are you going to do?"

"I want to inherit it all."

"What are you going to do?"

"You know."

"You won't dare. I know what you want. I'll speak to Max. I'll . . ."

No, she shook her head, agitated, her gaze cold, nobody will say anything to Max, nobody, because there won't be anybody, nobody but me, she kept saying with a maddened desire and a gaze of the most terrible evil, radical egotism, the certainty that the world is there to serve us along with the frightful uncertainty that the world might leave us out in the cold, a handful of dust in a chalky desert instead of the leafy paradise that was and had been the face of Asunta, two gardens in one or a single fierce wasteland of her youthful imagination . . . The face of Asunta Jordán. I don't know if the dying light of day gave her the almost mythological air of a great avenger: a Medea maddened not by sexual jealousy but by monetary jealousy, the yearning to be the heir to the vast amount, not knowing that money belongs to no one, it circulates, is consumed, and will end up in the immense ocean of trash. Perhaps because she knew this, she elevated herself from a jealous Medea to an enveloping Gorgon of power, queen of an empire that would slip from her hands if she did not endow herself with bloody eyes, a terrifying face, and hair made of serpents, crowned by this sunset and this ocean. Loved by Poseidon, possessed by our father Monroy, did she have to be killed so that from her blood would be born a gold dagger that would kill her before she killed me, Miguel Aparecido, Sibila Sarmiento, and Max Monroy himself, as she had perhaps already killed Jericó? In the flashing darkness of Asunta Jordán's eyes I saw the simplicity of destiny and the complexity of ambition. Or would Asunta Jordán have time to look at me and turn me into stone? And wasn't it true that . . . ?

"Even if you kill me, I'll go on looking at you," she said with a whiskey and lipstick breath when I moved away from her, called by the sound of footsteps on branches that increased behind me, giving way to the face of Jenaro Ruvalcaba, agile and blond, followed by a confused gang of sweating dark people, all armed with machetes, and Ruvalcaba himself swung his machete at the back of my neck, sending me with a bleeding head into the well of the empty pool surrounded by empty bottles and the grass that grew in a jumble from cracks in the cement . . .

Epilogue

ASCENT TO HEAVEN

H ere is my decapitated head, lost like a coconut at the edge of the Pacific Ocean on the Mexican coast of Guerrero.

My head not only misses my body. I don't know where I ended up from the neck down. Perhaps my headless corpse has also been put "in a safe place." Perhaps, however, the sacrifice of the body has been the condition for my soul to be liberated from a purely vegetative existence and assume a new life of connection. A life of connection: Isn't this the life typical of the animal? Is it wishful thinking to believe that now that my body is lost, my spirit will ascend to a region inhabited only by anima? And, to begin with, isn't anima animal?

Anima. How curious, how unexpected, the way the mind, if it does not return to, at least approaches knowledge acquired years before, the youthful readings I have mentioned so often in this my manuscript of salt and foam! Matter and form. Potentiality and act. Only death confirms for me that now I am no more than a potential act, matter in pursuit of its own form. Now I feel my soul as the promise of a restored sense, but without content now and therefore ready to receive all contents. I am something possible, I tell myself in this extremity of my existence. I do not yet exist. Even if I am, perhaps, immortal because of the paradox of having died, only for that reason . . .

Soul anima animal: My head lies on the beach, bathed by the tepid waves of the Southern Sea. I no longer know if I'm confused, if I speak of my anima and speak at the same time of my animal. But if I have once again become anima of animal, that means I have returned to the embryo, to the formation of animal and man, to the instant of similarity between species: their brotherhood.

I will stop there because the idea is enough to accelerate my mind and send me to an evolutionary aftermath I don't desire because I feel it moves me away from an obscurely recovered fraternity with the world, yes, but with my brothers as well. What were their names? How many were we? Two, three . . . ? The great ocean transforms my decapitated head into a seashell and repeats ancient stories to me that the sea alone preserves and the waves murmur . . . Two brothers . . . Their faces return, their bodies return, their names return in each beat of the benevolent, brutal surf that impels forward and drives back the entire movement of the universe . . .

An insane idea crosses my mind. Castor and Pollux. My brother Jericó and I enjoyed immortality only on alternate days. I feel terror. Can I keep immortality more than one day and consequently deny it to my brother? Can he do the same and leave me abandoned forever, adrift without one more day of life? I express this horrible thought looking at a mad rush of horses galloping over the waves shouting for water, water, though water surrounds them, you will not drink this water, you will gallop rapidly the length of this water, you will cut through the sea and protect the sailor with the fire of your memory setting the top of the mast ablaze, we, you and your brother, will give each other the emotion of life, love, combat, power, glory, the abduction of women, we will grasp the mast of fire and the steeds of the sea will drag us to a destiny I can see on the same beach I came to, already being there . . .

A pelican totters near the coast.

Its voice reaches me.

"The worm is an error," it says.

And these words are enough to return me to the site where I find myself and the terrible loss of life, the endless holocaust of the inexplicable death of us all, of human beings . . . And then not alternative immorality, or the horses of the sea, or the mast of fire, or the fear of killing or being killed when I am no longer immortal, none of that is present, only this lying here, a head cut off by a machete, and the thing that is not here, a lost body, a trunk of hollow cavities divided by the diaphragm, the mortal depository of the heart, lungs, pleura, antechamber of the stomach, liver, bladder, intestines, kidneys, what's left?

Aaaaah! I am satisfied. I am master of my head, no matter how decapitated it may be. Splenius, trapezius, trachea. The hyoid bone continues to hold up my tongue. My face has a mouth. My skull contains the encephalon. My brain, my brain lying here still has a cortex of gray matter that escapes through my nostrils, no longer encloses the white matter that comes out through my eyes. What happened to the cerebellum that controlled the movement of what I have lost: my body? What posture, no balance at all?

To breathe. Circulate. Sleep. What sorrow to have lost everything. What an illusion to believe new areas of my head can be lost only to give active life to the older ones . . . Skin. Orifices. Head. Trunk. Extremities. They were me. At first I saw myself in my bathroom mirror. I am twenty-seven years old. I caress my cheeks. I shave my chin and upper lip. I remember I must rescue my appearance before it is too late. I close my eyes. I imagine my face. An Indian thatch of black hair. Dark eyes sunk into the sockets of an almost transparent facial skeleton. Invisible eyebrows. A pleasant mouth. Thin. Smiling. Ears neither large nor small. A skinny face. Skin stuck to the bone. Hair sprouting like nocturnal thickets that grow at the bottom of the sea with the small amount of light that penetrates to the depths.

The great Sargasso of anticipated death.

The sea that ascends in brief surges, obliging me to swallow before it reaches the orifices of my large nose, big-nose, beak, snout, schnozz . . .

THEN THE IMMENSE black seaweed emerged at the same time from the sea and the sky and the miracle occurred: In the air, my unattached head and body reunited and the voice I already knew and recognized told me heaven is opening, the time of exile is over, the tempestuous winds carry us away, do you remember me? I am

Ezekiel, the prophet who joins the wings of the world and saves man from the fire and the waves, returning you, Josué, to the air that belongs to you and where you will have new companions: What a mistake, what a huge mistake to believe souls go to heaven or to hell, to new cloisters of cloud or flame! Souls do not fit into heaven or hell, which are enclosed spaces. Souls inhabit infinite space. Listen to the sound of my wings, listen to the voices of all that has existed. I will speak to you but you will see, Josué. You will see hard faces and unyielding hearts. You will see your rebel house. Your father. Your brothers. The whore of Babylon. They do not know there is a prophetess who watches them and protects you. They are seated on scorpions. They eat paper and believe it is ambrosia. They do not listen to you because they do not want to. Speak to them even though they do not listen to you. You are the great rumor, you are the great warning. The city is dying, you warn them, Josué, on the wings of the prophet Ezekiel who I am, the city will place obstacles before you, the city will be on guard because the spirit has entered you and therefore you disobeyed, you did not submit to the house of order, ambition, promotion, advantage, compromise, Josué, you did not lock yourself in your house, you did not cleave your tongue to your palate, you fasted, you saw the sanctuary defiled by plague and war, ruin and ignominy, crime, the desolation of the temples, the living corpses prostrate before idols, look, Josué, look from the air at the dolorous city, malodorous city, do you believe you have abandoned it forever? Do you believe you have left your house without finishing its construction? Ah, Josué, only death allows us to see the future; if we lived forever we would be the future and not know, if we continued on earth we would continue to believe in our individuality and not see the truth that accompanies us: the truth is another person, perhaps other persons, but undoubtedly there is one person, delegated by Providence, designated by the gods, made by Nature, the person who watches over you, not like an angel but like a good demon, the presence that accompanies you, the little devil you saw and did not see, knew and did not know, embraced and abandoned, the woman who gave herself completely to you, tested and proved you as a man and left you when it was necessary for you to draw near alone, as we all draw near, above all prophets like me, to the angels, to our destiny . . . She left. She lied to you so you would not miss her. She always guessed your necessity, Josué, your reason for waging war in the lands of Judea from the mountains of Nero and Pisgah to the edge of the sea, your personal war, Josué, the war of your unrepeatable but not solitary individuality, you have had a companion, Josué, the close assistance of the only person you really loved and who really loved you, with surrender, with rebelliousness, perhaps with vexation, always with passion and it was this, the passion that is a passage through life, suffering, enduring reversals, suffering disease, moving the soul to pleasure and to pain, desiring, becoming passionate, who was the demon of your passion?

Lost in the daily passage of life, perhaps you did not realize, Josué, that someone met you and from then on accompanied you, even in absence, invisible but always present: your woman-demon, your personal she-devil . . . Because when you lived, violence and habit, habit interrupted by violence, or vice versa, Josué, prevented you from distinguishing, until very late, until the final hour of your life, between the good and evil demon. Your ruthless guardian María Egipciaca, your fleeting nurse Elvira Ríos. Your contradictory, wise, and accommodating teacher Antonio Sanginés. Your dark brother Miguel Aparecido, imprisoned by himself and in himself. Your other brother Jericó, whom you loved so well, hated so well, and who in the midst of it all served you so well in measuring the infinite degrees of a man between love and hate. Your unknown mother Sibila Sarmiento to whom you can dedicate only the requiem of pity. Your distant father Max Monroy, so impenetrable because he is his own political party, the only party, so sure of never losing, turning lies into truth and truth into lies in order to move from there and affirm the power of the old, fearful the young threaten them, turning upside down the proven origin of all the things they created: This is what Max feared, he did not put you and your brother to the test to see if you waged war counting on all the comforts except that of knowing who you were, not because he wanted to avoid the brutal, inhuman destiny he imposed on Miguel Aparecido, no, but because of his fear of you if he set you free without the ties that eventually,

with crumbling sophistry, he imposed on you: I will give you everything to live except what threatens me. Asunta knew this, you know?
She knew the old man was afraid of you and perhaps, if she annihilated the two of you so you would not inherit, Max would understand it as another act of her loyalty: not so you would not inherit,
only so you would not present yourselves as what you were and Jericó once was: the sons of Monroy whom Monroy did not put in
prison, because in Miguel Aparecido's destiny you and your brother
Jericó must see not what did not happen to you but what could happen: fathers and sons devour one another, the rebel house will sit on
scorpions, desolate hearths will be extinguished, corpses will bow
before idols, and houses will be beacon lights . . .

"And Lucha Zapata?"

We were flying over the mountains of Mexico, destination unknown. The waters rushed from the hills to the sea, laying waste to
the high mesetas. I looked at salt marshes and swamps. I saw the
birds fleeing and the herds of bulls in the valleys and she-goats on
the rocks, we flew over a valley of bones, and Ezekiel said to himself,
prophesy upon these bones, such is the command of God, enveloped in a fierce sound of thunder and lightning, flying over the
mountains: prophesy, Josué, prophesy that all these bones will be
your house, and I rebelled, even at the cost of my life, because
Ezekiel could let me go and I didn't want to die twice without repeating:

"Lucha Zapata."

Perhaps it was a response to my plea—for Lucha Zapata was
now my final prayer—: in a cumulus of clouds I could see people I
knew; approaching me on our flight, I saw Alberto-Albertina returned to her condition as girl: naked, with the languid V of her
thighs displaying the limpid ↓ of her sex, she recognized me, greeted
me, and was joined by the waving hands of the children drowned in
the pool in San Juan de Aragón, naked Chuchita, delighted not to
have to dress anymore, Merlín who was part of the band of idiots
used to sneak into affluent houses, his head shaved, an idiot now
but happy, his mouth half-open and the snot running, Félix with the
sad face, stripped now of the ancient guilt I saw in his face when I

walked through the prison, but with his teeth always full of the remains of tortilla and egg. They greeted me with rejoicing, as if celebrating that I would be joining them, their condition still mysterious
to me, though the rapid transformation of the cumulus clouds into
luminous, dying cirrus clouds like a sunset and the announcement
of the dispersal of the clouds into strata indicated that the angelic
vision would not be seen here, that this sky was deceptive, that in
the end clouds are only ice in suspension, water vapor ready to return to its origin and destiny, which is the immense embrace of the
sea, from which I come, which I no longer know if I left, and to
which I don't know if I will return.

The children greet me and this makes me happy. It irritates me
that out of a half-ruined hovel on the side of a volcano, crouching,
dressed in black, holding a baseball bat in her hand, part of the volcanic landscape of black sand, comes my ancient nemesis María
Egipciaca, the jailer of my childhood, waving the bat and shouting
or screeching or whistling, a little old woman died shuffling the
deck, a little old woman died shuffling the deck . . .

I gave thanks. Elvira Ríos and Lucha Zapata were not to be
found in the cemetery of the air.

Neither was Jericó.

Neither was Asunta Jordán.

"Lucha Zapata!"

But Ezekiel paid no attention to me. We flew over the Meseta de
Anáhuac and from a place hidden among stones and underbrush,
leafy *pirul* trees and weeping willows, the voice I recognized rose
up, now with plaintive accents, now authoritarian, the voice of Antigua Concepción surviving the disasters enumerated by Ezekiel and
in open combat with the prophet, don't believe him, my boy, Josué,
you who have given me your companionship, now I hope nothing
more separates us, don't believe the false prophet who brings you
rushing through the air, damn charlatan, don't believe anything he
says, power is exercised wherever it can be exercised, in life or in
death, it is exercised wherever it can be, not wherever you want it to
be, that's my argument with this meddling busybody Don Ezekiel
with the big mouth and the black wings, ask him if there are any

politics with ethics, just ask him, ask him if something exists outside the palace of politics and the temple of money . . . ask him, Josué . . .

Ezekiel beat his wings too late, he said, not paying attention to Antigua Concepción who addressed us from her grave, be quiet old woman, there is no need to recruit troops at sunset, and she responded with a vast burst of laughter, the rights of a supplicant are sacred, since the beginning of the world, I beg you to return my grandson to me, let him fall, ill-omened bastard, damn prophet, let loose your prey, he is my grandson, he is mine, he is free to fall, or isn't he?

He is free to open the way to death, Ezekiel said with a sigh without driving back Antigua Concepción, let my children go, they are no longer Cain and Abel, they no longer fight with each other but with the necessity to which they must submit, do you hear me, wet-winged Indian? Each man is merely seafoam while he lives, grandeur is an accident death does not forgive because she is greater than everything, do you understand me, blubbermouth with wings? What are you going to give Josué? Not a *totopo* or a tortilla or a cake from the Shrine of Guadalupe? Miserable matinee magician, give me back my grandson, have pity, be fair! And the prophet: It is unfair not to know you are mortal and death is the justice of immortality, he is necessarily mine, shouts Antigua Concepción, necessity overflows you, Ezekiel responds, give me back Cain and Abel so they can reconcile in my bosom, the perverse grandmother wails now and Ezekiel: They are not battling each other but the desire and the destiny to which they will have to submit.

"They are sleepwalkers," the old woman shouted. "I'll wake them."

"They are destiny," murmurs Ezekiel, and he begins an even higher flight that leaves behind the grave where Antigua Concepción lies, shouting all is lost, don't deceive Josué, don't tell lies, don't weep and moan, look to your own house, leave another's alone . . .

The voice was dying out surrounded by smog and motors.

I insisted: "Lucha Zapata?" as if to dissipate the events that were suffocating me.

Then Ezekiel picked me up by the back of my neck and said she, she was your good demon, your companion, he said when we left the mountains behind and reached the height of the meseta and Mexico City stretched into infinity, brilliant in the lights of dusk as it was gray in the light of day, and Ezekiel murmured the words of God I will pursue your blood, blood will pursue you, blood will not hate you, and Lucha Zapata will be your avenging angel, Lucha Zapata is the only person who never betrayed you, now she will avenge you, look at her from on high, look at her go into the Utopia building without shouting, without naming you with each pulse of her heart and each beat of her lungs, at last sowing terror in the building, no one stops her, not even Ensenada de Ensenada, this breaks all the rules, this is not foreseen, Lucha is pulled in by the wind, no one can distinguish her from the air though everyone feels the fire of the hurricane until Lucha Zapata, breaking glass and splintering doors, enters the sanctuary of Asunta Jordán and surprises her with her nose in the computer and Asunta does not have time to resist the stab of a knife and another and another and another, stab of ice stab of dream stab of desperate wakefulness stab tearing the air to drive into the neck back breasts eyes of Asunta Jordán who resists by waving her arms, covers her skirt as if the stab had reached her sex, tries to clean herself off and falls facedown onto the computer that transmits a senseless prayer with no addressee . . .

They rush at Lucha Zapata.

They take her.

Don't look anymore, Josué. Don't look. Your destiny on earth has been fulfilled. The exterminating arrows have been shot. The names of the ghosts have been pronounced. Endure the crimes of the city. Prophesy against the city. And now, Josué, forget the great noise at your back and take a roll of paper to recount an incomplete narration . . .

These are the names of the tribes: They are spoken from the Aragón prison by your brother Miguel Aparecido, who still lives.

ABOUT THE AUTHOR

CARLOS FUENTES, Mexico's leading novelist, was born in Panama City in 1928 and educated in Mexico, the United States, Geneva, and various cities in South America. He has been his country's ambassador to France and is the author of more than ten novels, including *The Eagle's Throne, The Death of Artemio Cruz, Terra Nostra, The Old Gringo, The Years with Laura Diaz, Diana: The Goddess Who Hunts Alone,* and *Inez.* His nonfiction includes *The Crystal Frontier* and *This I Believe: An A to Z of a Life.* He has received many awards for his accomplishments, among them the Mexican National Award for Literature in 1984, the Cervantes Prize in 1987, and the Légion d'Honneur in 1992. He was nominated for the Man Booker International Prize in 2007.

ABOUT THE TRANSLATOR

EDITH GROSSMAN, the winner of a number of translating awards, most notably the 2006 PEN Ralph Manheim Medal, is the distinguished translator of works by major Spanish-language authors including Gabriel García Márquez, Mario Vargas Llosa, Mayra Montero, and Alvaro Mutis as well as Carlos Fuentes. Her translation of Miguel de Cervantes's *Don Quixote* was published to great acclaim in 2003. She received an award in literature from the American Academy of Arts and Letters in 2008 and was inducted into the American Academy of Arts and Sciences in 2009, the same year in which she held a Guggenheim Fellowship. In 2010 she published the book *Why Translation Matters.*

This book was set in Fairfield, the first typeface from the hand of the distinguished American artist and engraver Rudolph Ruzicka (1883–1978). In its structure, Fairfield displays the sober and sane qualities of the master craftsman whose talent has long been dedicated to clarity. It is this trait that accounts for the trim grace and vigor, the spirited design, and sensitive balance of this original typeface.

Rudolph Ruzicka was born in Bohemia and came to America in 1894. He set up his own shop, devoted to wood engraving and printing, in New York in 1913, after a varied career working as a wood engraver, in photoengraving and banknote-printing plants, and as an art director and freelance artist. He designed and illustrated many books, and was the creator of a considerable list of individual prints—wood engravings, line engravings on copper, and aquatints.